DE RIGHTEST PLACE

ACKNOWLEDGEMENTS

Thanks to special gifts that kept on giving...

My first thanks go to Rhiannon, Gareth and Carys who, every day and in every way, are the wellspring of my enduring joy in just being alive. Love. Love. Love.

Then there's Bernardine Evaristo, Ellah Wakatama Allfrey, Jennifer Hewson, Funso Aiyejina, Lawrence Scott and Jenny Green Scott, who variously mentored, edited, commented and guided this work through its many drafts. Huge thanks.

Alex Smailes and Gareth Jenkins of Abovegroup and Melanie Archer. Immense gratitude for the cover photo and design.

Helen and Andy Campbell gifted me the use of their Tobago flat, an escape from the insidious seductions of Trinidad and the internet, to get on with the serious business of writing and sea bathing. Couldn't have done it otherwise. Greatly appreciated.

My book club buddies and many friends who kept asking, so how the novel going? That splinter in my sole spurred a sprint to the finish line. Massive thanks. Hope you don't mind if I don't let you know what I'm up to next rounds, OK?

To Bocas Lit Fest – your very existence, your boundless energy in making real what once could only be imagined; they sustain and nurture me in this late life outing. I owe you. Big time.

To normal, everyday Trinidad, whose unique genius is to unceasingly produce real life stories that are too unbelievable for fiction. Carry on regardless.

Finally – Dear Hannah and Jeremy, Peepal Tree Press, bravest, most aware publishers, ever. Thanks for your faith in me and your courage in taking me on. Again.

The Hollick Family Charitable Trust and the Arvon Foundation put their trust in the uncertain possibility of this book by their generous award of The Hollick-Arvon Prize 2013. I am humbly grateful.

BARBARA JENKINS

DE RIGHTEST PLACE

PEEPAL TREE

First published in Great Britain in 2018
Peepal Tree Press Ltd
17 King's Avenue
Leeds LS6 1QS
England

ISBN13: 9781845234225

Supported using public funding by
ARTS COUNCIL
ENGLAND

CONTENTS

Prologue: I Cynthia – Belmont Maco   7

PART ONE
1. Float to Loftier Altitudes   13
2. A Place of Scattered Desperation   22
3. Soulmates   28
4. Get Up, Stand up   35
5. Making as Eef   43
6. Correct Costume Conquers Challengers   46
7. Licensed to Sell Spirituous Liquors   53
I Cynthia – Belmont Maco   64

PART TWO
8. The Gift with Unalluring Packaging   71
9. A Good Friday   75
10. Everybody Needs Somebody   85
11. Fortune Favours the Fearless   94
12. A Large Circle of Keys   102
13. Neptune in Pisces   111
14. Don't Deal   117
15. Fraught with One-Upmanship   125
16. Routine, Rhythm and Ritual   134
17. Strategic Battles   141
18. Hold to Your Convictions   148
19. A Quiet Place   158
20. Glad Tidings   165
I Cynthia – Belmont Maco   169

PART THREE
21. Madonna Mashes Mapepire   177
22. Inner Knowledge   186
23. Lunar Eclipse   196
24. Wet Paper Can Cut You   201
25. Karma   210
26. A Certain Amount of Harmony   214

27. Think of the Consequences   222
28. Deep in Thought   227
29. Home Sweet Home   234
30. Muddy More Water   238
31. Fool Yourself   243
32. A Long Range Vision   250
33. No Chick Nor Child Nor Parrot-on-a-Stick   262
34. Live, Love, Be Happy… Irregardless   265
I Cynthia – Belmont Maco   275

I CYNTHIA – BELMONT MACO

On the day I born, overhearing the Rediffusion that the neighbour turn up full blast so the whole yard could enjoy he good fortune – he being the onliest person in the yard to have radio – mih Marmie hear a nice song she never hear before and it go like this: *Who is Sss… what is she?* That Sss… is all she make out of the name, because right at that instant, Dou-Dou, she Martiniquan pwatique, bawl out from the lane, *Proviz-yoh, proviz-yoh fray.*

Marmie rush outside. She have to choose plantain to pound and dasheen to boil and fresh seasonings to put on the carite she buy from the fishman that same morning self. The first belly pain slam, *whattam!* And is radio-neighbour-self who have to run up the lane to get Nurse Brooks. Nursie rest she two hand flat on top mih Marmie stretch-out belly. She feeling round and round. She ent saying nothing. Mih Marmie ent have no experience in these matters, but when she seeing how Nursie only shaking she head, how she only pushing out she mouth, Marmie sensing things mussbe not right. Nursie saying to radio-neighbour, You stay right here. Then she say, This looking like real trouble, oui. She tell him, Do quick and run up by the Circular Road. Get a car. This is Colonial Hospital business.

See the three woman park up outside on the road, waiting for radio-neighbour to come back with the car. Dou-Dou, marchande, market basket balancing on she head, shifting from foot to foot. She don't know how to leave; she don't know how to stay. Nurse Brooks, big black midwife bag in tight grip, head jerking left to right to left like a frighten chicken looking to get to the other side of a busy road. And mih poor Marmie. She prop up on galvanise fencing, she two hand holding up she belly, like if is a big heavy pumpkin she carrying and she fraid to drop it and it buss open. Oh god, oh god, she saying. She bending over. Oh merciful father in heaven, she bawling. She squatting down on the road. Uh-uh-uh.

She calling, JesusMaryJoseph. Now is only a whimper: OhGordOhLord OhGord! And with that, I step out, foot first, right there on the road. Uh huh. Right on the crossroads. Right under Eshu watching eye. Yes, Eshu-self looking on as mih two foot touch the pitch road. Watch mih. I ready to travel. I ready to carry news. I ready for the road.

When she hear is a girl she make, Marmie decide there and then to call me Cynthia. What else girl name the man could be singing about that early morning? What other name starting with a Sss? What happen, though, is that when the christening party reach the head of the line Sunday morning, when I is six weeks old, Father Liam Pádraic look for my intended name in his book of saints. He look, and he look, and he look again, but nowhere can he find the name Cynthia. And in any case, he say he can't baptise children who born out of holy wedlock on the Lord's Day. With that he send back mih mother, Thalitha Charbonné, mih godmother, Angela Del Pino, and mih godfather, Sonny Deyal, telling them to come back next Thursday, the day for bastards. Which by luck and chance also happen to be the day of the week I born on. Thursday. The day for the child who have far to go. It give Father plenty time to look up in his older saints books and find out who is Cynthia and what is she. *St Cynthia is an obscure third century Catholic martyr, who was tied to a horse by her heels and dragged through an Egyptian city for refusing to worship idols.*

Well. Well. Well. Look at mih crosses! Three of them! Is like I is Calvary self? First, Eshu is my orisha, and he have plans for me – messenger, carrier of news. Second is the Thursday borning – traveller. And third is mih baptism name – *Cynthia*. Listen how that name they give mih sounding like if is two half: Sin and Thea – each half at war with the other. First half, Sin – to do with the Bible man-god thou-shalt-not commandments. Second half, Thea. I find she is a woman-god who doing whatever she want and letting you do what you want, too. Yuh business is yuh own business. So, from early on, mih destiny is to be open to everything and everybody. Ambidextrous: I using mih two hand equal-equal. Ambivalent: I seeing all two, three, four side of every argument; I give the devil his due; I turn the other cheek, and is I who facing all two direction on a journey. Don't ask mih to judge nothing. Put mih in front any competition – Carnival costume, pan side, Easter bonnet, poetry, baby, dog – no matter what, I find something equally good in everything. Up to me, everyone done win already.

If anybody ask, so where Cynthia is? somebody bound to answer, check out De Rightest Place. That is where to find mih when night come. I Cynthia, right there. I spending hour after hour drinking straight coconut water with a curl of lime peel, while everybody around me getting sweeter and sweeter, higher and higher, louder and louder. Empty rum bottles piling up and Bostic tired fulling up beer chiller and ice bucket as the night wearing on.

And what I doing in De Rightest Place? I minding mih business. And what is mih business, you might arks? Mih business is minding other people business. They call me the Belmont Maco, the see-all, hear-all of the village. Watch mih. I listening to all the talk, all the jokes, all the story that people relate.

Is Eshu-self put mih so when I born under he eye. Eshu, the one they say connect up the world of awakeness with the world of dreams, the one who link here-ness with there-ness. Eshu, spirit messenger of the gods, and I Cynthia, living messenger of De Rightest Place, ready to carry story from one to the next, like Eshu-self. I listening to everything people relating, yes, but I listening even harder to the stories they not relating. Under the waves of sound vibrations, I picking up the heart vibrations and the soul vibrations. I does travel from what yuh seeing to what hiding behind what yuh seeing, from what yuh saying with yuh mouth, to what yuh telling yuhself in yuh head, from yuh wide-awake self to yuh deepest dreaming self.

But while is me who know all and could tell *all* about the people and things going on in De Rightest Place, I Cynthia choosing to follow Solo example. Yuh see, most nights when he was here running things, Solo uses to have a small side playing panjazz. Everybody in the little combo getting a solo spot to riff and ramajay while the other musicians standing back. But check them – they supporting, they encouraging, they keeping the thing going. Everybody waiting fuh as and when they get the feeling to find they own space to do they do. For who decide which instrument, which player, yuh mus' hear and which yuh could do without?

And who is me to turn mih back on the establish custom of De

9

Rightest Place? When it come to people business, who is to say who story to tell and who story to leave out? Everybody getting a chance to take centre stage and give they side of the story. Even the pub itself. Yuh ever hear the saying *Walls have ears*? Well, the walls of De Rightest Place does hear everything that going on inside a there. If walls have ears, well then, it must have voice too, or else pressure inside would build up so high, head buss open and roof fly off.

Only thing is, the walls here build longtime. Old man McDavidson build this place for Florence, he onliest daughter, who he didn't let nobody get marrid to. Miss Florence school uses to be right here. With the rod of correction, lil picky-head chirren get bad English knock outa dey head and proper English knock in. Miss Florence, poor thing, musbe rolling in she grave to see how, after Independence and we own-own University, "bad English" get promotion to "home language" and "creole" and "patois". So, under Miss Florence instruction, is not only ole-time budding civil servant and politician, is the building self that learn to talk plenty-plenty proper English. So, when yuh see De Rightest Place trying its bes' with using The Queen's English, beg pardon, I hope yuh try and unnerstan where it coming from. Is the burden of history that real hard to put down.

As for me, the Belmont Maco cyah get leave out. I will step in and reveal as and when I see fit. Yuh see, yuh cyah always trus' people to tell the whole truth when is they themself that involve. I take refusing to worship idols very serious. As far as I concern, *No Man is an Idol*. And is not I Cynthia, nah, not me, is *this* story, the story about De Rightest Place that will get drag through the whole a Belmont.

So let we begin. Who we bringing on stage first? No question. Clear the way for none other than the bosslady of De Rightest Place, the woman who everybody does call Miss Indira.

PART ONE

1. FLOAT TO LOFTIER ALTITUDES

Is fifteen months to the day that Solomon Warner gone to Caribana and not come back. See y'girl Indira prop up on a heap of pillows on her side of the bed. But she can't stop her eyes slanting over to the picture on his bedside table. Opening night party of De Rightest Place. The two of them hugging-up, smiling for the camera. A stray blue streamer draped over his right shoulder. Her left hand caught in the act of reaching for it. She stretch over and pick up the picture. She looking at it hard-hard. She say, Solo man, the time has come for me to accept that it's all over. Because, while it's true they wasn't married in any legal sense, it looking like not in any other sense neither, since he could pick up himself, take off to Toronto with the steelband, and not come back with the others.

Was only Skeete, the iron man, who tell her that Solomon say he going solo. It really eat her up how Solo himself not even once try to get in touch with her. Not even a little *Dear John, oh how I hate to write* letter. She telling the picture, Solo man, how could you not send even one word, one paltry word, to say whether you're dead or alive? After all we've been through together? Seven and a half years. She rest back down the picture. She close her eyes. She say, If I don't recognise this is it, that I've been bit, this could drag on and on and I'm left here, lingering in limbo. Chuts, I'm vex with Solo, but I'm also sad. Regretful, but not bitter. Abandoned yes, but I'm not destitute. At least that is what Indira trying to talk up herself into believing this Sunday morning. She figuring, too, how she going to move on. She open back her eyes. From whence cometh my guiding light?

Y'girl bring to mind a TV show where an expert was giving advice, brandishing his book, *Everyday Economics for the Financially Fraught*, like if is some kind of Bible. It really rankle her that advice about how to use stale bread in forty different ways always

13

coming from people who don't even eat bread – bagels and croissants are much more to their taste. But anyway, the TV expert say that first you make a list of your assets and, while she suspicious of such advice, because of where it's coming from, at least it's a start. So Indira find paper and pencil and she quick-quick begin to make a list.

A List of My Assets. First asset, she say, is herself, so she write down: ME. After all, yourself is all you have when everything is gone and, although everything is not gone, it's good to look at yourself and see what you have that could work for you when the chips are down. It's not as if it's the first time she's down on her uppers and has to start from ME. So saying, y'girl sit up a bit straighter and glance across at the big oval mirror facing the bed. She lift an appraising eyebrow, then she add: *young, good-looking, nice body*. She look at her hands. Nails nicely done, sure. French-cut, white tips. But the hands are rough and red, scored and blotchy. Calluses on the palms. Was a time when she used to wear gloves when she'd be seen in public – though she'd turned that to her advantage in the retro playboy-bunny years when those long, above-elbow, black gloves was the signature nightclub hostess costume. She never fool herself as to the real reason. She look at her hands again. Battle-scarred. She slump down on the pillows, close her eyes a good while. She sit up, shaking her head. She look at what she's written – *young, good-looking, nice body*.

What next? *Bright*. Though how bright you could be when your man standing in front of you packing for Caribana in August and putting sweater-gloves-snowboots-coat in his suitcase, tell-ing you the internet say it cold no arse in Canada, and you only asking him if he have his creditcards-passport-cash-phone? If you can't read the writing on the wall… But she still leave *bright* on the list.

Another asset pop like fireworks in her head. Blink, blink, blink go the eyes. She bite the pencil, chew on it a bit, and, after a little weighing-up, she write down: *White*. There. She's com-mitted it to paper. But she still feeling she must debate with herself what she can't say aloud. The asset value of white. C'mon, she saying to herself. Don't be coy. Admit that white is the default skin colour for global acceptability. It is the get-outa-jail pass, the

14

win an extra-throw-of-the-dice. Yes. It's true. Take her, for example. Living in Europe, no one questioned her right to be there. To have been born in India was *interesting*; her singsong accent was *charming*; even her name, so foreign, was *unusual*. But she could blend in, go anywhere without alarms going off. And though here, in this country, she stand out, it was in a good way. People look at her and immediately assume she's well-off, has access, is deserving of deference. *Blonde, blue-eyed, white*. A veritable Holy Trinity of Privilege. Can't deny. Security guards bow and say, Ma'am, and open gates. It certainly gives you the edge, whether with barman or banker, police or politician, lunatic or lover. Not at all bad for someone who is marginally poor and lives in less-than-desirable Belmont, who lived with a black, pub-owning Rastaman musician.

But, hang on; waitwaitwait a minute, she think. Whose labelling am I adopting? I'm fooling only myself to call Solo *black* in this country. That's Europe; not how it is here. In this place, Solo *red*, up the scale by several notches, just below white and feel-they-white, somewhere in that jostling, fluid middle space along with light Indian, wealthy dark Indian and educated brown.

That whole *If yuh white yuh right* situation wasn't always so with her. There was a time, long ago, when her being white, its very *desirability*, wasn't good for her at all. When she was young. Too young. Defenceless. She hasn't forgotten, but she doesn't want to remember. Not now. She's not going there. Right now, right here, in this country, *white* is an asset. It has currency. She can't say it aloud. But she can write it down. *White*.

She tell herself, she should add *honest* to the list, because whitepeople in this place never want to admit they have privilege. No, no, no. In fact, they like to make out that they're hard done by. True. Take her friend, Suzanne. The one who says her family is French aristocracy, who came here with the *Cédula de Población*. The family tree hangs on her living-room wall. You look at it and is only French names and cousins marrying cousins and *Compte de* this and *Compte de* that. When Suzanne and her family get together for brunch on Sunday after Mass, the talk is all about the good old days, growing up on the fifteen hundred acre cocoa estate, *Qui Rit Bien*, that the ancestors bought with the Emancipation compensation they got from Westminster. What does the name mean? I ask her. She laughed. It means *Who laughs last laughs best.*

Yes. Well, one day, just last week, Suzanne is doing one hundred and twenty in her Mercedes, zooming past the Beetham on one side, the stink La Basse on the other, when a traffic policeman overtakes and flashes her down. Madam winds down her window, tells him that he should bear in mind that they, that is whitepeople, is an endangered discriminated-against minority in this island. And he, the stout, ebony policeman, so flabbergasted, he stands like a statue next to his motorbike while Suzanne winds up her window and speeds off.

But y'girl Indira is saying to herself that she's too smart to get suckered into that kind of mindset, because she, Indira, proud to declare to any and every body that she is *not* from here. And furthermore, though she and the local whitepeople share the same skin colour, she doesn't share with them their burden of selectively misremembered history, and so she writes down *honest.*

What else is there? Hmmm… maybe it's time to move on from the ME-myself-and-I concerns to more material things. She's looking around the bedroom. There's the clothes, the shoes, the handbags that filling up wardrobes in every room, but she's not about to do an inventory, so she just write *Plenty Clothes etc.* Solo left a whole heap of things behind, and, since it's looking like he managing quite well without them, she supposes they must be her assets now – but she's not business with such foolishness. One of these days she will ask Bostic to pack up Solo's personal effects and put them in the storeroom. Give her some breathing space.

Next: *Car.* A twin cab pick-up that Solo use to transport goods for the pub. The pub of course! The PUB! De Rightest Place. It's running on autopilot under Bostic since Solo gone. The few neighbourhood hardcore customers still there – you could even say they're living there – but from her vantage point, the upstairs bedroom window, she's seeing fewer and fewer people dropping in. It's like the spark to attract people gone. So, she has the pub, but it needs attention. And direction. Looks like Bostic is happy for it to tick over, but that's not good enough. She will have to nudge him or seize the reins herself.

What else? Yes, right here, right where she is, the apartment upstairs the pub, that she and Solo call home for years before he gone. Two more – *Apartment, PUB!* This building is the biggest asset of all. She have to rouse herself, make a critical assessment of it, see how it's really going and what it could do for her. No half measures. In for a penny… With that impulse, Indira get out of bed, throw on a wrap and go downstairs to take a serious look at the building. Outside, on the concrete forecourt, y'girl standing with her hands on her hips, looking hard at the building. Who could've guessed how things would turn out from the first time she saw this place? She was home, busy-busy. Big pot of pelau on the stove. Broom in hand. Phone rings. It's Solo. Come now, come-right-now, his voice excited and urgent. There's something I want you to see *nownownow*.

She turn off the stove, tie on a quick head-tie, divert a route taxi to the Belmont address Solo gave, and jump out when she spotted Solo's big rasta-stripes tam. He's standing next to a Chinese young feller outside an old rundown corner-shop. No name, no big sign advertising Broadway cigarettes or some such, like other groceries. Only a faded paper poster stuck up on a wall for JU-C Beverages, and a small sign painted on the front wall saying:

> HOWARD CHIN HONG
> LICENSED TO SELL
> SPIRITUOUS LIQUORS
> UNDER A GROCERY LICENCE

The paint on the wall beige and peeling, the plaster chipped and flaking off. The floor, inside and out, bare concrete. A tall wood counter. BRC burglar-proofing between long-gone customer and erstwhile shopkeeper; cut-out gaps for passing goods and money through. A dingy brown cotton curtain sagging from a relaxed spring rod spanning the doorway leading from the grocery to the back store. The back store so dark she could barely make out boxes, crates, tins, bags, piled high. Up a ladder through a hole in the ceiling to the attic upstairs, daylight threading a feeble path through dust-caked window panes, and, when they walking careful, careful, along the beams, bat guano, rat droppings, mouse pellets, cat dung, pigeon poo getting stirred up on the floor making her so sneezy-wheezy that they had to come back down quick, weaving their way through drooping cobweb drapes.

But the place looking solid – solid structure, solid location, and she agrees with Solo that it has potential. But that was after they got home and discussed the what and how and the why, but not the when of the decision to buy the place because the when was immediately, *Now-for-now*, said the Chinese young feller. He had to go back to university in Tallahassee where he'd come from in a hurry when his grandfather's will was probated and he found himself sole heir to the old grocery he hardly knew as a child. His own father had leapt up quite a few rungs on the merchant- class-ladder by opening a factory making breakfast cereals in the heady early years of the Independence drive for self-sufficiency. So the grandson, having no sentimental attachment to place or person, wanted to sell the place quicksharp, and Solo was equally anxious to set himself up as *Proprietor of a Pub*.

Hang on a minute. A pub? It's pub you saying? Indira ask. So why do you want to set up a pub? Why not a creole restaurant? People are always wandering around like bachacs looking for food and we could get somebody to cook, easy, easy. Or you could even convert it into two apartments, one for us to live in upstairs and the downstairs to rent out? But Solo want to show his father, God rest his soul, that it have more ways to skin a cat. When he start playing steelpan as a boy his father tell him, You see this steelpan thing that taking up all your time? Well, is a hobby, not something to take serious, and he pack Solo off to Dublin to study medicine. But he take up playing pan in the pubs at night and he find he most comfortable with himself on those occasions, so he drop out of med-school and start touring, playing gigs with a small side and now he want to recreate that music pub atmosphere right here in this place where people could lime and listen to live music and feel nice and mellow. He using the money his mother leave him when she die, right after she inherit from his father when he die.

So it's payback? You want to get back on your father for cutting you off when you dropped out of medical school? It's revenge that's motivating you? Solo say, no, no, no. Is for *me* to get the satisfaction of doing what I want, show the old man spirit that I could make a good living and a life doing what making *me* happy, same as being a doctor made *him* happy. And now I find the rightest place to do just that.

Now here she is, this Sunday morning, standing outside the building, thinking about those early days, of how she and Solo built up the place so people come all week long to spend time with friends who are like family, but, thank the good gods, are not. Dealing with the place is not going to be too hard, she thinks, but what about my own self, what am I doing about making a break with the past?

The Sunday paper lying on the forecourt where the delivery driver throw it. She unroll the bulky package and riffle through the pages.

Gemini: Like a hot-air balloon, you will be able to float to loftier altitudes once you release the sandbags of bitterness, resentment and guilt. Purification is essential.

Purification is essential. Hmmm… Back in India, people do ritual purification in the river. Here they go to the sea for healing and for baptism. Water to purify, to renew. But Indira feeling she wants something stronger than water. Y'girl don't want to just wash away the past. She reasoning that things you wash can get dirty and have to be washed again. What she wants is a real change. After the Noah Flood, even Yahweh himself said, not water but the fire next time. Fire changes things in a way they can't change back from. Fire gives light. Light takes away gloom, dispels darkness. She's glad that, as it so happen, now is year-end when the whole island looks to bring the light of fire to chase away darkness and sadness. She feels a lift of her spirits at the thought of fire. Purifying fire.

And so, on Divali night, Indira fill up some deyas with virgin coconut oil and put in cotton string wicks and lay them out in a big circle on the pub forecourt for herself and the bar patrons to light, making a ring of flickering flame as a sign of the unending chain of continuity in change.

Later, Indira make the All Souls pilgrimage to the cemetery at Lapeyrouse with Bostic, Cynthia and Fritzie, to light candles on the graves of their ancestors, because she herself doesn't have any laid-to-rest in this place – or anywhere else she knows of. She gone too, by herself this time, to Memorial Park on Armistice Day, to hear the blast and echo of military gunfire rousing the souls of the slumbering war dead.

She feel she have to demonstrate to herself that she have the strength to surrender to the reality of her loss, that she owe it to missing-in-action Solo to celebrate the victory he won through his courageous charging into battle against other people's expectations – hers too – to salute how he managed, against all odds, to triumph at making a living from making music in a pub.

After Indira do that exorcism, she walking back home to the apartment and the pub on that Belmont corner spot, making a reckoning of where she reach in her other journey.

She'd done her best to *release the sandbags of bitterness, resentment and guilt,* yet she's not feeling as light, as relieved, as she thought she would be. She doesn't feel as if she's got rid of any weight. Instead, she feels she's got no anchor, like she's drifting.

It's easy to count what you have, she thinks; it's counting what you don't have that is hard. Some things you've never had, so you don't know the shape or the size or the feel of them. From the time she was born to now, so many shapeless spaces. There are the things she did have, some snatched from her, and some she carelessly allowed to go missing. Things she held so close that the holes they left are like the spaces from lost pieces in a jigsaw. You know the shape, you know the size, but you can only guess at the whole picture. Her life before Solomon has so many missing pieces.

It was what had drawn her to Solo, something about him that made her look again and then look closely a third time – his assurance, how comfortable he seemed in his skin, how confident in what he had chosen to do. A sure, secure rock she could hold on to.

Solo, I felt that at last I could stop drifting with every passing current. I told you that I had lived many lives before you, that I could be born into a new life with you. Solo, Solo, why you didn't leave me something to remember you by, something living and growing? Why didn't I tell you that, with a child of yours, I would have a chance of atonement for losing that other one? If we had a child you wouldn't have disappeared without trace, your foot would have been tied. But those were things we never spoke of. Things you never asked about. In all the years we were together, you never showed any interest in babies or children, so it's hard to judge what kind of father you would have been. You laughed when I showed you *Perfect Partners Plan Parenthood*. You said, let's wait. Wait till we get settled somewhere. Wait till we have the time to do it properly. It's a big decision. Yes, Solo, a big decision we never made. But, there were some good ones we did make. In the time we lived together in this island, I believed I'd found the place where I could belong, and share a life with someone who belonged to me. I thought I'd become the Indira that I *could* be. I saw a possible life I could hold on to and put my trust in. And now? How does that faith, all that trust hold up now?

Float to loftier altitudes.

That's what she must do. Rise above her disappointments. A fragment of an almost forgotten prayer surfaces in her memory. Something about changing what you can change, leaving alone what you can't – the wisdom is to know the difference. She can't change the fact that Solo has gone. That she didn't have his child. That she lost the one she did have. What can she change? She needs to think about that some more.

It is high noon when Indira reach home. De Rightest Place standing tall, solid. She look up the full length of its height. How easy to see everything in clean black and white terms in stark daylight. No blurred edges, no grey areas. No questions, only answers. No doubt, only certainty. She straightens her back and stride across the forecourt to place both her hands against the worn, wide, barred, double doors. The thick wood is cooler to her touch than she imagined it would be. She leans against the door for a while, allowing its strength to take her weight. How solid, how reliable it feels. She strokes the surface of the door with her fingers, the whorls of her fingertips, the lines of her palm, the calluses under her knuckles, searching, finding secret echoes in the wood's curlicues and ridges, the knots and grain. De Rightest Place, she say, I'm talking to you. Yes, you. You who are so big and strong and tall. I am going to rely on you. And – I hope you're listening good – you will have to rely on me. We're in this thing together, you hear? Partners. You belong here and I belong here too. It's de rightest place for both of us.

Y'girl turn away, walk up the stairs, turn her key in the lock and push open the door.

2. A PLACE OF SCATTERED DESPERATION

Indira flings open the jalousie windows and pokes out her head. The nearby clouds are plump, creamy-white, huddled, hanging like cows' full udders. Craning her neck still further, she can just see, leaking at the edges, a rim of sky, the early morning thin blue of skimmed milk. Cows and blue are good omens, happy omens – puts her in mind of Lord Krishna and the gopis. The universe is saying: The time is right; make that fresh start. How? The answer reveals itself in the light of dawn: The only way to make a start is to begin. So, get going. Gird the groin for battle.

Twenty minutes later, shielded by the assertive armour of Yardley's Imperial Leather, and bolstered by the morning's horoscope: *Centre your energy so you won't approach any problem from a place of scattered desperation*, y'girl is downstairs, surveying the interior of the pub.

Dear gods, what a sorry sight! In one corner, on the small platform, dusty stacks of beer crates jostle for space with a metal bucket, out of which a mop and a broom lean askew. Above, on the wall, a hodgepodge of gilt-framed photos. Solo in his prime, Solo with the band, Solo with the drop-ins, Solo and Bostic as teenagers, arms around each other's shoulders, Solo and Bostic on opening night – Solo as *patron*, Bostic, *barman* – smiling as if they'd just swallowed both canary and cream, and she, herself, resplendent in African Trophy robes. Now, if you didn't know, you couldn't tell who is who and what is what, the glass so opaque with dust and grime. Hard to imagine that there, in that dismal corner, was the bandstand where Solo and musician friends would play for hours.

She closes her eyes to bring back how, on any given night, it could be Solo on tenor pan, Ming on keyboards and Andre on guitar, then Anthony on sax, and Colin on clarinet, each stepping up, segueing in and slipping away with the mood. Sometimes

Solo would cede pride of place to the Maestro Boogsie, and he, the big man himself, would nod an invitation to anybody who looked interested to come and riff alongside him. And if Chantal there, or Natasha, either of them would forwards up. It could be the seasoned Mavis or Ella, or maybe one of the youngsters, Vaughnette or Ruth, who would take the mike and scat along. And it was play. Real play, like the way children play. For love, for fun, for enjoyment. People passing on the street, old ladies with young babies, big man and woman and even little children, would stand in the doorway like shadows, slide into the pub, make space to sit down, order a drink and everybody could dingolay to the vibe. And y'girl, Miss Indira, the I&I Queen as they called her, she would play too: The Hostess. Smiling, greeting, serving, presiding, dancing.

Solo was the magnet for all that, and now, with both north and south pole gone, is up to me, Indira Gabriel, to *centre my energy*, be my own Equator, and do the do.

Like we have a visitor.

The voice startles her out of her reverie.

Oh. Bostic. Morning. Didn't hear you. Thinking about old times.

Uh huh.

But when old times gone, we have to deal up with new times.

It's as if he hasn't heard her. His attention is on inventory – replenishing the chiller, packing empties into crates, noting the spirits levels. Indira continues her survey – the torn and scuffed leatherette upholstered chairs, their peeling, black-painted metal frames, the scarred, water-ring-marked tables, the cracked and grimy tiles on the floor, the headgrease-stained walls, the ceiling, dingy yellow with ancient nicotine smoke. A pervasive *man-cave-odour* hanging about the place.

How long has it been looking so awful?

Her arm traces a sweeping arc over the scene. Bostic follows her gesture, but his matter-of-fact expression doesn't match her dismay.

Nobody bothering with that.

But, shouldn't it be nicer? For customers?

They come, they buy drinks, they talk, they make joke, they

play games, they go home. I clear up. I go home. Next day, I come. I set up. They come. They buy drinks. What it have to change?

Indira doesn't answer. She walks around between the tables, pushing chairs into place, packing draughts boards and pieces into their boxes, collecting ashtrays. She notes the dust balls along the edges of the walls, the smears of dried spilled drinks on the floor, the dusty tables abandoned along the back wall.

How many people come here? On a normal weekday night?

He looks at her. His face is stiff.

Hard to say.

Take a guess. How many tables?

Five, six.

Weekends?

Couple more.

People stay the whole time?

Usually.

What they drink?

He turns away, carries on with stacking the chiller, filling crates, moving them to the storeroom.

Beers, rum.

Scotch?

Some.

How much does it make?

Bostic rests down the crate he was carrying with deliberate care. He turns his back to her, goes to the sink and washes a couple of glasses. He picks up a towel and a glass and turns to face her. He pushes one corner of the towel inside the glass and pays close attention to polishing it for a couple of minutes. Then he holds it up for inspection looking at her through the glass. He places the glass on the bar counter and looks her directly in the eyes.

It making enough.

Enough for what?

Enough for new stocks, bills, pay me and make sure you have enough for yourself.

Maintenance?

What maintenance?

Indira waves an arm over the room.

Repairs, painting, lighting, new furniture, cleaning…

24

Bostic goes back to the sink, picks up a rag and begins to wipe over the bar counter. He stops abruptly, flings the rag into the sink and slams his palm on the counter.

You have a problem with how I running the place?

No, not at all. I…

Is over a year Solo gone and I here by myself. You stick yourself upstairs. Never come down once to see how the place doing. I carrying the whole responsibility. And not a single word of thanks. Not one.

He walks round the counter and comes up close, staring down directly at her. His face is red. A vein throbs at his temple. His lips curl into a snarl.

Then all of a sudden, this early morning, you walk in here. Finding fault with everything. What really going on?

As if she has been struck, Indira reels backwards, staggers and collapses onto a chair. Her face flushes, then blanches. She drops her head into her hands. Bostic walks away, towards the bandstand. He yanks at the broom, clanking it against the metal bucket. He drags the tables away from the wall, scrapes the chairs along the floor over to one side, stirring up the dust of ages as he sweeps. When that half of the room is swept, he goes to the storeroom, gets a dustpan, sweeps the dust into it and tips the dust into the bin. He gets the bucket, fills it with water and mops the swept area. Minutes pass, a quarter hour passes, but Indira is not aware of time or of Bostic's deliberately noisy busyness behind her. Her mind is blank. When his sweeping around her fails to rouse her, he knocks the broom handle against the bucket.

Excuse me. You are in the way.

She looks up at him, her face showing no sign of understanding. He continues.

You could sit somewhere else? I want to clean here now.

Indira gazes around as if she's just woken in strange surroundings. As she stares at Bostic, a small furrow forms in her brow. She gets up as if to leave. But instead of moving straight towards the stairs, she gazes around as if unsure of direction. Bostic sees her hesitation. He wonders why she doesn't just go. Just leave and let him carry on with his work.

You going back upstairs?

Yes.

She says yes, but her mind still does not connect with where she is. She is not sure where to go. Then her legs take over, guiding her towards the stairs. She mounts them, step by measured step, goes to her room, and falls on to her bed. Her mind unhinges further from her body, drifting away, floating to another time long ago, another place far away.

The gold thread follows the silver needle that follows her hand, running its own heedless way across the sari, a spice merchant's gift for his betrothed, the gold thread shimmying, shimmering through the fuchsia silk, iridescent as the wings of the dragonfly flitting across her view, drawing her eye and drawing her hand as she embroiders the pallau, her eyes, her hand, the silver needle, the gold thread following the path of the zigzagging dragonfly, straying from the set paisleys, flitting hither and thither every which way…

Ruined… totally ruined… Bad gurrl, bad gurrl, bad gurrl.

Indira sees, draped from a waist as lean and as mean as a pew, the long heavy silver rosary chain studded with jet beads, big and black as watching eyes. She fixes her gaze on the silver suffer-the-little-children Christ impaled on his own suffering big-man cross. She will not look up. She will not look at the thin pale lips that spit the words, the harsh bloodless lines that rasp the shape of the words over and over: *Bad gurrl*. She will not meet the cold blue eyes. She will not look at the white wimple drawn close around the face as hard and as white as a marble saint in the chapel. She does not feel the metal edge of the ruler that Mother Clement crashes down on to the knuckles of her right hand… Her mind floats away from *Bad gurrl. Bad gurrl. Bad gurrl*… A cold white marble hand waves the right hand away and summons the left… a matching pair of hands blooming instant crimson roses on the knuckles… That pair of hands made her a *Bad gurrl* today… danced her needle across the length of the silk, its threads spun by captive caterpillars, dropped in hot water to release their coveted cocoons. Her once-pale little caterpillar fingers… She looks at them, she counts each swollen one. *Badgurrl, badgurrl, badgurrl,*

26

badgurrl, badgurrl, badgurrl, badgurrl, badgurrl, badgurrl, badgurrl…
They are seared scarlet. Her penance for committing the mortal sin of tracing, with a silver needle and gold thread across shimmery silk, the dance of the dragonfly's iridescent wings.

When she comes to from this memory-dream, she looks around. What is this place? Where is she? Does the *bad gurrl* belong here? Is she the *bad gurrl*? Her hands run over her body. They encounter the heft of her breasts. This is she. She is the woman now.

The weak light strained through gauzy curtains casts thin wavery shadows across the room. But wasn't it bright and sunny before? Between then and now a gap of unreal time. She can't remember what brought her here, to her bedroom. She closes her eyes and forces herself to retrace her waking day. Where was she? Downstairs. The pub. Bostic. Arguing. She left. Before it was done. Must finish it. Get it done. Once and for all.

Laughter and the clink of bottles rise from below. Can't go now. Tomorrow.

3. SOULMATES

Out of a clear blue sky, she come in here, putting god out of her thoughts and start to find fault with me! The place looking awful. How much money you making? How many customers come in? How come it so dirty? Who she think she is? Who the hell she is anyway? A little nobody from nowhere. Nobody don't know a damn thing about her. She say she from India, but Solo tell me he meet her in a nightclub in London. And what she was? Owner? Bosslady? Nah. Guess again. Exotic dancer! Uh-huh...

When Solo buy the old grocery, who he look for to help him renovate it? Me! Me and he working day and night. *To-ge-ther*. Is me, Bostic he put to run it. His first. His only-est choice. And in the meantime, what she was doing? Flitting all over the place. Flinging her bleach-blonde rasta-braids. Flirting with everybody. Musicians, customers, *tout-moun*. Miss I&I Queen of No Account!

Since Solo gone Canada, Miss I&I Queen never put a hand, never put a foot, never put herself out to come downstairs to even rinse a glass. Not once. Months gone by, she upstairs, sulking. And now, she ketch a vaps and come down here, throwing her weight around. I not answerable to her. When Solo getting ready to go Caribana, he say to me, Bostic, I leaving you in charge. You understand what this place means to me. Take care of it till I come back. When you coming back? I ask. He say, I don't know. Maybe not for a while. You tell her you not coming back? No. This is just between you and me. And we go by the lawyer, and Solo hand me *Power of Attorney*. Nothing can be done without me. My agreement. My signature. That is how Solo and I does roll. Soulmates. You can't take that away. *Especially* not some interloping Indira-come-lately.

From day one, I, Terrence Bostic, and he, Solomon Warner, were best friends. From that rainy September morning, when Solo and I were put to share a desk in the kindergarten of Tranquillity Boys' Primary School, I think we sized one another up as rivals. I remember smirking at his Bugs Bunny blue lunchkit and flaunting my own red and yellow Star Wars model. But I have to admit he won with the pencil case and sneakers. Army camouflage print with magnetic clasp (*thups*, as it does itself up) easily outranks zippered (*rrrrr*, stuck, reverse, *rrr*, stuck again) pink peony print. And as for my Bata Bullets v his Adidas? No contest.

At recreation that first morning, we ran out together in the pouring rain to kick ball. A little classmate delivered a message: Teacher Mildred say come out the rain, now. Another message came. Teacher Mildred say, When she say *now*, is *right now* she mean. Then Teacher Mildred herself is standing in the classroom doorway, surrounded by a couple dozen jostling classmates, eager to witness one of life's hard lessons: *Disobey and You'll Get Licks.* It was the way the world worked at home, why not at school too? Smarting palms and up-welling eyes bravely, nah, stoically contained – together.

We pitching marbles in short pants; winning scholarship to Queen's Royal College and going Saturday twelve-thirty Roxy double feature in long pants; running away from home Carnival time to beat pan in Silver Stars panyard; captaining football and cricket teams as rivals. Two cocksure handsome redboys, smelling ourselves as man from early, having to fight off girls who were conniving to catch one of us, till death do them and us part. My mother, Solo's mother, both of them, drummed home the *Thou Shalt Not Go Causing Distress to People's Daughters* commandment as we walked out our front doors enveloped in clouds of Brut. People's daughters were the respectable light-brown Woodbrook girls. Our mothers didn't explain causing distress, but fellers at school exchanged information and we learned what kind of girls we could safely tackle – girls from places like Belmont and Gonzales, glad that boys like us were paying them attention. Girls who already knew the ways of the world from the men around them and the bosses of the places where they worked. Girls whose families were quite accustomed to having distress visited upon them. For us, for Solo and me, those encounters were just another subject in our education on how to be men in the world.

One evening, we were over by him, watching an old Western video. About an Indian Chief. Cochise, I think. When the movie was over, Solo went to the bathroom and came out holding a little yellow and white cardboard box in both hands, like if it was a communion plate. His eyes locked into mine. He said nothing. His fingers pulled out the thin wax-paper wrapper. The box fell to the floor. He unfolded the wrapper. The paper drifted down. I could not move my eyes from his. He held the blade in his right hand, his stare not wavering one blink. He lifted his left hand till it was right in front my face. In one stroke, he drew the edge of the blade across the pad of his left thumb. Blood, bright red heart blood, sprang out of the slash and flowed along his thumb into his palm. He handed me the blade. I did just as he'd done. We pressed sticky thumbs together, clasping wet palms. Together, we said, *Blood*. Just like in the movie.

Through all those years, we were like see one, see the other, inseparable. Until Christmas of the year we left school.

He whistled our call to get me out to the front gate and we stood in the early morning chill on the pavement outside my house. He said he wouldn't come in. He wasn't in the mood for Christmas greetings. He handed me a letter. He bit his lips and looked away, but not before I saw his eyes were full. I read the letter and handed it back. When? I asked. He didn't look at me. He looked up at the mist-shrouded Northern Range, as if looking at it properly for the first, and maybe, last time, said nothing for a long while, then said, Tomorrow. Neither of us said anything more. We didn't hug. We didn't shake hands. He wheeled his bike off the pavement onto the road, climbed on it and rode away. I imagined I saw water drops darkening the grey road, but maybe it was because my own eyes were blurred. I watched his bent back, the pumping motion of his legs, the narrow wheels on which he balanced, the white polo shirt billowing behind him, and while I wished that sail would blow him back, I knew his bike would turn at his corner and take him home as it had done a thousand and more times before. I stood there on the pavement unable to move as I watched him sail out of my life.

Solo's doctor father had decided that Solo should follow in his footsteps. He arranged for him to go to Dublin. It's your special

30

Christmas present, said his father. Plenty boys would be glad for this opportunity. To make sure Solo actually got there, his father took him himself. I suppose he did not want to risk a repeat of the Arnold incident. Arnold Samuel, a schoolmate of Solo's dad, was a legend to us boys, to our elders a warning about what wayward sons are capable of. The son of a prominent judge, Arnold was unwillingly despatched to London to study law. When the ship docked in Port Antonio harbour to pick up its cargo of bananas, Arnold jumped ship. Story goes he went to join the Maroons in Don't Look Back settlement in The Cockpit Country. Dr Warner wasn't taking any such chances with his only child.

And me? What do they say about a body that has had a limb amputated? It never stops feeling the missing part. For me, though, not always a limb. Could be eyes missing one day, and I'd be stumbling about, not seeing anyone or anything around me. Another day, hearing nobody, nothing. No taste for the things we used to do. No panyard. No football. No cricket. Instead, every rumshop in St James got to know me.

I think my mother understood. Malkadee, she called it. But when it lasted too many months, she got fed up. A big locho twenty-something man (how old you say you are now, boy?) still living in his mother's house and showing no sign of making a move to get a steady career? She contacted a distant cousin who was building a house in the country. Make him work till he too tired to think. So it was lifting bags of cement and sand. Toting clay blocks and wood. Fetching buckets of water and sheets of galvanise. I learned carpentry and masonry. I worked till I was tired. But not too tired to think. When the house was finished I was back home and at a loose end again. Then wrestling became a big thing. Every week, the Mighty Ray Apollon and Thunderbolt Williams played to a packed, screaming Jean Pierre Complex. I was physically fit and I tried that too – for a while and with not much success, as my mind wasn't in it.

My brother Stephen got married. He'd got his girlfriend pregnant. Aunties and uncles started asking me, What happen to you, boy? How you letting your little brother overtake you? I tried to make joke about it. Nobody ever asked me to marry them. But it did make me ponder. A wife. Children. Would that make

31

it easier? Would that give a purpose to my life? But then, after three children, *bam-bam-bam*, last one a baby still, *braps!* just so, Stephen's wife picked up herself and went to Canada to do a course. She sent him a letter to say she's bettering herself and not coming back.

Terry will help out, our mother assured Stephen. Is not as if he doing anything he can't leave. So I had to help out with driving children to school and their activities while Stephen was at work. My days and weeks and months and years rolled on, unremarked, like that. Then one nephew was old enough drive. That freed me from responsibility. I had plenty time to drink, to smoke whatever was available, time to do a bit of this and that, to drift in and out of the odd little building job, to work as a bouncer in the new nightclubs that were springing up everywhere, like fleas on a stray dog. All in all, looking back at that time, I don't remember clearly where and when and with whom I passed my time. Half a life spent as a sleepwalking alcohol and drugs-fuelled zombie. There were days I would wake up in places I didn't remember entering. Strangers shaking, kicking, shouting: Wha' yuh doing here? Eh? Nasty stinkin drunkard. Get out! Get out!

Through the haze I was aware that the new millennium had swung in. I heard that Solo was back. The talk was he didn't study medicine after all. He was a musician. They said he'd brought back some woman he met in England. No one was surprised that Solo came home with a foreign wife. A man studying abroad was expected to acquire such a trophy. It would have aroused ribald speculation if he had failed to do so. Solo's mother herself was an Irish bride, a quiet woman who settled into her new life and didn't make waves. But this woman of Solo's was stirring talk wherever she went. Town was saying that she walked taller than her height, her back straighter, her bosom higher, her cleavage deeper, her bottom tauter than women her age around these parts.

One day, I spotted them strutting about downtown. The two of them sporting dreadlocks. His long, streaked with grey, controlled by a tam. Hers waist-length and blonde, locked into a mass of thin beaded curls that swayed with her high walk and swung around her face with every turn of her head like sparking contrails flung from a spinning Catherine wheel on fireworks night. I ducked into a bar, afraid he would see me and recognise me, or worse, fail to do so. I couldn't bear the thought of meeting him and watching his horror at what I had become, or his not doing so and my having to say, Solo, Is me. Bostic. Schooldays. Remember?

They came into the bar. I held my breath and sat down quickly, facing the mirror so I could watch them without being seen. They walked to a table and signalled for drinks. I searched his face looking for the boy who had been my centre. I saw a man comfortable with himself and his place in the world. His eyes lifted towards the mirror and I turned away so that he would not catch a glimpse of me. When I righted myself, he'd bent his head to look down at his hands. As he did so, a few stray locks escaped from his tam and swayed forward. My wrists stung as if those ropes of his hair had swung across the room, like a lasso, to capture me. I felt my face, my body flush. I tipped my beer down my throat to quench the flames within me. When I calmed down, I looked at the two of them again. At her. I could see her waving her hands and dancing her fingers while she spoke, as if words alone couldn't convey what she wanted to say. She was a woman whose eyelashes fluttered like butterflies, whose eyes sparked fire. She was bewitching. A proper *Jezebel*. And Solo was under her spell. They left and I was able to breathe again. Able to relax the squeezing in my chest, slow the surging in my veins, quieten the throbbing in my head.

Was it after this that Solo started asking for me all over town? I have no way of knowing. People who knew us together, wanting to spare him the hurt of what I'd become, denied up-to-date knowledge of me. But ours is a small world. Word got to Solo. He found me. He held up his left hand. A bright white line, the scar of our pledge, gleamed across the whorls of his thumb. I held up my left hand too. A mirror image of his. We touched thumbs. We clasped hands. *Blood.*

We didn't reminisce about our happy, carefree boyhood years together. That was a closed space. You can't go back there – like the Garden of Eden. No, not Eden, it was more like being in the womb, some hidden place where you secretly became you. Now, it was picking up from where we'd left off and filling in blanks about what had happened to us – for me a lost half-life. Things hadn't been easy for him either. But the very music that had led him into a life of drink and drugs was also his salvation.

Music, he said, transcends reality, transports you into another dimension, makes you alive in a different way. It's as if your soul is what's real and the body just the vessel. Then, on sober days, he saw that the vessel was getting too knocked about and, if he carried on mishandling it, one day it would just fall apart. He had experience in detox and rehab – many, many times – but he still trusted music's ability to bring him peace. Go up to The Mount, he told me. Take a residential rehab. This is on me. I want you back. *I want us back*.

For six long dark months *I want us back I want us back I want us back* was my mantra. I emerged stone-cold sober, clean, and very, very vexed with myself for the wasted years. Then Solo bought the old grocery in Belmont and talked about his plans for a music pub. I threw my skills and energies into that project. They were the happiest months of my life since those teen years. I didn't want it to end.

I told Solo I wanted to manage this pub. You deal with the music. I will run the bar.

Is not a dairy bar. Is alcohol we serving.

Is only a Jehovah Witness you could trust as good as me to guard your liquor.

Solo told me he didn't need convincing. He knew that we had too much real life together for him to lay that aside. He handed the management of De Rightest Place over to me, his dearest, his *truest* friend, and I haven't let him down. We worked here together for over four years. We were closer, more in tune with each other than any other two people I know. When he was leaving for Toronto, it was only to me that he revealed his true intention. I'm not coming back. I want you to continue with the pub. And take care of Indira. Make sure she's OK.

With that, he left me a second time.

Who is she, to come down here and criticise me?

4. GET UP STAND UP

On this, the second day of my new life, I'm going to put into practice the lessons I was reminded of on the first. They are not new. I learned them long ago but I ceased to practice them, not needing them for years. Skills got a little rusty. But hard thinking is a great WD40, so I'm going to cogitate a bit and come up with a plan of action. A *strategy*. Lessee... what's the Core Four in *SSS: Strategies for Success in Skirmishes*...

First: *Know what you want.*

I know what I want. I want this pub. But you already have it. I want it to work. It doesn't? I want it to work in such a way that I am involved hands-on. I want to make it a huge social and financial success. You mean like it was when Solo was here? Gottit.

Second: *How are you going to achieve that goal?*

I'll have to take it over. Run it myself. The place is a disaster. A few people, a few beers, a few rums. Barely ticking over. That's not a pub business. That's a... parlour... a little street-side one-door booth-affair, old man 'n old lady keeping themselves busy lest-you-call-in-the-undertakers kind of enterprise.

Third: *What are the obstacles to reaching your goal?*

Money. Making it a vibrant place will cost money. Which I don't have. Yet! Plus there's Bostic. He could give trouble. Those old stick-in-the-mud types don't welcome change.

Finally: *How are you going to overcome those obstacles?*

Go to the bank. Take a loan. That'll take care of the money part. Then the manager-cum-barman issue. Get Mister Bostic to see the light. Might be tricky. He always showed a little hostility towards me. A little resentment. Always was *only* Solo's friend. I could never understand the schooldays male bonding thing, this loyalty to the past. But it shouldn't be too difficult to bring him round to seeing things my way if I put my mind to it. After all, he's a man, not so? A subject I have some familiarity with. And if that doesn't work, *Heigh Ho, Silver!* A good barman can't be too hard to find.

Get up. Stand up. Stand up for your rights. Y'girl singing with Bob as she showers, getting ready to go downstairs to brave the old lion in his lair. Lemme see, what to put on. What's the image? Businesslike proprietor, nah, *proprietress*, taking charge. In a casual setting in the morning. Sexy businesslike proprietress etc. Hmmm… Structured yet casual garments that show nice body. *Get up. Stand up. Don't give up the fight.* She can hear Bostic clattering around below. Give him a few minutes' grace to get comfortable, minding his business then… *Flash, bam, alacazam, Wonderful you came b*y. Y'girl checking herself in the mirror before going down. Tan slacks, slender croc-skin belt threaded through stylish X-loops accentuate still slim waist, further *ac-cent-u-a-ted* by sculpted white linen shirt that ends at the waist – scope there for slight movement revealing glimpses of smooth pale taut skin. Long sleeves folded to just below elbow, so that a bracelet – let's see… coral? Jade? Tiger's eye? – can slide unobstructed. Matching pendant on delicate gold chain… No… Thread it instead on the brown leather cord… Ah, better… nestles at top of cleavage… Undo that button… and that one… Good. Ring? No. None. Rings have a definite set of codes. Absence of ring leaves it open, signals a certain… *mystery*… a certain uncertain *availability*. Hair. Loose? Nope. Too obvious entrapment intention. Bun? Too severe. Off-putting. Ponytail? Nah. Don't want to act the ingénue. Plait? Hmmm. Single French plait. Start at crown and work down the back of the head right down the length to end in a paint-brush… tied in place with… with… this scrap of pink glittery gift-wrap ribbon… Ah ha, attraction-distraction! Footwear? Sandals, almost flat. Going to meet him standing. Mustn't rise above his shoulder… Can't risk seeming to challenge male dominance. Slide pedicured feet into brown leather, push-toe rasta sandals. Done? Not yet. Emphasize eyes. Today, forget-me-not. Gloss lips. Scent? What was it the one-n-only Coco said? *A woman who does not wear perfume has no future.* Uh-huh. Serious talk, that. The choice for this encounter is easy. Anaïs Anaïs. Y'girl never ceases to marvel how men's brains always hook that fragrance on to something elusive and evocative in the past. A gracious elegant mother, a big sister going on a date, the wistful tenderness of a first love. So much *emotional* connection with a woman, even if none of it was their personal experience. All the world's a stage and we are but candles in the wind. *Ready or not, here I come.*

Downstairs, she looks around, but she does not see him. She hears a flushing sound, a running tap, the clank of the paper towel dispenser, the sliding of a lock. She stands her ground as Bostic emerges from the washroom. He does not see her. His attention is fixed on tugging the zip of the frayed three-quarter cut-offs he's wearing. It seems to be stuck. He bumps into her. Anaïs Anaïs step up, do your thing. Focused still on his fly, he's bent over. *My gods. I'm above his shoulder. Postural disadvantage. He'll be defensive. Embarrassed by wardrobe malfunction.* He steps back, looks up, says, Oh excuse me, turns his back to her while continuing to wrestle with the zip. A brisk yank and he turns to face her. She looks at his fly, sees it's done up, lingers her glance just a small extra millisecond, gives a wry smile. *Hmm, close physical contact has not registered. Discernably.* She's not meeting his eyes – a tactical adjustment to demure-mode.

Morning, she says.

Morning.

So how you doing?

He grunts. Moves briskly away to do stuff behind the bar.

Oh-oh. Avoidance strategy. A stuttering start. This conversation is not going to move along under its own motion. It's up to me to kick-box it.

Bostic, I was wondering. Could we have a little chat?

When?

I was hoping now?

He looks pointedly at the clock above the bar. He looks around the room. He looks in the sink and back at the clock.

I've plenty to do before I open the place.

It won't take long.

He presses both palms on the bar and faces her.

Talk.

She walks over to a table, pulls out a chair and sits facing him, elbows propped on the table. The tiger's eye bracelet slides down a tanned arm and comes to rest against the fold of the contrasting white linen sleeve. She leans forward a little and the tiger's eye pendant pops from the shadow of her cleavage and swings a forward arc on its leather string, then returns to touch its nest and swing forward again. A hypnotic little pendulum that says, look-at-me, look-at-me, look-at-me. Bostic does not look. Instead, he turns to the sink, runs the tap over a sponge, squeezes it, comes to her table and begins to wipe it over, forcing her to move her arms and fold her hands in her lap. He then goes to the next table and wipes over that one too.

Talk.

No, no, no, no, no. That's not the script, Mis-ter Bar-man. This is a face-to-face, tête-à-tête, ring-a-ding, slam-dunk showdown we're having here.

I was rather hoping for more of a discussion, Bostic.

About?

This place.

You didn't do that yesterday?

Couldn't you come here for a few minutes so we can have a real conversation?

She pats a chair. He drops the sponge on a table and comes over. She holds his eyes while she hooks her leg round the chair leg and pulls it away from the table.

Please sit.

He slides into the seat and leans back. His eyes are averted, half-closed. He looks sort of... put-upon.

Bostic, please be open to this.

He looks at her and moves his head in an almost imperceptible nod. She leans forward. Bracelet and pendant again try to perform their trick.

Remember how the place was when Solo was here?

No answer.

It was busy. It had music. It had life. People coming from all over. Coming for the vibe, the energy, the joy of being here in De Rightest Place. At de rightest time. You don't miss that?

Still no answer.

If Solo was to come in now, you think he'd be happy to see how the place looking?

Bostic looks at the door. He looks around the room as if

searching for something he may have overlooked. He looks long at the pictures on the back wall. He looks at his hands cupped together on the table. He does not look at her. When he does speak, his voice is husky.

I wonder if you notice Mister Solomon Warner is not here.

Bostic, listen. Please. Wouldn't you like the place to be busy and vibrant again? Don't you want to be in lively surroundings with a flow of happy, *engaged* people? Not spending day after day, night after night with the same tired, dreary regulars?

Bostic gets up from the chair, lifts it and slowly, deliberately, places it under the table. His hands are clenched around the back of the chair, the skin of his knuckles blanched, stretched tight. He looks directly at her. His voice is low, harsh.

Misslady, now you listen to me. First. Those *tired dreary* regulars are all that's keeping this place afloat, and keeping you afloat.

He leans towards her, slamming palms down on the table.

Next. These exciting folks you fancy as your clientele. What will bring them in?

His voice softens, taking on a regretful tone.

Last time I looked, the big draw hadn't returned from his sojourn abroad.

Indira reaches over and places her hands on his.

You miss him too, don't you?

Bostic does not look at her as he slides his hands from under hers. He walks behind the bar, dropping his head over the sink. She hears him sigh. His voice is low, tired, drained.

What *do* you want?

Y'girl gets up and walks over. *If you can't lick 'em, bite the bullet instead*. He turns, facing her, but he looks down at the counter, not at her.

I want to be more involved. I want to get a life again. This place is all I have. It can do better than this. It *has* done better than this.

His head is still bowed. She goes on.

I know you've been carrying the whole responsibility by yourself.

You'll catch more flies with honey than with pepper sauce, Indira.

And I've not been pulling my weight.

He looks up. Impassive.

I will not let him rattle me.

Can't we let bygones be bygones?

His body language reveals nothing.

OK. He's playing hardball.

I'll come down in the mornings and help with the clean up and maybe we could work together in the evenings, too?

He raises an eyebrow.

A reaction!

I know I didn't do much before. But I can work you know.

Bostic turns away, his shoulders slump. She could barely hear him.

Do what you want. Nobody stopping you.

Bingo!

Give me a minute to get changed. I'll be right back.

It's not quite the outcome she hoped for, but it is a start. Y'girl not stupid. She recognises she's still at *First: Know what you want*, but at least her intention is now out in the open. She wants the bar and she wants it to be De Rightest Place again. An armed truce with her main obstacle at least has the potential for further negotiation.

While Indira biding her time, getting a better idea of the lie of the land, she and the Numero Uno Obstacle settle into a routine that's so precise that it seems choreographed. Y'girl going down about an hour after she hear him arrive – give him some space to be himself. Don't let him feel threatened. Go down when you hear he's pulled the tables to one side of the room and stacked the chairs. Exchange good mornings. Sweep and mop the floor while he's packing the chiller. Wipe down the tables while he's crating, storing empties and taking out the garbage. Do some washing up; he's putting the tables and chairs back in place. Go to the backyard to pick some of whatever is in bloom – hibiscus, allamanda, bougainvillaea, gloriosa superba, or some days, leaves – croton, sweet lime, coleus; he's filled jam jars with water and put them on the tables. Misslady, don't use my drinking glasses for vases, you hear? You know if any of those plants poisonous?

Retire upstairs… *Time longer than twine.* Let him deal with accounts, stocktaking, placing orders, managing delivery. Leave him to handle the lunchtime trade – mostly anxious folk having a single tense drink while waiting to see the PlayWhe draw on the TV. Return at sundown. Good afternoon, Bostic. Good afternoon. Replace the flowers with candles in pierced clay holders, serve drinks, chat with new customers, engage with the regulars. Be the animated life and soul of the pub.

★

I Cynthia feel that the word mussbe spread that De Rightest Place brighten up, because the clientele growing from neighbourhood hard-core regulars like me, to new regulars. Some is from Belmont self and some from outside. I Cynthia notice the new regulars moving in grappes. Each grappe coming on a different night. Bostic drag out the music set-up he did put away after Solo gone. Yuh could tell the day of the week by the music the new regulars want. Monday – country and western; Tuesday – pop song; Wednesday – calypso; Thursday – back-in-times. And weekend, is hot soca right through.

Cecil and Boyee say it put them in mind of the Wurlitzer era when every bar did have a jukebox and patrons dropping coins in the slot and selecting records and the *mood* they want to be in. Sandy, KarlLee off-and-on visiting American girlfriend, say that back in her hometown, her parents talk about themselves as teenagers going to the soda fountain to dance to rock 'n roll played on the jukebox. I Cynthia remind them that in the old days yuh could put a twenty-five cents piece in the slot and pick no-play when yuh in the mood for a few minutes peace and quiet to hear yuhself think. Cecil recollect how that use to get the patrons real vex and threaten to mash up the jukebox. Yes, say Boyee, remember that time when people in a bar in Penal did mash up one? A fella, wanting to impress a new girlfriend with his conversation lyrics, put a whole dollar, a whole four quarters, in the jukebox for no-play. Twelve minutes of silence was more than the patrons could bear. It spoil the party mood and them fellers them planass the jukebox with three-canal cutlass. When they finish, the thing can't play no record at all. Is only free silence coming from it. After that incident, Han Yee, the feller who did own the chain a jukeboxes, had was to remove that no-play choice in all a them.

I Cynthia feeling a shift in the vibe at De Rightest Place. It like

41

a echo of some loud noise, a distant thunder, coming from somewhere far-far. And that echo vibrating from Indira and Bostic. I watching how they moving when they in the same space. They dancing round another, each one watching the other like if they have eyes in the backa they head. Like spider and fly. Is like she think she is the spider and he is the fly and he thinking he is the spider and she is the fly. Each a them feel they is Anancy with all the tricks in they bag. What *really* going on with them?

★

Indira looking around the bar, smiles as she notes the change in atmosphere, the growth in numbers of customers, the increase in revenue, and she says to herself, I'm biding my time. I want to be sure that this is a steady, reliable trend before tackling Bostic about the changes I want to make. Then we will have another *conversation*. He may resist change, but if there is one thing I know about, it is *change*. Change – clothes, surroundings, even location – is what growth is about and I'm damn well not letting him stop me.

5. MAKING AS EEF

One evening, when I was a little girl, Uncle took Bai and me to the temple. The sun was going down. The river was gold. The temple was gold. When we entered the courtyard we saw two boys, no bigger than Bai, holding up a large patchwork bedspread like a curtain. Then something bobbed up and down behind the curtain. A bundle of gold cloth. Sometimes it appeared above one end of the curtain, disappeared, then bobbed up again somewhere else. Bai and I joined the other children, running back and forth in front of the curtain, laughing and screaming, trying to guess where the gold bundle would appear next. All at once, a loud stamping, like that of an angry elephant, came from behind the curtain. We ran shrieking towards our elders. The heavy boom of drums and the clash of cymbals drowned our cries. The boys holding the curtain ran off with it.

I see it now. There, in front of us, stands The Most Magnificent Huge Man. On his head is the gold bundle. A massive, stupendous gold turban. Look. His face! It is green! His cheeks are wide, stretched wider than his face. They are white. His chin is big and white too. He has the biggest red mouth you ever saw. His eyes are fierce with thick black lines around them and I felt myself pulled into the tight black circles right in the middle of the eyes. Those eyes are boring into my head and I feel that they can see what I am thinking. I am sitting on the ground, so near to what is going on that I feel I am with the dancers and the musicians. It is dark around us. But the stage is lit by oil lamps hanging from the walls and standing on the floor. The flames flicker and twist, rising bright, then falling dim. The shadows move across the faces of the dancers, making them look scary, and then, when there is light, beautiful.

Was I hypnotised by the moving light and shadow? I stopped being me. I felt I was the one encased in the elaborate costumes, the many-layered wide skirts, the swirling scarves and tossing tassels, the stiff embroidered jackets and the dazzling gilt decoration. I was gods and demons, princes and knaves, beautiful damsels and wicked seductresses, weaving stories without speech, stories told with mad shrieks and cries, with stamping feet and tinkling ankle-bells, with eye-rolling, whirring wrists, flicking fingers, tossed heads – stories about battles, fortunes shifting back and forth, fearful challenges, miraculous escapes.

Maybe I had simply gone into a dream, because I became aware that the performance had ended and I was in the temple court-yard. The crowd was drifting away and the evening rituals of temple life were starting. As Uncle made to take us children home, I spotted the performers coming back to the courtyard. I tugged away, running to where they were. Just as if they were going about their normal business, the actors shed their costumes, one carefully removed garment after the other, the scarves, the jackets, the skirts, building heaps, no longer bright, on a bench. As each piece was taken off, the fantasy spun through the long night slowly unravelled. Stripped to their everyday lungis and vests, the actors sat down on the floor of the porch to remove their make-up. I watched, struck dumb, as the hero tore off the paper glued to his cheeks and chin, his formidable face shrinking. He wiped away the dark green from his face, his black eyeliner, the white lines on his forehead and his wide red lips. As he cleaned, his noble character, his awesomeness, diminished. Gradually, what was revealed was an ordinary face, an undistinguished brown face, a face that could belong to any man in the village, even to our own Achan. I was so entranced by this revelation that I couldn't move, even as Uncle called me to go home. I looked on as the god removed his god-making trappings – his clothes, his mask. I saw him droop his head and release the tension in his back, his buttocks, his legs, as his posture slumped into that of a mere man, perhaps a fisherman or a carpenter or even a caretaker, like my Achan.

With that unmaking, I, the child Indira, imbibed lessons about the power of illusion and the possibilities of transformation that I did not then understand. But the magic of that kathakali performance stayed with me, so that things that were real around me felt unstable, as if they could mutate and become something else at any time and it was costume that imparted that power.

But here, in this Carnival Country, is there anything I could tell people about costume, about drama, *about making as eef*? Not a word. Not one solitary syllable.

In this place people can be themselves one minute, low-key, normal, normal. But next minute put them with friends and they playing themselves, large, large. Then, in front of strangers, they acting out who the stranger wants them to be or who they want the stranger to think them to be. And the thing is, as they do it, changing everything – voice, vocabulary, volume, posture – it's like they're not aware they're doing it. Yet everybody knows which of the personas they're dealing with and when, and everybody is segueing in accordingly. All that without even a stitch of costume. And when you put them in costume? Well. Yes. I get *that* from early o'clock. This place is in nonstop play-acting mode.

6. CORRECT COSTUME CONQUERS CHALLENGERS

Some months after her resurrection, see y'girl Indira in her favourite thinking space, her side of the King-size bed. She's doing a quick audit of where she's reached in her goals for her new life.

The pub is busier, livelier, as if, like her, it's thrown off the widow's weeds. The small steps she's taken have already yielded promising results. The new customers are changing the flavour of the place. She knows Bostic is afraid that change would discombobulate the core old-timers, but to her it's looking like Boyee and Cecil, Cynthia and Fritzie, KarlLee and Sandy, Anil and Feroze are as cool and content as before. And Bostic? What you expect, eh? Same old, same old. Taciturn as ever. Yet, on balance, she's taking a win there.

And what about herself? Well, she finds assessing the new-comers is an instructive exercise. She's refining her skills in discerning who to court, who to keep at arm's length without rudeness, who adds glamour, who adds class, who brings an aura of calm, who brings a risky edge, and, most importantly, who looks as if they're going to be real trouble *before* they become real trouble. That takes acumen.

The thought strikes her that her years before Solo were spent *in practicum* at The University of Male Psychology. She didn't know it then; she thought it was merely life. Now that she's on *that* subject, she's thinking that De Rightest Place always was something of male hangout. Is that desirable? Should it matter? C'mon, c'mon, she pulls her mind back to the matter in hand. Which is? Taking full control of the pub. She'll retain Bostic if he wants to stay under the new dispensation with she, Indira Gabriel, at the helm. She will steer the business forward to be more of a real pub, making real money, not just ticking over as a rumshop.

Frankly, she's calling it as she's seeing it. That is what it's degenerated into.

Getting ready to go downstairs to have Phase II, no, Phase III, of that ongoing conversation with Bostic, y'girl is wondering how to outfit herself. But since that man seems immune to female beguilement, should she even bother? *Waaaait-a-minute!* Is it only for the male gaze she dresses? What a preposterous idea! She doesn't need *Correct Costume Conquers Challengers*. Dammit, she could have written a better manual herself! So what should her attire say this morning for that *conversation*? That she's confident, relaxed, coming from a position of having the upper hand. Puff-sleeved (*maidenly*) purple embroidered muslin khurta, (*her irises reflecting healing gentian violet*), pink, three-tiered skirt decorated with little mirrors and beads from the Indian Expo, aqua canvas slip-ons, turquoise cotton headscarf tied British film charlady style. After all, she's going to work. Cleaning up after Sunday night's last lap of weekend's excesses.

Morning. Morning. Clean floor. Wipe tables. Decorate tables. Time to go upstairs. But y'girl doesn't. Watch her. Like she's determined to have it out with Bostic. She looking around and smiling. Yes. This is mainly a man's space. She goes to the chiller, pull out a Stag and an LLB, open them, place both on the counter, go round the other side and sit on a stool sipping her Stag. Bostic emerge from the storeroom bearing calculator and accounts book, and although he lift an eyebrow on seeing her, he making to carry on with his normal routine. She clink her bottle against the LLB and say, cheers. He nod, but he ent touch the bottle.

C'mon, she say. Relax. It's Monday. There won't be many in at lunchtime.

He turn his back to her.

I have accounts to do.

OK.

She take a couple of slow sips.

So, how's it going?

What?

The business. Picked up?

He move the book to the counter. He facing her now, but his head is bent over the book.

47

You here every night. See for yourself.

I think it has. I think we're doing very well.

He lift his head. Eye-to-eye. We?

Yes, Bostic. You *and* me and De Rightest Place. So much so, that I'm thinking of doing some refurbishing. Making it more attractive.

No comment, but both eyebrows fly up almost to where his hairline use to be in the full flush of his youth. She take a long breath.

I'm thinking, since so many of the new customers, *and* our old regulars, are men, we could make it more like a sports bar. You know? Buy a big flat-screen TV, put it up there on the wall. Everybody could watch cricket, football, golf, swimming, basket-ball… everything from all over the world… All the world cup qualifiers, all the T-20, India Premier League! And… Oh my gods! Beijing Olympics! Bostic, can you picture it? We could make the inside themed… you know… Sports pennants, caps, scarves… Man U colours one wall, West Indies cricket colours another wall, and T&T Soca Warriors… Isn't that a fantastic idea?

Bostic pick up his LLB. He swig half of it in one continuous swallow. He roll the cold bottle, dripping with condensation, across his forehead, across his cheeks and nose. He replace the bottle in its ring of water on the counter. She tip her bottle right up and drain the last of the foam. He looking straight at her, his face wearing a slight smile of satisfaction, a kind of quiet *gotcha*. He says one word.

Money.

Money?

How you paying for that?

I'm going to the bank for a loan. Tomorrow morning.

He clink his half-full bottle against her empty one.

Cheers.

Next morning Y'girl finds herself sitting outside the office of the loans officer, one Morgan Johnson, and she's trying to fit that last name into some sort of mental image.

She knows that JT Johnson was a longtime big store on Frederick Street. Owned by colonial-era British merchants; nowadays their progeny are in the highest echelons in banking, insurance, trade. Then there's Johnson's Hardware – Chinese Johnsons. Forebears' name corrupted on entry by an indifferent immigration officer during the empire's heyday? Maybe from *Jhang Sun*? Then there's Mr Morris Johnson, cabinetmaker of Erthig Road. African descent. His last name must've come from an enslaved ancestor who was owned by a plantation squire named Johnson? Maybe that first JT Johnson? Y'girl smiles at the delight she gets with names and what they could signify in this crazy, mix-up place. Not like India, where you could tell religion, caste, occupation, status and even village just by a person's name.

Ms Gabriel, the loans officer, will see you now.

Morgan Johnson's secretary ushers Indira into the office.

Good thing y'girl has been around the block a few times. It takes just a couple hundredths of a second, nowhere as long as the time between Bolt and the second placer in the one hundred metres, for her to take the hand that is offered. Oh my gods… Morgan Johnson is an Indian woman.

OK… lessee, indentured immigrant forefathers for sure. Johnson? Hmm… Morgan? Not as in *Freeman*! And that's not all. This young, slim, attractive woman is not sporting what she, Indira, has come to think of as the Bollywood-Trini-Indian girl's beauty trump card – those long, smooth, flowing, flick-a-dick tresses. This one's hair is cut short, very short. A three-millimetre spiky buzz-cut job. It's aubergine. The apparition's smile pulls a tiny pink butterfly tattoo into a fluttering of wings at the hinge of her jaw just, below her left ear. Its proboscis curls round her earlobe and plunges into her ear canal, as if whispering secrets about the gold filigree butterfly skewered to the loans officer's left nostril.

Oh yes. She's gotta concede that this girl is way ahead of her in pushing boundaries. Hair? Been there done that: Rasta, braids, scissor, razor, bleach, dye – all had their way one time and another. Nose ornament? An Uttar Pradesh great-grandmother's kali-pani heirloom? Niiiiiice touch. Not done the nose piercing… yet. Tattoo? Hmmm. Still associate tattoos with childhood fairs in Kerala where muscled strongmen flex and ripple their tattoos to life – flying fish leaping from flowing rivers, waving cobras raising their heads from baskets, naked women dancing.

Whatever early doubts y'girl may have harboured about her choice of Liz Taylor *Obsession*; the calf-length, back-slit, shape-sculpting linen dress of bold black-and-white stripes (with suggestive wrap-front), ample cleavage emphasised by a strategically-placed Gillian Bishop gold, garnet and moonstone pin; flirtatious peplum at the waist picked out at its frilled edge with scarlet satin bias-binding – whatever doubts the unexpected Morgan Johnson persona may have triggered are instantly dispelled. Y'girl comforts herself that she's adept at being all things to all.

She's also secure in the knowledge that her gold and garnet button earrings would send the message that she isn't no ketch-arse beggar. You have to show you have hard assets before banks would lend you money. And, no matter where they're placed along the gender spectrum, nothing can make a banker's eyes gleam more brightly than the sight of visible assets.

Good morning, Ms Gabriel. How can I help you today?

(*I want your money to fix-up my business place*) I've come to offer you the opportunity of investing in my business.

Tell me about the business.

(*A rumshop in Belmont*) It's a pub in an old Port of Spain neighbourhood that's experiencing rapid gentrification.

What are your plans?

It's a thriving business. Longtime neighbourhood regulars and lots of newer young people looking for a different vibe. The Avenue and The Boulevard have become a bit predictable, a bit chichi. My plan is that with so many sporting channels on cable TV, a sports bar would take off. Wimbledon, US Open, World Cup, Indian Premier League, Olympics. A comfortable afford-able bar becomes first choice to congregate with friends and engage with the event. Have a great time.

How much were you thinking of?

Let's say around eighty thousand. (*I really need around fifty, but say what? Right now, this same bank advertises loans up to thirty thousand dollars just for the carnival season. That's money for tickets for all-inclusive parties, different outfits for each one, gym membership to tone the body for display in a beads-and-bikini costume in a big-name band with premium alcohol and gourmet catering, air conditioned trucks for cooling down, loos, make-up artist, hairdresser, costume adjuster on board… They offering that to all kinds of folks. So why not me?*)

You have a contractor's quote?

Not in writing.

We can work with a ballpark figure… Over?

Over?

How long?

Let's say five years?

Fingers fly over a keyboard and the loans officer hands Indira a printout.

That's the monthly repayment on eighty thousand over five years at today's rate.

Y'girl has the composure not to gasp. A tiny frown winking above her nose bridge and just as swiftly dissipating is all. She's running an index finger along the line of figures – while checking that Morgan Johnson's eyes are tracking her huge gold, moonstone and onyx ring.

Looks doable. The place is doing very well now and will do even better as a sports bar.

She puts the slip of paper into her black Prada-indistinguishable knock-off handbag.

Morgan Johnson rises.

Is there anything else?

Indira Gabriel gets up too.

I'll bring you my contractor's quote in a week.

And the deed for the pub.

I have that here.

Indira reopens her Prada-lite, extracts a thick tattered brown envelope and hands it over. The loans officer pulls out a fat document and flicks her eyes over it.

It says here that the building is owned jointly by Indira Gabriel and Solomon Warner.

That's so.

As co-owner, Mr Warner will have to co-sign.

I'm the one taking out the loan. And repaying it.

That may be so, Ms Gabriel, but Mr Warner's property will be held as collateral. If the loan is defaulted on, his property will be at risk of foreclosure.

51

Y'girl has masks for every eventuality. She will not show disappointed, crestfallen, defeated. Instead she whips on a crisp businesslike smile.

I will deal with it.

They walk to the door and, as they shake hands, Indira points her chin towards the brass nameplate.

Unusual first name.

Born Meera. This one fits the corporate image better. Yours?

Born in India. Still works for me.

Y'girl presents the loans officer with a retreating view of shoulders thrown back, spine straight, skirt slit opening-revealing, closing-concealing, opening-revealing, closing-concealing. MM in *Some Like it Hot*. Super-high white sandals placed oh so coolly one in front the other. Pure *High Society* Grace Kelly.

Put that in yuh pipe and smoke it, Ms Morgan / Meera; Johnson / *YES! Jan Singh!*

7. LICENSED TO SELL SPIRITUOUS LIQUORS

Y'girl, not willing to reveal to Bostic the full story of her visit to the bank, gives him a partial truth – that the monthly repayment would be too high for the business to support at present; that she was sure that if they brightened up the place some more, just the front, maybe, they could keep on expanding the trade without too much investment; that until such a time as they had saved enough to go the whole hog and do it up themselves without worrying about a bank loan and repayment pressure, they should work within their means. Would he be agreeable to working out with her how much they could invest in a face-lift? He would. And who to do it? They know just the person. KarlLee, the infamous Belmont graffiti artist.

Next day, foreday morning, KarlLee at De Rightest Place before Bostic reach, before even Indira self properly get up. He bang the heavy padlock against the hasp and Indira look out the window. The white early morning light aslant on the face of the building, broad eaves casting deep, sharp-cut shadows on the forecourt when she reach downstairs. KarlLee standing there, taking in the austerity of the geometric contours, the unadorned walls, their subtle colours. Indira, respecting the artist's contemplative silence, lets him have his quiet appraisal. Then she tell him, I want a new look. KarlLee look at Indira. He taking in her bright hair, loose and bed-wild, curling around bare shoulders, the green muslin wrap printed with a tropical forest motif, drape under her arms and tie in a knot above her breasts. What's below the fine fabric is not clearly visible, but hinted at. He look at the building front and he look at her front. You have any ideas, he ask her. None, she say. Surprise me. He look at her again; he look at the building. Tomorrow, he say. Tomorrow.

★

53

I Cynthia surprise to see the pub close for a week. Indira say she want the artist to work without disturbance and interruption from customers and deliverymen. She say even *she* keeping outa the way. But I Cynthia concern more about we regulars. Indira didn't warn we that she closing the place for a whole week. For plenty a we, De Rightest Place is more home than home. Yuh cyah mess with that so easy. Take Cecil and Boyee. Them fellers life fix by a schedule. They waking up late-late. Yawning and stretching, hawking and spitting, yampie still in they eye, they stumble into De Rightest Place. Toss back a straight rum. Brrr! Ahhhh…ha! Shake they heads, dislodge the cobwebs, go to the lotto booth to play a mark they get from a dream. Come back to the pub, till home for lunch and siesta. Late afternoon back at the booth, place a nex' bet, then De Rightest Place till wee morning. Whosoever want them, know where to find them. Is looking fuh trouble to interfere with that.

★

Y'girl Indira upstairs, glancing up from her book, *Life, Lust, Love*, watching through the jalousies, as one by one they come to De Rightest Place. Cecil, one long leg folded like one of them Masai in *National Geographic*, prop against the lamppost for an hour while KarlLee apply a coat of white emulsion over the ochre, and one of white gloss over the lime green. She hearing the talk rising from below. *Tabula rasa* awaits inspiration, KarlLee say to Cecil, who nod in agreement. Maybe he's thinking that is the fancy designer name for white paint? Why you didn't strip off the old paint first? Cecil ask. Somebody has to preserve the historical record, answer KarlLee. Nobody in this here-today-gone-to-morrow philistine country cares about the past or the future. Only the present. Cecil express agreement. Is good to start small.

Afternoon come and Indira see Cecil come back and continue to watch paint dry. Boyee, also propelled by habit, gravitate to De Rightest Place. He bring a plastic Rubbermaid chair and park it on the pavement right by where Cecil standing. Cecil pull out his phone. He say, Kwesi, bring the small bench for me. Indira smile. True to form, Cecil is not letting Boyee upstage him.

A young man get out a maxi and make as if to head up the Valley

Road. He stop. He turn round, cross the road and walk towards De Rightest Place. He take off his tie, roll it up and put it in his pocket. He undo his top shirt button, fold up his sleeves. He stand up next to the two old fellers. He watching the action too. Indira looking through the slats in the jalousie. Nobody below aware of her. Except one. That young man.

Oh my gods. I've been spotted. The boy. He's looking up. Straight at me. How innocent he looks. His mother's milk still on his face.

Something, something, about him seems familiar. Has she seen him somewhere before? The way he holds himself. Is it reminding her of somebody? That stance, that turn of the head... She feels she knows it, but she can't place it. He seems a little startled by the sight of her. Her fluttering eyelids tell him, Don't say anything. This is just between the two of us. Kwesi stroll up with the little bench for his great-uncle. The boy look away and the moment of contact snaps.

More chairs and benches appear, the arrivals engaged in loud banter on what KarlLee should and shouldn't do on the newly blank surface. None of your usual fat-like-black-pudden lettering, yuh hearing mih? None of that 'De Mock Race E question mark' stupidness, advise Nelson, the grounded airline pilot, aka Admiral.

That night, when everybody disperse, every zandolie finding his hole, Indira comes downstairs to check on what the artist do. The plain white wall gives her a strange feeling. Like if she went to confession and the priest tell her, My child, your sins are forgiven, go in peace. She has been there before, sins forgiven, soul washed, but the go-in-peace part she never really took on because she knows that forgive is one thing, forget is another. She knows too well that while the past can be covered over, it is there under scabby layer and scabby layer of accumulated history, separated by gauze-thin plasters of forgiving – of which this is just the latest. Even so, even with this understanding that nothing is gone forever, just hidden, Indira feels a sense of calm, as if her spirit has some space to soar, and wants to find out how high it can go.

So, on the second afternoon, Indira, ever alert to new commercial possibility, tells Bostic to bring out an Igloo cooler loaded with ice and chilled beers. Now, Stag and Carib in hand, the spectators watch KarlLee as he open up a double-sided aluminium stepladder in front of the pub. He spread the two legs wide, so that the ladder straddle the entire doorway. He walk up the ladder on one side and, at its highest, in the middle, he extend his arm to reach the top of the wall, just over the closed door. He proceed down the other side, and when he reach the bottom, he go up and down again. He do this up and down a couple of times. The spectators start heckling. What you think you doing, man? Hurry up and start. We not here to watch you do gymnastics.

★

Two days pass and I Cynthia watching the stream of people rushing past mih front gate. I really wasn't expeckin' people to get such excitement from watching man paint wall. I figured I bes hads check it out fuh mihself, so I work mih way to the front row self. I see KarlLee turn to face we, bow down like he on stage, and pull out a tin from his pocket. KarlLee pick out a crayon. He stretch he arm out and he study the crayon good. He bring it back to his face, he lick the tip. Quick-quick he run up the ladder with the crayon in his left hand. He rotating his arm with the crayon trailing along the wall. When he reach the top, he switch the crayon to the right hand and run backwards down the other side of the ladder, his arm rotating and the crayon tip against the wall. He step back and we see a long black spiralling curl up one side of the wall, over the door and down the other side. Well, the people clapping and clapping. I Cynthia could barely restrain mihself from clapping too. I not seeing any artwork to speak of, but Jeezanages, the man could real do performance. KarlLee take a bow, then turn back to the wall. He draw plenty ovals. He draw lines. He draw dashes. He fold up the ladder. He res' it against the wall. Then, he gone. So, show over, I gone too.

★

Next day, Y'girl Indira ready upstairs. She peeping through the jalousie slats, craning her neck, looking this way and that. Searching for somebody? Checking to see if the boy came back? But she's not seeing him. Cecil arrive. He behaving like if he is the project manager. He walk towards the ladder prop against the wall. Next to it is a large cardboard box. He look inside. He glance around the pavement and forecourt and nod with satisfaction.

The national spirit of entrepreneurship strongly in evidence. Bostic there, selling beers from the cooler. Jumbo, the Nutsman, taking accurate aim, throwing bags of salt and fresh nuts at his customers. A tight cluster under a big red Digicel umbrella and Indira know is Jassodra spooning channa, tambran sauce, mango chutney, pepper sauce onto a barra, slapping another barra over, wrapping the doubles and passing it to Annette, who sliding the package and paper napkin into a brown paper bag, taking money, giving change – all in one swift smooth action. Miss Mabel is walking through the crowd, calling, Sweetness, come for sweetness. Tulum, pawpaw ball and tambran ball. Sugarcake, caramel and coconut brittle.

Chairs, little tables, benches, jostle for space on the forecourt, spilling onto the pavement. There is an air of festival, Indira thinks, like being at a cricket match at the Oval or at an entertainment with Nikki and Errol on the Brian Lara Promenade. People come up close to KarlLee sketch and are deep in discussion about what he do, what they guess he going to do, and what they think he should do. Bostic have cause to refill the Igloo twice before KarlLee appear.

This time the artist sporting a red beret and a long white outer garment over his T-shirt and khaki short pants. Boyee alert the crowd. Aye-a-yay. Look, KarlLee reach. Cecil call out, KarlLee, your granny just pass here looking for she nightie. Like you didn't arks she if you could make a borrow? The crowd erupt in laughter. KarlLee throw one evil cut-eye in Cecil's direction and make to turn back, to go home. Bostic catch him by the arm. Don't worry with them. They is a set a ignorant people. Admiral shout, Come, come nah man. People waiting to watch you do your thing. Bostic stride up, shoulders wide as a fridge. Cecil, I think you had enough beers for the evening. Cecil look at the ground, then up at Bostic, who continue, Tell KarlLee his artist smock looking nice. Cecil is somewhat chastened, but would not go so far. He meet the challenge halfway. Man, is true, you could pass for *Pee-car-so*! KarlLee, appeased, walk through the parted crowd towards his mural. He look at it from afar, then up close; he step back again, spread his arms wide and flex his fingers. Ladder! Bostic and a contrite Cecil set up the ladder, spread-

57

eagled, as it was the evening before. KarlLee hand-signalling some final adjustments, a little lower, not so low, and then an abrupt stop.

KarlLee stand back, take a slim paintbrush from the pocket of his smock, hold it at arm's length, squint at the wall, put back the brush in his pocket, stare at the wall, click his fingers and say, Marigold! Bostic look down into the cardboard box and lift out a can. He take it over for KarlLee's inspection, tilting it label side up, sommelier style. KarlLee give it a glance, a little nod and continue to stare at the wall. Bostic prise up the lid and take the open tin over to KarlLee. He pick up a wide brush, dip it into the Marigold and starting from the left side of the wall, he skip up the ladder running the brush not precisely over, but more a loud echo of the charcoal spiral of the previous day. He switch the brush to his right hand and run backwards down the ladder, transmuting the black curves into gold. He dip again and this time he run up from the right side and down on the left. The crowd, tiptoeing and swaying from side to side to dodge the heads of those in front, see that he replicate the first spiral, but further up the wall, both spirals intertwining above the doorway. KarlLee bow to the assembly, hand the brush to Bostic and then he gone.

The more inebriated among the crowd speculate as to whether KarlLee gone home for another brush, or to change his clothes, intending to return. Surely he not finish yet? Boyee call out to Bostic, I hope the bosslady paying him by the job and not by the day. The more sober of the spectators, some of whom may have stumbled upon PBS TV programmes on art and art critique, stand apart, stroking imaginary beards, pointing fingers, waving hands, while discussing brush-stroke technique, colour choice and rep-resentation. Admiral suggest the work not complete as yet. A budding copywriter in an emerging advertising agency disagree. He thinks it represent the upward and downward spirals of the country's oil and gas economic fortunes. That's why is gold over black. Admiral wonder aloud why the background white. Does it represent Indira herself, the white bosslady behind the enter-prise? Copywriter put forward that maybe it standing for the generations of plantation squires and slave owners whose control of land and resources is being challenged at present by the very

East Indians from whose country of origin the bosslady came. Cecil, listening at the edge of this group, size up Admiral and Copywriter and give his succinct opinion: Art-fart.

The following afternoon, spectators find a sheet of brown corrugated cardboard propped against the door of the pub. On three lines, in red capitals: RESPECT. ARTIST. AT WORK.

The artist reach to work dressed in his now yellow-spattered smock, a green beret perched on his head. Peacekeeping mission? Admiral murmur to Copywriter, claiming familiarity on the strength of their having bonded the evening before as the sole intellectuals among the ragamuffin gathering. Bostic cast a warning eye in their direction, forcing Copywriter to suppress a rising snigger. They hearing a rhythmic *clunk, clunk, clunk* of a vehicle trundling on wobbly wheels. Cecil step back from the crowd to investigate and he see his great-nephew, Kwesi, heaving up the gentle rise a supermarket trolley loaded with tins of paint, brushes, rags, an empty black plastic bucket and a large bottle of Perrier tinkling in a pewter ice-bucket beaded with condensation. What you doing? great-uncle asking. I is the artist intern, Kwesi say, puffing up his pigeon chest. Make room allyuh, make room, as he steer his vehicle through the crowd to KarlLee.

The artist not acknowledging spectators at all. His whole attention is riveted to the wall. He reach over to the paint trolley and pick out a small brush. He point at a tin. Cecil note for future reference the alacrity with which Kwesi lift the tin from the trolley and hold it out for KarlLee to confirm. He noting, too, how the intern, without further instruction, prise it open and pass it to the artist. From one open tin to another, the artist dip a brush and move swiftly along the wall leaving red ovals here and there, yellow splotches and lines, light green curves and dots, large blue areas, dark green and black mottles, more red in spirals. Nothing making sense to the crowd standing there quiet, quiet, like if they in church. Cecil watching how Kwesi moving from artist to trolley, miraculously anticipating the need for particular paint, for the correct brush. He finding it hard to believe this is the same boy who you can't get to do nothing home without you bawling behind him forty times.

KarlLee climb up the ladder. On the left wall he paint two

pictures that everybody could make out. One, a tray with three bottles and three glasses, and above that, a large black rectangle. The onlookers, as if at the cinema at the climax of an event – think Gary Cooper facing Ian Mac Donald outside the saloon bar in *High Noon* – look on in hypnotised silence as the artist come down, walk to the trolley, lift out the Perrier, unscrew the cap, lift the bottle to his lips and drink the entire contents *glug glugglugglug glug*. He turn the bottle upside down and, as the final drop hit the concrete, he plunge the bottle, neck down, into the bucket. People start to laugh and clap at the drama and style and maybe at the painting too.

Next day, Indira is surveying the scene. She is looking for the young man with the nice face, but she not seeing him. Looks like there is now a well-established viewing club with members, a camaraderie born of shared experience. They are buying drinks for one another, speculating and discussing in little groups. It is like being on a small ship on a long journey, a kinda *jhaji bhai* thing, she decides. Everyone has a reserved spot on the forecourt and pavement. Stray passers-by meet an amused tolerance from the in-group, who jostle them aside if they arrive to find some newcomer idly park up there. If a *nouveau arrivé* dare to say, W'appen, you own this spot? or even, This is a public pavement, well, if any of them says anything like that, see Bostic appear and watch how quickly the importunate upstart moves away and stands at the back of the regular seated audience.

KarlLee and Kwesi arrive early that day. The artist, in his now multi-spattered smock, still completely ignoring the multitude. Like he in a trance, working fast-fast to join splashes and dots, link curves, fill in circles and ovals and suddenly, magically, scarlet orange-edged heliconia, crimson pachystachys, golden allamanda climbing up the left wall; cashew, mango, chenette, pommerac glowing through thick foliage; mot-mot, hawk and parrot preening, bromeliad clinging, monkey and ocelot peering, iguana peeping and mapapire hiding. Hear the oohing and aahing and loud speculation. It looking like a horsewhip snake? Nah, w'appen? Since when snake have foot? You can't see is a zandolie? Cecil feeling like if *Life of Earth* being created in front of his very eyes, except that instead of the BBC's whispering David, Belmont is blessed with the silent KarlLee.

From her eyrie, y'girl Indira spots the young man with the nice face among the first of the spectators to arrive on the afternoon of the sixth day. He stands and looks at the right-side wall, now painted blue and covered with a myriad stars and swirling planets, comets and meteors in gold, red, blue and silver. On the left side is the tray of bottles and glasses; on the right wall, a sheaf consisting of seven pieces of paper – a lotto slip, a pick2 slip and one for PlayWhe, two phone cards and two playing cards, the queen of diamonds and the queen of hearts. Matching the black rectangle is an open book, its pages unfurling. She watching him as he looking at everything once, then everything twice, as if he reading a book in a foreign language of which he has only a smattering of the vocabulary. No, it's more like a foreign language film because the scene, the story, is unfolding even as he watching. But who, she thinks, is the one who is trying to interpret? She's never had anything to do with younger men. He looks so sweet. She wants to stroke him, like a kitten or a puppy. Hold him on her lap and cuddle him. Play with his fur. Tickle behind his ears. Brush his pelt. Kiss his nose...

Y'girl suddenly realises that she's got so absorbed in her riotous imaginings of what she could do to the boy that she has not noticed the crowd filtering quietly towards the front of the forecourt, thickening into an open-mouthed mass of humanity focusing on the scene unfolding before them. She spots an arm – weaving through the leaves, branches, animals and flowers on the left wall – extend a hand balancing the tray. Above, the fingers of another hand curl around the top of the black rectangle. On the right wall, a third hand clutches the book from below and a fourth arm reaches down the palm of its hand to display the seven sheaves of paper. KarlLee weaves wreaths of jasmine, marigolds, hibiscus and ixora into the four golden spirals. Below their meeting point, at the very top over the closed door, he paints a pink oval on a pink stalk, which descends to a point where the four arms emerge from a pink form that he has rapidly shaped.

★

I Cynthia, standing there with the whole assembly of people who gaping and shu-shuing while we watching KarlLee doing he thing, can't believe what I see. The man running he brush over the closed pub doors, and what we seeing emerge from under the brush is breasts, stomach, navel, belly, groin, thighs, knees, calves, ankles, feet – down to toenails with scarlet nail polish on them. Is a naked woman, Boyee shout out. All a we in the crowd fall into a hushed quiet like we is at Holy Mass and this part is the Consecration. I Cynthia was standing next to Jah-Son, Elaine grandson. I see he turn he head away from what KarlLee doing and look up at the window of Miss Indira apartment. He mus' be looking up see whether the inspiration there. Yes. She there. I Cynthia see them locking eyes. The boy look down. When he look up again, I Cynthia see Indira smiling. And she wink.

Everybody else looking at the mural. Cecil, who use to take out pictures when he was a youth, say that the vision on the façade of De Rightest Place is like a image rising on the surface of photographic paper when you put it into developer fluid. Of course, nobody but he-self understand what the hell he talking bout.

★

Y'girl Indira focusing on KarlLee again. She sees that no sooner had the nude appeared than the artist begin to clothe her in a swirling mist of milky white that lace through the fervid jungle on the left and the ordered constellations on the right. He gives her a smile as enigmatic as the Mona Lisa's. Above the whole, in curlicue cursive red fringed with yellow, he writes *De Rightest Place*, and with a final flourish, on the black rectangle, some words in white capital letters.

When the people have gone, Indira is standing alone outside. She's looking at the design. She see that is she that KarlLee painted on the door. But he gave her four arms. KarlLee made her into Lakshmi! Lakshmi, goddess of prosperity and wealth! But this Lakshmi is not sitting in an open lotus flower. She is standing up against the stout wooden door of the pub. And what is she holding? The tray with bottles she could understand – and the paper and cards. Those would be the source of wealth, of future prosperity. But the book? What kind of book is it? Hard to say. It's just a book-book, a big fat no-name book. Maybe it stands for her reading, her fonts of inspiration? And as to the other item, Indira is looking at it good-good. First she reads it to herself, line by white line, only with her eyes. Next she reads it in a whisper.

Then she reads it loud, loud, LOUD!

INDIRA GABRIEL
LICENSED TO SELL
SPIRITUOUS LIQUORS
ANYDAY ANYTIME

Y'girl stands there. She's smiling broad-broad. Look at the name there, she wants to shout to the whole world. Look who is licensed to sell spirituous liquors. Look who name there. IS ME! Indira Gabriel. Who the firetruck could challenge that now?

I CYNTHIA – BELMONT MACO

What a setta excitements when KarlLee was doing up De Rightest Place! Is like cooler fête every night, except fuh no loud music, thank you Jesus. But the picong was enough. Indira couldn't a pay fuh the advertisement she get fuh free. Yeah. Was nice. Excepting fuh one thing I notice that have mih a lil concern. Nah, not the painting, even though I find it too *coskel* for my taste. But like mih friend Gillian the jeweller say, in this country even coskel has its time and place. And since Miss Indira take over De Rightest Place, I Cynthia can tell you, coskel time and place really reach fuh true.

Nah, what have mih a lil unsettle is the look that pass between Elaine grandson down on the forecourt and Indira peeping through the jalousie upstairs. Innocent lil boy getting sweet eye from big hard-back woman – an jus at the exack moment when KarlLee, that good-for-nothing-scamp, paint she stark naked like a harlot for everybody tuh see. Huh! You think mih good friend Elaine would like to know I see something that could, maybe, cause trouble fuh she grandson and let it pass juss-so juss-so? Nuh-nuh-nuh. I don't want to cause no confusion in family business. So yuh ent go catch me rushin up no hill with no idle speculation to make she worry and add to she trials and tribulations. But I know enough about Elaine to know is my bounden duty to keep a close eye on the boy and make sure he don't stray from the righteous path he granny set him on. Yuh see, I know that chile from before he born.

Right from the very start, Grampa Felix call that chile Jah-Son, not Jay-son. He say, as the baby don't have no declared father, he has to be the Son of Jah, the Most High Father. Agnes, the baby mother, was badlucky enough to get pregnant and no baby father nowhere in sight. Felix say that kind a thing don't happen to no woman up to now except fuh Mary, so it hads was to be Jah doing.

Again. Agnes keeping she mouth shut. She not revealing the chile father name tuh nobody, not even tuh Elaine, she own mother.

One morning, Agnes bring she baby son up the steep dirt track. She carrying a white plastic Hi Lo bag. It have a few little vest, some disposable diaper, a feeding bottle, a tin a formula and a envelope with a birth certificate. Mother's name: Agnes Chance. Child's name: Jason. Father's name: Not given. Agnes put the chile into Elaine's arms. She hand the bag tuh Felix. She kiss the chile on he forehead, turn away and walk back down the track. Eight months pass before Elaine hear from she. She send a letter to say she working as domestic help and nanny to a couple in Upper East Side, Manhattan. Jah-Son reach two years before he see he mother for the first time since he born. Agnes say she come back home to fix up she papers. She going to graduate from illegal alien to legal green card holder.

The lil boy, wearing only a shirt too small to button up the front – if it had buttons – peep out from behind Elaine's skirt. The sole of he two foot fringe with mud; he thumb in he mouth, he nose running sticky snot, as he gazing in wonder at the strange woman. Gran-Gran say, Come out chile, come out from behind mih and give your mother a kiss, while she pulling he hand from he mouth and wiping he nose in she skirt tail. The chile bury he face further into that garment. He only a lil chile, but he see how the woman face look as if she going to vomit at Gran-Gran suggestion; he see how she turn away at the invitation to kiss. He not believing that this person with slick, black, shoulder-length hair; red lipstick; long red, patterned nails; who talking funny-funny, could be he mother. Agnes say she staying down the hill at a friend, Abdul, a name nobody ever hear her call before. She say it easier to get to and from the Embassy from where he living. She say you never know when the Embassy will call to give out appointment. Plenty, plenty people also waiting to hear and is best she stay where it have phone.

One Friday evening, Agnes sitting on the sofa in Abdul apartment. She watching the news on the TV. All of a sudden, the screen go black. When it come back on, the picture change. Some men, dressed in black from head to toe, with black facemask and carrying all kind a long gun, storm through the newsroom. At first

Agnes thinking is a trailer for a movie or some kind of weird joke. But then she hear: *Get down on the ground. Spread out your arms.* She know that voice. Is Abdul! She seeing him prodding the newscasters with the gun to force them to do what he say. What going on? Is a hold-up? But what it have to steal in a TV newsroom? And is strange to carry out crime in plain view of thousands of viewers. Then the screen go blank. When the picture come back, she seeing a tall man in long white robes and a white skullcap in the picture. The man talking into the microphone, just like the newsreader was a few minutes before. He say he is the leader. He say he making an important announcement to his fellow citizens. He overthrow the government. His followers have parliament under siege. He have the media, radio stations and TV station also under his control. He say: *Keep calm. Stay indoors and all will be well. You will not be harmed. Fellow citizens, you have been freed from this corrupt government who trampled on the rights of the people.*

The officials in government and in the army play it down. They want to take shame out they eye for taking torchlight to see in the day what everybody else in the country was long time seeing plain, plain, in the night. They call it *an attempted coup* and it last only one week. But some seven months later, when Abdul still in prison awaiting trial, Agnes make a next chile. Maisie. But the number of people in Elaine household get back to the same as before, because Felix pass away during the coup. Heart attack, the District Medical Officer say. But Elaine say she know full well is the shock of seeing big man, big woman and even little chirren toting all kinda electronic goods, household items, jewellery and groceries through smash-up shop windows in broad daylight, with no care for right and wrong, during the week-long standoff. It was much too much for poor Felix heart.

Before she leave for New York the second time, Agnes promise her mother, that she will send for her children as soon as she properly settle. She say her new green card will get her more and better employment options.

In the years that follow, I Cynthia see Elaine going down to the docks every so often to clear a barrel. When the two chirren watch she unpack the barrel is like something alien from outer space land in they house. What all them strange things their Mammy send have to do with them? The sneakers with backward ticks and racing black cats, the T-shirts and shorts emblazon with I heart NY and I heart Chicago Bulls? Them thing pretty and nice and new and clean, but how much use they have for that? Some clothes for Maisie too small. Is like Agnes don't realise the chile growing. Some things for Jah-Son too big. The boy not catchup yet with where he mother expeck him to be.

What them chirren could really do with is right size school uniform, school books, school shoes. Is Elaine self who have to locate them thing. She find sheself endow with more Tupperware and Amway than she have food and house to use them with, but find it hard to sell or give away the things Agnes send. She understand is she daughter way of trying to do she best, in the only way she know, to show love and caring for those she leave behind. So Elaine take out what they could use and leave the rest in the container they come in. Soon, the little house get full up with half-full barrel after half-empty barrel of crumbling, unused plasticware and never-worn clothes blooming yellow age-spots.

Is a real miracle to report that this boychile, son of the Most High Jah, grow in wisdom and stature, and in grace with God and man. He get what he have of those qualities by pure luck and chance – and by the hands-on training Gran-Gran mete out, reinforce, off and on, with broomstick, rubber slippers or pot spoon. Stature he mus' be get from the not-given father, cause the boy taller by far than any man on Elaine side of the family. As to wisdom, if is school that suppose to impart it, he not there often enough to get a share. As to grace with god and man, Elaine long since give up on the god of Christianity. She see *him* belonging to those who have, who is the oppressors of those who have not. She teach Jah-Son about kindness, fairness and justice – things she know he not getting from neither church god nor church people and she teach him to cook and clean and wash and iron clothes and to look after he lil sister, all of which, she figure, bound to stand him in good stead with mankind and womankind. About the ways of the world and the wiles of women, however, the boy get leave high and dry.

I Cynthia see this half-form boy, this Jah-Son, come from

work, get out the maxi and cross the road to watch KarlLee paint. Evening after evening, he not going straight home where he living with Gran-Gran, Maisie, and her little son, Small Man. He not going home to feed he pothound, Armageddon, a name he say he get from a movie. He not going home to attend to he songbirds. No. He standing there, still and quiet, like if he put down root in that spot. He not talking to nobody. He watching the artist. He watching the crowd. And I Cynthia watching him.

When KarlLee paint the woman naked, the boy turn he head up to the second storey. He eyes catch bright blue eyes looking down through the slats. Them eyes look directly at he own. Two eye meet two eye and make four. They exchange a look that say she know (and he know that she know) that he see she bare naked. The boy flushing and blushing. He look away. He look down at the ground. Then he and she eyes clasp on each other again. They latch on, tight, tight. Is like question and answer, call and response, passing from one to the next. Then she right eyelid come down slow, slow and squeeze shut, trapping that exchange deep inside the black hole in the middle of that bright blue eye.

Wait, nuh! Is wink she winking at him? Big woman can't be making sweet eye at that… that… *boy*? I Cynthia look around to see whether the sweet eye was for somebody else and if anyone else seeing what happen, but no, all eyes fix on KarlLee performance.

PART TWO

8. THE GIFT WITH UNALLURING PACKAGING

Early the morning after the painting finish, Indira comes down-stairs with the papers, folded open at the horoscope page. She's eager to get the place ready. She sees Bostic clearing up the forecourt, stacking empty beer bottles in their crates, sweeping up doubles wrappers, nuts bags, styrofoam food boxes. The place inside still the way it was, but she's planning to fix it up. Sound advice from *Persistence Pays Plenitudinous Premiums*. First thing, she tells herself, is to get KarlLee to take down the old pictures at the back, take them to Geoff, his photographer friend, and get him to do whatever he has to do to make them fresh and bright again and then hang them gallery style, with captions and so on. Was Solo who gave this place its being, infused the vibe that made it alive. Maybe paying tribute will bring it back to where it was when he was around?

Fritzie pass by to see what going on. She gone inside, grab a beer and fall in with the job at hand. Cecil and Boyee drift by. They figure the pub *hads was* to be open. After all, the painting done finish. No reason for Miss Indira to keep the place close up. Whole week big man have no refuge from the trials and tribulations of life.

Them two barfly see Miss Indira and Fritzie wiping down tables, unstacking chairs, they see Bostic fulling up the chiller. They look at one another. Cecil cock his head towards the door. Boyee lift his eyebrows. Cecil point his chin at Miss Indira. Boyee purse his lips and make to pick up one of the little wrought-iron tables. Miss Indira flutter her eyelids. Cecil pick up the next side and the two of them move the table outside, under the eaves. They go back in for two chairs. Bostic bring out two cold Stag. Fritzie bring out the draughts box. Cecil and Boyee, feeling like they reach home at last after a long and perilous journey, swig long draughts of the beer, wiping the foam from their lips with

71

the backs of their hands. Cecil, back in harness as self-appointed leader of the two, pick up a draughts piece, fold it in his palm, put his two hands behind his back, then cross his closed fists on the table in front of him. Boyee tap the right fist and when Cecil unfurls his fingers, is the right one for true. Boyee selects the black pieces, Cecil, the white, and they relax into the welcome tension of combat by draughts.

Fritzie daughter, Precious, drop in to tell her mother she off to school. Feroze, passing by on his way to check out another used Almera for his flourishing fleet of illegal unlicensed rental cars, slow down when he spot Cecil and Boyee. Like Miss Indira open back up, he tell himself. KarlLee bring Sandy, his long time visiting American girlfriend, to show her how nice the place looking and they pull out a table and two chairs, too. Feroze come back with the fella he buying the car from. They pull out two more chairs, ask Bostic for some beers and a pack of cards, and they start up a all-fours game. Bostic go back inside with Cecil and Boyee empty bottles and come back out with a table, then two more chairs and park them up on the forecourt, just to see what would happen. When he come back out with cold beers for the ole fellers, he see two mature women, looking like recent returnees – straw hats, floral dresses, sunglasses, faces immaculately made-up at nine in the morning, but obviously not going to work – sitting at the table he just put out. One of them signal him and order a latte and an espresso.

Bostic know these some kind of coffee drink – he watch enough episodes of *Friends* to know that – but it's beneath his dignity to show he doesn't know exactly what these ladies want, but he's too glad they're sitting there, glamorising the forecourt to tell them that this is a pub not a coffee shop, so he gone inside to relate his predicament to Indira and Fritzie. You didn't tell them here is a bar not a coffee shop? Indira ask. Go back and tell them they can have a cold soft drink. Fritzie don't see why they can't make some coffee for two visitors. All they want is a black coffee and a coffee with milk. So *you* making the coffee, Indira ask. That can't be too hard, Fritzie say. Indira tell her to go upstairs and take out the tin of Blue Mountain from the freezer and bring the kettle, but then Indira go upstairs she-self. She and Fritzie make the coffee, pour it into two nice ceramic mugs, whisk up some evaporated milk and pour it hot and foaming in one coffee, put the mugs, teaspoons and a bowl of Demerara Gold on a tray with two paper napkins. Indira open a packet of Bermudez ginger biscuits and put four on a small plate. She take the tray downstairs to the two ladies. They look up, smile and thank her. Indira halfway back inside when one of the ladies say, Excuse me, Miss, we'd like to have a look at your lunch menu. What's on the menu today? Indira tell them they don't have a menu, but they can have what they were making – sancoche. It's a thick soup. You'll like it. The women say they'll be back around one.

Back inside she laughing so much Fritzie and Bostic had was to wait for her to calm down before she could explain. Is years now I telling Solo we should be selling food. I tell him people *have* to eat food. They don't have to drink alcohol. Bostic interrupt. You really believe that? That people don't have to drink alcohol? Indira stare him down. Look, just so, just so, we have customers for coffee and for lunch. Lunch? Bostic ask. Who cooking lunch?

Indira pick up the paper and read out what her horoscope say. *Gemini: Discard not the gift with unalluring packaging.* She rest down the papers and look at Fritzie. Fritzie, you think we could make a pot of sancoche by one o'clock? Fritzie say, Well, since we have to eat, too, I don't see why we can't cook for a couple extra people.

Well, in two-twos split peas in the pressure cooker and the two of them chopping onion, garlic, chive, celery, peeling and dicing potato, carrot, breadfruit, pumpkin, kneading flour for dumpling and next thing you know, is a big pot of sancoche waiting for the foreign lady customers who say they coming back. One o'clock come, half past one come, quarter to two come, but the two women don't come. Meanwhile the aromas from the bubbling sancoche slip downstairs making Bostic salivate, rub his belly and sigh. Whiffs waft through the open doorway and out into the forecourt where KarlLee, Sandy, Feroze and his friend getting distracted from playing cards, Cecil and Boyee trying to play draughts until Cecil slam down the piece in his hand, stand up and say, This is torture, I going to put an end to it. He march inside and call upstairs. Run the soup, Miss Indira.

Soup intended for a generous five serve ten modest portions

that first day, leaving everyone wanting more. Tomorrow, say Indira, come back tomorrow. Next day, she prop up a little blackboard against the open door. It say:

HAVE A

SOUPA TUESDAY

WITH OXTAIL

From the outset Fritzie say they not having no styrofoam bowls, no plastic spoon. People must feel they home when they eating home-cook food. So, she pass in by Chung Wah and pick up two dozen blue and white china soup bowls, the ones with the pretty translucent rice grain motif, but she gone to Excellent Trading for the spoons, because those short-handle china soup spoons only good for fishing out things like wontons and little piece a pak choi from clear broth. Trinis like long-handle metal spoon so they can feel something hard in they mouth, something that can't break when they bite down on it, something they can use to cut up provision and dumpling in the bowl self. Because, Fritzie add, we not wasting time with any of them delicate little lightweight appetizer soup for people looking for something solid to follow. We making only belly-full soup. So if it isn't callalloo with coo-coo balls, is corn soup with cornmeal dumplings, or is beef soup with breadfruit chunks, or dhal with channa flour balls, or fish broth with cassava and green fig, or oxtail with sweet potato wedges, or coconut milk oil down, with mixed provision, or even a variation on the original first soup, pigtail sancoche with wheat flour dumplings.

SOUPA it always is and it draw customers from far and wide. It is with this lunchtime soup trade that Fritzie and Indira business partnership begin. Nice and smooth. Hand and glove. Thelma and Louise.

9. A GOOD FRIDAY

In later years, when he lying in bed by himself, KarlLee lose plenty sleep wondering whether forewarned woulda be forearmed that Friday. Maybe, if he'd put a raw egg white in a glass of water out in the sun and read his future there at midday, who know? Maybe that woulda help him out when he first set eyes on Sunity.

When Sunity walk in the pub that first time, the whole room stop, just so. We the people didn't turn we head. We didn't stare at she. We simply freeze, and slope a lowdown eye over she, tracking where she passing. KarlLee think that if she did imagine she could slide in here and blend in easy-easy, without anybody paying her any mind, well, it only go to show she either too green for words or not quite right in the head. But look she there, right in the middle of the bar room, causing this sudden hush, all a we antennae up. And she? She cool, cool, too far inside to turn away and walk back out, even if she did notice the effect she having.

And if she wondering if she make a mistake to come inside, who could've blame her for choosing this place as a refuge? From the outside the pub look so cute and inviting, just the kind a place someone in her position would choose to escape to. Look, the name alone announcing that you reach where you should be. And the sign saying *Anyday, anytime.*

But, it wasn't any day – it was Good Friday, it wasn't any time – it was four-oh-five in the afternoon, and Sunity, in her Good Friday church clothes – black sheath dress with a wide, white satin, pleated cummerbund, black fishnet stockings, black and white patent-leather high-heeled shoes, black pillbox hat with white grosgrain ribbon and black spiderweb veil – would've stop traffic anywhere, even in St Michael and All the Archangels at the Stations of the Cross vigil where she just come from.

Them stiletto heels beat a *plink-plink-per clink* on the terrazzo floor ringing through the room, like Rudolph Charles in the panyard signalling Desperadoes with his iron to come to attention to start the tune; the *plink-plink-per clink* marking time to her advance to the bar, where customers angle aside, guard-of-honour styling, to allow her space. Indira, looking up, controls her amazement and still manages to pour out a steady, creamy, foaming, black Guinness; Bostic, releasing a shower of small change on the counter near a waiting customer, glances down at Apocalypse at his feet; the Rottweiler herself stays quiet-quiet, lying on her side, but black eyelids now flip wide open and blacker ears twitch sideways; Bostic, on autopilot, slip off a left sandal and rub a calming bare foot along the bitch belly as he jerk his chin in Sunity direction and Sunity place some folded notes on the bar in front of her.

A tall merlot on crushed ice, with a slice of lime, please.

KarlLee, hear the voice. Afterwards, when we heckling him, the fellers and them say he *heed the call*. Its authoritative diction, precise enunciation and modulated pitch register in every listening ear, is true, but, according to KarlLee, it pick him out special, tunnelling into his ear canal, reverberating on the drum, vibrating the little bones, coursing through the cochlea and semicircular canals setting a storm surge of waves along the little hairs inside a there, then leap the synapses into the auditory nerve and startle his brain in a frisson of... he can't tell – all his years and years of experience can't tell him what. And then, as suddenly as her presence had conjure it up, the spell of silence break in an embarrassed outburst of excessive volume, as if to compensate. KarlLee, jerking out of his stupor, slam down the domino he poised to play with undue force; Boyee slug the last of his Stag and bang the empty beer bottle on the mosaic scarlet ibis adorning the table top; Fritzie and I Cynthia take up, more loudly the thread of the whispered conversation they having about Precious, and the room return to something like its earlier, indifferently welcoming, state.

The woman step across with her drink to the nearest empty table and perch at the edge of a spindly wrought-iron chair, as if she fraid to sit too far back. Under his eyebrows, KarlLee watching her profile as she flip up the veil on to the crown of her hat. She bend over, looking into her glass and, as her hair swing forward, a thick black curtain hiding her face, he turn his attention back to Boyee's play. He trying to convince himself she not his kind a woman. Too cool. Too sharp. Too sure. And too besides, he's not sure how long Sandy going to be away for. But is he, only he, still stealing glances her way, who notice when her elbow jolt against the table edge, and the red drink in her hand spill over the rim of her glass and onto the immaculate white cummerbund.

See how fast KarlLee bolt up from the dominoes game, sprint to the bar, grab a club soda and, in two-twos, reach her side. He pull up a chair, drag out a handkerchief, pour club soda over it and raise a quizzical eyebrow in her direction. All that commotion and she not looking at him. Her gaze fix on the handkerchief he holding towards her. He, taking her slight shrug of the shoulder as assent, begin to dab, to pat, to stroke, to rub at the stain on the white satin, and under his hand it fade from red, to pink to blush. Under his hand he feeling the rise and fall of her diaphragm. He thinking her breathing coming faster and faster as he work at the stain. He feeling the warmth of her breath flowing through his hair, tingling his scalp, as he bend over her lap. She not so cool, after all. He could smell the fragrances of her skin, her breath, her hair – cinnamon, coconut, peppermint, vetivert, and oh, KarlLee can't tell which is which, only it warm and nice and sweet, and he there, wrapped in the cocoon of that air, drinking it in, swallowing it, in and out, in and out. He rub and stroke and wipe at that cummerbund as long as he could and when the stain not fading further, he stop and look up at her face. He see her eyes red, moist, like she was crying.

He died for us. He died for all of us. Her voice comes out as a whisper; he have to stretch his ears to pick it up.

Who? he say. But immediately he catch himself, and he suddenly feeling stupid, thinking, but not saying, *What the fuck. Dammit. Fool me.*

Jesus, she say, in that soft voice again, Jesus. He died for all of us.

And that's why you crying?

He died.

She say it like if the shock and horror of it only now hit her.

KarlLee throw a little off balance, but he not a longtime smooth operator for nothing.

You know, he died a long time ago. Years and years ago. Thousands and thousands of years ago. Y'boy surprise himself at how gentle he sounding – patient, slow, repeating things – as if he talking to a lil child.

In church today, I felt as if it was happening right then.

He look at her face good. It looking real, real sad, the tears now flowing in two smooth lines down her cheeks. It remind him of raindrops catching a reflection of the world as they slide off a banana leaf, and he glance down, a lil embarrass, a lil shy, at being witness to such feeling. She still not looking at him as she carry on talking, soft, soft, as if to herself.

I was there with Him, suffering with Him, at each station of the cross.

Jeezanages, KarlLee thinking, *what have we got here?* But discretion overtake the thought and he say instead, You're feeling better now?

I prayed to Him to allow me to share His suffering. And He did.

For one tortured moment, KarlLee feel she going to open her palms and show him a pair of bleeding stigmata, and then what he could do? Club soda can't fix that. But the moment pass. Her hands stay foldup in her lap. He look at the delicate brown hands, smooth, catching the light like a fresh nutmeg shell. None of that false plastic nail and scandalous multi-colour pattern paint on, like Amber and Fritzie own. These little nails only have a slight gloss, nothing else. He well distracted, but she not noticing that. She keeping on with her story.

Collection time was coming up. I was kneeling. I reached for my handbag on the bench behind me. I took some notes from the wallet, put the wallet in the handbag, rested the handbag back on the pew bench and continued my meditation with my eyes closed, praying for oneness with His pain. I was so deep in meditation, I didn't notice the collection basket pass by, and the notes, my offering, stayed in my hand.

She open her palm. KarlLee look at it. He want to read her fortune there. He want to read if his fortune tie up with hers in the faint delicate tracery. He want that little hand to hold his hand, tight, like she did hold on to the collection money. But, in that situation, what else KarlLee could do, but nod? About the going to church thing, about the meditation and praying thing, he well understand. He use to go to church regular when he was a college boy. He reflect that he *had* to go to church in those far-off days, no argument, dress up in white long-sleeve shirt with blue school monogram embroider on the pocket, white long pants, black leather shoes polish so bright you could stand up next to a girl and place your foot just below her skirt, look down at the shoe-mirror and see…

I placed my hand on the bench behind me to reach for my handbag to put back the money until the end of the vigil, when I could hand it directly to Father, but when I patted and patted the bench behind me, I felt nothing there.

Shit, think KarlLee. Oh, no! he say, but he looking at the way her round bosom rise when she stretch out her arm demonstrating the patting action on the invisible bench. And her arm, smooth and firm and gleaming and…

I turned around and my handbag was gone.

Bugger! come in his mind, Gracious heavens! come from his lips.

It had vanished. She raise her head. Is first time they two head level and KarlLee see her face properly. She pucker her red lips something like a kiss, something like a Marilyn Monroe kiss to be exact, and then the lips blow out, phew, a puff of air. It vanish, just so, she say. So, maybe, it wasn't no kiss for him, but when KarlLee see the face, the eyes, the lips, well, he smile, because she nice. She nice, too bad. All he want to do is stroke that cheek, kiss those lips, feel those eyelashes tickle his body… but he catch himself quick. He have to show interest in the conversation.

You saw who was sitting behind you? Someone who could have taken your handbag?

There was a couple I had noticed earlier. A man and a woman. In the first hour of the vigil, they were there, but at the start of the second hour, when I realised the handbag had gone, I looked for them and they were gone too.

So, they must've taken it?

I thought Our Saviour was testing me. Sending me a taste of His passion, which He would stop when He saw I'd suffered enough.

She living in the real world? What kind a person go looking for suffering when it have plenty around, without conducting a search, eh? He himself have more than his share of suffering these past dry months. All a them people who does make foolish joke about male prowess and say, Red man always in season, never include him in any survey; nobody never asking him how he making out lately. But she, she like a angel, maybe she is one of them angel come down from heaven to help mankind? KarlLee want to be the mankind this angel come to take in hand. Oh god, he close his eyes, that would be so, so sweet. She talking about passion, but he *know* about passion, he is passion expert; he didn't forget passion, even if is a long time since he taste any since Sandy go back home. And boy, oh boy, he could give this angel a taste of his passion anytime, anyday. KarlLee can't open his eyes, he fraid she could read his mind with those impious thoughts next to her innocent words. He nod to let her know he still listening.

I prayed for the second hour, thanking Him for my anguish. In the third hour I heard a rustling in the pew behind me and when I shifted my position to investigate, I saw the man and the woman, the couple who was there in the first hour, kneeling once again in the pew behind me.

So, did the handbag come back too?

There was still no handbag. The test hadn't come to an end.

Did you get it back later?

After the third hour, the vigil ended and I went out to my car. It wasn't where I had parked it. I wasn't sure if that was another test, so I looked for it in case I had mistaken my parking spot. Most of the cars drove off and mine wasn't among the few left.

The car keys were in the handbag?

Yes. And my house keys too.

KarlLee know that not good. Real bad in fact.

Your driver's permit was in your wallet?

Yes.

The insurance certificate in the glove compartment?

She nod.

He spelling it out, slow, slow so she would get what he driving at. And, of course, your home address is on both.

Yes. And my phone with all my contacts is also in the handbag.

Like the penny drop, but he still don't want to spook her and make her run off in a panic.

You went to the police station to make a report?

No. I was walking around in a daze, but when I saw the sign, I came in here to settle my mind. To help me figure out if this is my test, to give up everything I have and follow Him as He bid us do. I even gave up the collection money in exchange for the wine.

Look, Miss...

Sunity. Call me Sunity.

Look, Sunity, first things first. By all means, give away all you own, but don't encourage people in stealing it.

So, what you suggest I should do?

Let me take you to the police station to make a report. Afterwards, we can figure out what to do next.

She look at him a long, long while. KarlLee say afterwards he feel he was going through a exam he hadn't prepare for and, while he willing to take a guess in a multiple choice, he didn't know what subject he was being examined in. She look at his hand, fumbling on the table top, still holding the handkerchief, stain pink like the cummerbund stain. She look at his face, now flushing even redder through the red-Chinese-panyol-African mix-up creole skin; she look at the eyes, into them greeny-amber up-tilt eyes that earn him the schoolyard nickname *cyat eye*, and she must see something there that she like, because she stand up and touch her hand to his own. They leave the pub together and all the hush and the sly glances that greet her when she walk in, come back again as the two of them walk out.

On the pavement outside, KarlLee hearing the buzz rise up in the bar and he know all a we inside talking about them. He wishing it could have something for them to wag they tongue about, but who knows, maybe, if he play his cards right in this next stage, who knows what it might lead to.

They gone to the police station in his car, the little red mini-moke convertible – the one that Sandy buy for he and she to swing about town in style when she actually visiting – and afterwards KarlLee offer to drop Sunity home to make sure everything all right there.

As his car turn into her street, she say, Look! That's my car there. In front my house. KarlLee see a black Sunny park up in front a white house and when he reach it, he park up too. She open the gate – it not lock – and they go up the path to the porch and he see that the front door wide open. She walk in first, and when he reach the porch and make to follow, she hold up her hand to stop him, but from where he standing, he could see what going on inside the living room. She squat down and she say, It's all right, Lucifer. I'm home. What've you been up to, eh? He see her patting and rubbing a big, big, white pitbull who only smiling, smiling, chops wide, wide, showing more rows of teeth than *Jaws*. She concentrating on the beast, but KarlLee, scoping out the room over her head, spot a nashy little feller crouch down on the floor, next to a mahogany glass cabinet, covering his head with his two skinny arms. She stand up and the dog stand up too. If you see how that beast big; it wide like a young bullcow. She and the dog walk towards the feller by the cabinet and she say, Stand up. You're a man, so stand up like a man.

The feller stand up, but his head hang down. He looking at the dog, who not doing nothing threatening, he only standing next to the woman. So, where're my handbag and keys? The feller try to talk, he try to point, he try to look in her direction, but is like he hypnotize by the beast. He can't do nothing. She put her hand on the beast head and the dog sit down next to her. She say, Where's my things? The feller say, K-k-k-kitchen. She leave the beast and slip past a counter and come back with a handbag, the exact match to the black and white stripe patent-leather shoe she have on. She open the handbag and look inside. Keys? she say and he reach in his pocket and pull out two big bunch. They jangle-jangle in his hand like Angelus bells, is so he shaking. She say, Rest them on the cabinet. What's your name? He say, P-P-P-Prakash. She say, Prakash, I want you to deliver a message to those people in the church, the ones who sent you here, in my car, with my handbag, to rob me. Tell them, Lucifer leads you into temptation, but when you sin, he doesn't let you out. She looking straight at the feller, but he not looking at her at all, he only looking at the dog. She rest her hand on the beast head and she say to the feller, And you remember that too. It's not too late to change your ways. Go! Now! The feller move slow, slow, scrabbling sideways, eyes bulging out he head like a mangrove blue crab; he scramble out the front door, down the path, out the gate and pelt speed down the road.

KarlLee mesmerise by the events, by the dog, by the woman. She look at him. She say, Come inside. It's over now. Let's relax. She sit down on the sofa, she lean back on some cushions and she pat a space next to her: Come on! He go inside, moving towards the sofa, but he, too, looking at the beast. She see that and she say, Lucifer, here! The dog come and she bend down, hold his ears and tell him something quiet, quiet. The beast walk out the room, flop down on the floor in the front porch, right in the doorway, put his head between his front paws, and watch them like they is just a movie.

KarlLee kinda relax now, too, and he go and sit down on the sofa next to her. She say, How about some red wine? He see that she smiling right up, right direct into his face. He smile back, broad, broad. He say, That sounding just right. He pause and carry on in that offhand way he have, But you don't think you should take off that nice dress first? She look at him in a sort a way that say, Where you coming from? He say, Well, we wouldn't want another accident to happen to it, would we? She laugh. Accident? What accident? KarlLee point at the faint stain on the cummerbund. She say, Oh, that? Yes! Oh yes. Ha, ha, ha. She laugh, he laugh, they laugh.

She kick off them spike-heel shoes and send them flying across the floor. She lie back on the cushions, close her eyes and let a long sigh escape. Aaaah. Then she snuggle deep into the sofa, moving her whole self in a slow unwinding dance. She raise her arms above her head, point her toes, stretching the arch of her foot. KarlLee watching the calf muscles swell and tighten; she push down her heels and the top of her thighs rise, pulsing rounded mounds straining against the black sheath dress. Point, push, point, push, point, push. But KarlLee don't unwind. He can't unwind. He get wind-up instead. He completely transfixiate on the action – his two eyes trap in the fishnet stockings, in the diamond mesh self, as it stretch open and close, open and close, like the mouths of fish beached in a seine. His brain lull into a trance under the sighing susurus of his hot red blood, surging from one chamber of his heart to another, forcing open the valves, closing them, in syncopated rhythm with the point-push, point-push, point-push. She pause in midpoint, she turn her head slow in his direction, she half-open her eyes and she say in a kind a dreamy murmur, Ummmm, I could do with that glass of wine. Stay here, I'll be back in a minute. KarlLee, he stay there, stranded at the edge of the sofa, gasping like he just get tumble and jumble by a Maracas wave, waiting for the backwash to drag him, straighten him out, waiting under Lucifer impassive gaze.

10. EVERYBODY NEEDS SOMEBODY

Indira looking out for Fritzie to come to work. It's Glorious Saturday. Christ not resurrected yet, so is still Lent. Yesterday was fish broth. Today would also have to be no meat, so maybe a nice ital corn soup? People like corn soup.

Indira getting well good with the menu planning now, but she still relying on Fritzie sweet hand for the real creole flavour. But is after ten and Fritzie not there yet. She and Bostic already pack out the chiller. While the regulars would not let a scrap of meat pass their lips on the sacred end days of Lent, alcohol is a different matter. Alcohol is like air, and like Boyee say, how you could forget that The Last Supper had wine?

Oh, there you are. Indira greet Fritzie in that kind of sarcastic way she picked up in England, as Fritzie push open the door. I was wondering if you were coming in today. She looking pointedly up at the clock hanging over the bar and then at Fritzie. My word. Aren't you looking special? Looks like you have something important on today.

Fritzie look straight ahead. Morning, she say, to no one in particular, go to the bar, fish in her carry-all and pull out a pair of flat shoes to wear instead of her red wedge sandals. She put on her apron and, without another word, she gone upstairs. Indira and Bostic exchange eyebrow lifts, mouth pouts and shoulder shrugs. They could hear the fridge door screeching open, things being banged on the counter, fridge door slammed shut, dried peas raining into a metal bowl, heavy stream of tap water hitting metal.

Indira hurry upstairs. She put on her own apron and stand at the sink, rinsing the split peas. She pour the peas into the pressure cooker, add water, put on the lid and weight, then she start kneading flour with baking powder and butter for dumplings. Fritzie chopping corn with the cleaver like if she wielding an axe at the root of the tree that bringeth not forth good fruit, peeling

85

eddoes and yam like if she flaying a lover caught in *flagrante*, grinding chives, onion, garlic, chadon bene in the little electric blender, looking as if she picturing somebody body parts inside the little plastic cylinder while the blades whirring.

Y'girl Indira knows better than to ask a person anything when they vex, because is her they would take their vexation out on. So, she just sous-cheffing with this corn soup until Fritzie ready to talk.

They make the corn soup in a silent intricate dance. Nobody stepping on nobody toes. Nobody stepping in nobody space.

Fritzie standing at the sink, washing the chopping boards and chopping knives, and she turn round quickly when she hear the pot spoon, which was balancing across the bubbling pot, slip off and clang on to the terrazzo floor. Too quickly she turn round, so the knife she washing slice through a finger and the hot stinging pain make her cry out, Fuck!

Indira say, Oh gods, what happen? Fritzie hold up a finger springing red. Indira grab a pantry towel and run over and she squeeze the finger tight. She pull Fritzie over to the living room sofa where they sit together, still in silence.

So, what's the matter?

I cut my finger

I mean what is *really* the matter?

Fritzie looks up but does not answer.

You came in late this morning. You're dressed as if you're going out. You're not talking to anybody. That's why I'm asking you, what is *really* going on?

Fritzie hang her head. Wet spots darken her apron where her tears fall. Indira puts her arms around her.

Is Precious.

Something happen?

School. They send for me to go in today. Precious get suspend for three days and I didn't know nothing. Every morning she putting on uniform and going off normal-normal, but then when she know is time that I leave home to come here, she tack back home.

How did you find out?

The suspension letter. The parent have to sign it and send it in with the child when she return to school. Of course, I never see it. When they check and see that the signature on the letter didn't match mine on her records, they send for me.

Why was she suspended?

Repeated disobedience and leading a boy astray.

Indira lean back and laugh.

Sorry, can't help it. Sounds just like you would expect from my borrowed goddaughter, and your daughter. Rebel.

Fritzie manage a smile.

Fruit don't fall far from the tree, eh?

Now *how* was our girl disobedient? And *how* was that hapless boy led astray?

That blasted cellphone. The students suppose to have them switch off in class, but apparently she spending all her time texting and taking selfie and after a couple warnings, the teacher confiscate the phone.

So far, so good.

Later, Precious make a boy go to the staffroom and pick up the cellphone from the teacher desk and give it back to her. When the teacher see it gone, she call in Precious, who confess. Both a them get suspend. The boy parents bypass the school authorities and complain direct to the school supervisor. The whole thing get blow up big-big.

She sigh.

Is hard to bring up a child alone nowadays. I wish I could just bite the bullet and make her father share the responsibility

Her father? Precious has a father?

Fritzie looks at Indira, who turn red and flustered.

I know about biology. I mean, her father is around?

He's around. But he don't know he have a child. I not even sure that he would believe me if I confront him one day. Is not like we was in a relationship. More like a couple one-night stands. Or, even if he believe me, whether he would want to help. Then I remember the story about the Tree of Knowledge. Maybe knowledge is the forbidden fruit for a good reason. Knowledge can be more dangerous than ignorance, sometimes.

Could that be true? Indira runs that thought through her head. If she had not found out the truth about what had happened to her baby, would she have been as tormented as she is now? Wouldn't she, long ago, have just let him slip away into her past, like so much else?

Indira give Fritzie a little twisted smile to show she in agreement. Fritzie is encouraged to continue.

Anyway, is too late now. I let the time go by and I do nothing for twelve years. One hundred and forty-four months looking for food, clothes, doctor, rent, uniform, books for this man child. And he don't even know. When I see him, I want to say, You don't see how we child, Precious, growing nice? This is the only child you make and look, you don't see how she even take a little after you? But I realise now that it's too late to lay fatherhood on him. Or bring a father into Precious life. It's just too late.

Indira brain is racing trying to figure out who could be Precious father. The child looks like her mother in print, and you can't find any feature to pin on somebody else. Indira closes her eyes to focus on her mental picture of Precious. She knows she is not as good as the people here at working out the fine fractions of racial mixing. Lessee. Maybe something around the eyes? Something a little bit oriental perhaps? She's looking at Fritzie good. Yes, and the skin. Precious skin. Lighter, more yellowish, kinda more dark honey colour. Not rich molasses like Fritzie's. And the hair. Precious hair. More open wave, less kink. Hmmm. Who put those ingredients in the pot? From what Fritzie revealed, it is very likely to be someone who is from around here. Could it be someone who is a regular? Something to speculate about later. The moment is calling for other urgent matters.

Look, Fritzie, let's talk about how to deal with Precious later. The multitudes are gathering downstairs. Soon they'll be making a set a noise, demanding food.

True. First things first. Where you keep your Band Aid?

After lunch cleared up and the patrons gone home, the two women sit with Bostic at one of the little tables to have their lunch. Amber, Fritzie's youngest sister, walk in with her baby and she pull out a chair to join them. They just come from the Health Centre. Akeel get his second set of shots and he fast asleep. The women take turns to hold and cuddle him. When Indira cradling the baby, Amber say, Yuh looking good in that role, yuh know. Yuh hol'in him like you is a real expert.

Indira say nothing, but she blinking rapidly. She stand up with the child and walk around between the tables, singing softly to him. She bends her head to inhale the breath of him, to take some of him into her, into the void she carries. When he stir, she take him to his mother who pull out a breast to feed him.

Easy to mind when they small, say Fritzie. Small children, small worries. Big children, big worries.

Is so they say. But ah don' remember me giving we mammie any trouble when ah was growin up. Ent, Fritzie? Ah was a easy chile. Not like your Precious. Ah see she mixing up with all kind a fren now. Neck and chest powder up, talking loud, loud in the road. What yuh going to do about she?

Maybe I should send her to you, Miss Perfect, to get straighten out.

Amber turn to Indira and Bostic.

The two of allyuh ent have no idea what going on. No child to confuse allyuh life. We know Miss Indira don't have no chirren. But what about you, Bostic? You have chirren?

None that I know of.

That is the real difference between man and woman, eh? Woman does know when they make a chile, but a man does have to have a woman come forward and say a chile is he own. When a woman tell a man she pregnant, he could say, So what you planning to do? Yuh throwing it away or yuh keeping it? As if the decision is she own only and she will have to bear the conse-quence whatever she decide. Man always say they don't want no chile until they settle.

Fritzie add her two cents.

Settle usually mean he prepared to leave his mother house and move in with a woman who he expect to take over from his mother. The poor woman then find herself having two child to mind – a big hard-back man plus the baby they make. But you get lucky with Akeel father. It looking like he is a devoted father.

Yes, Amber agree. Nowadays them young father and them like to show off that they could make a chile. He does take Akeel wherever he going. All that Viagra talk have them young boys

89

frighten about impotence. They want to prove they could get it up and they not shooting no blanks.

The women laugh. Bostic pick up the empty soup bowls and glasses, go to the bar and start to clear up. Indira hold up a copy of *Popular Porn Princess Positions* for their inspection.

It says here that modern young men are learning about sex from watching internet porn and that they are expecting their girlfriends to behave like porn stars. All kind of weird sex practices from the get go. Some young people never even get to experience the ordinary missionary position.

Some of it is the girls too, eh? Fritzie adding. They have a different approach to sex, to commitment. Plenty girls who in casual relationship with fellers don't mind getting pregnant. It show that they not no mule. Nowadays, it not like long time when it was a shame thing to be making baby. Lemme tell you, even married woman used to cover up and disguise they growing belly with long blouse and thing. Now everybody exposing they big belly, naked, naked, whether they married, single, horning, loose, no matter what. Nobody don't care.

Amber continue the quizzing.

Miss Indira, yuh ever did want to make a baby?

Is a question that Fritzie never ask, just as Indira never ask who Precious father is. Fritzie interested to hear how Indira answer Amber question. But Indira not answering. Instead, she get up and say, I think I'd better give Bostic a hand.

When Amber gone, Fritzie see that Indira not pleased.

Amber too fast and out of place to ask you your business. She interfering in me and my child business, too. I hope you not vex.

Indira pat Fritzie on the shoulder. It's OK. You're not responsible for her tactlessness. She's feeling good to have a husband and child. It is an achievement. Look, she say, you want to go upstairs and continue our conversation from this morning?

Upstairs, Indira stretch out in the hammock, Fritzie on the sofa.

So what are we going to do about Precious?

Is hard to say. I don't want to lay down too much a law because then the other children might tease her into joining them in worse things than cellphone disobedience, or she might rebel by herself if she feel she getting too much pressure from home.

You're doing your best.

I try my best, but look at the other influences around her. Take yesterday. That woman who walk in the pub. Nobody know who she is. She come by herself but she didn't leave alone. That kind of behaviour is like normal now. People see one another first time and they hook up, just so.

What is it with that KarlLee? Sandy has just gone back home. Her plane has hardly landed in Houston or Pittsburgh or wherever, and he picks up right away with another woman. It's like he has to prove that whenever he slings a hook, he still can catch something? I bet you anything he spent last night by that woman he pick up.

Fritzie look down quickly. She concentrating on her finger. She peel off the Band Aid. She blow a puff of air on the cut.

Indira, you ever think about getting another husband? Is how long since Solo gone? A year?

Almost two. But no, not really. It would be nice, like you say, to have some male support, somebody to discuss things with. It's hard to make good decisions on your own. Or to make any decisions at all. Look how long it took me to fix up the place, just a little bit, after Solo left.

That is all a husband for? Making decisions? Don't tell me you don't feel the urge to have a man? Solo was so much older than you. He and Bostic was schoolmates, not so? And Bostic is *a ole man*! Gone through! You is still a young, attractive woman, and you going to waste. You don't feel the urge for a younger, more virile man?

Indira look far away, lost in thought.

Fritzie continue: I see your face when you holding Amber baby. Like you missing something in your life. How much time you feel you have remaining to make a child?

Indira look across at Fritzie's earnest face, and she laugh.

Dear Agony Aunt, where in my day-to-day life will I find this mate you think I need? Just check out the fellers I see every day. Which of the deliverymen, regular customers, the occasional newcomer, you think suitable? You've already dismissed Bostic. Not exactly a big pond to fish in, eh?

Maybe you need to get out more.

Like you looking for company to go trawling?

Nah, just speculating on what could work for you. But it looking to me like you get all the advice you could want from your horoscope, anyway. I never see somebody so hook on astrology.

Girl, I was born in India. I grew up there. That means I was born and grow up in astrology. The day and time you're born determines everything about your life. To choose a husband or wife, horoscopes have to match. The day to get married, astrology decides that. To open a business. To write a letter. To go on a journey. To apply for a job. To host a special puja. Everything is determined by astrology. It's part of the religious practice. More than that, it is life. What do *you* rely on to guide you?

Church, I suppose. And prayers. Like the song say, *Everybody need somebody to lean on.*

She check her phone for the time.

I better go home. Shouldn't leave Precious too long. Satan find mischief. Midnight Mass tonight, so I better get some shut-eye now or I'll be of no use to myself later.

Indira stays in the hammock, pondering. A man and a baby. That's what Fritzie, and perhaps everybody, thinks she needs. Maybe they see her devotion to De Rightest Place as a substitute, that the energy she pours into the place could be better spent on a man and a child – if only she could get them. What would she want with a man, eh? She knows what a man would want with her. She's known since she was a little girl. And she quickly learned how much they'd be willing to part with for it, what they'd be willing to do, what risks they'd be willing to take. Except Solo. Solo was different.

It was his many differences from the others that had caught her off guard. She feels a little ashamed now at how she behaved then. And so she should, she tells herself. It was his first night playing in the club where she worked as an entertainer. When he finished his set, people stood and applauded and called for an encore, which he graciously granted, playing riffs on *Yellow Bird*, that all-time tourist-in-the-Caribbean favourite, making runs on his tenor pan that sounded almost classical, or maybe a parody of classical music. When it was over, he picked up a pint of bitter and walked towards an empty table in the semidarkness.

92

And there was I, Indira Gabriel. Spangly silver clinging halter-neck, back-slit evening dress, long black gloves above elbows, a *Breakfast at Tiffany's* Audrey Hepburn, sitting at a table, having a drink with a customer, an occasional client. Solo tripped against a chair behind me and pitched forward. I was drenched in cold beer. I spun around, not knowing who the culprit was, just mad and wet. Fuck you! I said. Know what that man said? I think we should get to know one another better first, don't you? And he took my hand and led me to the dressing rooms. He stood me at the washbasin and he took off my dress. He pulled out his handkerchief and sponged me down. Me standing like a manne-quin in underwear and gloves. Then he said, Go get your coat. I'm taking you home. And he did just that. Dropped me home and left me at my door. He wouldn't come in for the cup of coffee I offered him. I didn't shower that night. I wanted to cling to the sour smell of beer that lingered in my hair and skin. For weeks afterwards we would meet at work, we would chat and dance and he would leave me at my door. I saw no other man, I entertained no other man in all that time. I didn't want to. Then one night I said to him, Do you think we know each other well enough now? He said, Do you? I didn't answer in words. I simply pulled him inside and shut the door. I took off my gloves for him. Solo was the first man who made me hungry. He was my second love.

But she never retells this story to anyone, not even Fritzie.

Ah, she sighs, it's better they believe that my life began when I came to this island with Solo.

Her thoughts drift from Solo and are pulled to him, her *first* love. His birthday, the twenty-fifth of March, is the feast of the Annunciation. So she named him *Gabriel*, bringer of glad tidings. He would be a young man now. She conjures up his newborn self, his precious little face and the completeness of his small body, his miniature perfection, his infinite promise. She wonders what his promise became, where he could be, in what part of the world. Who was bringing him up? Was he at college or out at work? Is he loved as she loves him? Does he wonder about her? Does he want to know her. Has he tried to find her? Did the people who took him tell him where they got him?

11. FORTUNE FAVOURS THE FEARLESS

Indira fell asleep in the hammock where she lay thinking of him, her eyelids rimmed with the salt of dried tears. Overhead, the *rat-a-ratta-tatta-tatta* of heavy raindrops, barrels of bullets clattering on corrugated galvanise, weaves into her sleep. The gurgle of the downpipe outside her window becomes a tumbling cascade where she, kneeling at the water's edge among the bulrushes, spies a basket floating just out of reach, and, intuiting the scene from that Bible story in the orphanage, *Basket Brings Bounty*, she knows what is in the basket and that she is the one chosen to make the rescue and, as it is writ, she seizes a stick and tries to hook one end to the floating basket, to pull it towards her.

Outside, in the awake world, the dry season's sudden cloud-burst explodes, scattering shrapnel raindrops that pierce through leafless trees, pitting the dry, caked laterite, loosening dirt from a million tiny craters to form a web of cocoa-brown runnels that rush onward, carrying mud, dead leaves and parched grass, styrofoam cups, Favourite Fried Food boxes and plastic water bottles, racing towards drains already full and clogged, bursting through into the streets, ripping off sheets of asphalt, dense grey-black islands transported on raging road rivers.

People going about their Glorious Saturday business before Midnight Mass race for shelter beneath the overhanging eaves of shops. From behind screens of water pouring off the roofs, they watch the scene of devastation flowing past, even as the floodwater climbs over the curb on to the pavement, over shoes and ankles until, as one, the people pound on the siesta-shut doors of De Rightest Place, just as Indira pulls the basket towards her and she sees, as she expected, a wrapped bundle. As she reaches in to lift it out, the pounding below smashes into her dream. Her eyelids flip open and, still in a sleepy stupor, she stumbles down. Who is it, who is it? Wait. Wait a minute. I'm coming. She opens the doors and a group of half-drowned impromptu guests come flooding in. She puts on the kettle and an extra large saucepan to brew coffee and tea and cocoa to warm them up.

Among the washed-up flotsam, there's a tall young man. She's seen him before, she's sure of it, but where is it she knows him from? Hmmmm, Where? When? Chuts! Now she knows. It's the angle of view. He's the boy on the forecourt during the painting, he's the one whom she'd looked for every day – and still can't figure out why. She remembers the delicious tremor pulsating in her groin, and the guilty urge she felt to stroke and cuddle and caress his innocence. Now he is here, and he seems to take charge, running up and down the stairs, ferrying hot drinks and towels and a hair dryer from her to them below, in a silent pantomime. Clothes are flung over the backs of chairs and soon De Rightest Place is transformed into a refugee camp. The rising water laps against the street door, where towels rolled along the bottom edge yield to the onrushing tide, and seepage rises first an inch, then a couple inches, then several. Then the lights go out. Oh! A huge collective gasp. Does anybody have matches? Who has a torchlight? Where is the door? Don't step on my foot. Watch where you going.

Be quiet a minute, please. Stay right where you are. No need to panic.

A male voice rises over all and there is a hush. She knows it is *his* voice, though she hasn't heard it before.

Miss Indira, you have candles?

Yes.

You know where to find them?

I think so. They're upstairs. I'm standing on the stairs now. I think I can feel my way up.

Soon a wavering light floats down from above. The more superstitious make the sign of the cross across their chests, as the thought *Soucouyant!* flashes across minds that hold terror of the supernatural. Indira hands round a packet of a dozen candles and a box of matches and soon there are lit candles on the tables and people are sitting around, like in a cave of much, much earlier times, relating, through rumbling thunder and flashing lightning, competing and complementary stories of famous power cuts, legendary floods, memorable Easter weekends, while the rain

95

continues outside and the waters rise inside. Then, a silence as compelling as noise. The rain stops as abruptly as it started.

The hostages to inclement weather step tentatively down from their chairs, wade with care through the calf-deep water, open the doors and peer outside. Road and pavement, drain and verge are one. All is one sheet of still water in which the newly waning full moon, a melting disc the lustre of white gold, seems to lie just below the surface, gilding the water in concentric rippling circles. All is calm and all is bright. As they emerge, holding hands, feeling for where door sill ends and pavement begins, where pavement ends and curb drops to street, her guests, a flotilla of silent pirogues, drift over the moonstruck water. The boy says, Goodnight, Miss Indira, thank you for everything. Happy Easter, as he leaves with the others.

She watches his retreating back, as he leads the way, finding for his followers the obstacles, the hazards, the sudden drops in that waterscape of undivined bathymetry beneath the calm smooth surface. She is washed with an old familiar sense of abandonment, of being left behind, of not being one with the people she finds herself among. She is but a stop on the way to their destinations. She watches them as they wind their way homewards. In an awestruck silence, she reflects. There was a time. There was a time when…

The moonlight breaks into long ruffles on the calm black water. She is sitting on the floor of the wide verandah of her first home. Amma is on a low stool behind her. She is snuggled deep into Amma's thin lap. It is her turn to have her hair combed and plaited for the night. Her hair is wild and wavy. Amma works slowly from the ends to the scalp, smoothing the rough waves.

Amma, I want hair like yours.

But your hair is beautiful, daughter.

I wish it was black and straight.

You have what the gods gave you when you were born.

Why did I get this? Sita and Rajpati… and Bai too… got hair like you.

Your mai had hair like yours. When she brushed it out, sitting right where you are, it looked like the sun was hiding in it.

Why were my mummy and daddy in this house?

They came from England. They wanted to know India. They stayed here for a long time.

I was born here?

Yes, you were. In the village clinic. Just like Bai.

Where did my mummy and daddy go?

They went out in a boat one day. A storm came and took them away. You were just a little baby. You were safe here with us, and now you are our daughter.

Like Sita and Rajpati.

Yes.

How many times did she have this conversation with Amma? It seems like it was an evening ritual, her childhood bedtime story. How many times has she repeated it to herself as a child, as an adult? From those bare bones, she fleshed out in her head many versions of her own story, of how she came to be with Amma and Achan and Sita, Rajpati and Bai in that old colonial guesthouse on the banks of the backwaters of Kerala. Those fantasies were the stuff of her other life that dwelt in the dark nights of her growing-up years when she was no longer in the old colonial guesthouse, but in the workhouse orphanage for deaf-mute girls. Even now, in her adult years, still water and sudden storms flood her consciousness with that amorphous past.

The following morning is Sunday, Easter Day, and there is sun. She reads an inspirational passage from *Fortune Favours the Fearless* before facing the day. The scene of wreckage outdoors greets Indira as she surveys, from the vantage of the pub's corner spot, up the Valley Road and along the Circular Road that fronts De Rightest Place. The Valley Road is now a road in name only. It is a rutted-gutted, gouged-ploughed, trenched-wrenched surface. The water having drained off, the Circular Road is where everything has come to rest. Hillocks of rubbish, moraines of mud, long trailing eskers of branches and twigs, trapped residual pools, car tyres, a broken plastic chair, the rusted door of a fridge, black plastic garbage bags – some still full, others empty – tattered rags, contents mixed and mingled, sorted and strewn, a frying pan, its teflon coat pitted, a blue tricycle looking quite serviceable and, grinning up at her from the debris, the rictus smile of a pair of gleaming white false teeth. The stench of long forgotten, discarded things, of dead animals cast into drains, plastic bottles and foam containers, slick with old slime, chicken guts and duck feathers, disposable diapers for young and old disgorged from the underground drains where they had accumulated. Their reek fills every crevice of the air. Indira stands on her threshold and wonders what perfumes and unguents, spices and herbs would have been needed this day, those millennia ago, to mask that smell, perhaps not unlike this one, that would have wafted from the sepulchre when the stone was rolled away after three days if He had not got up, pushed aside the barrier, and walked away Himself.

With that thought, she looks up again at the Valley Road and sees, loping in long strides, *that boy*, the young man of the night before, the one who took charge, the one they called Jah-Son, and he is looking at the ground, finding secure foothold, as he leaps from one ridge to the next, making quick headway. She turns away to go inside so that he does not see her watching him, does not see her neck flush and her face redden, does not see her eyes widen and her eyelids flutter. She feels a surging in her chest, a pulse throbbing in her loins. What the firetruck is going on with her? This is a boy!

Inside, she pushes the tables along the wall and begins to stack chairs on to the tables in preparation for sweeping out the water that has pooled a foot and a half deep in the pub. Her thoughts drift to her co-workers, to their common predicament in the aftermath of the flood.

Would Bostic be able to get out of his house up the hill to come by, even if it's Sunday and a special one at that? There must be landslides up there for the volume of mud down here. Both cell phone circuits are down, maybe just too much traffic for the systems? Landline down too. Water in the lines, always the same story, even if is only two-drop-a-rain that fall. So she can't call him, can't expect Fritzie to come and help. She have her own place to clean up too. Sunday papers not delivered yet, but Indira laughs: Bet you the horoscope for today telling me to *Rely on my own resources*.

She smiles wryly at her own prediction. She is still smiling to herself when a shadow at the door causes her to lift her head, and she sees Jah-Son. He is standing there, knocking at the open door. He is smiling back at her and his smile pulls a bigger smile right across her face, her eyelashes doing their dance.

Want a hand, Miss Indira?

She doesn't speak. She lifts her shoulders and spreads her arms wide in front of her, palms up, as if asking for benediction. He looks around the pub, lifts his head and laughs, a laugh so deep and full and rich that it fills the room with a warmth that drives out the pall of damp and desolation that hangs there, with an energy charged with the strength of his white teeth, the firm lines of his jaw, the power in the tendons of his neck. Indira feels her spirit infused with a lightness that is almost like being as young and as hopeful as youth is said to be, and she's suddenly sure that all shall be well, that all manner of thing shall be well. He comes over to help her move the tables. Together they work without talk, piling tables and chairs, sweeping out the malodorous water, scraping off mud, hosing down furniture and walls and floor, dragging out onto the pavement soggy cardboard boxes of pulpy books and ruined rugs, soaked appliances and spoiled foodstuffs.

As they work, the light framed by the open doorway shape-shifts and swings from one side of the room to the other before they are done with the cleaning and the pub is restored to some semblance of normalcy. Even so, business can't resume; electricity hasn't come back, drinks are warm and few, and there is no ice. The water, too, has not come back. The tank they were drawing down from would, by now, be almost empty. But, as they stand and look at the result of their labour, a sense of relief and gratitude washes over Indira.

Here is someone who, out of the blue, unbidden, has come to be her helpmeet, again. She has a sense that she has willed him out of the ether, as if he's had no life before she first saw him and will disappear once she's finished with him. She must keep him for a while longer. She wants to let him know how much she appreciates his help. How much his presence means to her. She smiles at him.

Hungry?

Could do with something, yes.

Come, let's see what I can find.

Upstairs, he won't sit. He's too dirty, he protests. He'll mess up her nice furniture. You have bread? Cheese? A sandwich would be fine. You don't have to cook anything. I'll be all right. No, no, no – you've been working hard all day. You must be starving. I can do better than a cheese sandwich, she insists. Look, tell you what. Why don't you have a shower, then we can sit properly and eat something more substantial. We can have an omelette with a little salad and some bread. There's lots of man clothes you can change into after. Come, let me show you where.

What are you doing? What do you want of this boy? Ah, m'girl. You know full well what you're doing. You know where this is leading. You *know*.

J'ouvert morning and you in a mud-mas band, you in a paint band and what you looking for? You looking for a clean wall to smear with defiant mud, handprints, footprints. You looking for a freshly painted surface to print your multicoloured body on, to leave a rainbow of hues, the imprint of your painted pelt. And you, the clean, the unsullied, the untouched? The blue devils want to rub on you, the jab molassie want to rub on you, smear you with their blue-painted bodies, their black-painted bodies, smear your face and arms and your nice clothes. Is you they looking for in the crowd, you in the crisp fresh clothes. At Phagwa, the abeer water guns spray on you, you in immaculate white, who trying to run away, to hide. The urge to desecrate, to sully is let loose in the madness of sanctioned release, pre-Lenten, pre-spring. You lay claim to the wall you have sullied, the body you have blued and blacked, the clothes and skin and hair you have stained. I've left my mark. It is me who was there. The graffitist, too, knows the burning compulsion to say his say, leave his stamp, mark his territory, claim his space, the spoor of two-legged beasts.

She leads him to the shower in the guest bedroom. She turns on the water in the stall and adjusts the temperature. She leaves, saying, Get in while the water's still hot, there won't be much left with the power gone so long. Five minutes later, she gives a little knock and opens the door. He has just stepped out of the shower and she has brought him a towel, one as large and as soft as the one she's wrapped in.

She kneels in front of him and begins to rub dry his feet, his calves, his knees, his thighs. She strokes a finger along the bright red birthmark shaped like a coiled snake on his right thigh. He says, It's OK, Miss Indira. I can do it by myself, as he tries to turn away, tries to hide from her the effect this ministering of hers is having on his body, things he knows he cannot control. By then, her hands are cupping his buttocks, and, when she buries her face into his groin, into the tangle of tight moist curls there, nuzzling deeply into the tender hanging pouch which tightens at the touch of her tongue, a groan issues from him, unbidden.

12. A LARGE CIRCLE OF KEYS

A man say, Is me who break she in. A man say, After twelve is lunch. A man say, I am the first.

From the bedroom window the bloodied sheet hangs. An uncle plunges a finger to prove that all was intact for the bridegroom. Jubilant rifles fire in the air. All must know I am the first. Marry her off at ten, twelve, fourteen. If she is broken, send her back. The bride wears white. The chastity belt is locked. Cut off the clitoris. She must not know the joy of sex. Who knows what she would get up to if she does?

A woman say… this woman say… *I have done no better than was done to me… It is not right… his innocence was not mine to take away… I've done wrong.*

What has she done? Did she do to him, as was done to her? Can a woman do to a man as a man can do to a woman? Did she steal something from him? Did she give him a gift? Is it different for him from what it was for her?

When the silver needle did not curb its straying, when it flew across green silk, red silk, yellow silk, blue silk, following the flight of a bird, the jump of a grasshopper, the flutter of a butterfly, the leap of a frog, when her fingers were so swollen they could no longer hold the errant needle, they bundled her into a van along with stacks of flawlessly-embroidered saris and despatched her to where she would no longer be a nuisance to them. Through the long dusty journey she sat in silence, staring ahead, seeing nothing. The van turned off the main road to follow a long driveway. It came to a halt outside a very big house.

The van driver spoke to her. She didn't respond. He took her hand and led her up the steps to the verandah. There was a lady seated on a big chair in the shady verandah. The lady spoke. The child did not try to lip-read what she said. She stood stock still, staring at nothing, neither near her nor far away.

Come here, child. Let me look at you.

The lady beckoned. The child did not move. The driver came forward and led her onto the verandah.

What is your name?

There was no response.

The lady turned to her husband. She looks like a Persian princess with those eyes and that hair. Where did you get her?

From an orphanage.

Why doesn't she answer me?

She's from the deaf girls' orphanage.

She can't hear? She's dumb, can't speak?

The husband nodded.

She did not disabuse them.

That's not a bad thing. She won't spend her time gossiping with the servants or tittle-tattling our business with the neighbours.

Hear no evil and speak no evil taken care of, said the husband.

Why doesn't she smile or look sad or anything? It's like she's sleepwalking.

Give her time. She will get accustomed. They all do.

She did not get accustomed to him at night. He crept into the room, got onto the charpoy and lay down behind her as she lay awake, curled up, facing the wall. He pressed her tight against the wall. With his arm around her waist he squeezed her from the back. He grabbed her long thick plaits. He pulled on them like reins. She lay like a stone. A stone that was falling down a deep, dark pit. A pit that stank of slug slime and dead fish, a pit that squeezed and rubbed and thrust against her. Falling, falling, eyes open, seeing nothing but the darkness of the unending pit, not knowing the moment when he grunted, released his hold on her, got up and left as silently as he had come.

Next morning the ayah found her lying, curled tight, facing the wall. The woman, pulling at her shoulder, turned her round. Seeing her eyes wide open, the woman gestured that she should get out of bed. She not moving, not seeing, and evidently not hearing, the woman pulled her up, led her to a room, showing her a bucket of water and soap, gesturing that she should wash herself and the chemise she was wearing – stiff, sticky and crusted.

She did not move. The woman pulled off the chemise. She dropped it on the ground. She dipped a cup in the bucket and poured water over her hair and body. She soaped and rinsed her as if she was a baby. She washed the chemise, squeezed it dry and threw it over the towel rail. She dried her and dressed her. She undid the two damp plaits and brushed the loose hair until it shone like a veil of spun gold. She led her upstairs.

She did not get accustomed to the days either. The lady clapped her hands, smiled and laughed with delight at the sight of her. She took her hands in hers. She stroked her long mane. She caressed her cheeks. The lady's lips were moving constantly, forming shapes she could not read. It was a jumbled puzzle of pieces that made no pattern she could understand. That first day, and the days that followed, the mistress of the house would brush her hair and style it, weaving ribbons and jasmine garlands into her plaits, wrap the plaits around her head like a coronet, or leave the hair to hang loose with circlets of flowers on her crown. She would dress her in costumes. She'd be a fairytale princess with a starry wand and sparkly wings; a little cowgirl in jeans, checked shirt and cowboy hat; a Hindu goddess with bracelets, anklets, golden sari, hennaed hands; a Renaissance angel, white robe and feathered wings. She was a doll to dress and play with and the lady didn't mind her silence or her lack of engagement. It was as if her passivity only served to enhance the game, making her more doll-like, an automaton that walked and could be fed and changed, but couldn't act out will or feelings.

Not to be with her body was already a habit, formed in the other place, the deaf girls' orphanage. She had learnt the art of letting her sensing self separate itself from one world and be in another. Now, here, there was the world of the daytime living doll and the nighttime rocking-horse, which were outside her. In her head, nothing but a dark, blank, cloudy space where no memory surfaced, where no thoughts sprang, where no feeling arose. Trapped between those two, somewhere there was another self which had become slow and limp in its movement, its skin turned translucent, the blue of its eyes faded to a pale, still, unseeing gaze.

Unmeasured time passed this way until one morning the ayah came in to find her lying on the charpoy, her head a mass of wild and uneven spikes of hair. Strewn all about the little room, long ropes of curls lay in disarray. She did not move to get her up and ready that morning. Instead, she picked up the scattered hanks and the pair of scissors lying on the floor and took them to the lady. She was not led upstairs that day. No one came to her room that night. Times of light and times of darkness passed, but she lay there not knowing, drifting through deeper and deeper pits of nothing for unknown time. Until. Until she is sent away again.

Until she is jolted from that nothingness into a bright, odoriferous, frantic, hubbub space where she is bombarded by the pidgin polyglot of children brought from all over the country, who seem never to have been children, a space that assaults her eyes and nose and limbs and ears and head with too much sensation. Overloaded, overwhelmed, she sinks to her knees, her body curling forward, rocking from side to side, rhythmically, mechanically, repeatedly, transporting her to another place, an earlier time, to relive a journey that seems a long, long time before. Was this when she was taken from Amma and Achan?

boat rocks   badman took me   in boat   boatman looks at me   nods   points with eyes   at water   again   looks at me   looks at water   looks at me   looks at water   rocks the boat   badman turns   turns back   boatman rocks   badman looks   turns back   boat   rocks   badman not turn   boatman nods at water   afraid to go   afraid to stay   slip over side black water   oh oh so dark   can't   see feet   badman shouts   swim hard go under   stay under   mangroves   badman shouts   boat is coming   deep breath   dive black water hiding mangrove roots huhhuhhuh

It is dark. The water is cold. She is frightened. The trees drip tears on her. She hears a whistle like a birdcall. It gets closer. She sees a figure on a boat silhouetted against the bright water. A whistle. The boatman calls softly, Little daughter, come with me. He calls in a whisper, The badman has gone. I will take you somewhere safe. She chooses to trust him. She swims towards the boat. Cold water, tired, heavy clothes. She thinks she can go no further.

He reaches out the pole towards her. He pulls her in. He points towards the floor. She lies there. The dark trees above, crowns closing overhead, form a long dark tunnel. He punts through the lagoon. Thick forest. He stops. He points to a path, a gap between trees. She climbs out. The boat slides away.

She comes to a high wall with a wooden gate. She knocks and knocks again. Her knock is feeble. There is no answer. She finds a stone and uses it to knock and knock and knock and knock. Still no answer. She gathers small stones and throws them over the gate. She hears them fall on the other side. She throws another handful and slumps to sit against the wall. She hears a key turn and the gate opens. She sees a hand carrying a lighted candle. It lights up the face of an old woman. An old pale face and a pale hand. Then a long white dress and a white veil. A large circle of keys hangs from a cord around her waist. The old woman says nothing to the child, but she waves a hand to invite her in. The girl stumbles in and falls.

The light is bright. She can see white curtains. She watches them fill with breeze, coming in and falling back when the air is still. She thinks the curtains are breathing and as they fill, she breathes in with them, exhaling when they fall slack. She wants to raise her arm, wants to sit up, wants to turn her head, but she can't do any of those things. The old lady swims across her view. The old lady puts a cool palm on her forehead. She goes. She comes back. There is a cup in her hand. She puts an arm under her shoulders and helps her to sit up. With the other hand, she reaches the cup to her lips. The liquid is dark. She sips. Bitter. Like black tea without sugar. She turns away her head. The old lady nods and she tries again. She takes quick gulps. She slips back onto the cot. She drifts to sleep. In and out her dream she can hear people moving around her. She is too tired to open her eyes.

There is noise that is sharp and cutting, smells clanging and heavy, light stinging the nose and burning the eyes. It hammers through her skull, through eyes and ears and nose and mouth. She remains crouched, curled up, unaware of how long or even that she is on the floor. Someone touches her shoulder, shakes her shoulder, grabs her elbows and pulls her up. Her hands are pried from her face, thumbs lift her fluttering eyelids. She sees nothing.

She does not see, close up to her own face, a pair of black eyes and a mouth that make a big circle O, then a wide smile. She does not feel the taking of her wrist, the leading to a stool, the pushing down on her shoulders, forcing her to sit. Something is pressed against her mouth. Her lips touch a coldness, a hardness, a smoothness. Her tongue feels a swirling around each papilla, her mouth feels a soaking through its thin membranes, her throat yields to the rushing tide surging through it. And the water courses like a living thing, touching every part of her, awakening dormant cells, opening closed pores.

Tuesday, nine o'clock in the morning, Bostic return to De Rightest Place after the long Easter weekend. Electricity, water, phones, all come back too. He pick up three days' newspapers lying outside. He try the door. Is locked. He knock and call but no answer. Fritzie join him and call, her voice shrilling to higher places than his. Only silence from above. She pull out her phone and call Indira cell. Voicemail come on. I think it switch off, she say. Bostic tug at the service gate. I'll have to go round the back. He climb over the gate and go along the passageway to the back door. His knowing hand reach through the grille for the key hanging on a string from a nail hammered into the wall. He open up the back, walk through, unlock the front door and let Fritzie in. She rest the newspapers on the counter and look around. Except for a hint of mustiness, which open doors and windows would soon dispel, and a certain unnatural air of tidiness, there is no evidence of the flood of Glorious Saturday night. Bostic go to the storeroom. Only a few full crates of beer and rum and a huge pile of empties. Many more empties than he'd left on Saturday. I'm going to check on Indira, Fritzie say.

She find her in bed. She has a fever Indira tell her. She can't move. Fritzie place a cool palm on Indira's forehead. It does not feel hot. She ask her to stick out her tongue. It is pink. Can she cough? That sounding normal. Maybe I feel normal outside, but inside, I'm burning up. Would you like a drink? Yes, coconut water. When last you eat? I don't remember. I'm not hungry. Just thirsty. OK, I'll get you something to drink. You looking messy. How long you lying in bed? You don't remember? Maybe you had a fever and you now recovering. Lemme help you get out of bed. Look. Go and have a warm shower. Make you feel better. I'll change the sheets. Then you can lie down feeling nice and fresh. And shampoo that hair same time. It looking well dada.

For the next two days, Bostic and Fritzie running the pub and the cooking. Indira showing no sign of wanting to get out of bed. Is like after Solo leave, say Bostic. She spend months doing nothing. I had to do everything by myself. I wonder what happen? say Fritzie. All this talk about having a fever and not leaving her bed, and as far as I can tell, nothing wrong. No temperature, no aches and pains. Maybe she catch some strange virus in the flood? Plenty nastiness was in that floodwater. People who was here that night say the water real deep. Maybe she pick up something that sap her energy. But how she get the place clean up so good? If she do it all by herself, is no wonder she tired.

She opens her eyes. The sunshine is still there outside. The curtains fill and empty. She breathes with them. The old lady gives her another drink. She sleeps again. She does not know how many days are passing by, how long since she has been in this room with this fever and the old lady with her bitter brew. But soon she is awake for longer spells. The old lady comes in and when she opens her mouth to speak, the old lady puts a finger to her lips. She takes her by the hand and leads her to a room. There is a bucket of water, a dipper, a small bar of green soap and a towel. The water is cool. The old lady brings a white smock, which she pulls over the child's head. She leads her back to the room and shows her a chair. She sits and waits.

Fritzie comes in with a bowl of soup.

Hello! Hello! What's this? Like you can get up and move around now? Nice.

Indira looking at Fritzie's lips all the while. She look puzzled. This making Fritzie uncomfortable.

What's the matter? Like you don't know me?

Indira run her tongue across her dry lips. She whisper.

I had a bad dream. Maybe two dreams. Mixed up dreams, except not really a dream. It was about a long time ago.

You've been sick for a few days and all by yourself. Look, here's some nice soup. Let me help you with it.

Indira swallow as Fritzie feeding her and she can feel the warmth opening her throat and soothing as it goes down.

When I was sleeping, did you give me some tea in a cup too? Did you give me water?

No, you had coconut water. Not in a cup. In a glass.

I had a fever in the dream, so maybe I woke up thinking I had a fever?

Lemme tell you, girl, those sheets were soaking wet. Stink with stale sweat too. I think you *did* have fever. But like it gone now.

I want to lie down. I feel tired.

Yes, rest. I'll check back later.

Indira drift into a sleep.

A little girl stands facing her. The girl touches a finger to a thumb on her right hand and touches her own chest with the left. When she looks puzzled, the girl does it again. She copies the gesture and points to the girl. The girl smiles. The girl then does a movement like ripples on water with her right hand and points at her with her left. She copies the movement and points at herself. They smile at each other. The girl brings other girls in. One by one they sign their names. The girls sleep in the long room with her. There are two old women in white. She slips into their sign language and soon she forgets that she can speak. She's still young enough not to wonder at her life. Night happens. Day happens. Life happens.

Her day life is spent with the other girls. In the shade of an open verandah they sit cross-legged on a carpet in a wide circle so they can face one another and chat with their hands. In the middle of the circle is a large basket. From it, each girl pulls an endless stream of shimmering silk, on which her deft fingers embroider intricate patterns with beads of precious stones, gold and silver threads and shining sequins to decorate the cholis and pallus of saris. She remembers a bullock cart from long ago, its big wheels spinning as it races away in a dust cloud and she thinks she is in a magic wheel with the circle of girls at the rim and the shining colourful silk streams, the spokes radiating from the bright hub of silk. So the days find her lulled into a silent unaware contentment, busy in the rhythmic dance of her work, without a thought about what is outside the walls. But to her, and to her alone, the wild pure clear songs of birds and insects, frogs and lizards, water and wind ease through the hush, making even her daytime world a private cloistered dream.

Until, one day, her needle, entranced, follows the darting dance of a luminous dragonfly, skips away from the paisley pattern on the pallu she holds, and traces a wavering highlight of gold thread across a length of fuchsia silk.

13. NEPTUNE IN PISCES

Indira's fevered state lasts a week. When it end she go downstairs to get back on track with the demands of the pub. *Uncertainty and confusion* must not be allowed to intrude. Seize the reins. Bring some certainty and order. That's the plan.

Bostic tell her that KarlLee send a message that Geoff has the newly restored photos ready to hang. Very auspicious. She'll have a little get-together, just the regulars, and drink a toast to celebrate survival and a new start. She'll bring down a couple of bottles of her own stock of champagne. Not today, tomorrow. Kill plenty birds with that one stone. First and foremost to recognise Solo, wherever he is, as the one whose realised dream this pub is, and to which she owes her grounding. A thank you to through-thick-n-thin friend, Fritzie; a bow in the direction of the stalwart Bostic, a recognition of the artist in KarlLee, an appreciation of Cecil, Boyee, Feroze, Cynthia, for their loyalty and oh yes, Geoff, the photographer. Better get out that tin of *Eau de Nil* emulsion, get KarlLee to slap on a coat of paint today, no drama, make everything look crisp and fresh.

So said, so done. The little event go off nice-nice. The photos, hung gallery style, brighten up the place and create a buzz, an energising link with what was and is to be again. Except that, as Indira surveys the scene, she recognise that Fritzie seems a little frazzled. It must've been hard for her. She was looking after the daily soupa alone *and* caring for me while I was sick. Plus of course she had her own flood damage to clear up, and there's always Precious adding to her worries. Fritzie must've read her mind.

Indira, I need a few days to catch myself. You think you can manage now?

Indira knows she can't, but she doesn't say so. Fritzie's sweet hand is what makes the lunchtime soupa the success it is.

Yes, girl. It's time you take a rest too. I couldn't have managed

111

without you when I was sick, but I'm OK now. Come back when you're ready.

Next day, a procession of disappointed customers pass through the pub. People stop to drink yes, but those who would usually have their lunch there have to forage elsewhere and they don't linger. By one o'clock the place empty, and when Bostic suggest they close for siesta, Indira quickly agree and she go upstairs while Bostic lie down for a nap in the hammock slung between the trees in the backyard. So, when a knocking comes at the door, it's only she who hear.

She looks out the window and there, below, is the boy. She calls out, Up here. He looks up and then quickly looks down. He turns his head and shuffles from one foot to the next as if debating whether to go away or stay. She's wondering what he thinking, whether he's embarrassed at seeing her again, or, worse yet, ashamed.

She can feel herself softening, becoming flushed and feverish, just by looking at him. She's afraid he might turn around and go. He's probably thinking the place is closed, so why is he hanging around? He could be wondering whether she feels he's somehow done something wrong. He could be fumbling for a reason he can give for being there. She's afraid that if this moment isn't seized, he might never come again. What can she do, what can she say to make him stay? What do you want? Can I help you? Is there something you'd like? None of the above, she decides. Too crude, too flippant, dismissive even.

She calls, Can you wait a bit? I'll come down.

She opens the door and they stand facing each other. Like a re-enactment of the way they stood in the bathroom that day. He remembers too. He's looking at his feet, where she first touched him, but even looking at feet not safe, he thinks, as his blood rises and his face glows. He says, Miss Indira, you have any soup left? She shakes her head. She waves her hands, she makes a face in a 'no, sorry' way. He looks crestfallen. She says, Hungry? That question again. It sends a shockwave through his feet and up to his head. His feet remember where the question led. His head remembers too. Could do with something, yes. He looks up and he sees her face in a broad smile and he smiles back. Is not for me. Is for Gran-Gran.

She's standing there, smiling and leaning against the doorway, listening to him, savouring his being there and enjoying the effect her being near is having on him.

He knows he is talking too much, but must say something to give a reason for coming to see her again. Gran-Gran not too well. He knows he's sounding foolish. I was thinking I could carry some of Miss Fritzie soup for her and Maisie and for the little boy. He knows he's sounding like a complete babbling idiot and only nonsense coming out. But it look like soup finish early today.

We didn't have soup today. Fritzie's taking a break. She had plenty to do last few days.

Thanks, Miss Indira. Well, I going home now. I'll cook something. Is not a problem.

You can cook?

Yes. Why he not stopping there? He done answer the question. My grandmother teach me to do everything. Oh, god, I talking too much again. She say she getting old and one day, when she close her eyes, me and Maisie would have to fend for ourself and Small Man, Maisie little baby.

So, what can you cook?

His heart pumping fast. His mouth dry up. His palms oozing sweat. His head feeling light as if his brain has shrunk or disappeared. What does he like to cook? He can't think of a single thing. He runs his tongue over his lips. Maybe, if they're lubricated, words can come out.

One-pot.

One pot?

Cook-up. Cook up with rice. Rice and other things. Meat. Peas. Other things.

You want to show me what you can do?

Miss Indira, I can't stop. Gran-Gran home by herself and she not well.

But you will have to cook when you reach home, not so? So why not cook here and take it home with you?

She stands aside to allow him free passage even while he is wondering whether he should stay. He don't know whether he want to go in or to run away. Is not just Gran-Gran. Is what he getting himself into. His body telling him what it want him to get

113

into. His brain not telling him anything at all. It must be in a coma. He shakes his head to wake up his brain.

No? Indira asks.

No? Oh, no, I didn't mean no. I was just shaking my head. Yes?

He drops his head. It is more an admission than an agreement. He goes in and follows her up the stairs.

In the kitchen, she pulls out a bag of rice from a cupboard and rests it on the counter. She opens the fridge. See anything you can use? He bends down, peers into shelves and pulls open the vegetable drawers. A bag of carrots, a bundle of bhaji, a half dozen ochroes, a large chunk of pumpkin, half a purple cabbage, four pimentos, a lime. He takes out everything. He opens the freezer door. Meat? She comes closer and pulls out for his inspection first a leg of lamb, then a tray of chicken thighs, and finally a bag of chicken breasts. He's shaking his head. Not enough time to thaw and season any of that. He reaches over her shoulder and lifts a packet of boneless saltfish from the door shelf. This will do.

He washes the excess salt from the saltfish and puts the fillets to revive in a bowl of cold water. She takes out a large cast-iron pot and the cooking oil. He chops onions and garlic, slits and de-seeds the pimentos. She picks chives and oregano from the window box, her hand brushing his while she passes the herbs. He puts the pot on the stove and pours in some oil, adding the onions and seasonings while she rinses and shreds the saltfish. She drops the pieces of saltfish into a bowl. She shows him her hand to which fragments of salted cod still cling. He takes her hand in his. He spreads open her hand, like the parting of the petals of flower, stroking one finger at a time, until her palm lies flat in his. He brings her hand to his lips. His tongue traces a path along her timeline, her love line and the girdle of Venus. Its tip searches the clefts between her fingers. She feels the path of his tongue run in a surging current from each finger, each groove and cleft, each traced line, to flicker and flare in her groin. He sucks her thumb, licks clean her fingertips, its fishy saltiness tasting like tender, private skin sheened with new sweat. Then he measures and washes the rice, adds it to the aromatics, puts in the saltfish, chops and adds ochroes, pumpkin, bhaji. He shakes out half a packet of coconut milk powder while she's stirring the pot. He stands behind her, holds her hand, guiding it round and around the sizzling pot while she stirs. She leans back into him, pressing the length of her back and the width of her back, against his chest, his hip girdle, his thighs. He reaches across and picks up the water jug. He pours just enough to cover the contents of the pot and an inch to spare and together they stir the pot, right arm along right arm, a slender vine on a sturdy tree branch, his left hand pressing flat across her navel so that he can feel the surging in her belly and she feels the heat of his palm radiating to her core, melting her marrow, the fingers of her left hand running tingling circles along the back of his thigh, behind his knee, until bubbles appear, breaking on the surface of the liquid. He guides one last deep stir bringing to the top what had settled below, puts on the lid, lowers the flame, takes her by the hand and leads her to her bed. The book she's been reading, *Failed Fathers and Successful Sons*, slides off the satin bedspread to land face down on the floor.

The one-pot is ready in twenty minutes, the liquid absorbed by the swelling rice. Then, even on the low flame, the liquid dries up further and the base of the food begins to stick to the dry surface of the heavy cast iron pot. A smell of toasting rice wafts through the kitchen door and slides downstairs where it sails into the nostrils of the still slumbering Bostic. He wakes up and shakes his head, dislodging sleep, trying to figure out what woke him, and then trying to trace where the smell of burning rice is coming from. The scent also finds its way to the bedroom, sliding under the door where it mingles with the aroma of fresh sweat and body juices, to be eventually discerned by a post-coitally dazed Jah-Son who leaps out of bed, runs to the kitchen and turns off the stove, just as Bostic reaches the top of the stairs.

Jah-Son stands dumbly looking at the apparition, risen from below. Then, remembering the manners his Gran-Gran instilled in him, he says, Good afternoon Mr Bostic. Bostic looks at him, eye to level eye. He takes in every inch of the boy as if taking a picture in slow motion, from the top of his head, even in height with his own, his face, his neck, shoulders, chest, down past his trembling manhood, which Jah-Son, too stunned, does not shield from Bostic's eyes, the examination continuing down,

Bostic's gaze faltering, his face blanching at the birthmark of a coiled serpent on Jah-Son's right thigh, then down to knees, calves, feet and toes.

Bostic, his voice trembling, utters, Good afternoon, and turning, he stumbles back down to his hammock. He lies there for a long while, too shaken to get up and open the pub on time for the evening trade. His own right thigh throbs with a searing heat, as if the serpent coiled there has struck its fangs into his flesh and the venom is already coursing through his veins. He needs time to allow the thoughts and ideas tumbling about in his head to settle down. Then, only then, can he try to plumb the gravity of what he's seen and can't, now, unsee.

14. DON'T DEAL

Early December, Fritzie get a Skype call from Sandy asking her to find somewhere for her to stay as she coming for Christmas. Fritzie ask why she not staying by KarlLee as usual, and Sandy say the place is only for a few days; she will stay by him later on. She want to surprise him.

That is what Fritzie relate to Amber in a soft, soft, voice because they sitting in De Rightest Place and KarlLee there too, with Sunity. The Sangre Chiquito Serenaders blasting out "Anda Parandero" on the radio, is true, but Fritzie and Amber quite right to not take any chance – the deejay could cut in any minute, and people would hear their business if they talk at normal volume.

They look over at KarlLee and Sunity. Since that Good Friday, the two of them stick together like Velcro. KarlLee, who use to sport a thinning John Lennon ponytail, now shave his head clean. Fritzie say is a sure sign of what middle-age men up to when they shaving head but growing beard. Amber say, True. Well, KarlLee face looking like if he eh shave for a few days. Fritzie laugh and say it's a pity he can't do better than that pitiful lil Fu-Manchu that sprouting. Amber say, Talking bout hair, yuh remember what colour Sunity hair was first time she come in here? Black, say Fritzie, black like a Toco night. Both look over at Sunity's honey-blonde tresses, which she flicking back from her face every time she lean forward. Like she eh know where selling hairgrips? Her problem, not mine, Fritzie say. Mine is what to do about Sandy.

They sit silent for a while, sipping Carib and pondering the situation. Man-woman business always complicated, as both of them know full well.

Fritzie, is how long Sandy coming here?

Solo was still here first time she come, and he gone nearly three years. So maybe four, five years?

And she with KarlLee whole time?

117

Well, she come with her husband first time. To study Carnival, they say. Yes, is true. People does come here from foreign university to study Carnival. But last few years she coming back regular, regular, by herself. And not just for Carnival, neither.

Five years is a long time to be in a relationship with somebody at long distance, Amber thinks. Even if yuh coming and going regular. What could be the reason, especially if yuh have husband and yuh leaving him to come and stay by a next man?

So what she does come for?

Fritzie give her a 'I-can't-believe-you-asking-that-question' look.

It have to have a better reason than jus that.

Well, for one thing, she think KarlLee is a genius. That if he was living somewhere else, he would be recognise and be a millionaire long time.

Fuh painting them slogan and picture and thing on people wall?

What happen? Like you doesn't watch cable? You don't see them people in foreign? People does pay real money for other people to cover big, big building in cloth. Then after a weekend or so, the artist take off the cloth. He gone to cover a bridge in a next place. Contemporary Art, they does call it, but I say is Temporary Art. Only thing not temporary is the big cheque the artist does be dropping into his bank account.

That call for more reflection. Amber look at the two Carib they drinking. By now is only a warm frothy dribble left. She make sign to Bostic for two more. The first ice-cold sips wake them back up to the chilling reality of Sandy coming, unannounced. Amber pick up the conversation.

She know bout Sunity?

You think KarlLee would tell her he have a next woman? The man know where his bread butter.

Even if he getting jam elsewhere.

The two women laugh. They look at one another and laugh again, like they imagining the jam sessions between KarlLee, well-known fifty-something roué and prim-prim Miss Sunity, thirty-something schoolteacher. She not the first woman he giving private lessons to, but she's the most enduring. Fritzie

118

point her lips towards the couple. I find she putting up with him long.

Could be she in love?

Fritzie look at Amber and curl her lips with all the cynical knowledge of her years and years of man experience

Amber, life is not a TV soap. Love? Nah, she looking for excitements. Slumming in the ghetto with a artist. KarlLee is a ole hard-back man. He not going to be able to keep up with this. When he burn out, he will get fed up with her clinging. You wait and see.

Amber look at the two lovers. She nodding as she factoring in the new insight. She turn back to the matter in hand.

So what yuh going to do?

Dunno. I can't ask around here about a room to rent for a visiting friend, because people going to ask bold face, who is the friend. I can't lie, but I can't say is for Sandy, because her name will leave my mouth one minute and next minute KarlLee will know.

Amber know that only too well. She herself is the mistress of identifying when a piece of information so hot you have to pass it on quick-quick, to the next person before it burn your tongue.

You eh think KarlLee should know? He go have to make some adjustments before she reach.

Sandy want to surprise him.

Amber think on that a little. Surprise is what Sandy saying, but, maybe red-handed is what she have in mind.

Maybe she suspeck something going on? He and Sandy does video Skype almost every day. Check him. You eh think she see how he change hairstyle, growing beard, dressing like he young?

Fritzie look appraisingly at Amber as a realisation coming.

You mean she might be suspect he have a next woman?

Same thing happen in *Bold and Beautiful*.

And how they sort it out?

She suspeck. She visit unknown to him and ketch he with the woman.

Fritzie consider this option. Let life follow art? But these are real people, not actors who can simply walk away from screen disaster and go back to a different life.

I can't let that happen.

Is them business, not your own.

But I am involve.

Just tell she it have nowhere to rent. She could stay at the Hilton.

It will be like watching a car crash in slow motion.

Amber drain the last few drops of her beer. She stand up and put her hand on Fritzie shoulder.

Look girl, I going to work now.

Fritzie continue to stare at her bottle. Amber know she disappointed, but she can't take on Fritzie's anxiety.

Let them sort it out. Them is big people. Should handle they own stories.

No comfort in what Amber say. How could a girl like Amber, life running smooth, smooth, husband, child, all nicey-nicey, how she could know how torn apart she feeling about KarlLee and Sandy? KarlLee and Sunity? Even about KarlLee himself? Fritzie agree that Sandy have husband in Baltimore or Philadelphia or wherever, and really shouldn't be claiming exclusive rights to KarlLee, but, on the other hand, is Sandy who does big him up, make him feel good about himself, encourage him to get artistic exposure. And too besides, is she who does give him money, pay bills, stock up fridge and freezer, buy his medicine, so he owe her something for that. If what she want is exclusive rights to his loving-up, well, she earn it.

KarlLee and Sunity laugh out loud, drowning out The Sangre Chiquito Serenaders, who move on to "Alegria, Alegria". Everybody having a good time. It nice when that happen. She move back her thoughts to her dilemma. Who know what Sandy and her husband does be doing back home in the States, eh? Is true they is two ole people, ole like KarlLee, although age don't seem to slow down that ole goat. But you know, Sandy really have no right to expect man here to be celibate when it have so many hot, hungry, young women around tempting them. She look across at Sunity, who stick up tight, tight, under KarlLee armpit. Young, sexy, fun. Giving KarlLee a little April to his September. Can't begrudge him that. And, furthermore, KarlLee is from here. Local woman should get first preference. Not that she like Miss Sunity, eh, but she can't identify with foreign women who feel they could just walk in and throw money around and pick up who they want and furthermore expect local women, like herself, to be on their side, helping them, when they want to cause botheration.

It looking like she have to decide who to choose to be loyal to – Sandy, a woman like herself, who supporting a man in his work and his life, but is a rich foreigner, or KarlLee, a man, a player, ketch-arse and happy to be supported by a woman, but he from here self. But there is another choice. Like Amber say, let them sort out their own thing. But if she do that, she will get the blame from both of them – from Sandy for not telling her about Sunity and from KarlLee for not warning him that Sandy coming unexpected. Oh god, like she can't win no how. How she find herself in this comesse?

Indira, seeing her friend sitting by herself, comes over.

Penny for your thoughts.

A cent would be plenty.

So bad?

Her voice fall to a whisper.

Sandy coming.

When?

Any day now.

Oh, my gods!

And she don't want KarlLee to know.

Indira point her chin up and the two women stand. Indira call out to Bostic that she going upstairs and to call her if he want her. In the apartment, Indira move *Don't Deal. Duck! Circumventing Challenges* from the sofa to make a space for Fritzie. Indira ask Fritzie what she wants to drink and Fritzie say coffee and Indira ask, espresso or latte? They laugh as both remember how that was the start of their relationship. Plenty water under the bridge since then, Fritzie say, and Indira say, bridge over troubled water, more like. And more troubled water about to pass under this bridge with Sandy coming, Fritzie add. Indira ask her how she know Sandy coming and, for the second time that day, Fritzie relate about the Skype call, the request for a separate place for the first week or so and her dilemma in all this.

I wouldn't want to be your position.

You feel I cool with it?

121

It's not going to be nice for you when the mark buss. One side is bound to blame you. Actually, both sides could blame you.

So what to do?

You could do as Amber says and let them deal with they own problem.

You don't have no other suggestion?

They sipping and they thinking. Indira sees her friend's forehead is as furrowed as a canefield in June.

Well, instead of weeping and wailing and wringing our hands we could work out some scenarios.

Fritzie steups, a short fed-up steups. What I need right now is some way of avoiding this scenario altogether.

As far as I can see, the problem is Sunity, Indira say. If she wasn't in the picture, we wouldn't have this problem.

Is there some way of getting rid of Sunity?

Kinda drastic you don't think? And for Sandy who you don't even like?

Fritzie bark a harsh laugh. Well, in a less permanent way.

Sunity has family in Canada, yes?

Yes. A sister in Ottawa. The one who always arksin her to visit for Christmas.

Maybe this could be the year?

Indira reach over for the newspaper and flip through to the horoscope. The opposite page is the travel section. Check out this, Fritzie. I spotted it this morning. She pointing to an ad.

Fritzie read out: *Caribbean Airlines: Dreaming of a White Christmas? Special fares to Toronto for travel between 15th and 29th December. Offer ends 06th December… visit our website…* She look up from the paper. What's the date today?

Fourth… Hmm, two more days… Indira gone over to the cd rack, pull out, push back, pull out, push back then pull out a Bing Crosby album, *White Christmas.*

They talk some more, pick up the newspaper and the album and go downstairs.

There, Indira kill the volume of the parang soca on the radio, put the cd in the player and Bing singing, *I'm Dreaming of a White Christmas, just like the ones I used to know, where the treetops glisten…* Indira join in, dueting with Bing. Fritzie say, outloud for everybody to hear, White Christmas. That is something I always want to see. She call out loud, loud, over Indira singing. Indira! You ever see a White Christmas? Indira stop singing and answer. Yes. When I left India and met Solo, we spent a while in Frankfurt. You have to see a White Christmas to believe it. Pure magic. It's like all the angels in heaven have come down to cover the world with their wings. KarlLee say, I spend years in London and I see plenty Rainy Christmas, Sleety Christmas, Foggy Christmas, Cold-no-arse Christmas, but never White Christmas. Bostic say, all I ever see is Red and Green Christmas. Caribbean Christmas. What about you, Sunity, Indira ask. You ever see a White Christmas? Sunity say, no. She add, her voice wistful, My sister always bothering me to come up for Christmas and every year I leave thinking about it until school close. That is when you find out the airlines booked up and all they have is executive class at top dollar. Where your sister living? Fritzie ask. Ottawa, Sunity say. Last night, Indira say, TV news show snow deep, deep in Eastern Canada already…

At this juncture, Bing burst through with *Sleigh bells ring, are you listening, in the lane snow is glistening, a beautiful sight, we're happy tonight, walking in a winter wonderland.*

Indira look up from her newspaper. Would you believe this? Fritzie look at this! She hand the paper to Fritzie who read aloud, slowly, as if she seeing it for the first time: *Caribbean Airlines: Dreaming of a White Christmas? Special fares to Toronto…* Sunity rush over to Fritzie and read aloud over her shoulder… *for travel between 15th and 29th December. Offer ends 06th December. Visit our website…*

Sunity whip out her phone, go to the website, click and click and she say, Oh my gosh, only two seats left at that price. What to do? All you, help me out here, what to do? KarlLee say, You sure your sister will be there? It mightn't be convenient for her. Indira and Fritzie want to slap him, but exercise restraint. Indira say, only one way to find out. Call her or text or email. Phone quickest, say Sunity as she scrolls, finds the number and dials. A loud squeal. SassyWassyJassy, is me… Hahahaha. I hope your children not around when you call me that name. Quick question, is OK for me to come up for Christmas? You sure? I thinking some time between… she looks at the ad… between fifteenth and twenty-ninth, yes, this month. Gosh, we in December already, you realise? Gosh, just imagine, I only now see this ad, is like Fate taking a hand. Yes, yes, yes! We still the same size. Everything. I'll need everything. Boots, coat, gloves, hat. Yes, I will book now. Gosh, only hope those seats not gone already. We can Skype later. Mwah, mwah, mwah... Love you... see you soon... bye. She fiddle again with the phone, pull out this card, that card from her wallet and in just twenty minutes after Bing's first warble, Sunity pay for her ticket to Toronto and onward to Ottawa. It's done. Fifteenth to twenty-ninth.

You leaving me for a whole two weeks? KarlLee objecting. Over Christmas? What I going to do with myself?

Indira come over and puts an arm around his shoulder. You will do what you usually do for Christmas, KarlLee. Tell Sunity.

I spend Christmas right here. In De Rightest Place. German style Christmas Eve dinner, Christmas morning Trinidad style Christmas breakfast, then later on, English style Christmas dinner complete with crackers and plum pudding.

He take Indira's hand and kiss it. Indira, I am remiss. I have been negligent. Forgive me. I want to thank you for all the years of making my Christmas happy.

So, you're not going to be neglected when I'm gone?

You go and visit your sister. I shouldn't begrudge you that. Folks, we better be going now. A lot for us to... ahem... discuss before Sunity leave.

Fritzie call out, What name she call you that make you go red and laugh?

Sunity chants like if is a nursery rhyme, Sunity, Sunity, where yuh leave yuh panty?

KarlLee squeeze her arm as they go out the door.

Let's go and see if we can find it.

Fritzie give Indira a high-five. Yippee! Girl, you is class.

Bostic say, what was that about?

Woman business, say Indira.

15. FRAUGHT WITH ONE-UPMANSHIP

I Cynthia park up mihself in De Rightest Place as per usual. And I listening hard to the vibe of the place. Because it looking to me like it change it tune again. You see, in the days with Solo and Bostic, was like total harmony. I uses to think that Bostic could read Solo mind and Solo know what Bostic thinking. Is a back and forth, one with the next, and with we the people. Laughing, joking, chatting, smooth-smooth, whole time. Then Solo gone, and, fuh Bostic, is like he rhythm section close down. Is only bass yuh hearing – pom-pom, pom-pompitty, pom-pom, a thump low down in yuh chest, like a deep heavy heartbeat. But since Miss Indira come back active in the bar, I find the tune change again. Bostic there still, but he beat subdue and sometimes yuh eh hearing the bass notes at all. As for she, well, she singing all kind a tune, following every band that passing. First is she and Fritzie with Soupa every lunch time and in no time flat, watch how we chipping along to a steady beat. Steady crowd, steady menu. But yuh did hardly get accustom to that, than she pick up with Elaine grandson and everything turn ole' mas. The two a them doing fancy dinner event every weekend. Every day is a different menu. Every day is a different crowd. We regulars don't know whether we coming or going, is so we confuse. Sometimes I does feel I at a crossroads with Eshu and he trickster self, with four steelband coming from all directions towards me – All Stars coming down playing "Curry Tabanca", Despers on a nex road with a "Borodin Polovetsian Dances", Exodus with "Rainorama" on the third road, and Phase II coming down the last road doing "One Love". All converging on me. Is pure cacophony.

And it have a next thing I cyah let pass. It does stick in mih craw to see how that lil boy, Jah-Son, totally bazodee over Indira. The poor boy rushing home from work on a weekend, tired-tired, to take up work in she kitchen till all kinda hours. He following she round, sniffing-sniffing behind she, like a lil puppy dog. If she say, Bark! he say, Yip-yip. I not unsympathetic to Indira, yuh understand – plenty cobweb mussbe collect for he to brush off since Solo gone. But a lil boy? Nah! That is pure advantage.

I Cynthia looking at Bostic too. I don't see how he could be too happy about any a this. Fuh instance, the thing between Indira and Jah-Son. Bostic bes fren, bes-bes-bes pardner getting heavy-heavy horn in front he face and is nutten he could do. Let Bostic only make a mistake and open he mouth among we regulars about what we all seeing going on there and nex thing yuh know, Boyee will start to speculate whether Bostic jealous and want Indira for heself and Anil, who mind never far from the gutter, would wonder what Bostic and Solo did have going on between them for Bostic to be so uptight about what Indira doing when Solo not around. I Cynthia not the only one who feel things changing too much. I checking out Bostic, and he not looking happy at-all, at-all. You don' need candle to look in the dark for what showing clear-clear in broad daylight.

★

I looking around and wondering how things get out of hand so fast. Give an inch and she take a mile. Fix-up the front? OK I say. Do different things inside? No problem. Lunchtime soup? Sure. Now is outdoors she gone. Pavement café. Bistro. Inter-national cuisine, Indira says. Internet translation, I say, because it looks to me like all she and Jah-Son doing is finding on the internet ways to fancy-up our Trini food to attract the different clientele Indira always looking for.

I looking at the menu and what I seeing is that you can take an ordinary pelau, take out a few things, add a few things and it becomes Risotto alla Milanese, or Paella de Andalucia. Fish broth is Bouillabaisse Marseillaise. Stew pork and beans? Call that Moroccan Cassoulet when you here, OK? All very well and good, I say, to have your fun and games. But what about me, Terrence Bostic? And what about Solo's pride and joy, De Rightest Place?

At the front of the pub, on the forecourt, Indira and her team set out half a dozen tables with tablecloths, fancy-fancy napkins and candles in expensive clay holders. Jeezanages! I look out and all I seeing is string after string of white *fairy lights*, lacing through big pot after big pot of bush making a thick screen. Is Ficus, palms – madam put only yellow-stemmed, eh – small leaf bamboo and sweet lime, separating dining area from the road. *Al fresco*, she say. What else? New staff. Yes, Indira bring in Precious and Maisie. The two young ladies in ole-style creole garb of white frilly broderie anglaise blouse, black skirt or pants and madras plaid apron and kerchief headtie. Miss I&I Queen back in business, flaunting her international closet of costumes. Flamboyant dashikis, colourful kangas with matching turbans, floating shalwar kameeses, sleek long black tube dresses with jewelled waist chains – as varied and as unpredictable as her clientele. And who are these people Miss I&I dressing to impress? A set of here-today-gone-tomorrow never-see-come-see floaters. Young people who say they are *professionals*. Hear them talking about degree in Management, degree in Business. You ask me what they managing, eh? As far as I can tell they managing to still be living at home with Mummy and Daddy. And what is their business? Their business is spend, spend, spend. On things and more things. On *adventure*. When they pull up in their flashy cars and trucks and SUVs, all I seeing is Nina, Pinta and Santa Maria. And I'm sure that *moving on* is going to follow the rape and pillage, sure as I am that the sun will come up over Laventille Hill tomorrow.

I can imagine them in their offices, boasting to one another in that pretend modest way they have, Don't look for us on The Avenue; *these* days we liming in Belmont. Raised eyebrows meet smug smiles. Yes, Belmont. You should try it. And to think that I'm expected to supply an upmarket atmosphere where these overindulged folks feel they're being rootsy and edgy, but nonetheless, safe.

★

Indira, warned by her horoscope that things were not going to be plain sailing – *Gemini: The Five of Wands in this position indicates that once harmonious relationships could now be fraught with one-upmanship and negative comparisons* – had not really been surprised when Bostic give her his reaction to the new situation. No, he don't care for the new bistro scene out at the front. All of a sudden De Rightest Place and in particular, he, Bostic, have to deal up with

127

the sort of customer who demanding pinot grigio – merlot, shiraz and sauvignon blanc being *so last year*.

He tell her she spending a lot of money fixing up for that night trade, but how long she think it will last? Those kind of people very fickle. They here today, gone tomorrow. The minute another new place open up, they taking off. They jumping in their SUVs with their credit cards and you not seeing them for dust. They don't develop any loyalty to anybody or anywhere. For them is only a scene to be seen in. He only hope, for her sake, she'd make back her investment before they move on.

So, while he, Bostic, willing to expand his cellar to cater for the new palate – and he even bring in and train Curtis as wine waiter for the bistro crowd – he careful to restrict his domain to the original space – dominoes, cards, lotto tickets and Play Whe – secure in his old role of listening to the problems, adjudicating the arguments and parting the fights of the day-long, year-round regulars. So, he sailed along, looking askance, but in the main, prepared to remain an observer. Until the night of the dogs.

★

This was when KarlLee and Sunity, feeling a lil peckish after Lucifer advanced aggression training class in the Botanic Gardens, decide to go to De Rightest Place for supper. With their pitbull on a leash, the three of them occupy a table near the door where Bostic could see them and exchange a lil banter. A superb lamb tagine ras-el-hanout and its accompanying Rioja so mellow-out Sunity that she relax her attention and is only when she hear screaming, see people scattering and tumbling over chairs, that she wake up to the fact that something not quite right. Is then she realise that Lucifer leash not in her hand. She look up and she see her dog standing, all four legs firmly plant in the doorway. He looking straight ahead, nostrils flaring, and a weird whinnying sound issuing from his throat. Is as if he see a jumbie or some other invisible presence. What Lucifer senses pick up, what vibrations tingling him, quickly reveal itself to all. With a single bound and a flash of black and tan, Apocalypse vault over the bar counter. Bostic pride and joy Rottweiler then proceed to walk as sedately as a nun at vespers towards Lucifer. She place her dark muzzle against his white one and, turning around, her stump of

128

a tail twitching, she present her rear end to him. What gallant gentleman could offend a lady by refusing an advance like that, eh? With the gift of love is so gracefully offered, Lucifer, ever the sensitive one, not hesitating for a second. He mount, he deliver a few swift and frantic thrusts and they tie. After they separate, they lie down side by side, both of them looking like they well happy with an unforeseen but enjoyable encounter.

★

I Cynthia sitting there among we the people, watching the bistro customers. All I could say is that is a good thing them people does spend plenty time and money in the gym. I never see so much a jumping on table and chair as when that ferocious man-eating pitbull let loose. But when they see that he doh business with them, that his interest is elsewhere, they form a ring around the mating couple. I Cynthia never hear the bar so quiet. Like they is watching a leatherback turtle laying eggs on Grande Rivière beach or looking at a TV show of a human baby being born. Mouth open, but nothing coming out. And when the dogs done fix-up, if yuh hear how the young men start clapping and shouting, yuh would think their football team just score a goal. The young women with them looking a lil embarrass, but they join in the merriment when the young fellers call for a next rounds of cocktails, to celebrate. Celebrate the dogs or inebriate the girls I wondering. I suspect the young fellers and them was hoping this public mating thing would encourage the young ladies to throw caution to the winds later that night. We regulars go straight back to we games, we drinks and we conversation, just as if nothing unusual happen. Is only Sunity and Bostic who looking put out.

KarlLee gone outside on the forecourt. He holding on to Lucifer leash real tight. The two dog owners way down at the far end of the counter talking hush-hush, both of them looking as serious as The Virus. Sunity turn round and leave, but from the way she face set up, I know this not the end of that business.

ϒ

The following afternoon, I close the bar at siesta for a conference. There's a little group seated around a table. KarlLee, Sunity and Indira and a fourth chair for me, but I not ready yet. My mind in an unsettled mess. Is a good thing Indira decide she will control the discussion. Don't know what I would say or do otherwise. Deep breaths, deep breaths. Indira mussbe read my mind. She tap her glass and I sit down.

We are all friends. You agree? she say. We do. Do we want to stay friends? Again, nods all round. Can we then agree that we will not let two dogs spoil that friendship?

Lucifer is not just a dog, Sunity interject. To me, he is a person.

The blood rush to my head and I, forgetting that I had plan to be calm, rise to the bait she throw for me.

And you think Apocalypse is less than Lucifer?

Just a minute, the two of you, Indira break in. I am the only one here who has no vested interest in this. So, if it's OK with you, I'll tell you when you can speak so we can settle the matter amicably. OK? She wait for the two of us to agree and she continue.

Sunity, you speak first.

Lucifer was here quietly minding his own business when *his* dog – she pause to point dramatically at me – *his* dog jumped out of nowhere and raped Lucifer.

Is a struggle to stay sitting down and not pick up myself and walk out the room. I catch Indira eye. I see her fighting to keep her face straight. Like she finds it funny. I see the humour now and I'm ready when she address me.

Your turn.

I hope nobody here seriously believing that a female dog can rape a male dog. Everybody here see what happen. Her dog climb up on my dog and sexually assault her. Not the other way round.

She jumped over the counter. She jumped over begging for it.

You should a have your animal under stricter control so he wouldn't go around interfering with other people's females. My Apocalypse was in her own home. Your animal was an intruder. Breaking and entering.

Wait, wait, wait. This is getting us nowhere. Everybody saw that the two dogs mated willingly. Consenting heterosexual adults. No law against that. So, what is the real problem?

Pups, I say.

Puppies, said Sunity.

What?

Lucifer is a registered prize sire. When he is mated, his puppies get a certificate showing that Lucifer is the sire and they sell for at least two thousand US dollars each, depending on whether the dam, the mother, is also of a high pedigree. I don't let him mate with just any and every bitch.

I hope is not my Apocalypse you referring to as any and every bitch. She has papers too. Rottweiler papers. Pure breed. From a dam and sire with papers. And now she is contaminated by some…

Contaminated? Did you say contaminated? You know how much is the fee for Lucifer to line with a bitch? A carefully selected pedigree bitch?

I looking from Sunity to KarlLee and back again. Is on the tip of my tongue to lower the tone and note that Miss *Very Particular* Sunity doesn't seem to be quite so fussy when choosing her own mating partners. My mind fly to imagining Sunity demanding to see KarlLee's papers and checking *his* pedigree before consenting to a coupling and this image make me laugh outloud.

Look, Sunity, the dogs did their thing. You not happy, but I even less happy. Your dog do his business and for him it done and over with, but is my poor little Apocalypse probably now impregnated with half-breed pitbull pups. And to make matters worse, this is the first and only time she ever mate. Last time she in heat I take her to a proper Rottweiler stud to line, but all she do is sit down and only snapping, snapping at him when he come round her sniffing. She just wouldn't consent and you can't force her. Our two dogs choose each other. What you want me to do?

Take her to the vet. Get an abortion.

Abortion? Abortion? I could hear wine glasses rattling on the bar counter. You mad or what? Indira, listen. Like your friend here totally out of her freaking mind. You hear what she say? She want me to take my Apocalypse to the vet for him to put her under anaesthetic, cut her open, take out whatever in there and then what will happen next? I'll tell you what would be the consequence. Even if she come out alive, she won't be the same dog again. And, too besides, she wouldn't be able to have any pups afterwards. You expect me to do that to my Apocalypse?

Look at it from my point of view. Lucifer's stock will fall if word gets out that it is diluted by cross-breeding.

Just then, who should push open the door and come in to start work on the evening's supper menu, but Jah-Son. He signal to Indira that he's going upstairs and she motion him to wait. KarlLee has been silent throughout. Indira turns to him.

Tell me something KarlLee, what breed are you?

Breed?

Well, race then.

Hmmm… Human? OK! OK! … I see you not in the mood for jokes. Well, from my father's side, pure Chinese, from my mother's, African, Portuguese, Warahoon they say, and I not sure what else.

Jah-Son, what are you?

Me? I suppose African. Mixed.

What about your mother? Your father?

My mother? Who is that? And as for father, worse yet. I never even know who my father is.

Anybody here see anything wrong with KarlLee? Anybody can find fault with Jah-Son? Nobody? Well then, Sunity, I don't understand what all the cross-breed angst is about.

Indira, you're talking about people. We're here to discuss dogs. People are free to breed how they want, but you can't allow pedigree dogs to do that.

Well, Sunity, it seems to me that your dog and Bostic's dog really believe they are people too. Come Jah-Son. Let's go. Excuse us, folks. She picks up her book, *Fifty Fantastic Frolics featuring funghi, farfalle, fou-fou and falafel.*

Indira go upstairs with Jah-Son, and Sunity and KarlLee take their dog home, leaving me sitting there – the one left with a most likely pregnant bitch. At least I know who the pups' father is. And what a Rottweiler and Pitbull mix could come out like. Ah, well. What's done cannot be undone. But that, bad as it is, is the least of my worries right now.

When this boy, Jah-Son, calmly say he don't know who his father is, all I could do is sit there like a dummy. He drop that bomb just so, and nobody flinch. Like it's normal. But not me. That bomb explode in my guts. I had to hold my belly. I looking at the table. I looking at my hands. I looking at the floor. I making sure not to look around. I don't want nobody, nobody, to catch my eye because I am sure, sure as my eyes didn't deceive me when I saw that birthmark, that I would be bound to reveal something in my eyes, on my face, that would make them look at me, look at him, look at me again and connect.

★

Upstairs, Indira's head is full of the talk about dogs and breeding and people and choice and offspring and abortion. Surprising how such subjects can be discussed in that clinical way, she thinks. The matter with the dogs wasn't really settled, but perhaps all concerned might reflect on it in a different light after the discussion. All she can think about is how often new life starts from an impulsive or accidental act, and how, whether puppies or babies, most people are instinctively drawn to young things, to hold them close, to feed on the force of new life. And yet, some people can look at a baby, look at a puppy, and see it as a commodity, with a price tag, an item for trade in the marketplace.

Perhaps that's what had happened at the Mary Magdalene Home for Unwed Mothers. That they saw in Gabriel, *her* Gabriel, an item for sale to the highest bidder. A male child seemingly with pedigree? With his pale skin and light eyes, he'd have a market price that could be afforded only by one of their anxious wealthy waiting clients. Was that what happened to him? Was that how she came to lose him?

16. ROUTINE, RHYTHM AND RITUAL

Was a time when I use to go straight home after work on Saturday afternoon and just hang out whole weekend with Gran-Gran, Maisie and Small Man, with Armageddon and the birds. If I ketch a vaps, is a lil sea bath here, a lil river lime there. Everything cool, everything fluid. Then back to work Monday. But since this thing with me and Indira start up, weekend begin on Thursday. Between working evenings at De Rightest Place and every day except Sunday at Stephenson & Sons Hardware, I hardly spending any time home at all. And when I there I ent have no time for nobody. Is only sleep I sleeping. But I not complaining, eh. I learning new things, new ways of doing old things and I living like a man, not a boy. I notice that Gran-Gran and Maisie looking at me different and treating me different, and I know is not because I hardly there and bringing home nice food and extra money. Nah, is not that. Nobody telling me nothing but I know is because they know things different with me. I doing big man thing with big woman.

So I settle into this new life. I arrive at De Rightest Place after work. Straight away Indira and me begin to work together, prepping the ingredients for the evening menu. Then we go to the bedroom for man and woman business. We come out afterwards to set up the main courses, ready for finishing on the stove or oven. Then I carry home dinner for Gran-Gran and Small Man. As I leaving, Maisie coming in, ready to wait at tables. Is a fixed schedule. But I not complaining, eh. Pleasure, work and duty, each different, each in its place and time.

But then something change. After all the talk downstairs about the dogs and who is what race and breed and so on, Indira standing next to me while we peeling and chopping vegetables, seasoning meat, choosing herbs and spices, but is like her mind far, far away, not on what we doing. We finish and I looking forward to the bedroom break. But no. Indira start the cooking. Maybe, I think, maybe it's her time of the month or something. I don't make no comment, I ent ask no question. Food ready earlier than usual and I reach home when Maisie now dressing to go down. Next day, same thing happen, and that is the case on the third day too. Now, I really puzzle. I looking around for what she reading to see whether that could give me a clue, but the only book I seeing is *Routine, Rhythm and Ritual,* and that mean nothing to me. This apartment too full of self-help books. How is a confuse person to know which one is the guide for today, eh? I scratching my head, searching my memory for anything I say or do to cause this change in the woman behaviour. I trying to read her face, to interpret her body language, to work out whether somehow I cause offence. But no, she just as friendly, she chatting as usual, she discussing the menu, she smiling and laughing – if there is something to smile or laugh at. Normal, normal, except for that one thing. We living like priest and nun.

Maybe she find church. Maybe she find somebody else. Maybe she bored with me. But I don't think so. I not seeing any signs – no prayer book, no chaplet, no pictures of a man, no secret phone calls or trips out. We still laughing and talking good-good. No matter which way my mind go, I can't find a explanation. First I'm puzzled, then I start to feel uncomfortable since it looking like if what we had going on between us never happen at all. Like if that time fall into some kinda amnesia gap in her brain. Then I decide, oh ho, two can play this game. Back to basics. So now is a light kiss on her cheek, I calling her Miss Indira, I not chatting about Cecil and Boyee or any of the bar patrons. I ent making no jokes or relating about work or home. We only talking about the task in hand: May I have the peeler, please? Thank you. You're welcome. If it's not too much trouble, I'd appreciate if you could turn on the oven. Certainly, no problem. Much obliged. Don't mention it.

But that could go on for only so long. It eating me up real bad. Resentment growing inside a me. What the hell is the matter with the woman? I didn't do her nothing for her to treat me so. I do everything she want me to do. I thought she was enjoying herself as much as me, but is like she want to finish with me. Blowing hot one minute and blowing cold the next. Is she self who start up this thing. She must be see something in me she like and want. So what going on?

On the journey from work in the maxi I working myself up into a state of vexation. I not some shoe she could just wear out and throw away when it get mash up and ugly. Wait a minute. I not mash up and ugly. And, too besides, at no time could she say I wear out. I make up my mind to have it out with her once and for all. She will have to tell me what is going on. I not playing no more games. When I reach De Rightest Place, I see the lunch board still up, but the soup offering rub off. Instead: Closed for dinner today. Private function. Open tomorrow as usual.

I run up the steps two at a time. Is now I boiling up with rage. She couldn't even warn me that we have an event this evening? It looking like she feel she big enough to handle the menu planning and cooking by herself. So she pushing me out there too. Dissing me. Enough is enough. I push open the kitchen door, banging it against the wall, then I slam it shut. I could feel my heart pounding hard-hard. Knocking my ribs. I ready for this fight. But... but... but... with who? With what? The fridge? The oven? There's no sign of her. No sign of food preparation. No menu stuck to the fridge door. I stand there like the smoke showing where the last fireworks explode.

Then my nose pick up a smell like incense, my ears hearing a sound, ohmmmm, ahmmmm, ummmm, ohmmmm. Soft soft chanting, not words. Her bedroom door is slightly open.

I go in. The jalousies are closed. The curtains too. The light is dim but I can make out her iPod in its dock on the dressing table, and next to it a thin spiral of incense smoke. She sitting up in bed holding a book: *Kool Kama Sutra Secrets for Western Women*. She's wearing a red silk wrap, tied in a knot above her breasts. She look up at me, her eyelids fluttering, showing only flashing blue slivers. She pat the space next to her on the bed. Sit, or lie, I don't know which, and I don't want to guess, so I stand there like a statue. I still not moving when she beckon me. She will have to do more than that for me to come in. I am not her puppy dog to sit and beg at her command. She have to acknowledge that she hurt me. She have to make up for that.

★

136

Her decades of experience with men have not gone wasted. She reads his bewildered anger in the twitch of his jaw muscles, the pain in his eyes, and his weakness for her in his shoulders. She puts her book down, gets out of bed and goes to him. She stands on tiptoe to put her lips against the hinge of his jaw, to kiss his eyelids, one then the other. She unbuttons his shirt and pushes her hands in to cup and rub his shoulders. She leans her face into his chest. She touches each nipple with the tip of her tongue.

He can feel his resistance draining but his rage is still trapped in his chest. He will not let her decide how this will go. No, no, Miss Indira, you will not turn me around so easily. He parts the red silk to reach in round her waist, lays her on the floor and kneels across her, straddling her. He undoes the knot in the wrap so she is lying on a sea of scarlet silk. He knows she is waiting for him.

He starts at her feet, licking his way up to her groin. She spreads her legs for him. His tongue draws a circle around the tender inside of her thighs to her mound. She grabs his hair to keep his face there and to move his mouth to where she craves him. No, no, Miss Indira, you can't use me like you want. He is already licking behind her ears, her fluttering eyelids, his tongue darting at the corners of her mouth. She turns her head to try to catch his mouth in hers. No, no, Miss Indira, this is me, Jah-Son, the man. I am the one in charge here. His tongue traces a tendon in her neck down to the hollow at her clavicle, curving in wide arcs under her breasts. His tongue lashes deep into virgin territory – her armpits, her navel, the backs of her knees, under her curling toes. Then he gets up, buttons his shirt, walks out the door, crosses through the kitchen, down the stairs, home.

Next morning Indira call through the bedroom door to Fritzie that she has flu. She doesn't want to expose anyone to it.

But I immune to those things.

Maybe. But in any case, I'm too weak to be of any help.

What happening with supper?

There's no answer.

When Bostic comes upstairs to collect the garbage, he spies a clear plastic bag that look as if it contains something that shouldn't be thrown away. He puts the black garbage bag out on the pavement, the clear bag in the storeroom.

Fritzie and Bostic don't see Indira when they come to work on Monday. They see Sunday's paper lying folded on the table. A note scribbled in the margin reads: *Will be back sometime. Don't worry.* Something circled on the page catch Fritzie's eye. *Gemini: Saturn brings you the energy of its pulsating rings today. These vibrations will push you to finish up something in your sentimental life.*

The message, with its implications, loud and clear to her.

She knows how Indira does rely on horoscope to make big and little decisions '...*finish up something in your sentimental life*...' There it is! I don't have to wonder where that advice take her today.

★

Early Sunday morning, before even cock self get up to crow, I am at his house. I wait as Gran-Gran goes to wake him. Mornin, he says, and I turn my head and see him standing there. I almost do not know him. It is as if he has grown in stature and in strength, standing here in his own space. He is not the growing boy of before. He is a grown man. All that I came to say, all that I came to demand, makes no sense any more. I find myself saying, Morning. Just dropping by... to see how you doing. He inclines his head a little and I don't know whether that means, Yes, that's why you came, or yes that's what you're saying about why you came, but at least it's an acknowledgement that I'm here. He looks over my head, his eyes following the steep dirt track to the paved road below, as if to try to understand the concept of dropping by, way up here, foreday morning. He says nothing. I look at the sky. The sun, the colour of a ripe Julie mango, squeezes its way up from behind the range, spilling its juices across the sky and the city below. He beckons, come. He leads the way along a dirt path between fruit trees. I could hear them before I see them. They're in a shed. From the frame of the carat palm roof hang a couple of dozen cages of split bamboo, terite, cocoyea, balsa wood and wire. He leads me to a long wooden bench and leaves me there. The whistling, the trills and runs, call and response, solos, choruses, the ramajay of his songbirds is all around me. When I close my eyes I am back at the house of silence where there was no human voice, but the voices of birds. So many lifetimes before this.

When he returns, he has a basket of fruit and seeds. He puts it on the bench beside me. One at a time, he takes down the cages. He whistles its song. The bird calls back to him. They duet while he cleans its cage, replenishes the water, puts in halved fruit – sucrier, pommerac or sapodilla for some; for others, a handful of seeds, sprays of seed-headed grasses. The nesting cages are bigger, housing a male and a couple of females. There are nestlings in the boxes. A parent bird is feeding them, beak to beak. He lifts out a little one and cups it in his hand, bringing it towards me. He opens his hand and there is a ball of fluff. He blows gently across the top of his hand and the down sways with his breath. I hold out my cupped palms and he slips the nestling into it. The little creature is almost weightless, it shifts itself a little then settles. I blow a little puff of air across its feathers and it opens its eyes and looks at me. Its little beak opens and out comes a tiny *cheep*. It is the most tender, the most trusting little face I have seen in the many, many years since *his*. I cannot stop the tears that are flowing down my cheeks. He takes the little bird and puts it back in its nest, then his thumbs are under my eyes as he smooths away the tears. He pulls me into his arms. He blows across the top of my head. His breath flowing over my scalp is a comforting breeze over parched earth after harvest. He holds my head tight into his chest. He rubs his palm around and around my head. I can feel my crown chakra wake from its long sleep, its energy coursing to every organ, every tissue, every cell, igniting glands and vessels, tingling nerves and pathways, until all of me is alive.

He takes me to the hammock slung between the trees and lays me there. He brings a soursop which he pulls apart in his hands. The white cottony flesh tears, sticky white juice running between his fingers and down his arms. He places half the fruit on the ground and he sits beside me. He scoops white pulp with his fingers and puts it in his mouth. He leans into me and passes the sweet tangy flesh from his mouth to mine. I suck the flesh and membrane and I pass the black seeds into his mouth. When there is no more pulp and the green prickly skin folds over, empty, he climbs into the hammock with me. It is big enough.

★

As the days rolled into a week, and still no sign of Indira, Bostic is sorry to see the bistro collapse, even though he'd foretold its demise. A few of the SUVs and flashy pickups still stop for beers but now they move on early in the evening to pick up their elegant escorts for the newest scene elsewhere.

It was easy for Maisie to go back to her old job at Favourite Fried Food, popularly known as 3Fs. Those *Join our Service Team, Excellent Salary and Prospects* notices stuck to the glass façade of fast food outlets never come down.

For Fritzie, the problem was Precious, though she'd been in two minds about the effects of the bistro on her daughter. Under Indira's training she'd learned how to conduct herself with customers, how to be pleasant without being servile, and friendly without being overly intimate and above all how to hold her temper in the face of rudeness. But there was a downside. Precious was now accustomed to money, to disposable income as opposed to pocket money, and was not at all happy at that source drying up.

I have to get another job.

You underage to work.

So what I was doing in the bistro? Playing?

You was helping out your mother and your godmother.

She not my real godmother.

True. But she is the only person willing to help me deal with you.

So, is only you and Auntie Indira I could work for?

That's right, my girl. Until you old enough to pick and choose.

So what I suppose to do while I waiting?

You can get on with your homework and do well at school.

Why I have to write on paper? I have a laptop. We have wifi. Why I can't do the work and press send? Nah. The teachers still wanting pen and paper. Real backwardness. Why government bother to give we laptop if they don't give school internet? With a long, succulent steups and a cut-eye at her mother, Precious slap her books on the table and flop down to start her homework.

For the other ex-employee, Curtis, former bistro sommelier, the closure was more a new beginning than an end, as Bostic discover the next morning.

140

17. STRATEGIC BATTLES

Bostic pointed to the large metal drum mounted on its side and standing on a wheeled frame fashioned from reinforcing steel rods.

I come to work good, good, this Friday morning and first thing I see is this thing park up right here.

Fritzie agree that indeed the thing is parked up, on the forecourt, where tables for dinner were set up a scant week before. She walk towards the drum.

But who would bring this and plonk it down here just so?

She lift the handles and the drum opens half-and-half along back hinges. There is a metal grill set into the lower half over a bed of charcoal.

Like somebody set up and ready to barbeque. But who?

Who becomes clear that afternoon when a pick-up pull up on the forecourt and Curtis and Kwesi jump off the tray. Together they tug off a big maco cooler box, the kind on wheels, a folding table, a cardboard box and two big bulging blue plastic bags. The pick-up drive off and the two fellers set about moving this and that until everything is to their satisfaction.

Fritzie upstairs busy clearing up after the daily soupa lunch trade. That still continuing, Indira or no Indira, and she nearly ready to go home – she have to be there when Precious reach, to keep her on her toes with the schoolwork. Bostic, inside the bar, all the while watching the antics of the two young men, but he not going to demean himself by going out to ask them what the ass they think they doing trespassing on people property, and who give them permission to be there. Time longer than twine, give them enough rope and they will hang theyself, and other pearls of hard-won wisdom come to mind. So he biding his time, waiting it out. And soon enough, Curtis come in.

Afternoon Mr Bostic, how you going? I just come to full the bucket.

Bucket?

This bucket here. To wash hand and thing.

Wash hand?

Hand does get sticky with barbeque sauce.

Barbeque sauce?

Yes, Kwesi and me, we trying a lil ting. With the bistro gone through and everything. Man have to live. Y'unnerstan?

Yes, man have to live. So, what you and Miss Indira agree?

About what?

The use of her premises, the water, the washroom, because I guessing you boys not going to do your business in the bucket, eh? And your customers might want to wash hands too. Barbeque sauce does be real sticky. Ent?

Mr Bostic, I come in here, nice, nice, to ask for a bucket of water and you giving me a setta talks. If you don't want to give me the water, just say so. I sure Miss Cynthia down the road wouldn't mind if I ask her.

When you down there, ask Miss Cynthia if you could use her gallery to set up your business too.

Why? We on the public pavement outside a here. We not on anybody private property.

My advice to you, young man, is to fill the bucket and go back outside. When you reach there, I want you to check exactly where you set up. Follow the line of the pavement round and see if you entirely on public property. Now go and fill the bucket.

Fritzie come downstairs. She ready to go home. Bostic call out.

You talk to Indira since she gone?

No, it looking like her phone gone dead.

Come. Tell me what you think about this.

Fritzie following him into the pub and down to the storeroom. He bring out a clear plastic bag and he show it to her.

This was in her garbage to throw out.

Fritzie gasp. Her hand fly to her face. She take the bag and open it. Yes. It is really stuffed full of long thick hanks of blonde hair.

Look at that length. Like she cut off all. You see her before she go?

No. You have any idea why she do this?

Well is hard to say, but she and Jah-Son had a little coolness between them. I never ask why and she never tell me.

142

You think she gone up by Jah-Son house? Up by his granny?

She never went up there before as far as I know. But, I suppose that is where she is. I can't think where else she could be.

Do me a favour. You could pass in by 3Fs and tell Maisie that if Indira up there, tell her we have to talk? Tell her to say, is urgent, OK?

Something wrong?

Fritzie, girl, I feel if we don't do something quick about those two young fellers, we going to have a problem. I want her here on the spot when I sorting it out.

When Bostic reach to open up De Rightest Place next morning, the barbeque pit is still in position where the young fellers leave it the night before. The newspaper not on the forecourt. There is light coming from the bedroom window upstairs. She must be reach back and pick up the papers already. He also seeing half a dozen or so bird cages hanging from the branches of the guava tree in the backyard. Hmmm, like Jah-Son here too.

Indira come downstairs about an hour later. Bostic take one look at her head and point his chin in her direction.

Like you trying something new?

You like it? Like you trying something new too.

Bostic look puzzled. He touch his own hair. No. What you mean?

I see a barbeque pit set up on the forecourt, so I figure you doing something in the evening.

You see it? Good. That is why I send for you. Is not me doing something.

Who then?

Curtis and Kwesi.

Those two young fellers? They're showing some enterprising spirit. Nice. They talk to you about using the space?

That is the problem. Curtis say is public space and he don't have to ask nobody nothing to be there.

I looked at it properly when we got here and it is directly on the forecourt. My space. Our space. That is why I thought it was you. You or Fritzie.

So you agree the fellers trespassing.

143

No doubt about it. They say when they coming back?

No, but is weekend. Everybody looking to buy food. So, they bound to be back later.

What you think we should do?

They sit and talk and when Fritzie reach, she join them. Soupa Saturday lunchtime trade come and go. Then evening come. Indira makes it her business to be relaxing with a gin and coconut water on the forecourt, where she and Bostic and Fritzie moved back the tables and chairs, the potted plants and the fairy lights to their bistro location. When the pick-up draw up with Curtis and Kwesi, there is only the pavement for the big maco cooler, the folding table, the cardboard box, the blue garbage bags. They can barely see their barbeque pit, enclosed as it is within the boundary screen of palms, ficus, sweet lime and croton. They do see Indira, but she's so engrossed in her book, *Micro-enterprise Manual for the Budding Businessperson*, that she doesn't even look up at their clattering arrival. The two young men hold a brief conference out of sight and Curtis approach her, a big smile on his face.

Hello, Miss Indira. Like you come back. You had a nice holiday?

Oh, hello Curtis. Yes. A nice break. How you doing?

I all right.

Glad to hear that. Take care.

Indira turn her attention back to her book. Curtis is confused. That didn't go quite as he expected. He gone back behind the hedge for a hurried, whispered exchange with Kwesi. Then the two of them return to Indira, who still not looking up, even as they are standing right in front of her. Curtis clear his throat. Uh-huh-huh. Excuse me again, Miss Indira.

She look up. Oh, Curtis. Hello, Kwesi. It's a while since I saw you. My, my, you're getting to be quite a grown-up young man. How's Uncle Cecil?

Uncle Cecil fine. He and Boyee gone up Arima. It have horse racing today.

Oh, yes. Nice, nice. Well, good to see you. When you reach home, say hello for me. She turn back to her book.

The two young men look at each other. Kwesi taking the lead this time.

Miss Indira, you could spare us a minute? It have something we want to talk to you about.

Sure. She rest her book face down on the table and lean back in her chair. What's up?

We could sit down?

Yes, of course. But before you do that… She tilt her glass reflectively, examine the scant half-inch of liquid left, and toss it back. Before you make yourselves comfortable, could you go in the bar and ask Mr Bostic to bring me another drink? She pass the empty glass to Curtis. And get something for yourselves too. On the house.

She's not reading when Bostic and the two boys come out. She motion them to sit. You too, Bostic, please.

What can I do for you? Her face is serious. The boys sit up straight. They rest the ginger shandies they were sipping on the table. Bostic is leaning back in his chair with his lemon, lime and bitters. Her gin is untouched.

Miss Indira, when you was away, we start up a little business. Kwesi and me.

Well, congratulations. So what you doing?

We doing barbeque evening time, for people to take home.

Good idea. So where is the business? St James? The Avenue? Belmont.

Oh, nearby your home. Well, I'm sure people in the neighbourhood appreciate that. Well, good luck. She pick up her drink and makes to clink her glass with their bottles. Cheers!

The boys do not touch their bottles. They are looking down at the table. They look defeated.

Curtis slide a glance at Bostic. Mr Bostic, please tell Miss Indira what happen.

Bostic look at them. Is a long, long time since he was their age, but he hasn't forgotten how brash and cocksure he was. Riding roughshod over old-people ways of doing things. He'd had to learn and so would they. They just need some guidance.

Indira, yesterday when you wasn't here, these boys drop off that barbeque pit. He pointed at it. Indira shifted her position so as to see it, as if for the first time.

Oh, that? It's not yours, Bostic?

145

No. Is theirs. I wasn't here when they drop it. Nobody didn't ask me no question. In the evening, the two of them turn up and start to light fire, smoke up the place, and selling barbeque whole night. People coming in and out the bar wanting to use wash-room, wanting toilet paper, hand-wipes, soap, glass of ice water to drink. I don't even know what time they finish, because when I lock up the place and leave, they was still here. This morning when I come back, the pit park up same place.

Like you had a good night's business?

They do not answer.

So, what's the plan for tonight?

Still no answer.

Curtis, Kwesi. Look at me.

They look up.

Answer me.

Well, we have chicken quarters season up and ready in the cooler. And some pig tail. People was asking for that last night.

And?

And we was planning to do the barbeque again.

Where?

Same as last night.

Where the pit is parked?

Yes.

On the forecourt of my business place?

The two fellers don't say anything.

And your customers? You getting port-a-loo delivered for them to use?

Kwesi is emboldened. He sees an opportunity to score a point.

Miss Indira, is street food. Street vendors don't have to provide facilities for customers.

That's true, Kwesi. But your barbeque business is not on the street. It is on my property. Your customers were using my facilities last night and will no doubt expect to do so again tonight.

Curtis recognise defeat.

Miss Indira, what you want we to do? We done start already. It looking like it will do good. Whole morning we cutting up, cleaning and seasoning chicken. People expecting we to be here tonight.

Bostic what you think we should do about this situation?

Bostic drain the last of the LLB. He squinting at the residue of foam sliding down the inside of the neck of the bottle. He rest the bottle on the table, fold his arms and appraise the two young fellers.

OK, this is what we will do for tonight. And tonight only. You can move the plants away so you can reach your barbeque pit easy. I will allow your customers to use the washroom. Miss Indira and I will talk about this tonight. Be here tomorrow morning before Miss Fritzie start serving her soup. We will talk then.

Bostic and Indira do not let Curtis know that they've see him wiping his eyes on the sleeve of his T-shirt. Bostic pick up his bottle to go back to the bar. Kwesi say, thank you, Mr Bostic. Curtis say, Mr Bostic, sorry about last night. Indira say, drink up your shandy, boys, before it gets too warm. She take her glass and her book and she follow Bostic.

She is thinking how right was that morning's horoscope: *Gemini: Accept a coming challenge only if it will benefit the greater good. Avoid becoming self-righteous and moralistic, but hold to your convictions. You can raise others' sensibilities by choosing strategic battles that illuminate important moral or ethical issues.*

Bostic return to setting up the bar for the evening trade. He's relieved that Indira is back and has taken charge, asserting her position as bosslady of De Rightest Place. He's long decided it's best he simply ticks over. Keep a low profile. He's the barman. Nothing more. He has too much cocoa in the sun to call rain upon himself. There's Jah-Son and all the ramifications of that revelation. There's his promise to Solo to look after Indira. And there's his responsibility towards the prudent exercise of that Power of Attorney. Yes, he saying to himself. You just keep the boat steady.

Upstairs, Indira is off on another mission. She rummages through her bookshelf. Let me see. Hmmm. Ah, there you are. *Citizens Collectives: Inter-Generational Initiatives for Grassroots Growth and Sustainable Synergy.* If you don't want to lick them, better you join them. She and Fritzie can carve out a new business venture from this opportunity. Street food management. Expand or you'll shrink.

18. HOLD TO YOUR CONVICTIONS

Jah-Son deep in thought as he unhook the bullfinch's cage, open the cage door, and absently whistle its call. The little bird jerk its head towards him and it whistle back, *twee-eeee, chirrup-chirrip, twee-eee*. It hop onto his outstretched index finger and he stroke its sleek black feathers. It flutter under his touch and the sudden flash of white at the base of its longer wing feathers bring a smile to his face.

A shard of sunlight pierce a gap between the leaves of Cynthia's breadfruit tree. It ricochet off the line of broken bottles embedded along the top of Mr Aneel's wall, and shine in Jah-Son's eyes as he clip a fistful of grass stalks, heads sagging under full sprays of seeds, into the bird feeder. Sun up already. Time to go upstairs to get ready for work. Is only Friday. Still Saturday to go.

Was a time when you step in a maxi and say good morning and people would look up and answer, Mornin', and somebody would move a bag to make room for you to sit, and somebody would say something to anybody, everybody, nobody-in-particular about something they seeing outside the window, or hearing on the radio the driver have on, and a conversation would start up. But not nowadays. No. Everybody have cellphone in they hand, they earphone stick up in they ears. You could be on a desert island all by yourself. Every man is ah island on this island. Same thing at work. People in they own world. They don't want to have nothing to do with nobody.

Look at me. Since I leave school I working Stephenson and Son. Monday to Saturday I there, week in week out, year in year out. Checking goods coming in, checking goods going out. And supervisor checking me. No conversation, no joke. He just making sure I doing my work. And the boss watching him to see that he doing his work. But is not everywhere like that. I see how Miss Indira and Fritzie working. Talking and laughing, bigging

148

up one another whole time. Even Mr Bostic, who kinda gruff most of the time, the women and them can get him to make a little joke sometimes. Everybody sharing the work and everybody sharing the benefit. Even me. I come in and meet everybody there already, but is like I jus wash mih foot and jump in the team. When I first start working Stephenson and Son I was glad for something to do, to be independent and to bring a little help out to Gran-Gran. But since I start at De Rightest Place, I not feeling right at work. I not comfortable. I can't ignore it as before. I seeing everything that wrong. I know how to fix it. Make it a nicer place for the workers. But who is me, eh?

The boss is in the warehouse when Jah-Son clocks in. George had a stroke and is in hospital, Mr Stephenson says. Dirk is taking over from him. Jah-Son looks at his new supervisor. Dirk has been in the company for all of six months. He's been shown what to do and how to do it by Jah-Son. Dirk runs his fingers through his long straight hair. He picks up George's clipboard. OK, he says, fête over. Back to work.

In the lunch break, Jah-Son goes to the boss's office.

Mr Stephenson, I'm handing in my notice.

What you mean handing in your notice?

I'm leaving.

What you mean you leaving?

I'm leaving the job.

Mr Stephenson rises from his chair. His face is suddenly red.

All these years I give you a job and now you leaving? How you could be so ungrateful after all this company do for you?

Jah-Son is taken aback. He hasn't imagined that Stephenson & Sons feel they are doing him a favour. How could it be a favour when you work and then get paid?

Mr Stephenson, with all due respect, you give me a job and in return I give you my labour for five years. Same job, same pay for five years.

Same job, same pay. What you expect?

The company growing with my work, but I not growing too. Everybody around me growing and I staying small. Is time I start to look out for myself.

149

What you feel you could do, eh? Counting what coming in and what going out? There are machines to do that now. Your job was going to finish anyway.

Well then, it's a good thing I giving in my notice.

Don't bother with notice. Don't bother to come back.

You firing me, Mr Stephenson?

No, you tell me you leaving, so I letting you go. Collect your pay for this week from the accounts clerk. Tell her I say to pay you for tomorrow too, even though you not going to be here. And when you catching your tail to find work somewhere else, don't come crying to me to take you back.

Jah-Son walk back to De Rightest Place with mixed emotions. To the people on top, the people below are disposable. Like toilet paper, use and then flush away. How could he have put up with that for so long? Everything was fine until he decided not to be exploited any more and then the true colours of the masters came out on show. Is like if these people feel that you should be glad you getting pay at all. After all, generations of your ancestors worked for them for hundreds of years without pay, so you lucky. On the other hand, he was relieved to have escaped. He was a free man. But what's was he going to do now? What would Indira say?

Thank the gods, was what she say. This thing has been giving you horrors for some time. He was surprise to hear that. You mean to say you know something wasn't right? How could I not know? You've been bite-up for weeks now and I didn't know why. I thought it was to do with me. He reach over and take her hand and look at it. Well, it was only to do with me. I'm all right now. I didn't know I was giving you worries about me. Sorry. She give his hand a squeeze, so that he would look directly into her eyes. Promise me next time something bothering you, you will tell me? He smiled. Yes. And you do the same too. OK?

Well, there is one thing. A couple of things, really. The first one is to do with Bostic. The pub business doing well and that's a good thing, but it means he's working harder with hardly a break. You think you could give him a hand?

You think he would let me? Everybody know the bar is Bostic territory. He might not like me coming in. And the last thing I want to do is get on his wrong side.

150

Why don't you help in ways he will let you and see how far you can go? You may be surprised. I feel that secretly he'll be glad for your help.

What is the next thing on your mind?

We need to be in a different frame of mind for that. But I promise you, I'll tell you as soon as the time is right.

That afternoon, Jah-Son work alongside Fritzie and Indira clearing up after lunchtime soup. When Fritzie leaving, he go downstairs with her. Bostic stacking the chiller and packing up the empty crates. Jah-Son watch him for a while to see how he going about it, following his flow. He know that everybody have their own rhythm, their own way of working that their body already work out. He know Gran-Gran's housework rhythm, his own bird-care rhythm, the soup-making rhythm with Fritzie and Indira. If you try to do it different, your whole body objecting; it hurting in strange places; you fumble, break things, you slow down. Even your mind get tangled up when the body rhythm change. It's even worse when another person break into your flow.

So, his observation of Bostic is to find a place in his flow where he might be glad for some help. Bostic lift a crate of bottles from the storeroom, cart them to the chiller behind the bar, unpack the bottles into the chiller, then take back the empty crate and bring out another full one. The packing of the chiller is clearly a technical task; it require a knowledge of likely sales of each type of drink, ease of access, shelving position and the different temperature requirements – intelligence that Jah-Son could see he couldn't pick up just by looking – but the lifting of full crates from the storeroom and carrying them to the chiller, that was pure labour and that is where he could try to make a start.

What you want next?

Bostic look up from packing Stag. Malta, he say.

Jah-Son go into the storeroom and bring out a case of Malta. He move away the empty Stag case and put the Malta into position.

This going back in the storeroom?

Yes, put it with the others.

Jah-Son find where the empty case should go and call from the storeroom, What next?

151

Carib.

And so they go on until the chiller packed, the only conversation being what to bring, where to put things. Jah-Son intrigued by the decision-making that go into the packing of the chiller, so he comment on how much more of one brand Bostic called for. Bostic tell him that he sell twice as much of that brand as the other beers, and that lead to a conversation about customer preferences, gender and age differences, time of day choices, spirits versus beer. Is the longest conversation they've ever had.

The next morning, Saturday, about half an hour after Bostic arrive, Jah-Son come downstairs. He dressed in shorts and a T-shirt. Bostic greet him.

What happen? No work today?

I leave the job.

The conversation end there. Bostic turn away, go behind the bar and start to do things out of sight. Jah-Son wondering whether it's Bostic's deliberate intention to put up a barrier to exclude him from his domain or whether it's simply what he did at that stage of the morning. He don't let it bother him. Normally, he would have tended to his birds and gone to work long before Bostic arrive at De Rightest Place, so they were not in the habit of meeting on mornings. He had purposely come down later than usual, so that he could see to the birds as well as observe Bostic. He doesn't offer to help. He go upstairs to work alongside Fritzie and Indira with the soup of the day.

In the afternoon, he go down and this time he ask Bostic directly whether he would like some help. Bostic assign him the same task as the day before. Jah-Son take the conversation to the barbeque activity on weekend nights.

Looking like Curtis and Kwesi doing some business outside.

Uh huh.

It going good?

Look so.

Jah-Son leave that line of talk for a while, then come back to it.

Plenty cars park up.

Where?

When the barbeque going on.

Yeah.

I see their customers coming inside and walking out with beers. Some.

Different crowd from the bistro dinner lot.

Uh-huh.

Looks like Bostic don't want to talk about the barbeque or its effect on the pub. Or maybe he just doesn't want to talk to *me* about it. So Jah-Son go quiet until the chiller packed and Bostic retreat behind the bar. Jah-Son taking that as a signal that he not open to any more engagement, but he still persist.

Mr Bostic, anything else I can help you with?

I can manage.

OK.

Jah-Son go back upstairs. The evening progress, the barbeque in full swing, soca blasting from a system set up on the forecourt, cars pulling up and parking on the street, customers in and out of the bar. The Belmont Bes BBQ Boys, as their sign identify them, keeping busy filling orders. Jah-Son sitting inside the pub, liming with Feroze, yes, but really paying attention to Bostic's flow. He seeing that Bostic could hardly keep up with the stream of passing-through customers. While the regulars sit and sip and chat and play board games, the transients only want to get a bottle or two and leave. Most times they calling out their orders as soon as they enter, without so much as a please or a thank you, not looking to see whether someone else being served or waiting for service. Bostic serve those intruders quickly, as if to get rid of them. The regulars are a tolerant lot, but Jah-Son could see from the looks they giving that they not happy with the situation, that they feeling side-lined in what they regard as their own space.

Sundays there is no barbeque and the pub closes by nine o'clock. On Monday morning, his first weekday as an unemployed person, Jah-Son feeling strange to be getting up and not going to work – which you really can't call the little bit of help he giving Bostic. The last thing he want is to be living off Indira, like some sweetman. Man have his pride. When woman minding you, you don't have any grounds to call any shots. She on top and you better fall in line. He see plenty men suffer that fate. Take Mr Aneel next door. Every time he and Mrs Aneel have they disagreement, she does start cussing him: Yuh is a good-for-nothing mamapoule man. If it wasn't for mih ma and pa, we would a be living on the street. Is mih mother and father hard-wuk what minding we. The likkle bit a money yuh does be bringing in from them kiss-me-arse kite you does be making can't buy enough food to fill the space between yuh own teeth.

What abuse will Indira hurl at him if his idle state continues?

He gone downstairs. He do his do with his birds and he come over to the bar to do what he did on the past two days. It looking like Bostic not too happy to see him. When he offer to help, Bostic say, All these years I doing it by myself, I don't see why I can't continue by myself. Tuesday, same thing. Wednesday, Bostic say, I have to ask Indira if she feel I suddenly become incapable. Thursday, Jah-Son didn't even try. Instead, he gone up by his grandmother to find out how things going and to check on his nesting birds. When she ask how he doing, there was no way he could avoid telling her that he leave the job in the warehouse. So where you working now? I helping out in the pub. In the bar with Bostic? Well, not exactly. I mostly helping with the lunchtime soup. Why not the bar? That is man work. Gran-Gran, Mr Bostic say he can manage by himself. Listen, Jah-Son, he must be feel you arrive on the scene and want to take over. Don't forget, he running that place with and without Indira for years. Two man-crab can't live in one crab hole, remember that. You be careful.

Friday come and Jah-Son position himself on the forecourt to take in the scene. The barbeque blazing, cars pulling up, parking, driving off as usual. He watching customers running in and out with bottles held by their neck and he get a idea where he could be of some use. Next morning, he brace himself to approach the topic. Bostic's back turn to him, but he speak anyway.

Mr Bostic?

Yes.

You think you could spare a minute to hear a idea I have?

Bostic turn to face him.

Well, I was looking at how the barbeque customers does have to come quite in here for their drinks.

No comment.

I was wondering if we could try out a idea I have.

Bostic not saying nothing.

You still have that big cooler you had on the forecourt when KarlLee was painting? I watch you a few afternoons and you sell plenty beers from that cooler quick-quick.

Silence from Bostic, but Jah-Son decide, in for a penny…

I was wondering, if you still have the cooler, if I could full it up with a mix of drinks, put in plenty ice and sell it directly to them outside.

Go in the storeroom and look for it. If it there, you can borrow it.

It is there. Jah-Son brings it out and washes it in the backyard.

Mr Bostic. It clean now. Can I fill it up with drinks?

What drinks?

From the storeroom.

You put drinks there?

Jah-Son know that question don't need no answer. Of course he didn't put drinks there. Bostic continue. You say you have a idea, but like it begin and end with getting a cooler. What is the next step?

Jah-Son is torn. He doesn't want to be rude to his elders, but Mr Bostic is not being fair. He wasn't taking that from Mr Stephenson and he don't see why he should take it from Mr Bostic.

Mr Bostic, I not doing this for myself. I don't want anything from it. I want to do this as a help out to this pub. I watch what happening here and I see two things that need fixing. One, the barbeque customers does come in here like they in a ten items or less line in a grocery. They hurry, hurry and they rude. They upsetting your vibe. You does have to be fixing them up first just to get rid of them. Second thing, the pub regulars don't like it. They feel their space is invaded by aliens who do not respect them. If I deal with them outside, then both problems solve one time.

Bostic taking his time to answer. He thinking about what Jah-Son say, but he thinking more about how he say it. How he able to stand up for himself without getting angry or disrespectful. He feeling a little ashamed for pushing him away, but he don't know how to change his manner to be more accommodating. He don't want to encourage this boy, or allow himself to develop anything like a friendship, because where would that lead? Far better to keep his distance.

OK. Take what you want from the storeroom.

I really don't know what I want, Mr Bostic. Is only you who know what those customers want.

Bring the cooler.

They pack the cooler together and Jah-Son looking on good-good.

Where the ice?

We only have enough ice to put in drinks.

So where to get ice, then?

You will have to go out and buy ice.

You know I can't drive the pick-up, Mr Bostic. I will have to take taxi.

Bostic took Jah-Son for ice and they stopped off for coconut water by the Savannah on the way back. They sat on a bench opposite QRC. You know, is over there I went to school, said Bostic. Happiest days. Solo and I were at school together. Solo? asked Jah-Son. Solo, said Bostic. The red rastaman who starring in all those pictures hanging up in the pub. Solomon Warner, Indira Gabriel's husband and Terrence Bostic's best friend. Best friends then and best friends forever.

Where he is?

Canada.

Jah-Son didn't know what to make of this disclosure. Why was Bostic telling him this? Was it a warning that Solo could come back and take back Indira? Was he saying that he didn't approve of Jah-Son's relationship with his best friend's wife? Was he telling him that to depend on De Rightest Place for his home and his living was a risky thing to do? Was Bostic saying he was a foolish little boy for not wondering about the man in the pictures or about Indira's life before him? But he didn't know how to say to Bostic, Why are you telling me this? He had to make of it what he could.

Bostic left him to deal with the cooler on his own, as if he wanted him to succeed or fail by himself. That night, foot traffic flowed more easily since all the customers' needs were met on the forecourt. Some bought drinks while waiting for their barbeque and bought again to take away. By the end of the evening, Jah-Son was exhausted. He felt he'd done more than a full day's hard labour in the seven hours that he was selling drinks and refilling the cooler, selling drinks and refilling the cooler. But he was happy that his idea proved to be successful.

Bostic didn't say anything to Jah-Son about the way things went, but on Sunday afternoon, when he and Indira were doing the weekly inventory, he introduced the subject.

You see we had a new outlet last night?

She looked up from the books.

How was sales?

Better than usual.

She tapped her pencil on the table for a while, reflecting.

You know, I was getting worried about your regulars feeling their space was invaded by the barbeque crowd.

Bostic glanced away from the column of figures he was working on. He made a tent of his fingers. He leaned his chin on the tent ridge and lifted his eyes towards Indira.

You know something? That was my worry too. Fellers like Cecil and Boyee was getting restless. They was seeing these people coming in, behaving as if they own the place, demanding instant attention. But last night everything was fine, like the old days. Cool scene.

So, you OK with Jah-Son helping out?

As long as he stick to his part and don't get in my way, I cool.

19. A QUIET PLACE

*Gemini: Find a quiet place to escape with your honey today. In the midst
of all the hustle and bustle, you can get cozy in your own private nook.*

Indira folds the newspaper and places it on the bedside table, takes
off her reading glasses, and rubs her eyes. Yes, it is here at last. The
green light she was waiting for.

Jah-Son, how do you feel about not knowing your mother and
father?

His index finger stops drawing circles around her navel. He
shifts his head from her breast to look up at her face. Her eyes are
wide, their pupils huge, dark and deep. She not making idle
conversation here. She want a real answer to her question.

It don't feel no how in particular. Is not as if I know them and
they gone away or die or anything like that. If you show me a
picture of my mother, I wouldn't know is she. And as for father,
I don't know if my father, whoever he is, know he have a son and
the son is me.

He looks up at her again. I tell you who I know tho'. I know my
grandmother. That is mother plus father in one. I don't know if
I miss out in anything. When I growing up, I know plenty
children with they mother, some with they father too, and they
didn't seem to be any better than me and some was worse. So I
never study that too much. I was a child then and now I am a man,
so I reach where any mother and father would a expect me to
reach. I don't think it matter who raise me.

He resumes drawing his circles and she strokes his head. Lazy
Sunday lie-in pillow talk, but Jah-Son feels a weight in her hand,
senses a certain distractedness in the rhythm of her stroking,
hears her heartbeat speeding up. He wonders why she asking him
that question and why his answer affect her so strangely. It come
to him that her question is an opening to something she has on

158

her mind, and that he is meant to pick up and carry on the conversation.

What about your parents? They still in India?

Indira doesn't answer. He waits a while. He feels her shift. He looks up. Her face is turned away, sunk into the pillow. He adjusts, supporting his head on his elbow, to see her better. She is crying. He sits up, leaning his back against the headboard, and he pulls her head on to his lap. He lets her cry long, streaming, silent tears. There is no sobbing, no shaking, just an upwelling and a draining. He can hardly hear her voice.

I don't know.

He thinks about that. She doesn't know where they are? She doesn't know what?

You lose touch with them?

There is another long silence. Then, she wipes her face in the sheet and looks at him directly. She gives him a weak smile.

That's one way of putting it. Yes, we lost touch. We also lost sight, hearing, smell, taste.

What you mean?

I never knew my parents. Except what the people who brought me up told me.

In India?

Yes. I was brought up by strangers. It was the caretaker and his wife in the boarding house where my parents were staying. I called them Achan and Amma, like the other children.

Sisters and brothers?

They had three children of their own. One was a boy my age. We were babies together. We were like twins.

Jah-Son lets this sink in, gives her breathing space.

What happen to your parents? They get sick or something?

Amma said they were living there for just a few months before I was born. She thought they'd been in India a long time. Travelling. From England. Young people.

He can't breathe. He's so fearful of breaking the spell.

One day they went out on a boat. There was a storm and they never came back.

Where were you?

I suppose they'd planned to go out for a short time because

159

they didn't take me with them. When they didn't come back, Amma and Achan took me to live in their room.

An English baby? You mean to say nobody reported an English baby, a white child, abandoned in India?

I've thought about that a lot, and I think I know how, for a time, nothing happened – no report to authorities or anything. I read up about that period in India. To put myself in their shoes. There was a lot of political upheaval at the time. A state of emergency that went on for years and years. It was a very bad time for everyone. So people were keeping quiet, not making any trouble for themselves. You never know how things could turn out if you call the attention of people in authority to yourself, especially if you of a lower caste, like Amma and Achan. You have no power. Maybe they were terrified they'd be accused of murder or kidnapping or something. So I suppose, one day passed, one week, one year and then how could they report it? Too much time had passed. They just kept me and brought me up.

She falls silent for a minute or two. Then she continues.

You know what? I didn't even have a name. Amma said they didn't know my real name. They didn't know my parents' names. They called them sahib and memsahib. After my parents disappeared, Achan and Amma called me Indira. Amma said that when my parents were talking in English, one word she could understand was *Indira*. So they named me that. I think my parents were discussing politics. Indira Gandhi was the Prime Minister around that time. From what I've read about her, she wasn't a nice person. She put her people under a lot of pressure. It must've been a frightening time for Amma and Achan.

They were afraid somebody would report them about you?

Yes, that's what I believe. And, another thing, it was a girl child they were left with. Girls didn't count as having much value. In fact girls are a burden. I was lucky they decided to keep me. At least, I think so.

He strokes her forehead.

You think about them?

My parents or my adopted parents?

Both, I suppose.

I imagine my birth parents a lot. I have my own fantasy about them. I think about them going to India like they're on some big hippy adventure. You know, flower children, taking drugs for spiritual awakening. Seeking a guru, or a Maharishi for enlightenment. Following in the footsteps of the Beatles...

Jah-Son looks puzzled.

You don't know what I'm talking about, do you? It's long before you were born.

Maybe. But it still interesting. And your adopted family?

They are stuck in my head just like they were on the day I was taken from them.

What happened?

For a long while, she doesn't answer, and when she does speak her voice is heavy with sadness.

I can't talk about it.

With that they both fall quiet. Indira gets up and goes to the bathroom. Jah-Son goes to the kitchen to make coffee. They get back into bed, sitting up and sipping the morning brew.

Jah-Son, you ever think you would like to have a child?

If Jah-Son was wondering how the conversation would go next, it wouldn't have been in this direction.

I never thought about it. I suppose is not something fellas does talk about, or think about. From what I can see, the normal thing is for a fella to become a father by accident. People say: So and so make a child for so and so. Or a girl would tell a fella that she making baby and is his own. Why you ask me that?

Let's just suppose that I say to you that I want a child. How you would feel about that?

You mean like *plan* to make a child? Decide in advance that is what you want?

Yes. How would you feel about that?

I dunno. I haven't thought about that.

He stops to think for a few seconds then turns to her abruptly.

You asking a serious question. You not pregnant?

No. I am not. But yes, it is a serious question. Because I would like to have a child.

Just so?

It's not just so. It's been on my mind for a while.

I never think of you as the kind of woman to want a child.

161

What kind of woman doesn't want a child?

An independent woman. Like you.

He looks at her, at her earnest face. He gives a little laugh and tickles her chin, making her look up at him.

What happen? You feel time passing you by?

That's partly it. But it's not all of it. I want a chance to find out what it is like to be a good mother.

But you expecting the child father to help too? To be around?

It's something I can do by myself if I have to.

So how I come in this?

I would like you to be the child's father.

But you don't mind if I not around when the child growing up.

I didn't say so. But if you're not ready for the responsibility, I would understand. I will look after the child myself.

Jah-Son rests his coffee mug on the bedside table. He turns with deliberate care to face her directly.

Wait. Hold on a second. What going on here? One minute we talking about how not having parents could mess up a person's life. How I lucky I had Gran-Gran to fill in for mother and father. How you don't want to talk about your childhood because of whatever happen to you. And next minute you want me to make a child with you, and it don't matter if I not around to help raise it?

Jah-Son gets out of bed. He reaches for his clothes and begins to dress.

Jah-Son, wait. You don't understand. I didn't mean it that way.

You could manage by yourself you say. So you happy for me to be the kind of father my own father was. Wham, bam, thank you ma'am. Is this how you see me?

He sweeps his arm over the bed, over Indira, her eyes now wide and alarmed.

That's what all this is about? I is just your stud? The sperm donor?

He is almost at the door when a pillow catches him on the back of his head. He swings round in time to catch the next one Indira flings at him. She is standing on the bed, hair wild about her tear-stained face, reaching into her arsenal of bedclothes for a third pillow when Jah-Son lunges at her waist, pulling her down on the bed, where he too falls, beside her. He rolls over on to her, pinning her under him.

Now, he says, games over. I going to make breakfast. When you catch yourself, come out and eat. Then you and me, we going to have a serious talk.

They sit across the table from each other while she seeks, in the morass of her unsorted feelings, to find words to express some of what is in her heart – the trailing hauntedness of a life of disconnection with place and person, her wanderings through India and Europe, then finding this island, her feeling that she could be at home here, her many fleeting attachments and relationships with men, with women, her finding Solo and the years of reprieve from being an unanchored solitary, and her need, now she's approaching the use-by-date for women, her need for someone who is hers, not a spouse or a partner, but someone who is hers entirely, whom she can love unreservedly.

She says, I have to confess to you that I tried to become pregnant by you without asking if it was OK. I was trying something I'd been reading about – the rhythm method, abstinence until my fertile time. You didn't know what I was doing, why I wouldn't go to bed with you for days at a time until that day when I tried to seduce you, but you didn't fall for it. Maybe you felt I was playing games, hot and cold. But it was all selfish biology and I should have discussed it with you first. It backfired on me. I deserved that. I am sorry.

Some things she does not tell him. She does not tell him about the evening the tax collector came along that dark Kerala backwater and, glancing up at the old colonial guesthouse, spied her on the verandah having her hair brushed out by Amma. How he came upstairs and demanded to see their papers. How they had none. How they could not convince him that she was not a stolen child. How he grabbed her saying he would take her to the authorities. How Amma and Achan and Rajpati and Sita and Bai fought and cried. How he lifted her and carried her down and placed her in the boat. How he shouted at the boatman to move faster along that dark Kerala backwater, how the boatman helped her to an escape of a kind.

She does not tell him *everything*, even about those things she will speak about. She tells him some of the things about the cold orphanage, about the hot kitchens, about living by her wits in India. She tells him a little about what she had to do, the people she had to persuade, by any and every means, to come by the false documents that got her the right passport to freedom. She tells him a little about getting by through her wiles in Europe, about meeting Solo, about coming to this island.

She does not tell him about the Mary Magdalene Home for Unwed Mothers. She does not tell him about Gabriel or how she came to be pregnant with him. She cannot tell even herself about Gabriel. To utter words about him would make him into a shaped story with a beginning, a middle and an end. That would be too final. It would make of him something that she could not pull out at will and keep on ever refashioning to her heart's desire.

Jah-Son listens. He has never before had someone speak to him for so long and in such a personal, revealing way. He cannot look into her eyes. He wonders how his innocent, unquestioning, simple, one-day-following-the-next, carefree life has become woven so intimately within this knot of unfathomable complexity and he marvels at his fate to have been there on the forecourt that day when KarlLee was painting the wall and he chanced to, fleetingly, lock eyes with the enigmatic woman peering through the jalousie window upstairs.

20. GLAD TIDINGS

At night her sleeping body frees her mind to burrow through memory, to tunnel into fear and desire.

In a faraway place in a long-ago time where she is…

See her chop and wash and scrape and peel and strain and grate and scrub and sweep and wipe and lift and polish and carve and sift and drizzle and pour and knead. Watch her remember she can speak through shouts and clouts, through looking and listening. See her burnt, scarred, cut and peeled hands. See her eat plate scrapings. See her sleep on floors.

Is she ten? Eleven? Is she twelve? She doesn't know. The days, months and years pass unmarked, unremarked. In time to come, in a place where birthdays are celebrated, she will decide on a date to mark her birth, from a half-remembered story about seasons and rain and wind, told by the woman who did not birth her, and who had no way of knowing the names of days, months or years.

The children change. Some go. Where they go, no one knows. New ones come. Where they come from they do not have a name for. One day they take her.

See her sitting on a white satin cushion. Ylang-ylang woven through bright spun-gold hair. Eyelids, forget-me-not. Lips, musk rose. Jasmine garlands encircle her neck. Sprays of tuberoses perfume her lap. She remembers being dressed up before. Now there are more of them. Silent men. Plump with power. Gorged with greed. Lip-licking their lust. Lakhs of rupees pile up. One by one the men get fewer. Only one is left. See him rub his hands. See his lips curl. See him lift the filmy gauze curtain. See him enter. Even at eleven she knows what is to follow.

They repair the rent. Another viewing. Another bidding. Another entry. Another repair. And again. And again.

Soon no man dares to lift the curtain. Blue zombie eyes warn of the depths to which they are destined to fall, foretelling the failures in their futures, sounding the death-knell that awaits their souls at night.

In the house of girls there are special girls. She is striking. She is different. She is a special girl. To be with her, to possess her, to subjugate her, adds stature to a man. She masters the wiles of wanton women; she invents new tricks for the trade. She is a chameleon – compliant and submissive, eager and adventurous, defiant and rebellious. She dons a myriad costumes. She wears a multitude of masks. She is all things to all men. Each performance brings a standing ovation. Encore.

She senses there is another self. It is deep, deep inside. It is space without shape or form, without feeling. Still, quiet, empty.

Sometimes a girl disappears. When she returns, she is weak and pale. She rests. She has no guests. I was sick, she says. Now I am better. Sometimes a girl does not come back.

When she gets sick, she is taken away. The sickness lasts for a while, then passes.

Then she feels a calm on her skin like a cool breeze, a warmth like morning sun, a tingling like new rain. She hears crickets in concert, leaves whispering their stories. She can see the air pushed aside by a bird in flight. She can smell an ant hurrying by. A yellow carambola on the branch pricks her eyes, tickles her eardrums, blisters her nostrils before its waxy skin can stroke her fingertips, before its sharp juice sears her throat.

This new being she knows is herself. Her inside self that has come alive. A butterfly flutters in her belly. It touches a nerve that sends a wave to her groin, which answers the touch in a long upwelling that rises and breaks, rises and breaks, surging back and forth, refreshing the fluttering in her belly, restirring the wave in her groin. A fish swims in her belly. She can hear the sloshing; she can feel its thrashing tail. It glides around the wall of her belly, round and round; its overlapping scales ripple against her inner-most skin. Her insides squeeze and relax, squeeze and relax, exciting the fish to swim in all directions.

Her outside self sees the new place. There are other girls here, round-bellied girls like herself. They have come from many places. They speak many languages, but in whispers. There is a

166

rule of silence here. Their tongues slide and slip, the words mix and morph with the comings and goings of the girls. Malayalam and English glide into Tamil and Urdu sprinkled with smatterings of Kannada, Tulu, Hindi and Bengali. And there is Latin. Latin of church, Latin of prayers, Latin of the nuns who are in charge of the place where the round-bellied girls live.

The round-bellied girls are fallen women. They have sinned and are carrying the fruits of their sin. They must pray. They must do penance for their licentious lives. They are debased creatures who have wantonly strayed from the path of righteousness, yielding to the call of the flesh, loose whores of the devil, unworthy of being called ladies – unlike Our Lady. They work in the busy convent laundry, washing and ironing the clothes of the unknown and unseen who leave their sacks of washing at the gate and pick up fresh, folded garments later. They work in the garden, growing vegetables and fruit. They tend chickens for their eggs. And they pray for forgiveness for their sins. They pray that the fruit of their wanton ways will disappear so they can start anew.

She does not share the unhappiness around her. She does not feel debased. She moves from task to task, placid and aloof from every insult, each attempt to make her cowed. What is around her is not her life. Her life is happening inside her. She now knows that she is carrying a child. She now knows how the child got inside her and how it will come out. When she prays she tells of her wonder at having – living and breathing inside her – someone who is hers and hers alone. She talks to the child. She tells stories of her life. She tells the child of her love. She feels knees with her fingers, the crown of its head with her palm. When she sings, the child dances to the song; when she strokes the elbow trapped under her rib, the child shifts and settles. She places one hand to feel the beat of her own heart, while the other hand, on her belly, pulses with an answering echo. They are one, one within one.

She is in the garden, under a tree, when the first pain slashes across her belly and she yields to it in a deep crouch. She feels the force of his weight pressing downward. She feels a twist, a stretching, a widening of her canal. There is an urge to push, to force against the pain that rips through her squeezing belly. She raises her head, looks at the sky, at the light filtering through the leaves and she does not know sky or light or leaves. Nothing exists but her pain. The pain finds its way up her throat and her mouth opens in a bellow that relaxes that other deeper throat so that it too opens wide. She looks down to see what is leaving her with such urgency, and she sees his head, then all of him as he flows out in a rush of blood and slime. She stretches out her hands, and he is there, caught in her cupped hands.

She says to him, Oh, my love, you are here, my love. At her voice, he opens his eyes, a mirror to her own, and he looks at her, listening, with an intensity that makes her think that he knows her and has known her a long time. She wraps him in her skirt, lies under the tree and cradles him to suckle at her breast. They lie there, he in her arms, as she slips into oblivion.

For days and days she lies in a bed. She is in and out of sleep, unable to stay awake for long, unable to move. Someone brings him to her and he suckles deep, as if to swallow all of her. Gabriel, she calls him. Gabriel of glad tidings of great joy. What has gone before is no more. This is her salvation, her reward for enduring all that was bad before. She has made something good. She has made someone that is hers to love.

She wakes one morning and waits for him to come to her. He does not come. Her breast hungers for him. She calls, Gabriel. Someone says, Hush. He will not come. Someone says, He died. Someone says, That is what they always say.

I CYNTHIA – BELMONT MACO

One thing about this island, eh. Nothing, nothing stay the same. Yuh blink and something change in that split second that yuh wasn't looking. It have a saying here, *The Devil don't sleep*. We does also say, *God don't sleep*, but evidence fuh the first saying a damn sight stronger than fuh the second. Bear in mind, shark don't sleep neither.

New government come in. Is a coalition. Suppose to represent tout moun. But from where we sitting it ent looking so at all. Story in newspaper and TV news suddenly stirring up argument and discussion in De Rightest Place. People pointing out how all the plum ministry portfolio, where they have opportunity for kickback and patronage, going to one kinda people. All state board position going to one kinda people. Cecil say that is the problem with we blackpeople; we too easy to fool. Instead of looking after weself like everybody else does do, we only making space fuh everybody else. We small up, small up to accommodate so much is like we come invisible, even to we own self.

Feroze get a contract to drive party supporters in party jersey to line the street wherever the Prime Minister car passing, so they could wave flag and cheer, fuh she to have people to wave back to and smile with. We tell him a better contract would be to fly a squadron of helicopter, because it looking like she more up in the air than on the ground. He say is OK, he already too busy, thank you. His taxi fleet taking supporters to surround all a them helipad that now lay down in more place than all a them girl working in Bronco & Bull Recreation Club in Central, put together. Is we turn now, he say.

One time, I hear Anil tell Indira, You are the only true-true Indian I know. All of us born here and father and grandfather too. We only playing Indian because is a good mas that working for us. But you are the genuine article. You born in India, you grow up

169

in India, you even talk Indian. It have a new vacancy as Head of the National Secret Security Service. They had to fire that young girl, who theyself did put there, when the mark buss about nepotism and who frennin with who and lack of qualification. You want me to put in a word for you? You will be jus what they looking for. You know how we Indian people love whitepeople even more than we love ourself.

Well, we making joke and laughing about serious thing, because, as Fritzie say, sometimes you have to laugh to prevent yuhself from crying. But then thing get real serious and hit home, and was plenty crying all round.

When the State of Emergency declare, people only asking, W'appen? W'appen? Is true big cultural icon, Pat Bishop, gone to her Maker with heart attack the day before. Cause for State of Mourning, we say, not no State of Emergency. We asking w'appen, because, as far we can see, nothing outa the way happen. It ent have no attempted coup, no black power march, no shutdown in essential utilities, no strike in public service, no walkout in senate or in parliament. Then we hear is because the Prime Minister get death threat. Steups. We here know all kinda people, down to Cyclops, the one-eye vagrant, who does get death threat and we wondering why police can't deal with that by theyself and leave we ordinary people to go about we business without interference. But nah. One time is hotspots identify and curfew impose. And guess where is hotspot? Guess where is lock-down? Uh-huh. Belmont, Port of Spain, and all along that narrow strip where half the population, and almost all the black people living, choke-up, choke-up. Where the drug lords living, KarlLee say, where the money laundering taking place, where the guns and ammunition passing, where the deals with ministers and financiers happening, authority not bothering them. Is business as usual.

We have to agree. It hard to see how all the lil vending business selling jersey, pants and panty, fruit and vegetable, food and drink, pirate CD and DVD, and false-hair extension and incense, all night from stall and tray and shopping trolley on the pavement and road self, have to pack up and leave early. And furthermore what is the use? Trade done dry up. Customers staying lock-up in they house, not venturing out, except to go to work. Police and army driving around in open jeep with big big gun pointing out on all side, day and night. When they passing, see how people scattering like cockroach when light turn on. Is pure dread sufferation among poor people. And nine o'clock, when curfew time reach, every bat in they cave *or else*.

Was only six o'clock Saturday afternoon when Curtis and Kwesi get a share of *or else*. They pack up early because business slack, but the Belmont Bes BBQ Boys have so much chicken leave back in the cooler that they looking for somewhere to store it, so it wouldn't spoil. De Rightest Place ent have no space in fridge or freezer. Kwesi call the feller with the van who say he have room in his freezer, but he not home in Barataria yet. If the boys could get transport, they could take the chicken there and the wife will fix them up. The only transport around is the pub van. Bostic and Jah-Son still working, so Indira tell them they could borrow the van but to make haste and come back quickly because she wants her van back where it belongs before curfew.

They passing along Piccadilly. Town like god-res-de-dead. Quiet, quiet. When they reach near Duke Street corner, is sudden traffic jam. They see fellers pelting speed up the road. A couple of them jump over the wall into the Dry River and is only screaming and *pottow pottow* yuh hearing. One feller, sprinting towards them, legs and arms pumping like he is Ato Boldon self, all of a sudden, at the same time as a loud *pattack pattack*, jump in the air, arms and legs spread out like a back-up performer leaping off the stage for a crowd surf at Machel Monday, and the feller fall *blaps* face down on the pitch road, limbs grappling for purchase to keep on going, back heaving and pumping a thick red tide, and the road, like Mayaro beach, sucking it up it nearly as fast as it coming out. *Wheeeeeeee whoopwhoopwhoop.* Spinning bluelight, blue-n-white van pull up. Trunk pop open, two man jump out, throw feller in trunk. Two more man with big maco highpower jump out and start walking slow slow. *Wheeeeeeee whoopwhoopwhoop.* Van reverse down road full speed. And the two man walk up slow slow to the van, one to the driver side, the nex one Kwesi side.

Is police or it ent police? Who arksin' when man point gun and move the barrel sideways just a inch and yuh know that mean get out, hands in the air? Flick the barrel up two inch and yuh walking ahead, hands still in the air. Reach Duke Street and is a procession of hands-in-the-air yoot yuh joining. Twenty or so yoot line up, face touching wall outside All Stars panyard. Arms and legs spread against the mural of the band in red and white officer costume, with gold-fringe epaulettes and buttons, big sign saying Woman on the Bass. Nobody ent say nothing to nobody about nothing. Is only gun sign language they talking. One man pass along the line a yoot, and, as he pass, he slam the gun stock into the back of random yoot knee. Yoot and them pissing, shitting in they pants, but they stay standing up because they could hear man stamping on body and yoot screaming when they fall down. The yoot get signal into pick-up and van and nobody see or hear bout them, and nobody know where to look or who to ask.

When the State of Emergency finish, not a word about if they catch the death-threat maker. And like Prime Minister she self forget. On TV, we only seeing she staggering around with she foot tie up with bandage. W'appen people arksin'. She tell media that two tin a cornbeef fall out a cupboard on to she foot.

Town have it own story as to why State a Emergency was call. Town say was so that hundreds and hundreds of lil black boys, including Curtis and Kwesi, could spend weeks lock up in a concrete block of a pigpen way out in Quitea Quitea, that government rent for millions a month on a long lease from a big party financier. Nobody eh get charge fuh nutten. In State a Emergency, people does get lock up fuh no reason and is nutten yuh can do about it.

I Cynthia say it ent fuh no reason. It have solid reason. To frighten all the poor people and dem so they ent go do nutten when they fed up and vex with all the thiefin and corruption government doing. You tell me, who going to march or protest when police and army have power to shoot yuh dead, no question arks?

When the Belmont Bes BBQ Boys get release, they come home to a heroes' welcome, but they not the same cheerful happy-go-lucky fellers they uses to be. They only looking down on the groun and glancing sideways at each other and not answering when people ask them what happen to them when they was gone.

Papers and TV not reporting anything of what really go on, but then arks yuhself, who own the media eh, who controlling what to show, what to tell? All the media telling, all they showing, is how happy people was with the lock-down, how safe some people was feeling during curfew, since they could sit out at night in they verandah and watch the stars without fear, and how sorry they is that the lock-down stop. One woman even declare that she wish the lock-down had last till after Carnival so she could play her mas' in safety.

But what couldn't get lock-down was the internet. Enough lil children in long school holidays with free government laptop get a real education. Whole day, whole week, they sharing plenty story, plenty report about first-hand experience from brother, sister, cousin, neighbour. Is plenty lesson them lil chirren get about power and lack of power. And they study them lesson good good. I Cynthia fraid, fraid too bad fuh dis place when them lil chirren reach big enough to teach we older people some a the lesson they learn during that State of Emergency.

And what about we at De Rightest Place? It take we a lil time, but, lil bit by lil bit, we adjust to a new normal where we a lil more jittery, a lil more careful, a lil more frighten than before. Is like we add on a invisible but conscious *Anybody Anywhere* to *Anyday Anytime* to the sign outside.

PART THREE

21. MADONNA MASHES MAPEPIRE

Indira stretches an arm over to the other side of the bed but finds only the warm impress of his body lingering in the mattress. In the first weeks after he'd moved in with her, neither had a particular side of the bed; it was their playground and the mattress rebounded to its original contours as quickly as a trampoline. Now they were like a settled couple. The shallow spidery imprint of a restless, gangly youth had morphed into the deep curve of a confident, relaxed, grown man. He's already downstairs. She, too, must be up and about early today.

Easing herself gently to the edge of the bed, she gets up, flings wide the windows, and hooks back the white gauzy curtains filling with the inflowing breeze. In its low-slanted beam, her bare skin laps up the sun's newborn energy; she raises her arms in salutation, and then brings her hands together in a namaste of thanks. Soon, soon, she will resume her early morning Surya Namaskara. Not yet though. The gynaecologist warned her that she should not do anything too vigorous for a couple of weeks.

It was only a small operation, just a womb scrape for an old trouble, she'd told Jah-Son and Fritzie. That half-truth made her nervous and uncomfortable, and, coupled with the after-effects of the surgery, the cramps and the bleeding, she'd been feeling unusually fragile and vulnerable. But today she has an important mission. She is going to visit Immaculate Mary. An auspicious day like this is best for making a request of a deity, for making bargains with those more powerful than oneself. Today is Ash Wednesday, the day for repentance.

She has spent more than half her lifetime, not in repenting for what that religion deemed sin, but in regret for what was lost, and in guilt for allowing it to happen. Today she will ask for a sign that she can forgive herself. She will ask a favour, too, and leave an offering to remind Immaculate Mary of her plea.

She kneels at the chest of drawers, pulls open the bottom drawer and delves beyond the thick folded sweaters until her hand touches the hard contours of a box. She lifts it out. How could something that presses down so heavily inside her be so light? She sits on the edge of the bed, staring at the box. An ordinary shoebox, somewhat scuffed at the corners and edges. It has moved across continents and over oceans with her, but she hasn't opened it since she packed it, a lifetime ago. She looks through the open window at the pale sky beyond. She picks up the box, pulls it on to her lap, breathes out, opens it and plunges her face right in. She draws in his trapped fragrances. Oh, would that her lungs, her blood, her heart and every cell could bind with it.

What has she kept of him? A little white muslin chemise with a double row of blue-thread smocking at the front. From Vindra. The little white bonnet she'd knitted herself. She'd followed a pattern – repeating knit, purl, knit, purl for a long while. Then, losing concentration, she'd done a double purl and not noticed till afterwards. Could she find again the place where she'd gone wrong? She searches the little garment as if looking for a lost treasure and there it is, at the back of the bonnet, where his tiny crown once rested, where her hand once cupped, the place where the pattern falls apart, where the row of stitches, instead of aligning in a continuous flow, is broken by a cross line out of sync. She didn't unpick and reknit that errant line. She'd kept that mistake. What else? One pair of knitted booties, blue, unflawed, a little plastic clip, like a clothes peg, clasping in its teeth a curl of something dry, crisp, yellow-green. For just a moment, a frown creases her face, then a flash of knowledge clutches at her throat. She knows what it is. The remnant of what linked her to him for nine long confusing and joyous months. Whose is it, this umbilical scrap? A piece of her or a piece of him?

Indira? Jah-Son calls out. Nearly time to go. She repacks all but a single bootie and reburies the box at the back of the drawer. She drops the bootie into her handbag. Coming in a minute, she calls.

They pick their way up the long stretch of narrow, winding, concrete steps that leads up to the shrine. At the threshold, she pauses a little, blinking. The harsh outside light, filtered through high, stained-glass windows, transmutes into a rainbow of hues, ruby and peridot, amethyst and amber tinting everything – the white marble altar, the communion rail, even the air itself so that she feels she has entered a surreal, transfigured space. Jah-Son pauses, too. His nostrils have picked up a medley of aromas that are both familiar and strange. There is the dark mustiness of incense, the lingering acridity from wicks of extinguished paraffin candles, but there is something else, a smell that doesn't quite fit. He turns and sees a thin plume of blue-grey smoke rising and quickly dissipating on the hillside opposite. Dry season clearing of land for the brethren to plant when the rains came, that's all. Perhaps they had started it a little too soon. With lots more dry time ahead, the bare land would scorch, turn to dust and blow away quickly. He looks at the smoke, then follows Indira inside.

She walks along the aisle, moving slowly from one statue to another, seeking the blue-veiled Immaculate Mary, with the babe in her arms, her bare heel crushing the head of a poised, forked-tongue serpent, described in the local handbook to the Magnificat, *Madonna Mashes Mapepire*. But she couldn't tell which was which, or who was who, because the statues are hidden under purple sacks and she can no more lift each shroud to find the one she seeks than she could lift her own skirt in this place. How could she, after all her years in convents, forget the Catholic practice of covering up statues during Lent? But she will not turn away and leave. She's had the sackcloth, now she will stay for the ashes. Dust to dust, ashes to ashes, the priest intones, smearing a paste of charcoal ash and chrism in the middle of their foreheads, branding them with his wide, smudged thumbprint. Our days are numbered, we knoweth not the hour.

The pungent smell of wood smoke again catches Jah-Son's attention as they leave. The smoke is denser, greyer. The little plume of flame has spread to form a ring of fire, enclosing mainly lastro – bois cano, gru-gru boef, bamboo and razor grass. The crackling of dry twigs as they are consumed by the encroaching fire echoes across the hillside like sporadic echoing gunshots. Jah-Son watches the wind pick up speed across the slope and sees the line of flame shift to the left, stretching the circle to an oval.

He had not thought it could swing round the spur to threaten the little cluster of huts up there. But again, there is bamboo ahead of that line of flames, and with bamboo, well… Maybe is time for them fellers to out that fire.

They are two blocks away from home when a whoosh sucks the air from around them in a rush, snatching up litter from the roadside gutter. Styrofoam cups and an open food box, along with some scraps of discarded doubles wrapping-paper swirl and duck skittishly; a plastic grocery bag, filled with air, scuttles along, then floats upwards like a jellyfish bobbing on a wave. A heavy boom bounces off the buildings around them. It is not gunshot. They are used to *that* noise and can recognise it. It is a deeper, more hollow sound, followed by another and another. With each bang, showers of sparks spray skyward, releasing a flurry of feathers of pure light that swirl in the air above, circling, turning to red, then blackening as they float down.

Jah-Son looks up. The danger is real and immediate. He has to get there at once. Indira cannot walk any faster and in her state could not help. He lifts her off the ground and runs with her in his arms along the road to De Rightest Place. He sets her on a chair under the awning. His high shrill whistle brings Armageddon bounding from the yard to run with him towards the fire that is racing through the clumps of bamboo on the slope above. A rain of hot, soft, black petals of ash settles on his head and shoulders as he runs, clings to his eyebrows and gets trapped in his nostrils, but he runs, his chest burning, his face streaming with sweat, running as if his own life depends on it. He knows that it would take just one floating bamboo leaf taper to alight on a carat-palm thatched roof, parched to straw in the long dry season, and the roof would go up like a flambeau. If the fire encircles the small cluster of huts up there, all who live in them will be trapped, and that's Gran-Gran, Maisie and Small Man and the shed that houses his nesting songbirds.

Indira signals Bostic to bring her a drink. She wants something to match her mood. Campari and coconut water with a wedge of lightly-squeezed lime trapped under the floating ice cubes. Just right. Bittersweet, sour and chilled. She savours the first sip. She tries to understand her mood. What is it? Concern for Jah-Son and the fire, of course, but more powerful than that, she has a longing for an ease, a relaxation, a letting go, if only for a while, of awareness, of the world, this island, these people, this pub of hers, this body, this mind, even this craving soul. So many things have happened to her, things she had no say in and no control over when she was very young. Then for years she's been in charge. *Sexual Solutions for the Suppressed and Scarred Psyche* had been her manual for survival. In those years, she'd made decisions, she'd bent things to her will and it was tiring, often frustrating work. Fate didn't always comply. Sometimes it seemed to want to thwart her.

Take this morning's visit to that church perched up there, with only steps to get there, not even a road for cars. Was she, like some desperate invalid on a pilgrimage, seeking a miracle cure? All that bother and every statue swaddled and useless, and to think that all the priest could talk about is sin and the wages of sin. What sin? Whose sin? How does it go again? *Let he who is without sin...* Indira shakes her head to remove an intruding rumour about that particular priest and his particular brand of sin. The inspiration for *Pederasty and Prurient Priests*? No, she hadn't gone to the church for the priest. Priests are only human, after all, and subject to the same frailties, and when you consider the ridiculous restrictions in their lives, well, who can judge them? No, the priest didn't matter. She had gone for Immaculate Mary.

Some of the female habitués of De Rightest Place had attested to her powerful intervention in cases of female infertility. Indeed, Ursula swore that her brood, after long years of childlessness, came by way of Immaculate Mary's miraculous intercession. Indira noted, but only to herself, that while Ursula had indeed made three children, she wasn't too convinced that husband Ziggy was present at any of the conceptions. None of them seemed to have taken anything from him in appearance. She smiles. Perhaps that's why Immaculate Mary Conception pilgrimages work? Maybe she herself won't need a miracle from Immaculate Mary after all. Now that her minor surgery is done, nature might just take its course.

But how is Jah-Son getting on? Would he have got to Gran-Gran's in time? Igniting bamboo clumps shoot sparks like fireworks, high, far and wide. The carat-leaf roof of the bird shed would be at greatest risk. She focuses on the noises. There is loud crackling like crumpling cellophane; that would be fire chewing its way through razor grass, but no boom of bursting bamboo. Maybe that is under control. She looks up at the hillside to see a few darting tongues of flame licking at what was left of the vegetation. Dark smoke rises straight up from a glowing patch – probably stumps of bamboo. Jah-Son and the others would be beating out the remnant flames with cocoyea brooms and palm branches; they would be passing buckets of water from the standpipe in relays to the smouldering pile, though what could there be left for fire to consume? There is nothing she can do to help, not in her state. She will sit there, sip her drink and wait for Jah-Son to return – and let her meandering thoughts find their way back to Immaculate Mary.

Behind the bar, Apocalypse stirs in slumber. Her ears stand up and twitch; she lifts her mighty head, eyes blinking and nostrils quivering and her stump of a tail jerks from side to side, a signal that Armageddon is nearby. It is almost five minutes, though, before two figures come into view, dragging their feet along the pavement, and another couple of minutes before Jah-Son stumbles under the awning and sinks into the nearest chair. The little pothound, coated with ash from his nose to his tail, slides under his chair and flops out on his side.

If you didn't know Jah-Son real good, you wouldn't recognise him, Bostic observes. He look like a black devil mas from J'ouvert just woken up from a two-days' stale drunk. His janx curls hang in black greasy clumps, bloodshot eyes peer from a smudged and streaked face from which runnels of sweat flow. His shirt has lost its buttons, his belt is missing from his rolled-up pants; bare arms, bare legs are smeared black, slashed ragged with cuts. Bostic draws two Stags by their necks from the chiller with one hand, flings a white hand-towel over his shoulder with the other, and moves towards Jah-Son more quickly than his bulk suggests possible. With a flip of his thumb he opens one beer and passes it to Jah-Son, who is ready for the second by the time Bostic has it open. Jah-Son presses the towel to his face, the sweat and grime leaving a dark greasy smudge in the middle. Keep that safe, Bostic, he says. From what I just been through, we should call it the Shroud of Belmont.

Bostic fills the dog's water bowl and watches as Armageddon dips his muzzle into the cool water, lets his tongue, long, thick and pink, like a slab of veal, flop out and soak for a bit, then lap at speed until the water is all gone.

Bostic pulls out a chair by Jah-Son. You get your birds?

First thing.

Where you carry them?

By Kobo.

You have to go back for them quick. That feller crazy. Next thing he will say is his own.

Is the best I could a do. One thing, though, he understand birds. They safe with him.

Bostic picks up the two empty bottles and Indira's glass, goes back to the bar and returns with a fresh Campari for Indira. He calls over to Jah-Son.

Allyou manage to out it?

I leave them finishing it off.

How much get burn?

Is what didn't get burn.

Jah-Son gets up, raising his arms above his head in a long stretch, and pulls out a chair at Indira's table.

Everybody all right?

Nobody get burn.

Bostic returns bearing another Stag and a jug of water.

What about their house?

Maisie and Small Man roof halfway burn.

So, how they making out?

They have to move back in with Gran-Gran.

He sees Indira making to get up.

You want help?

No, I'll manage.

As she makes her way slowly upstairs, Jah-Son and Armageddon go round the back of the pub. He strips off his bedraggled church clothes, picks up a bar of blue soap and the end of the hosepipe and lathers and scrubs himself and his dog, bluish suds turning a slatey-grey slurry as the water run off them into the

183

open drain. They shake themselves and stand in the sunshine to dry off. Bostic comes out back and his eyes are drawn again to the birthmark on Jah-Son's thigh, where drops of water, catching the sunlight, glitter like new scales after a sloughing. Again, Bostic feels his right thigh itch and tingle; again the coiled serpent has sunk its fangs into his flesh. He scratches the spot and feels its hot tingling surge towards his heart.

He longs to lay claim to the boy, to come out and say, Jah-Son, you are Jah's son, but you are also my-son, Bostic-son, my only begotten son and I am well pleased with you. Ah, but it is not possible. He would have to admit he had known for a long time and was too cowardly to say so; say he was sorry for not looking back, not following up in the places where he'd dropped his seed to check whether any had taken root. He would have to apologise for his early rough treatment of Jah-Son, even when he knew he was his son.

Bostic hangs his head and closes his eyes as he collects his thoughts. Then he shakes his head to dislodge them and turns back to the task in hand – the pub.

Last night was las' lap. People, stretching out Carnival till the last possible minute, didn't want to go home. He was still serving drinks and collecting bottles when dawn broke and the last revellers staggered out, singing snatches of what they could remember of the tune that was sure to be declared the road march.

And today? Bostic glances across at the lamppost. Its shadow, reduced to a small black oval, hugs its base. Midday already. In a short while the regulars, having placed their Play-Whe bets, would start drifting in.

KarlLee would be sitting by himself, speaking to nobody, while he scrapes the silver film off his scratch cards. He'd become morose since Christmas, after that last tempestuous visit by Sandy. When the benefactor of your electronic devices is the one who set up your password, you should expect that you have no secrets, muses Bostic. It wasn't long before Sandy worked out that KarlLee was involved with a woman called Sunity, and stormed off back to her husband in Boston or Minneapolis or wherever, cutting off contact. But perhaps the cash flow has resumed, since KarlLee is back on track as a regular. The ole fellers, Cecil and Boyee, would be filling in their lotto slips, debating every number as they chose. That night's draw promised twelve million dollars. There'd be plenty customers this afternoon and night. Lent had a way of making people thirsty, as if they fear they're about to spend forty days and forty nights fasting in a desert. He better get his act together and clean up the place fast.

22. INNER KNOWLEDGE

Heavenly House of Asha Ashram
Come to your true home
Pune, India

- Are you suffering right now at this moment? Look at yourself in your physical form, your feelings, your perceptions. Are you in pain? If your pain is linked to the past, you must free yourself from that Past. Do not let the ghosts of the past dominate you.

- Heavenly House of Asha Ashram offers daily practice in meditation to release you from past suffering, bring you to Mindfulness in the Now and clear a path for Future Happiness.

- At the Heavenly House of Asha Ashram, we heal your Body through Ancient Ayurvedic Medicine. Make it whole again. Women's Woes a speciality.

- You will learn how to remove the three obstacles: the Obstacle of Earthly Desires, the Obstacle of Karma and the Obstacle of Retribution.

- In just four weeks, you will be imbued with the Roaring of a Tiger and the Chanting of a Dragon. You will be a New Person.

- Are you ready to experience these Miracles in Transformation of the Body, Mind and Spirit?

- At Heavenly House of Asha Ashram, skies full of Benefit will smile upon you. Rains of Joy will soak into you. The Radiance of the Sun will empower you.

- Read testimonies from our former guests <u>here.</u>

- Claim your right to be as fulfilled as they are.

- Book <u>here</u> for one of only twenty places on our Monsoon Magic special this August at the Heavenly House of Asha Ashram.

- Secure your place now with a deposit of only 25%.

- Use the Paypal option <u>here</u> or the wire transfer option <u>here</u>.

Is it true, then, what that book says – *WWW: Wondrous World of Wi-Fi* – that the answers to life's problems aren't to be found in books, but on the Internet? Here I am, still stale from sleep, still in my deshabille, just idly browsing and I come across this – Monsoon Magic. Roaring Tiger, Chanting Dragon, Smiling Skies Raining Radiance… How does it go again?… Anyway, the Ayurvedic healing sounds just right. Women's Woes. That is exactly what I have. Heavenly House of Asha Ashram, Pune, India.

Left India, how many years ago? Twenty? God, that's a lifetime… Maybe it's time for a pilgrimage. Go back to roots. What's the cost again? Should be able to manage the deposit, but the 'pay the balance by the end of June' part could be a little tricky. Could get on one of those Our Mother India Tours – Searching for Ancestry and Dharma – organised by Amaralee & Famalee Travel and Tours. I'll have to stretch every dollar to make a hundred for that. Those tours usually end up in Uttar Pradesh or Bihar, but I could always take a train from there and make my own way to Pune.

Indira! Fritzie's voice, soaring up from below, breaks into her reverie. What happen? You not going to the Oval again, or what?

Indira ketch herself. OMG, I can't believe I forgot. Is cricket today. She calls out, Fritzie, just a minute. Almost ready. Coming down right now. Tell Bostic to give you a drink … and fix one for me too… Rum.

They settle in their seats – not late, but they've missed some of the pre-game ritual. Watching the teams limbering up is always good for picking out players, calling out to them and waving and sending kisses and laughing at their antics as they show-off. They've missed, too, the serious stuff, the rolling of the pitch, the captains examining it closely for signs of how it would play. They've missed the toss, but reach in time for the first ball. They there for the cricket, yes, but is really the atmosphere they come for. The excitement of the crowd, the banter between rival supporters, the knowledgeable commentary about line and length and movement, moisture in the air, the condition of the outfield, whose shoulder is suspect still, who that blasted stupid captain – what the hell he thinking? – should bring on to bowl and so on, historical comparisons to other players, other memorable matches.

There's the people-watching, too. Just check out them in the corporate boxes. Uniformed waiters serving champagne, smoked salmon, Johnny Walker Blue whole day. Who really watching the match over there? They making deals, is all. So, that's how the other half lives? No girl, it's the other one percent. We in the ninety-nine percent. Well, we here on a workday, so we must be in the top something percent of the ninety-nine. You're right – we're the buffer class, between the one percent and the rest.

A lull in the game for the water wagon and a Mexican wave breaks loose in the Carib Stand and runs around the ground, rippling over the Trini Posse Stand, the DJ blasting soca, the wining Digicel girls in red spangly bikinis, waving red and white pom-poms – You would let your daughter be one of them winer girls? You mad or what? Let Precious come with any talk about putting on skimpy clothes and shaking she body in public – and is not Carnival – she will find she suddenly have a break foot and can't go *nowhere*. The wave fails to draw in the leather-shod toes of the *suits* of the corporate boxes, but it slips below them, a subterranean wave, and picks up energy again, surging around, as it crashes into the stands and round to its jubilant starting point.

The water cart goes off, the game resumes, and there is an announcement for a doctor to come at once to the pavilion. The excitement's been too much for someone? Someone fainted? There is mild speculation and at first no one bothers too much. Then a tremulous, murmurous, rippling wave travels through the crowd, and it fuels a mad shifting of people, a scrambling, tumbling, rumbling of people out of their seats, all running in the same direction. In less than two minutes, a long, long line snakes along the aisles between the rows of chairs, now empty of spectators. The story goes that someone in the Scotiabank stand suffer a heart attack and he die right there and then, and this news propels thousands of people to stand in line, some patiently and silently, arms folded as if hugging a guilty secret, others shamelessly phoning friends and family to tell them what happen and what to play, all waiting their turn to reach the Lotto booth to place bets on the day's Play Whe and Pick Two. Everybody and their dog betting on Number 4, *Dead Man,* because the last time that happen at a cricket match, a couple years back, when a man drop down dead in the concrete stand, and people play *Dead Man,* number four come down in truth and the payout so huge they run out of money, and punters had to wait to cash their tickets next day at the Lotteries Control Board downtown.

Indira and Fritzie make a killing that day. They play *Jackass* – number 36 – because they figure that anyone who believe that man falling dead at a cricket match will *always* equal dead man in Play Whe has to be a jackass. The Jackass play to prove them right. Is not rocket surgery to figure that out, Indira asserts.

If what she won had been enough to cover the trip to India – booking the Heavenly House of Asha Ashram, buying the Amaralee & Familee Tours and Travel ticket, the train ticket, living expenses, out of pocket and shopping – the matter might have ended there, but while the takings was good, it couldn't cover the whole expense. So, since it was gambling that had got her so far, Indira decides to trust gambling to take her the rest of the way. And she did have further encouragement from a trusted source.

Gemini: There is a part of you that harbours a deep understanding of how things work. You are someone with inner knowledge above and beyond schooling, who may even be able to contact the spirit world on your own behalf and of others.

Fritzie, Indira say, I feel a kind a Zen, a kind a vibe, about this. How could we just be in the right place at the right time, eh, if it wasn't Fate that guided us here? I feel this could work for us. I'm not talking about the lotto booth outside. That pays big money only twice a week, and only to who wins the jackpot. There are plenty places where we could go and do much better. I'm talking about the casinos. They have all kinds of things, slot machines, roulette, blackjack, poker, you name it.

Indira, I rather just hold onto what I have. You forget I have Precious to mind? Is plenty things you have to get for a teenager so she don't feel left out among her friends. I really don't want to jumbie this lil piece of luck I get.

Fritzie, look, you had just a few dollars before; now look how much you got. You could afford to invest a little back.

OK. But no more than two hundred dollars for me. When that done, I done too, you hear?

Monday mid-morning, when working people working, the two of them find theyself in Film & Fantasy Mega Mall, where the casino never closes and the bank never loses. In just three hours, Indira's winnings at the Play Whe are reduced to naught. Too tired to object, she allows Fritzie to call a taxi to take them back to Belmont. There, the full implication of the day's adventure sinks in. She's gambled away all her money. She's broke. She cannot pay to go to Pune, to take her Woman Woes for healing at the Heavenly House of Asha Ashram. Her woes have grown plenty more.

It's not the horoscope she turns to next morning, because a story on the front page of *The Spectre* catches her eye.

Police and priest to protect pilgrimage

In an effort to control the massive crowds that flock to the sleepy southern town of Siparia for the annual La Divina Pastora celebrations, Fr Anton Las Lomas, parish priest, and Superintendent Suruj Ram of the Southern Division spent several hours in talks yesterday.

When they emerged, Fr. Las Lomas spoke to *The Spectre*. "This shrine is a holy place for veneration of the Virgin Mary by Catholics. For many years we have accommodated the numerous Hindus who see it also as a place of worship of their goddess, Kali. They call her Siparee Mai. For both groups it is a holy place. On her feast day, pilgrims come from all over the country to make their offerings to her and to ask for favours and blessings.

"In recent years, some of the pilgrimages have become little more than party excursions, an excuse for people to get on a bus and go for a lime. We have had to endure loud carnival music, fêting, obscene language, vulgar behaviour, drunkenness and more, on the procession route. We have therefore had to appeal to the authorities to provide this holy event with some measure of protection when we celebrate next Sunday."

She didn't continue reading. The rest was only predictable phrases about what the police said they would do. Her eyes keep going back to '...*pilgrims come from all over the country to make their offerings to her and to ask for favours and blessings...*'

This country never ceases to amaze her with its alchemy. Dross to gold, every waking day. Here she is, frustrated at every turn, wanting one thing and looking in two widely separated places – the shrine of the Immaculate Mary in Belmont, and the Heavenly House of Asha Ashram in Pune – and right here, in this country, is one place that combines both. The Shrine of La Divina Pastora – Siparee Mai. Well, well, well. Look at ting, as they say.

And so, on the morning of Siparee Mai, Fritzie and Indira wait for the bus at City Gate to take them to San Fernando, where they will get a maxi to Siparia and the church. They are the only passengers for whom this is a maiden visit to the Virgin. An easy camaraderie is soon established and Indira becomes more and more excited as tales of earlier visits are exchanged, revelations about changes of fortune and desires fulfilled. And what did they ask for? A good girl for a son to marry, success for a child taking exams, prosperity in a business, renewed health for an aging parent, a womb blessed with a longed-for infant. And what if you don't get what you ask for? Well, says one, maybe it's not come yet; another says, maybe it's not meant be. What were they asking for? Indira and Fritzie exchange sidelong glances, embarrassed about exposing their longings. When their maxi empties at a metal barrier across the main road, they follow the stream of fellow passengers to merge with the larger surge of chatting and laughing women, men and children, all heading in the same direction.

As they enter the narrow roadway, Indira clutches Fritzie's arm and stands stock still. Good gods, she says, eyes opening wide, arms waving to take in the scene before them. This takes me right back. Lining the narrow road are tents and tables set up to display a multitude of goods – abundant teddy bears and other soft toys, incense, kites, long balloons twisted into deer, giraffe and dog shapes, jewellery of gold, silver, gemstones, T-shirts, shorts, dresses, shalwar kameezes, saris, combs, rugs, rows of James Plaignol olive oil in square bottles, rice, kitchen utensils, candles, slippers, potted plants, flowers, and stalls selling food and drink. Only difference is, says Indira, if this was outside a temple in India, every vendor would be following you, wheedling you into buying something, and as soon as you buy from one, the others feel entitled to a sale as well. But why would anybody come here to buy some of these things? Plants? Cooking oil? Rice? I have no idea, says Fritzie, but I'm buying two packs of candles for us.

A little street-side activity catches Indira's eye. A little boy, a baby not yet two, she reckons, is sitting on a tall stool. His little hands are clutching the sides of the seat and he's looking anx- iously at a smiling woman. She – the mother? – is trying to get him to engage with a teddy bear she is waggling a couple of feet away. As they watch, a man steps towards the child. He combs the child's soft black hair and begins to snip. An older woman – Nani? Aji? – shuffles forward, following the barber as he works his way around the stool. She's catching the falling feathery curls in her orhini, which she's stretched out like a safety net. The child makes no sound but continues to look troubled. At the end he leans over to fall into the arms of a man – the father? – who's been looking on, filming the scene on his phone. The old lady shakes her orhini to gather the snippets of hair and puts them into a clear plastic bag. The man hugs the child, now a big boy with a big boy

192

haircut, nods to the barber and passes him some crumpled notes. A waiting line has formed and the stool is already occupied by a fresh little customer. Indira stays rooted to the spot. Her eyes follow the little family as they move on.

Who took Gabriel for his mundan? Who amused him when he was anxious? Who has his first soft curls? She looks up, blinking into the bright sun, willing the tears to stop. You OK? Fritzie asks. Indira squeezes Fritzie's arm. Yes, she says. I'm fine.

She follows Fritzie into a courtyard, but can still hardly read the sign announcing *Siparia Boys RC School*. The wide concrete platform that fringes the school buildings is a blur. She can barely see the beggars, the lame, the halt, the able, the young and the old, the meek and the bold, a motley crew of the dispossessed who sit listlessly on sheets of flattened cardboard boxes and rags. Others stand leaning against the walls and pillars, some stumbling about with sticks, trailing their bags and rags. With bodies unkempt and untended, sore and broken, they present their abject condition to the pilgrims. It is midday. The shade has shrunk, but although the wide eaves now offer no refuge from the suffocating heat, the sufferers, protecting their turf, guarding garbage bags stuffed with things they've already been given, do not move. An odour rises of stale, long-unwashed bodies, soiled clothes, informal toilet arrangements, sour regurgitation from unaccustomed bellies, decomposing, discarded food. Flies, drunk with choice, alight on every surface.

The two women join a long queue that winds back on itself twice. It goes under a covered walkway leading from the school buildings near the gateway to a gap between the buildings on the opposite side. They join the queue though they don't know where it's heading. Their companions are freshly showered, well-dressed, orderly, cheerful, fragrant. They are carrying candles, bags, bottles, flowers. The air of fairground expectancy, easy friendliness and bursts of drama draws Indira back to her earlier self.

A short little man, whose round belly gapes in hairy brown lozenges between the straining buttons of his white embroidered shirt, leads a small procession through the courtyard. Behind him are two men carrying a long table, and three others, each bearing a brown cardboard box on his head. They pull a white cloth from one of the boxes and spread it over the table. The main man slicks back his thinning hair and beckons to the men carrying the boxes. It is a signal to the hundreds of eyes following his movements. The crowd of sufferers, surging from the platform all around, hides some of what is going on, but Fritzie and Indira can see small brown paper bags being passed overhead, so that even those at the back get something, though those at the front come away with handfuls. In under two minutes, the performance is over. The sufferers go back to their posts, the cloth is removed, the table folded and carried away. The empty cardboard boxes are repurposed by the beggars.

Another man, taller, burly, pulls from his pocket a fistful of folded dollar bills. He fans them out like a deck of playing cards and walks around the edge of the courtyard offering them to the beggars' outstretched hands. A little girl, waist-length hair held back by a sparkly tiara, shyly holds a sheaf of money. The sequins in her stiff, pink net skirt catch the light as she bends forward to hand banknotes out, one by one, to the beggars' seated children. The girl's black patent-leather shoes and her starkly white socks shine against the dusty bare feet of the beggar children. A woman in a bright yellow sari, her face alight with pride, watches over the little girl. Darshan, says Indira, gifts to get favours from the gods. So this – Fritzie indicates the candles, bottles, bags in the queue with them – all this is darshan too? Yes. It is.

At the front of the queue, a guard permits the entry of small batches of pilgrims into a schoolroom whose smoky darkness is relieved only by a glow in one corner. That is where she is. A small dark wood statue, illuminated by innumerable flickering flames. La Divina is wearing a long dress of white fabric embroidered with gold. On her head she carries a veil and a crown. At her feet, a layer of coins and paper money has built up, little handwritten messages among them. Under the watchful eye of a priest and a nun, bottles of olive oil, bags of rice, flowers, plants, new clothes, jewellery, bottles of honey, jostle for space on a table nearby. Yes. Darshan. Indira feels ashamed that she's so unprepared that they've brought only candles

Ahead of her, devotees make aarti to Mary. She is Durga-Kali's avatar today. Mary is unperturbed by this transformation; she's still smiling her wooden smile. When her turn comes, Indira cups her hands over the flames of the massed candles and brings the warmth to touch her forehead, her lips, her heart. She clasps her hands in namaste. She makes her silent request. She touches Mary's feet, looks into her wide-open eyes to let her read what is inscribed on her heart. She has left nothing. No note to let Mary know what she's come for. Nothing personal, nothing tangible to remind her that Indira was here with her longing. Her pack of white candles joins the other darshan on the table as they leave.

They spill out into the bright courtyard of the adjoining La Divina Pastora church, from which the Virgin was taken for her day as Siparee Mai. There are no worshippers in the church. Indira and Fritzie wander in, read a notice or two, genuflect, make the sign of the cross at the altar, and leave. On the road that parallels the one they came by, there are few people about. Early limers patronise the fast food outlets and bars; the real night scene won't start for a couple hours. By then the earlier pilgrims will be on their way back to the four corners of the island from which they'd travelled. Indira and Fritzie are silent on the return journey. Indira feels disappointed with herself for being so ill-prepared. She hadn't even thought to bring the little bootie to this Mary. Fritzie is cocooning her own wish, but at the same time, she's wondering whether, for her at least, today was a day of faith infused with cynicism or of cynicism tempered by faith.

23. LUNAR ECLIPSE

The Lunar Eclipse will stir things up for you. Passionate opinions or fiery tempers could take their toll. A friend might move away.

Not what she wanted to read this morning. Indira tosses the newspaper to the foot of the hammock, pulls off her reading glasses with a weary sigh, rubs her eyes, picks up her mug of coffee and looks across towards the shrine perched on the hilltop. She can hardly see it. Early morning glare, diffusing through early morning vehicle exhaust fumes, makes a spectre of the shrine. She's been there, to Immaculate Mary, to Siparee Mai, and nothing doing. She's been to a gynaecologist for the D&C and nothing doing. So what chance was there of anything happening now? If it did, it would be a miracle, an Immaculate Conception in truth, Jah-Son never being around much of late. All because of another woman.

You're being silly and over-dramatising, she chides herself. Only literally could you label Gran-Gran *another woman*. She raised him from a baby to the big man you trying to claim exclusive rights to. And it's a man who's taking him away – Small Man. Gran-Gran is sick, Maisie has to work, Small Man has to be taken care of. Jah-Son is effectively unemployed, so he has to fall to and help at home. So, Indira, pull yourself together. She pats *Positive Pronouncements: Perspective & Purpose*, which lies on the side table.

But oh, I do miss him. I love going to sleep with him there, waking to find him around, pottering with his songbirds. I love seeing him take time to work through situations new to him. With me, so much is an already well-worn path, while he is still clearing the bush to make his own track. All well and good, but practically, how is this affecting me, apart from my empty bed?

First there's the bar. After a shaky start, I see how Jah-Son has earned Bostic's respect and confidence. He lets him take on much of the heavy work now. He can stack the chiller, place orders with the best of them. It wasn't planned that way, but he is now Bostic's trusted deputy. Then, there's the food business. Since he learned to drive, he's taken over the shopping for the lunch soup. It was getting way too stressful for Fritzie and me, dealing up with traffic, bandits and frayed nerves. He's working hard. Bostic wouldn't say so, but I know he's seeing Jah-Son as an equal. We've all come to depend on him. But now, Gran-Gran's sick.

Going down with age was Gran-Gran's own diagnosis, and that was true. She just couldn't do what she did before. Then came a mild stroke and she needed active care. Jah-Son was even less at De Rightest Place. He could be there only when Maisie was home and Maisie could work only when he was home. She and Bostic had gone along with that arrangement until the increased demands of the pre-Christmas trade exhausted them both. It couldn't continue that way; she had to broach the matter with Jah-Son.

How things?
Gran-Gran holding on.
And the others?
Maisie now home with her. Small-Man in a preschool nearby.
Jah-Son returns to preparing vegetables, putting away dishes, clearing the counters for food preparation. Indira still stands, arms folded, leaning against the doorframe. Jah-Son looks across at her. Her body language makes him uncomfortable and it isn't just the madly fluttering eyelashes.
Something the matter?
I'm waiting for you.
Her face is rigid; her mouth set in a thin silence.
What? For what?
To ask me, how things?
So, how things?
She looks him up and down, goes into the bedroom, slamming the door behind her. Jah-Son continues in the kitchen, then the bar, until siesta. He leaves without seeing Indira. The next day he doesn't see her at all. And the next. He asks Fritzie if Indira is OK. She seems fine, Fritzie says, only a little quiet.
She vexed with me. I wondering what I do wrong.

You ask her?

I don't see her.

You know where to find her. Go and talk to her.

When she bite-up so? Could make matters worse.

It could be worse?

He doesn't answer, but when Fritzie leave, he knocks on Indira's bedroom door. A muffled, Come in. The room smelling stale. It is dark. The closed jalousies chop the daylight into thin slices that illuminate nothing. The bedclothes in disarray. He calls softly, Indira? Now he can see her form outline below the bedspread. He tiptoe towards the top of the bed.

You afraid of me now? Her voice is a whisper. He goes closer. Her face is pale, her cheeks sunken and when she open her eyes, the blue seems dull. He reaches over and strokes her forehead. Her eyes glisten, tears cup in the lids until they spill down her cheeks. He strokes them away but they flow faster. She move aside and he slips between the sheets and holds her until her sobbing cease and she fall asleep. He stay there till she wakes. I thought you were a dream, she says. I 'fraid you find I'm more real than you want, he replies. What's wrong? Tell me what's wrong. Nothing, she says, right now, nothing is wrong.

They lie there together for a long while. He tell her about Gran-Gran, Maisie and Small-Man, about how hard it is for him to juggle his responsibility to them while working at De Rightest Place and being with her. He sorry he hasn't spent enough time with her. He miss being with her, but he can't leave his family, especially his grandmother, now she in her last days. Without her he would be on the streets. Indira hug him, says she understand, that of course he must look after his family.

She wants to tell him about her own early life, about how it was damaged early. It is chafing like grit in her heart, but she cannot reveal this yet. She isn't ready.

As he walk up the hill on the way home, he see Maisie with Small Man at the preschool. Why you here? Who with Gran-Gran? Gran-Gran get another stroke. She's in hospital. I just now come from there, she says. I have to go to work and Gran-Gran need clothes and toiletries.

198

At home, Jah-Son feed Small Man, pack a bag for his grandmother, and set off for the hospital. Children are not allowed in the ward, so Small Man get leave out on the balcony of the fourth floor, silent and afraid, while strangers rush by on their way to see their patients. When Jah-Son return, he burst into tears. I want to see Gran-Gran. I want to see Gran-Gran. Jah-Son lead him to the aluminium louvres nearest to her bed, and lift him so he can peep through. He call in his little voice, Gran-Gran, Gran-Gran, I can see you. She open her eyes and smile at him, so he go away happy.

Next day Maisie go to wash and dress her grandmother and to ask about her condition from the medical people. The nurse say she can't divulge what is on a patient's notes, only the doctor can. Where the doctor? Gone. At his private practice.

Jah-Son does the afternoon shift, again with Small Man out on the corridor. After a week, neither Maisie nor Jah-Son have learnt anything about Gran-Gran's condition or what, if anything, the hospital is planning to do. Jah-Son's visits are tense – fearful that the child might fall off the balcony and down four storeys.

A couple days later, Maisie appears at De Rightest Place, Small Man in tow. School close for mosquito spraying, she tells Jah-Son. I have to go to work now. Small Man look listless. Jah-Son give him a cold soft drink and sit him at a table. When next he check, the child's head resting on his folded arms on the table. He feel hot. Jah-Son push two chairs together, lift the sleeping child, and lay him along the chairs.

Jah-Son does not visit Gran-Gran that afternoon. Is too risky to leave Small Man waiting alone on the balcony. He is still working when the child wakes, hot and disoriented. Jah-Son lifts him to go home. Indira asks, Small Man, you want soup? Small Man nods. I'll take him upstairs. Later, when he goes upstairs to get the child, Jah-Son find him on the sofa in one of his T-shirts, like a long nightshirt, and Indira is reading him a story. After a bath and food, he seem better, she say, Would you stay on and help Bostic in the bar? Small Man is fine here with me.

Next afternoon when Maisie drop off Small Man at De Rightest Place, Indira tell Jah-Son that the child could stay with her when he went to hospital. On his return, Small Man bathed, wearing new pyjamas, and having a story read to him.

On Christmas Day, the nurses allow Small Man to go into the ward with Maisie and Jah-Son. Is good they could be together, for when Maisie go to the hospital on Boxing Day, Gran-Gran's bed empty and the nurse tell her that Gran-Gran died the night before.

One morning Maisie says she wants to talk.

Things missing from the house.

Like what?

Kitchen stuff. Pressure cooker, the big nonstick frying pan, toaster.

When?

Two or three days.

You sure?

He look where the utensils were kept. They aren't there.

You didn't lend them to nobody?

No. Up to last week everything right here.

Jah-Son don't want to say aloud what he thinks has happened. It would put them and their situation in a place he doesn't want to go.

You feel somebody come in here and take them?

Everybody round here know that nobody here during the day, now Gran-Gran gone.

Maybe I could secure the place more?

This making me real nervous.

Lemme think about it, OK?

He does not have long to think about it. That evening, when Maisie arrive at De Rightest Place to meet him and Small Man after work, she's out of breath, dishevelled and in tears. After they calm her, she tells them what happen.

I wait for transport til I see a PH taxi come along with a woman passenger in the front seat. I get in the back. I feel safer as is two of us. But she get out not too long after and then he stop to pick up two men. One sit in front, one come behind with me. The one in front ask the driver to take him off route, but the driver say no, he don't go off route at night. The man pull out a knife and say, Tonight, you going off route. If you behave yourself, you could

201

get a piece of she too. The driver slow down, he so frighten. The man in the back hold onto my arm. I don't know what get into me, I bend down and bite him and open the door and jump out and run till I reach here.

No one needs to have the implications of Maisie's story spelled out. The incident is too common, too everyday to be shocking.

Coulda be worse, Bostic say. Remember the story in the papers? The one where the woman get gang raped by men in the taxi with her. And when she gone to the police station, the officer tell her she can't come in the station in *that* condition to make a report. He tell her to go home and put on some clothes and come back.

She naked?

Yes. They rip off her clothes when she struggle.

What happen to the policeman?

Nothing.

How come?

He only following rules for entering a public building. No bareback. No barefeet. No sleeveless. No revealing clothes.

And when you phone to make a report, what they say? No vehicle, no officer available to come.

Police is no blasted use. Only thing they do is tow parked cars.

And arrest and charge people for one lil ganja cigarette.

Don't forget arrest for using obscene language

Indira take charge.

Enough. What are *we* going to do about this situation? Jah-Son?

Maisie can't work nights. Is too much a risk.

You get away this time, Bostic add. Next time you mightn't be so lucky.

Night did suit me when Small Man wasn't in school. But right now, when I in a position to switch to day, it eh have no day vacancies.

She look around as if she just remembering something.

Where Small Man anyway?

He's sleeping on the sofa upstairs, Indira say. He's fine. He's quite accustomed now. Maisie, maybe tonight isn't the best time to work out what to do next. Go home and get some sleep and we can talk about it in the morning.

Jah-Son, Maisie and Small Man walk up the Valley Road to their home to find two bird cages gone, and the TV, cd player and small valuables missing – jewellery, ornaments.

Wet paper, Maisie say.

Wet paper?

Gran-Gran use to say that when your luck turn bad, wet paper can cut you.

We not going to get cut with no wet paper. We not going to behave scaredy.

Jah-Son, we have to face facts. Somebody coming here when we not here. Little by little, they cleaning us out. Like here not safe any more. What if they come in the day or in the night when you not here and is me alone? Is me against them?

Maisie, sorry. I not thinking straight. You right. But we should be safe tonight, so let's lock up the best we can and try and get some sleep. Tomorrow is another day.

Jah-Son set out early next morning. He know Kobo took the birds; he's done it before. He also figure that if anybody knows what's going on in the neighbourhood, is Kobo. Not bless with much sense, *not all there,* people say, tapping a temple with a finger, so people talk and behave around him like he can't see or hear or understand, like if he really not there. Gran-Gran use to say, God give that poor boy only half the sense he give everybody else. He looking on to see who down here helping the least of his brethren.

Listen, Kobo. I know is you take my two cages with the picoplat and semp. Bring them here for me now.

Kobo scamper off and bring back the cages.

D-d-dey g-good. Ah-ah-ah f-f-f-feed d-d-em.

Thanks, Kobo. But don't take them again. OK? I will mind them myself. You understand?

Jah-Son make as if to leave, walk a few paces, then turn back as if a thought just strike him.

I have little semp coming up nice. I will give you him when he ready to move out the nest. You will like that?

Kobo jumping up and down. G-g-g. Gimme B-b-b bird? Is mines? Jah-Son t-take b-back?

No, Kobo. I won't take it back. It will be yours. I go bring it for you. Let it get big first, OK?

Kobo twist his face into a look of delight. But Jah-Son isn't finished.

I need you to help me with something.

Kobo look up at Jah-Son, cocking his head to listen.

When you up by me, you ever notice anybody going in Gran-Gran house? Anybody who not suppose to be there when Maisie and me out?

Kobo hang down his head. No answer. Jah-Son realise he know something but can't talk.

They threaten you?

Kobo cover his mouth with his hand.

What they say they will do you? Eh?

Kobo shake his head back and forth.

You know Bostic? The wrestler feller? He and I is good friend. I will bring him for them if they threaten you.

Kobo make a downward slash with his hand.

C-c-cut off my balls. They go c-c-cut off my b-b-balls.

Bostic go tie up theirs in knots if they threaten you again. OK? So, is them young boy and them by the bridge? You don't have to answer.

Kobo nod. Jah-Son pull a note from his pocket and hold it out.

Look, here's a twenty. Keep an eye out for me, OK?

Jah-Son leaves. He won't risk spending too long with Kobo. Who knows who watching and noting?

As soon as he enter De Rightest Place, Jah-Son plop down in the nearest chair, his shoulders slumped, his hand propping his chin.

Bostic say, What's up?

When we reach home last night, more things missing.

Your birds?

I get back the birds from Kobo already. No, is the things in the house. Plenty things disappearing from the house.

The dog not there?

Armageddon? He know everybody and everybody know him. He don't make no fuss if is Kobo in the yard or any neighbours. He does bark, but is like he saying, Hello, glad to see you.

Who you think?

Is the young boys and them who does be liming on the bridge and who know everybody movement. They thiefing thing to sell to buy weed, crack. They threaten Kobo so he wouldn't tell me who.

They always thiefing lime, mango, zaboca, all kinda thing off people tree to sell. That not new. But thiefing from people house? *That* is new.

Is only since Gran-Gran die. People respect Gran-Gran up there. She use to say, I come here first. Everybody round here come and meet me here.

She gone and respect gone too?

Maisie and me, we come like easy prey. This coming on top of what happen to Maisie. Is like a message I can't ignore. Home not safe again.

Bostic pulls out a chair and sits at the table with Jah-Son.

I have to agree.

If I could find somewhere for us to go, I would move tomorrow.

That will be hard. Finding somewhere big enough for the three of you and for all your stuff, right away.

True.

Jah-Son staring at the floor. After a while, he lift his head and ask, You think it have space anywhere here where I could at least store what they not thief yet?

Not offhand. No.

What about the storeroom?

Well, I don't think it have too much extra space.

I could look?

Jah-Son tidy up the storeroom, piling up crates, putting out crates of empties for the delivery van. He create enough space that could store boxes of clothes and household items, but not enough for furniture. He ask about the shed in the back yard that seems full of old car parts. Bostic tell him Solo allow a mechanic to use the space as a storeroom, but the feller die even before Solo go away. Jah-Son ask whether he could tell a mechanic friend of his to come and take the stuff away to use whatever he wants. Bostic say it's fine by him, but he'd check with Indira to confirm and let him know.

The two men work side-by-side in the bar until Jah-Son leave at siesta time to go up the Valley Road to collect whatever household items and personal effects he figures could fit into the space he's made in the storeroom.

★

I Cynthia sitting in De Rightest Place with Feroze and the ole boys, Cecil and Boyee. We four already into we first rounds of drinks and cards. We see Jah-Son bring in box after box of books, pots and pans, crockery, cutlery, fans, clothes and bedclothes and pack them in the storeroom. Miss Indira watching him. We watching him. Everybody watching him.

Indira say, What's going on? Jah-Son say, We have to move out of the house. People only thiefing things and we don't know what they going to take next. Indira say, Jah-Son, I thought we were going to discuss what to do, but it looks like you've made your own decision already. He answer that he don't have no choice, that life turn around and bite him and he have responsibility now, with his sister and nephew to take care of, so he not in a position to lead the kind of carefree life he have before. Indira say, So how long are you planning on leaving those things here? It's a storeroom for drinks and we'll have use for it when things get busy. Carnival season coming up. Jah-Son look at Bostic, Bostic look at Indira and he say, As soon as he find a place for all three of them to live, he will move out his things. Is only for a while. Boyee say, So where all you sleeping? Jah-Son tell him he didn't have anywhere yet, but Maisie asking people at work if they know of a place to rent and now he asking them in the bar if they know anywhere. Cecil whisper to Boyee, Like it have no room at the inn? And them two old rascals laugh, slap they skinny thigh and snort out they beer through they nose.

I Cynthia hear them and I feel bad for Jah-Son. So I say, Is OK for Maisie and Small Man to move in by me fuh a few nights until you find somewhere, if they don't mind sharing a bed, but it can't be fuh too long, because family coming from The States fuh Carnival season and is by me they staying. Jah-Son say thanks, he'll talk it over with Maisie, but he sure she'd be grateful. Feroze offer a room for Jah-Son quite up Aranguez. Jah-Son say thanks, but it too far for him as he have to work and look after Small Man so he better be nearby. I Cynthia feel that in he heart, he hoping that Indira will offer for him to move back with she, but I guess he don't want to be a charity case with *she* bed the only port in a storm. I see Jah-Son glance across at she, but she head bend over the sink. She busy, busy, washing glass. How the boy to read that? Is she waiting for he to arsks she, or she tryin to avoid eye contact so he wouldn't arks? She eh looking too happy with the things in the storeroom, so how he could arks about moving back in?

I Cynthia conclude she aggrieve that the decision about storing things in the pub and about where he and the others living arrive at without discussion with she. But how the boy could know that? How he could know that maybe she feeling like she don't count. That he, Bostic, Maisie, Feroze and I could take upon weself to work things out, and treating she like if she opinion not required. Perhaps she thinking that if he not arksing, she not offering, and furthermore, all of we could do what we want, just leave her out of it.

Jah-Son puzzled by her silence. When in doubt, do what he always do. Go and look after the birds. As he cleans out their cages, and feeds and waters them, his whistles pour out how unmoored he feel now that Gran-Gran, his rock of ages, has gone, how unprepared he feel – not with caring for Maisie and Small Man, he can do that – over the threats to the house, his insecurity with Indira, how it feel like he cannot do the right thing or what are the wrong things he must avoid doing. His semp and his picoplat comfort him with their songs. In his heart he hear them say, Jah-Son, Gran-Gran looking out for you still. Have patience. Things will work out.

In the afternoon, on her way to work, Maisie drops Small Man for Jah-Son to take care of in the bar. Later they will meet her at work and travel back together – safety in numbers. When Maisie leaves, Indira goes upstairs. She does not offer to take Small Man with her. She does not give him a meal. She does not bathe him, read him a story or put him down for a nap. She does not come back down all evening. Let them stew in their own juice. They made their bed, they must lie in it.

The next day, Maisie and Small Man move in with I Cynthia.

Just for a few days, she tell Jah-Son, until yuh settle yuhself. She would like to help out more because Elaine was her friend. But this was the bes' she could do in the circumstance.

Jah-Son continue to sleep at home, up the Valley Road. What else is there to do? Two, three days go by; the stand-off between he and Indira continue. They not arguing, but they only talking about the bar and business, nothing personal. Only his birds talking with him, asking him how he spend the night, if they thief out everything yet, if Maisie and Small Man doing OK. And is only to them he relating how he lonely and sometimes frighten, how Small Man crying a lot for Gran-Gran, how he have to buy a rubber sheet to put on the bed because the child start wetting the bed like he is a baby again, how the little preschool say that Small Man spending the day by himself, he don't want to play with nobody, how he drifting off to sleep sometimes; and as for Maisie, she don't want to travel in taxi at night unless he with her, and even then, she picking and choosing which car they getting into. He tell his birds he don't know how much longer he can keep this up, but like Gran-Gran use to say, the longest rope have a end, and he waiting to see if he reach the end of this rope that testing his patience and hope, because he really feel he can't take no more.

And Indira? She has Jah-Son on her mind every day, all the time, thinking how hard it is to watch him pulling into himself, making himself smaller, as if he's afraid his body's taking up too much space. He's squeezing himself between boxes and chairs and tables, not letting his body touch anything or anyone. Even his lips not stretching across his face to smile at the ole' boys' lame jokes. His words are few, forced between lips as grudging as a post box slit. It hurts to see him shrinking, diminished.

She knows the regulars are discussing her, judging her, making her out to be a heartless bitch. Even Fritzie is avoiding small talk. I've become a pariah. And why? Because I'm standing up for myself. I'm not letting myself be disrespected. *My* storeroom, *my* pub. Nobody saw fit to ask me about using it. Everybody else's mouth is in the decision. If you leave me out of the problem, then leave me out of the solution. Furthermore, after all these nights I'm taking care of Small Man, feeding him, bathing him, reading him stories, putting him to bed, and just so, *Cynthia* is the one chosen to look after him. Like I'm not good enough. And as for Jah-Son. Well if he wants to show he is man by going up to sleep in that house where people breaking in and stealing, who am I to stop him?

She's been taken advantage of too often in her life; she has to harden her heart. She won't be a convenience for Jah-Son and his family. She'll tell him so the minute he steps in the next morning.

But, that morning, Jah-Son does not step into De Rightest Place. He call Bostic to tell him he going with an estate agent to look at a few properties for rent in and around Belmont and Gonzales, but that he'll be sure to be back in time for when Maisie drops off Small Man on her way to work. Except that he isn't and Maisie arrives at De Rightest Place with Small Man and no Jah-Son there to hand him over to. She can't take him to work and she can't leave him, and Jah-Son still not there when her shift start. The 3Fs manager call and she tell him she can't come yet, she has nobody to leave her child with, and the manager say we short-staffed, you too undependable, and this is a warning that if it happens again, don't look to come back to work. Maisie sorry that all her investment in the company so easily dismissed because she in a bind, but in her heart she glad he behaving so, because it have nothing for her in that kind of work. She made to feel like she is a easily replaceable item like one of the Made In China plastic food trays they use. She knows the manager only pulling rank and making grand-charge because why else they always looking to recruit people eh? Nobody don't last no time in that work, so she don't know what he feel he accomplishing with that kind a threat.

25. KARMA

Well, well, look at this. Other people have Thought for the Day, Bible Verse for the Day, Mantra for the Day, or even Nam Myoho Renge Kyo. What luck mine is Horoscope for the Day. How do the stars know in advance what is going on with me? It's one of life's great mysteries. Just look at today.

You have the means of finding a certain amount of harmony because you are capable of creating goodwill around you. Your karma requires that you give, give, and give, without counting.

It says my life is without harmony. And it's right! Disharmonious in the extreme. And why? Mea culpa. I haven't been creating much goodwill lately. Jumbieing my own wellbeing, so I'm feeling jinxed. What goes around comes around. What's that book called? *How Hostility & Hate Corrode Karma.* Yes, you mess with karma and see how fast it will turn round and bite you in the backside when you're not looking.

I have to stop focusing on how this situation with Jah-Son, Maisie and Small Man is affecting *my* life. It's petty and selfish. Do unto others, not so? When Jah-Son comes this morning, I'll be ... what it says here? ... *generous!* ... that's it. He and I and Maisie and Bostic will tackle this homelessness thing together. Together we aspire, together we achieve, as the national motto says. Should be my personal motto.

Indira goes downstairs to get the bar ready for early customers and to wait for Jah-Son to arrive. She will wrap him in the warmth of her generosity and harmony. She looks up at the bar clock. Ten to ten. She starts work. The beer is chilling, ice in the freezer for shots and chasers. She checks the clock. Half past ten. She arranges the chairs around the tables. Eleven. Bostic wonders what she's anxious about, but he not asking. She asking, though.

210

Jah-Son was here last night? Bostic tell her he reach late. She ask what happen with Maisie and Small Man and she hear that Maisie take him over by Cynthia, that Jah-Son come by saying he spend the day checking out places, but all he could find was all kind of hovels. So far, so far, Indira puts in, quick, quick, as if she is the twelfth fairy, cancelling a curse. Bostic look at her and ask, What make you think things will improve? She don't have no solid answer to that.

Jah-Son *does* come to work, but late that morning. He jump out of a van, walk in and say, Good morning, then go straight to the storeroom and start pulling out the boxes he put there just a few days before and carry them out to the van. He say to Indira and Bostic, Thanks for letting me store my things. Sorry for the inconvenience. He jump in the van and the driver take off. When he is back half an hour later, he goes out to the birds to feed them and clean their cages. He tell them how he renting a room in a house in Gonzales and it have a cot so he could sleep there and store the things till after Carnival when the owner plan to do some renovations, as the workmen don't have no time till the fêting done. I buying time, that's all, he tell them. Then he gone back inside to work in the bar until siesta, when he go for Small Man.

★

I Cynthia tell him I going to look after Small Man so Jah-Son and Maisie could work. Is best, too, I tell him, that he could go for Maisie without dragging that poor little child in the dew for him to catch cold. Miss Cynthia, Jah-Son tell me, thank you; this is the first time in weeks I feel I could breathe.

The bar busy, busy. It's less than three weeks to Carnival and every night there's some show, some party, some competition. Indira rent a big maco plasma TV to hang on the wall, so the patrons could enjoy the pre-Carnival events live. With Panorama steelband competition preliminaries on that night, I know no-body will go home till two or three in the morning. When Jah-Son pick up Maisie, he go back with her to the bar, so they could both help. His irregular hours of late was no doubt a bone of conten-tion with Indira, so he trying to make up for it.

So I Cynthia stuck at home. As the night go on, I feeling leave out of the excitement, so I call Maisie and say I want to lime in the bar and watch the steelband competition, too. Could she come and take over staying with Small Man? When I get to the pub I see Jah-Son still there. I can understand why. Where he going, eh? Some dingy room and small, folding canvas cot surrounded by cardboard boxes of stuff? No profit in that. He better off right there watching the steelbands, serving drinks and clearing up. Indira half-watching the steelband action. She band, All Stars, from the heart of the city, gone already, and is Phase II from Woodbrook – where she feeling no affiliation – who on stage now. I Cynthia find she looking at Jah-Son a lot. I feel she want to talk to him about his family and the house issue, but the circumstances not right. She must be realise that earlier she miss out on discussing it in a friendly, helpful manner. I cyah help but wonder why people does spoil they own chance of happiness because of bad mind.

When I look at Jah-Son, I see he watching she too. But is like they taking turns and two eyes and two eyes don't make four. Then she mussbe notice that the clock on the wall time not matching the time on the TV, so she climb up to fix the clock and like the little stool she stand on topple, and she with it. On the way down, she grab a tray with a couple beers on it and everything fall with an explosion of shattering glass. Jah-Son rush over to help she up from the broken glass and spill beer. She leg bleeding and he just lift she up and carry she upstairs. Cecil say, That boy is a poultry guest. What you mean? I ask him. When he explain, I say, Oh ho, but I hear people on TV does pronounce that word pol-ter-geist. And furthermore, I tell him, if Jah-Son really is one, he woulda arrange for a helpful spirit to clear up the mess. Bostic say, Is all right, I have that under control. Cecil say, You see how much powers the boy have?

Is nearly an hour that pass before Jah-Son reach back downstairs and all a we watching how he playing he eh see the nudging, the eye rolling, the eyebrow lifting, the smirking that accompany his return. He start washing glasses at the sink, crating empties, taking crates to the storeroom, like he don't business with we.

Upstairs, in sleepy half-awareness, Indira hears the slurred goodnights of the departing customers, the scraping of chairs and tables being stacked for ease of the morning clean-up, the clink of the last empties being stored, the front door being slammed shut. She is listening for Bostic to leave by the side door, listening for his usual, See you in the morning, and she is listening for Jah-Son to slide the final bolt in place, the flurry of clicks as he turns out the lights. She is waiting for him to run up the stairs, fling open the bedroom door, tear off his clothes and slide in beside her.

When she hears the front doors shut and locked from the outside, when she hears Bostic and Jah-Son on the pavement bid each other goodnight, her mouth is filled with the bitter slime of aloes bubbling up her throat. She knows it is her own doing that has led to this.

Tonight, every bird in its nest. Bostic in his home nearby and Jah-Son in the crowded room and narrow cot in Gonzales, because, even though it looking like he and Indira kinda make up, if having sex can be called making up, he not taking it for granted that he welcome to move back in, to live there. If he want to say he is big man, he can't depend on no woman who feel she could be blowing hot and cold on him. It can't work so. And with that thought Jah-Son fall into a restless sleep.

26. A CERTAIN AMOUNT OF HARMONY

The newly minted Belmont Action Committee for Conscious Holistic Ancestral National Arts Liberation approach Indira to use De Rightest Place for a Devil Mas' Competition to take place Saturday night, two Saturdays before the Carnival weekend. Because the committee include some pretty useless old stagers like The Admiral, and gadfly opportunists like Anil, Indira not inclined to take it too seriously, but when the councillor for the district, a certain Mr Junior Ramluck, comes by in a three-piece suit and wilting party tie in the midday hot sun to make the request in person, and he's quoting the very attractive figure the council prepared to invest in the venture (within the portfolio of their Freetown United Concept Kickstart Uhuru), and he outlines what they would want from the premises and from her staff, she's quickly rethinking her position. Let me discuss it with my associates, she says, and I'll get back to you in a couple days.

Y'girl eh waste no time. Quick-quick, she calls a meeting with Bostic, Fritzie and Jah-Son and puts the proposal to them. They want to know how the event going to affect them personally – what they will have to do, what they will get.

Bostic ask, They want the place to open till what o'clock? Two, three in the morning? Like nobody getting no sleep that night. It will be so much a people to deal up with. Indira say, No problem. St James has at least five such events every Carnival season for years now, and all the bars open late.

Fritzie ask, Is how much food they want for the competitors and judges and all a them politician hangers-on it bound to attract? Is boxes of chicken pelau and coleslaw and snacks all night, you saying? Is real cooking have to go on. Indira say, We could start the pelau early. Prepare the chicken and freeze it and it will be less work on the day itself. The snack boxes we could assemble from ready-made items. We can buy samosas, mini roti,

214

bake and buljol, cake slices, cheesecake squares, and fix it up nice in little plastic snack boxes. Drinks we always have. Is just to add more stocks so we don't run out and make sure we have enough Johnny Blue, Jack Daniels and Grey Goose for the officials and their entourage. Rum and beers for the contestants.

Jah-Son not saying anything. His head working out the child-minding arrangements he would have to make when Maisie also at her 3Fs job and, of course, Cynthia bound to want to be in the middle of the action at De Rightest Place. And ohmihgord, Cynthia's family! If they hear about a local devil mas' right there in Belmont, they sure will want to come and stay by her, and maybe Maisie and Small Man would have to move out sooner than expected. Jeez, like is sleeping arrangement, too, to work out. But where? His cubbyhole in Gonzalez, the only place he can lay claim to at the moment, you can't even bend down to tie yuh sneaker laces without bouncin' yuh head on something.

When Indira tell them the amount of money she giving every-body, Bostic look up at the ceiling and whistle, Fritzie two eye open big-big, but Jah-Son still in his dream world and no reaction. Indira ask him, You OK with that, Jah-Son? All he could say is, Yes, whatever you say. So, everybody agree? Yes, we good to go.

Indira calls Mr Junior Ramluck, aka Village Ram, and asks him to come by to finalise the arrangements. When he arrives, Bostic offers him a drink and, armed with a Johnny Blue on ice, he joins Indira at the table. She puts down her phone and asks Ramluck if he bring a contract for her to review. He pulls back in the chair, twirls the glass in his hand so the ice goes *clink, clink, plink*, like a ole-time cash register, sucks in his belly so the buttons on his jacket relax a little, pouts his lips and says, Contract? No. My word is my contract. He leans forward and puts down his glass. I'm a councillor in this district for the past fifteen years and nobody can say a bad word about my word. Indira says, OK. Well let's get down to word-of-mouth business then. She reads out some notes about what they discussed at the first meeting – what she is to do, what he is to pay, when he is to pay and so on. He says, Yes, yes, yes to everything, nodding so his jowls surge forward and back like plump little wavelets on the shoreline of his jaw. She asks him for the deposit cheque. He says he couldn't get the cheque because the accountant didn't turn up for work – you know how it is with these people – sigh – and it needs the accountant signature too, and he will bring it during the week, Wednesday; he will make sure and do that. His word is his bond. Ask anybody. Shake hands.

Wednesday comes and no call or visit. Indira can't get no answer on his phone, only voicemail. She leaving message and getting vex. These blasted kiss-mih-whatever politician monkey know what tree to climb, but she know all the brass monkey tricks. If he know what good for him, he had better watch his step with her. For all that venting, she still forging ahead with preparations because the event advertising on radio and TV with De Rightest Place as the venue. So, as far as she concern, it going to happen on the said date and, like it or not, is her call to be ready like Freddie. The Councillor calls Friday night saying he have the cheque, but it done late already and he still in a meeting. I will bring it for you tomorrow morning, bright and early. Final payment to come the Monday after the event.

No sign of said councillor Saturday morning, but the tents, tables and chairs, lights and sound system arrive midday in a council truck. The eight-man work team jump off the back of the truck and head straight into De Rightest Place, sit down and order beers. When time to pay, they tell Bostic that the bossman councillor say to put it on the tab. He would fix up later. And when they smell the chicken pelau cooking upstairs, they say they hungry and they entitled to lunch and how the bossman councillor tell them they could put lunch on the tab too. They eat and drink. Time passing, and Bostic find they taking long to start putting up the tents. He ask them when they planning to go outside and get the place ready. One of the fellers look at his cellphone and say is only three o'clock and they not starting work till after four when they expecting the supervisor to come and tell them where to put up the tent and open up the tables and so on. When the supervisor come, he thirsty too, he hungry too, and is another set of drinks and food all round and five o'clock reach and they playing cards and dominoes and eating and drinking and not a tent up, not a table or a chair in place, everything still pack up on the truck.

Fritzie come down and announce to everybody and nobody that she serve up eighteen boxes of food already, and not one of them going to a single official intended guest, and so-help-me-god-kiss-the-cross-and-hope-to-die, not even a grain of rice pass her lips. Is whole day she slaving over a hot stove and the place outside not even set up yet and she going out to the supermarket now to get more chicken and peas and rice and vegetables because she going to run short with the food and embarrass the good name of De Rightest Place. How was she suppose to know she catering for all these extra so-called workmen who, as far as she could make out, not doing a stroke of work and she can't understand why they come so early if they not doing anything yet.

The supervisor say they have to wait for the sound man and the lights man to tell him where things should go, and both of them have a Kiddies Carnival gig in the Savannah, but they coming just now, so why she fretting up sheself? All this quarrelling go make she look old before her time. She should cool down sheself before she drive up she pressure. Sistah, don't dig no horrors. Fritzie look the man square in his face, put her hands on her hips and ask him how she get to be his sister, because as far as she know, her mother make only her and Amber – no brother – and even though she know her father was wild like a quenk in heat in his day, she know what her father look like and she can't see no resemblance. With that she stalk out.

And Indira, where she? Upstairs. Look. Y'girl lying in bed, eyes closed under slices of cucumber, face plastered with a homemade organic avocado and oatmeal mask. Check the feet. Toes spread out like if she spend the whole of her childhood walking barefoot in zapatay mud, the toes separated by little balls of cotton wool, the nails a fresh, bright, gleaming scarlet – same shade as Sir Elton John's 1987 *Ferrari Testarossa,* at least that's what the label claims – and the fingernails matching too. With her hair turbanned in a white towel, amber roots newly-lightened to *Mystic Citrine,* y'girl making sure she will be looking her best for the dignitaries who going to be her guests this evening. Behind the cucumber slices she's seeing the picture now. A glamorous white woman, a busty blonde at that, serving drinks to those self-important hubris-bloated political types. She'll wear something nicely low-cut for leaning over to pour drinks. See, but don't touch; is not a buffet. How those pipsqueaks will be wetting themselves when she around. She could even go burlesque – it's Carnival after all. Not blue. Not black – that's for the devils. Red.

This pleasurable reverie is shattered by a loud commotion outside. What the firetruck is going on? She bounds out of bed, shedding cucumber slices, to look through the jalousies at the forecourt below. A tug-of-war is in progress. Kwesi and Curtis are holding tight to one end of their glowing barbecue pit while two burly men are pushing it away from its habitual parking spot. She can make out the council's logo on the men's T-shirts. Dear gods, who forgot to tell the Belmont Bes BBQ Boys that the forecourt is booked for another gig? Jeezanages, I completely forget about them. She phone Bostic and ask him to sort it out. No, she can't come downstairs. Tell the boys to put the BBQ pit somewhere in the back… Come back later… spectators would be hungry. With that thought she gone to the kitchen to check on said pelau and snacks and find Fritzie not there, only a big empty iron pot soaking in the sink and a note on the countertop saying, *Workmen eat out half the food. Gone grocery with Jah-Son for supplies. Back later.*

Which workmen eat out food? Indira phone Bostic again. He tell her he settle down Kwesi and Curtis for the time being, and he now supervising the workmen who there since midday eating and drinking and playing cards and now they on overtime pay they setting up for the event, and it already six o'clock so lights and so on have to set up too, and could she tell him when she planning to come downstairs to make sure everything going according to the agreement with the councillor, who not reach yet either, although he supposed to be the chief organiser. Maybe he waiting for double-time pay, too, to get his ass in gear. Indira tell him hang on, she'll be there in a couple minutes, just let her get herself respectable first.

The scene of disarray on the forecourt of De Rightest Place slaps y'girl in her freshly cleansed and tightened face.

What's with all this comfuffle? Who is the person in charge here?

From the middle of the melee, a short, slim, youngish man turns to face her. His hair, a spiky bleached blonde, rises like startled quills above gold-hoop earrings framing the edge of an ear. He wears a tight orange T-shirt and tight white shorts. In one hand he holds a clipboard from which a pencil on a coiled yellow cable dangles. He fishes in his pocket, hands her a card, a violet card, tucks the clipboard under his arm, and extends his free hand and a wide smile in greeting. His voice is high, excitable.

I am the event co-ordinator. It's all under control here. The tent will be ready in about fifteen minutes. Then we'll set out the tables and chairs and be all set for when the special guests arrive.

He lifts his arm close to his face to peer at one of the massive steel studs on a wide black leather wristband and announces: The actual competition will start at nine, but I've told the competitors to be at the venue by eight. He taps the clipboard while looking around him.

So where are they going to assemble while they're waiting to go on stage? he asks.

Who?

The competitors.

That Indira is flummoxed can be read only in the double crease flickering between her eyebrows, mirroring the synapses firing in her brain. Assemble before going on stage? No one told her about that. Forecourt, food, facilities and drink. That was the deal. Now they coming with backstage expectations too? But she won't allow herself to appear less competent than this trumped-up little squirt. No clipboard, is true, but she has plenty business savvy.

The competitors? Follow me.

She leads Mr Event Co-ordinator along the path at the side of the building. She waves an arm around. It takes in the large backyard, the guava tree with its hanging birdcages, a concrete jukking board sink and the Belmont Boys Bes' BBQ pit parked alongside the old storage shed.

All here is available. You see we have enough space behind here for everybody to get ready for the stage.

He looks at the space, looks at the clipboard and he ticks one or two boxes.

Washrooms?

The regular washrooms are in the bar. Those facilities are for my customers and your judges, politicians and guests.

Competitors' washrooms?

You will appreciate I cannot allow access to the bar washrooms to any person or persons whose body is painted with blue paint and black paint, or is covered in grease and reeking of gasoline.

She looks him in the eye. I take it you've ordered port-a-loos for the competitors?

He checks the clipboard, turns a page, goes back to the first page, flicks that one over again. Yes. Good. Excuse me. I must get back to see what's happening with the setting-up in front.

Indira leads him back to the forecourt. He can't see the satisfied smile on her face or see it broaden to a grin when he whips out his phone and starts to speak into it with much stamping and arm waving. He joins her where she's watching the workmen assembling tables and chairs under the big white open tent, the electrician slinging lights and the soundman setting up mikes and speakers. Everything buzzing smooth, smooth, like a hive of worker bees.

A port-a-loo will be arriving shortly. I'll get them to set it up in the back.

She gives him a thumbs-up, goes indoors to soothe Bostic's irritation and then heads upstairs to see how Fritzie and Jah-Son are getting on with the new batch of cooking. Then she must get herself ready to greet her guests.

But she can't. At least, not right away. In the kitchen she finds Fritzie and Jah-Son cutting up chickens, the counter littered with a half-dozen or more plump birds awaiting dissection. Don't ask, says Fritzie. Just don't ask me nothing here today! Jah-Son tells Indira that the grocery run out of cut-up portions. The first batch of pelau was made from legs and thighs. Look how much whole chicken we have to cut up just to get breast and wing and leg and thigh, and a whole set of back and neck to find room for in the freezer. Plenty more work and time running out.

What else could y'girl do? Indira take a last look of regret at the glory of her *Ferrari Testarossa* fingernails, grab an apron, a cutting board and a knife and set to work dismembering chickens. Two hours later, when the big iron pots bubbling with coconut, ginger and thyme-scented pelau, one huge frying pan sizzling with plantain slices, a massive bowl of coleslaw chilling in the fridge and the DJ soca music blasting from below rattling the kitchen crockery, Indira slips into her bathroom to cut her distressed fingernails short, wash her hair, have a shower and contemplate what next.

What to wear? Too weary to be bothered, too late to make a fuss, Indira pulls on a clinging black silk, long-sleeved, cowl-necked top and black palazzo pants, and drapes her Janice Derrick long silver double chain round her neck. She hooks more links through her earlobes, applies an iridescent translucent powder to her face, accentuates the sculpted lines of eyebrows, frames her eyes with kohl so they pierce through like twin blue diamonds, slashes on red lipstick – *Vampire* says the label – slips on black, strappy sandals – at least the toes still stunning – and, exuding *Fracas* from every pulse point, down she struts. When the brash Blond Ambition, over-heated Madonna plan falls through, you can always fall back on the cold fire of classic minimalist Marlene Dietrich.

As she steps outside, Indira can barely recognise the forecourt. Night has fallen. Through the dark, the steady pinprick glow of fairy lights strung across the front of the building, and the flickering flames of flambeaux on bamboo poles lend the space a magical atmosphere. The white canvas tent, more canopy than tent, stands ten feet or so above the ground. Below the canopy is a long table draped with a spotless white cloth on which lie the accoutrements for judging a competition – notebooks, stop-watches, pens and pencils, clipboards with tabulated sheets attached. A dozen or more chairs are placed behind the table. Below the table and a short distance in front of it is a vivid green Astroturf mat on which are set huge containers of palms, crotons and ferns.

It looks like an altar awaiting the high priests and priestesses who will perform the sacred rite of sacrifice. The faithful are already there, behind a row of steel crowd-barriers. They are standing, sitting, chatting, drinking, laughing and eating. Many are dancing to the DJ's sweet soca music. Everyone is in a state of excited anticipation. But when Indira looks again, the scene that flashes through her mind is The Last Supper, with the baying crowd ready to choose Barabbas.

27. THINK OF THE CONSEQUENCES

Today's Gemini Moon suggests good intentions, limited attention spans, and, perhaps, being deep in thought for a whole minute. That said, it's important to think of consequences before taking action.

Soon the dignitaries are seated – the three judges in the middle, flanked by two council officials, the three executive members of the Belmont Action Committee for Conscious Holistic Ancestral National Arts Liberation and an indeterminate number of political hangers-on. All but the judges seem to be a bit worse for wear, but that doesn't prevent the call for Johnny Blue from one end of the table and for Jack Daniels from the other. We can pour we own drinks. Just leave the bottles with a bucket of ice, a jug of water and some glasses. A fluid camaraderie quickly develops and much chatting and loud laughter distinguishes the two ends of the table from the middle, where a quiet discussion is taking place.

The judging panel comprises two women and one man – a veteran mas' designer, an eminent mas' historian and a highly respected authority on traditional mas' choreography. While they may have wished to dissociate themselves from the rest of the group at the table, they are well aware that he who pays the piper calls the tune, and the fee they've been promised for this gig – though a minute fraction of the bar bill these others were going to rack up – would go some way to keeping up the appearance of being relevant to culture and society, albeit in genteel poverty. Thus, their distaste for the company they're obliged to keep can be discerned only in their adherence to coconut water, neat, as their beverage of choice, and the serious, businesslike set of their faces.

The councillor, who managed to avoid eye contact with Indira when she greeted him and his entourage, opens the proceedings with a long ramble about community spirit being fostered and kept alive through his good offices, about community skills and talents being recognised and rewarded by his good offices, about community employment and revenue being generated by his good offices. He would have gone on for longer if Cecil, behind the control barrier, hadn't shouted out, Sit down. We come here to see the devil mas' not listen to you. The cry was picked up by Boyee. Village Ram, he shout out, why you don't go and have some fun in your *good offices*? This generates some fist pumping and shouts of agreement from the crowd.

It is high time for the MC, Mr Event Coordinator himself, to take the microphone and welcome the burghers of Belmont to the First Annual Devil Mas' Competition. Let us put our hands together and thank our hard-working councillor for his perseverance and diligence in making this event happen. The said burghers oblige with clapping, catcalling and whistling, which mollifies the spluttering councillor sufficiently for him to call for the Grey Goose at his end of the table.

Indira goes to check what is going on in the backyard. She thinks she's fallen into a space-time fissure and entered a different dimension. She has to lean against a wall to steady herself. For a fleeting moment, she is that little girl again, back in the temple compound with Bai and Uncle, watching the kathakali artists as they morphed from gods, kings, queens, damsels, dragons into ordinary, everyday people. Here, in her own backyard, clusters of common run-of-the-street men and boys are transmuting into mythical creatures. The disorientation lasts a split second, but the feeling lingers that somehow an otherworldly synapse has flashed across from life then to life now.

Rapt, she looks at the scene before her. Flaring flambeaux underlight almost naked beings as they daub blue body-paint and Reckitt's blue, molasses and grease onto one another, from hair tips to toenails. Blue wings and black wings, single pairs and double pairs, hang like resting pterodactyls from the guava tree; tridents and pitchforks, ropes and chains, whistles, horns and masks lie in heaps beside big biscuit-tin drums. Boys are filling beer bottles with kerosene, inserting cloth rags as fat wicks to make the flambeaux they'd use on stage for their fire-breathing acts. There is subdued laughter, drinking and the telling of tales – an atmosphere of such easy camaraderie that she is unwilling to break it by going into their midst to ask if all is right with them, and whether they need anything, so she slips away, back to the forecourt, to await the start of the competition.

His mouth dripping thick red, the first winged blue devil bursts on stage with a massive shriek and a giant threatening leap towards the crowd, who scream and run backwards. His accompanying imp pulls at the rope tied around the devil's waist to restrain him, and the crowd surges back, laughing at their own fear. The next one who comes on shakes his hips, causing his rope tail to swing lasciviously. He blows a piercing whistle while his imp beats a rattling tune on a biscuit tin. Another devil crawls like a crab along the ground, snarling and making feigned snatches at the calves and ankles of the onlookers. Others come on in fearsome hairy, fangy masks, provoking delighted screaming; others wave pitchforks, making jabs and stabs with them, swing heavy chains, shriek and jump, yell and prance. One sprays a mouthful of kerosene at a lighted flambeau held at arm's length, shooting an instant dragon's flame from his lips. For the finale, the gates of hell are open as these demons emerge on stage, looking as if they are ready to drag sinful mankind back there with them. That all – performers, spectators, judges – are veterans of Devil Mas' matters not one wit. The drama, the fear, the fun is still as fresh as the first time someone put on a pair of horns, a pair of wings, daubed mud all over, grabbed a pitchfork and played jab-jab on a long-past j'ouvert morning.

While judges and onlookers weigh the merits of each performance, Cecil calls out, Miss Indira, like the devils making Hell in the backyard. Boyee say, Nah man, that fire too big. Fire! Fire! come shouts. Folk push aside the barrier and rush to the backyard where they find masqueraders tossing buckets of water against the shed, trying to out the fire climbing up the shed door.

By the time the fire tender arrive, the shed fully ablaze. Sheets of corrugated galvanize curl, pop and wrench themselves free from the rafters, flying off the shed like magic carpets. A thick coil of intense black smoke rises up into the air, a dense sooty canopy, studded with firework sparks. Jah-Son and Bostic work with the firemen, smothering smouldering timbers with buckets of sand, and wetting the main building to prevent it catching too. Flames throw shifting shadows over the upturned faces of silent spectators who stand in awe, as if Judgement Day has come and their fate is in the spectacle before them. The fire is finally put out, but the Devil Mas' competition has been forced to an untimely end. Spectators, dignitaries, masqueraders begin hastening their way home.

The place is soon deserted. Indira, Bostic, Fritzie and Jah-Son wander through the backyard in a daze, surveying the destruction. It is not hard to see what happened. An overturned gas bottle was probably the cause. Add to it flambeaux, rags, embers in the barbeque pit, inflammable materials in the shed. Not rocket surgery, as Indira puts it. To bed now. Tomorrow is another day and we must face the melody then.

Back on the forecourt they survey the scene of abandoned revelry. Not our problem, Indira says. They have to come back to pick up their stuff in the morning. Bostic gives Jah-Son the keys to the pick-up. Would he drop Fritzie home and keep the vehicle overnight? He himself will walk home, not far. He needs to unwind.

In the bar, he and Indira have a drink, mixed and swiftly despatched in a couple of urgent gulps. After a long exhausted silence, Bostic says, Plenty clearing up outside.

I'll go personally to the councillor Monday morning. Their stuff can't be left cluttering up the place.

And what about payment?

Indira rises to go upstairs.

He'll have to pay what he already owes. Plus some sort of compensation for the damage caused by the fire.

Good luck with that. Look, I'll just clean myself up a little before I go.

OK. Goodnight. See you Monday.

Yes, Monday.

Upstairs, she kicks off her shoes, puts on the kettle for a camomile brew, drinks the hot tea, lies on the sofa, but she's twitching with tiredness and can't drift off. Maybe a second rum and coke will settle her swirling brain? She heads down to the bar to mix her drink just as Bostic is emerging from the washroom.

He is wearing only his Y-fronts. The clink of ice cubes falling into her glass startles him. He lifts his head before he can cover himself with his towel. He sees her eyes light on the bright, red, coiled serpent on his thigh. The words tumble from her mouth before she is able to stop herself.

Jah-Son has one exactly… Oh my gods! Oh my gods! The thought shapes and connects.

He takes the glass from her hand and leads her to a chair, making her sit while he fixes the drink. He pulls out a chair next to her and waits, his head hanging low, his fingers interlaced on the table before him. She doesn't touch the drink.

You knew.

He does not answer.

How long?

Not long.

You didn't say anything?

He stays silent.

Why?

He makes no response.

You knew all along, yet you stood by and did nothing when that boy was going through so much trouble. All by himself. The job. Gran-Gran dying. Nowhere to live. Sister and nephew to take care of. You knew and you didn't try to help. Didn't even try to take some responsibility.

She stands and pushes the chair back under the table.

What kind of man are you?

He gets up and goes to the washroom. When he comes out he is fully dressed. He locks up and leaves by the side gate. Neither he nor she utters a syllable or exchange a glance.

28. DEEP IN THOUGHT

First thing Monday morning, y'girl puts in a call to Councillor Mr Ramluck. The secretary says he's at a meeting and would she like to leave a message? She says she would. Let the councillor know that *The Spectre* is coming to interview her at De Rightest Place at two o'clock that afternoon to talk about about the Devil Mas' Competition event and the fire and perhaps he'd be interested in dropping in sometime before then?

Y'girl made sure to be dressed, ready for the councillor before she phoned, so she's not surprised when his chauffeured Range Rover pulls up within fifteen minutes. She's watching him bustling from the vehicle, stopping to take in canopy, table, chairs and all, still in place since Saturday evening. Then he knocks, looks round the open door and says, Morning Miss Indira, hahaha, so how things, today? He's rubbing his hands together, laughing like they're best friends and he and she accustomed to liming in the pub Monday mornings. She smiles. Things looking up already. He looks around. So, where everybody? She says, I decide we need a couple days to get ourselves back on track, so no customers today. She motions him to join her at the table. Jah-Son, she calls, come and get a drink for the councillor and me. What are you having? He looks at his watch, frowns, says, Perhaps a small Jack Daniels.

They clink glasses. She says, What can I do for you? He says, I hear the papers coming here later? What's that about? She says, Well it looking like some keen young reporter checking how the city money being spent at events that various councillors hosting at Carnival time. Looks like they think money is being diverted to line the pockets of friends and family. There's even talk of money going to fund criminal activities. You know – protection, gambling, drugs, guns and so on. The whole transparency and accountability issue. The press hot on that nowadays.

227

He's frowning, pouting his lips, crooking a finger over his mouth.

Well. Imagine that. No one can say *our* arrangement is anything but completely above board, can they? Hahaha.

True. But they may wonder why there's no paper trail and suspect something underhand. Why no money has changed hands even though an event has happened. They may want to ask about responsibility for the fire. What precautions were taken with flambeaux and gas everywhere – the risks to people's lives and so on. You know. The OSH rules and all that.

So, what are you going to tell them?

The truth, I suppose. Isn't honesty the best policy?

He raises an eyebrow.

I'll say that we agreed on a reasonable figure. They'll want to know what I provided and for whom. That list I can provide. And a list of the persons there.

He's still saying nothing and she continues.

I'll say that I waited for a cheque on Wednesday and was disappointed and that on Friday and Saturday I was also left high and dry. My staff will be at the interview too, to express their dedication to the cause of reviving Belmont's long history of craftsmanship in mas-making. They'll report how they went beyond the call of duty, even without pay, because they did not want their fellow Belmont people to be denied the opportunity to display their creativity, just because of a councillor's reluctance to follow through on an agreement.

He's not saying any thing. The place quiet, quiet. Then he looks up, eyes slanting kinda sideways, and he says, How much we agree on? She says, Let me refresh your memory. She picks up her phone and presses a button and the councillor hears his and her voices loud and clear, and they're discussing the cost and the food and drink. He's getting paler and paler, squirming in the chair, like he has worms. That's enough, he says, and he's gone to the car.

He comes back with a official chequebook. She sees pages and pages with two signatures already on them and he writes out the two cheques, one dated Monday self and one backdated to Wednesday gone and he tears them out and hands them to Indira. She studies them carefully; says thanks. When he stands up to go, she tells him, I'm sure the TV cameras will film the condition of the forecourt – two days after the competition. He says, Oh, yes. That. He takes out his phone and arranges for a crew to come right away to clear and restore the area. We will have to rebuild the room at the back, you know, Indira tells him. He says, We'll talk about that later. She says, The press was very interested in the competition. They'll be sure to ask about the results. You've got those, haven't you? He looks unsure. She says, Go back to your office and get that sorted out. Come back at quarter to two and we will have a joint press conference to talk about the success of the event – about traditional mas', innate creativity finding expression, about public-private initiatives etc. In the meantime, I'll go to the bank and deposit these cheques. Jah-Son will supervise the clean-up crew and ensure order is restored.

When they shake hands on parting, he catches a whiff of a woodsy fragrance, something with a slightly masculine energy. She sees him sniffing the air, as if trying to trace some weapon that has by-passed his defences. She goes back upstairs to refresh her pulse points with *Miss Dior*, best scent for levelling the gender imbalance on the business playing field – and for laughing all the way to the bank.

The councillor acquits himself handsomely at the press conference, exuding bonhomie and civic pride. How well the event had gone, how much community spirit had been incubated, nurtured and developed, how much foresight he had in imagining such an event, how much skill in bringing it off. No mention of the fire; not a peep about damage. Indira lets him prance and parade – the cheques have already cleared, her money safe, so why put on public view any of the twists and turns it took to get there? No profit in that, she thinks. Why embarrass the man by picking a public fight, eh?

Later, as she picks her way through curled rusted galvanise, blackened posts, charred, sooty walls, warped pvc water piping, melted wiring, she berates herself for her naivety. Tut-tut-tut… with so much life experience, yet so naïve, Indira? Surely you didn't need the gift of prophecy to know that without a public announcement from the councillor concerning the fire and compensation, you're going to be burnt if not cremated for your role in separating the said councillor from a portion of the largesse he'd counted on creaming off for himself? Where to begin? The legal route, suing him, was out. She was naive yes, but not so foolish as to imagine that lawyers, magistrates, judges are immune to corruption. A cabinet minister's son could beat up an unarmed elderly man with a cutlass and the case get put off and put off so many times that the old man die from natural causes before the case comes to court; a drunk-drive high court judge get off on a technicality about the breathalyser law itself. The law is not an ass – is the poor sufferer who looking for justice who is the ass. The law serves power. She is outside the charmed circle of the powerful.

Here she is, taken for a ride by a wily old ram and there is no way she can make him own up to his responsibility to her and to De Rightest Place. She can say what she likes about Health and Safety laws, and about him, but she knows he won't take any notice of her. If she's not careful, he could turn round and get a QC from England-self to serve her a pre-action protocol letter threatening to sue her for defamation of character. That seems to be the norm nowadays. No. Nononono. Not her in that.

She surveys the damage again. Gods alone know what it would cost to repair it – more than her share of the Devil Mas profit for sure, and where would she get the balance from? Ms Morgan Johnson at the bank out of the question. Mr Solomon Warner nowhere in sight to co-sign for a loan. A-lone. That's her. No rich financier lover in sight, even if she was willing, at her age and stage, to go back there. For starters, too much teen and twenty-something competition out there flaunting their wares at Woodbrook nightspots. Hold on, hold on, girl. What you think-ing? She shakes her head. She'd better derail that train of thought before it could arrive at a stationary.

She enters the bar and slumps into a chair, signalling Bostic for a drink. He guesses Campari with sour lime juice and soda. He brings a soda and bitters for himself and they sit silent, taking desultory sips, eyes drifting over the table, the ceiling, the floor, the condensation rings made by their glasses, looking everywhere but at each other, for what is there to say? Unfinished business hangs in the air between them.

A rubbish truck rumbles by on the road outside, the grinding mechanism sending the sweet-sour stench of fermenting vegetable waste creeping under the closed doors of the pub. They strain to hear the slide and slam of a maxi door, the running footsteps of children late for school. The tick of the wall clock measures their long silence. Her drink is all but finished. She swirls the ice in the glass, tilts her head back and drains the last drops of meltwater down her throat. An ice cube dislodges, slides down too. It is too large. It freezes shut her gullet and sticks there, squeezing her windpipe flat. She can't get air. She stands, stumbles, waves her arms. Bostic rushes round, slaps her hard on the back, the ice cube shoots out, flies through the air and lands squarely with a metallic *per-clink* in a glass on the bar counter. They stare, stupefied, look at each other, then hoot with laughter. Lady, says Bostic in his best fairground huckster voice, you have just won a prize. He brings refills to the table. No ice.

Talk, he says. I see you walking round the back just now. What you think?

She's propping her elbows on the table, knitting her fingers; a headache bands her forehead. Her voice is weary.

It's a mess.

Yes. I done check it out too. Can't even walk without getting juk or slash or trip up.

She does not even nod agreement.

So, what we going to do?

She lifts up her head. She looking around, as if to get her bearings. *We?*

We. We-self. What we going to do?

What you think?

It can't stay so. First is the clearing up. Move out everything. Take down the shed. Clear out the whole space.

Then?

See what the space looking like. Then decide what to do.

Pick yourself up, dust yourself off, start all over again?

Uh-huh.

When?

He looks at the wall clock. It's showing ten. He points to her drink, still untouched.

Ten past ten?

She gives him a weak smile, downs the drink in a single gulp and stands up.

One minute past ten. Come.

They go into the backyard and survey the wreckage. Now, with someone else on board, it does not seem so insurmountable.

Two fellers, plus me and Jah-Son, a truck making two-three trips to the La Basse, and we sorted in less than a day.

He reaches into his pocket for his phone.

Lemme see who I can get.

Hang on a minute. I got an idea. Let's go inside.

In the bar, she fishes into her handbag and pulls out a violet card. She picks up the handset of the landline and punches in the number on the card. He might be what we are looking for.

Oh, hi there. How are you? Busy, busy? Oh, things quieter now? That must be a relief. Plenty on your plate lately… Listen, I'm glad you've got a moment to spare… The clearing up here still not finished… Yes, I know it's not directly in your portfolio. But I don't think Councillor Ramluck would want to be associated with mess left after an event… His image… Oh, yes, I'm sure yours too… Look, why not take this on? Manage it. Take some pictures. Put it in the newspaper…

Her voice rises to italics.

'It's not done till the clean-up's done' or *'Leave a Clean Scene'*… you know… that kind of thing… Yes. Here the whole day. Uh-huh. Looking out for you.

I don't trust that little pipsqueak further than I can throw him, she tells Bostic. But I think he's got the message.

An hour hasn't passed before a council truck pulls up. Out jumps Mr Event Coordinator, a camera slung round his neck. With him is a council official. Indira and Bostic lead them round the backyard. The council official makes a call and soon another truck and two workmen in jumpsuits arrive. They set to work – a demolition and clean-up crew of two, one supervisor – and one event coordinator who filming the whole exercise. By nightfall, when the final truckload of debris moves out, the backyard is as clear as the Virgin Mary's conscience when she married the neighbourhood carpenter.

So, by the time Jah-Son arrives for the evening shift at the bar, he finds Indira and Bostic sitting at a table chatting like old friends. He, wound up in his own problems, now feels even more on the periphery of the companionable life of De Rightest Place. What's painful to him is that nobody seems to notice or care.

29. HOME SWEET HOME

It is soon after the Devil Mas event that Maisie call Jah-Son to tell him that Cynthia say she need back the room because her people coming from foreign. You remember she said it was just till her family come? Yes. I know. Is just that time fly and I didn't get nowhere yet. I will work on that today. Don't worry, sis, we'll get somewhere, OK?

Easy to sound positive with Maisie, but Lord above, how to convince himself all will be well? He hasn't felt so discouraged since Gran-Gran died. Is just one thing tumbling down after another. Maisie and her job, the incident in the taxi, the thiefing out Gran-Gran house, the moving from one place to another, the stops and starts with him and Indira and, on top of all that, deadlines for everything. Now it's urgent. He must find somewhere for them. He doesn't want much. Two rooms. But is like looking for two honest politicians.

These are the things playing in his head as he's walking down the road, hoping to get a maxi before the rain – if heavy cloud overhead any guide to the weather to come. A car pull up alongside. He hear his name. Is Feroze, in another of his buy-to-run-as-taxi purchases. Jah-Son jump in. Feroze say he's detouring to look at a car, if is OK with Jah-Son, who tell him he has no real place to get to. Still looking for somewhere for himself and Maisie and Small Man.

The car Feroze go to look at is a Toyota Corolla. Why you selling it? Feroze ask the lady. Nothing is wrong with the car, she say. Is just that she can't drive at night any more. After one time, is two time, as her dearly departed mother would say. Living alone, coming and going in a car is not safe any more. Satan busy finding mischief for idle hands. Bandits prepared to take your car, your purse, even your life. Has happened to two women friends. No. Not life. Praise be. Only car and purse.

Now they have to take taxi everywhere. But it's not so conven-ient. She does five-six different things when she goes out. Can't do that unless you hire the taxi for the whole day and who can afford that? Not someone on a retired teacher's pension, thank-ful though she is for small mercies. No chick, nor child, nor parrot-on-a-stick. The Lord giveth and the Lord taketh away. Blessed be His name.

All the time she talking, Feroze walking round the car, kicking tyres, sniffing tailpipe, shaking bumper, bouncing bonnet and trunk. While he checking out the inside, the first fat drops spatter the windscreen. The lady and Jah-Son getting wet so they hustle to stand under the eaves of the outbuilding. The two a them standing there quiet, quiet. Jah-Son figure the outbuilding where they standing is most likely the former servants' quarters. No-body is no 'scrvant' now. Not since Massa Day Done. But plenty old-style house still have quarters behind them, getting more and more dilapidated like this one.

She say how strange the rain came down so quickly without warning and he agree. She ask if he's living nearby and he say no. She ask if he's working with Feroze and he say no. She ask where he going and he say he don't know. Does he know that Jesus is the way the truth and the light? He say he hear so, and she ask if he seeking the Kingdom. He look up at the sky and say, Nothing so grand, just somewhere for himself, his sister and her little boy to live. She look at him good and say nothing, looking ahead again, checking the rain falling from the galvanize in long streamers. She ask, Can you drive? Do you have a license? He answer yes. She say, That's nice and is that the work you do? He say, Sometimes. She say what's your name. He tell her. She say her name is Miss Holder and an idea has just struck her. Would he tell her what he thinks about her idea. Come, she say, and Jah-Son follow.

She lead him into the outbuilding and Jah-Son find himself in a room full of broken-down, leftover, can't bear to throw out, can't bear to give away dining-chair, table, stool, cushion, standing-lamp, standing fan, pedestal fan, stove, kettle, washing machine, cardboard box, morris chair, folding bed, spring mattress, book-case, hardcover book with missing spine, more cardboard box, market basket with frayed handle, then into the next room where he seeing wardrobe, desk, desk-lamp, more bookcase, TV, TV-stand, Home Sweet Home pitch-oil lamp, more cardboard box, bed headboard, bedside table, coffee table, Encyclopaedia Britannica Vols. 1 to 26, deck chair with wooden knees folded to canvas body, picture frame: everything pile-up, heap-up, dust, dust, and more dust, cobweb and rat droppings. And here's the bathroom, she says. No seat on the stained toilet bowl, dripping single tap in rust-streaked cracked washbasin, the shower a concrete floor depression with open bent overhead pipe.

What do you think? she ask him. Jah-Son face blank. She say, What do you think about it? Think about what? The place, she say. It could work? For what? She say, For you. For your sister and her son. Jah-Son look around at all the confusion and he say, It will take plenty work to fix up. By the time the rain stop, Miss Holder already decide what's what and she tell Feroze she not selling the car after all. Feroze drop Jah-Son at De Rightest Place and Bostic lend him the pick-up. He pass and collect Kobo and Ghost, and in two-twos they reach the house in Gonzales.

Miss Holder park up herself on a chair in the yard to oversee what the fellers doing. OK, Jah-Son say, We will bring out the things and you will decide what you want to keep. Quick-quick a massive pile build up in the yard. Miss Holder walk towards the pile and touch an old clock, pendulum hanging outside the mash-up face. This was my father's; he used to wind it every night. She touches a dressing table, mirror broken, one leg missing. My mother got this as a wedding present from her parents. She pull out a Home Sweet Home lamp, point to a cardboard box at the back for Ghost to lift up, ask Jah-Son to pick up a bentwood rocking chair. She say, I don't want anything else.

Jah-Son transport everything to Kobo brother *Second Time Around Treasures* yard. He negotiate for help with fixing up the place in exchange.

When the place looking and smelling nice and clean, Jah-Son ready for his little family to move in. First he must bring down their things from the Valley Road. Not a moment too soon. There he find that the thieves start stripping off the galvanise sheets from the roof of the little board house. Next morning, he borrow the pick-up from Bostic and he and the fellers move out all the things that they need right away and at last Jah-Son, Maisie and Small Man move into their new home.

One morning Maisie turn on the shower and no water coming out. When Jah-Son check the tank, he find that it empty. They manage for a week with buckets from the standpipe, and then the water come back. But next time it gone, Jah-Son decide to collect the water tank and pump that still there in Gran-Gran yard.

At the end of the pitch road, he park the pickup next to a van piled high with coconuts. A strange dog rush out at him from under the van. It tie with a long piece of rope to the door handle, but it barking, snapping and snarling, tugging hard at the rope. He walk up the hill to Gran-Gran's house. He see three or four flags fluttering on bamboo poles outside the shed where he used to keep his nesting birds. A woman peep out the doorway from behind a curtain. She turn away and he hear her say, Somebody outside. A burly man, carrying a cutlass come out. He stand by the door and say, Wha' yuh want? Jah-Son say, This is my grandmother house. I just move out some of my things. I come for my water tank and pump. The man say, I eh know nutten about dat. Me eh know nutten bout no tank and no pump. Jah-Son protest. I born and grow up here. I live here all my life. I can see the tank from here. I buy that tank and the pump. Is mine. The man walk down from the house and reach a couple feet from Jah-Son. He raise the cutlass. If ah chop yuh up today, ah go say yuh was trespassing on mih property and how yuh threaten mih. Magistrate eh go do me nutten. The police eh go even let the case reach courthouse. Don' leh mih ketch yuh here again or it will be the last time yuh ever walk, yuh hear? Yuh cyah say me eh warn yuh.

Jah-Son look at the man face. He reading there, in the narrowed eyes and twitching jaw hinge, serious intent to inflict grievous bodily harm. The raised cutlass, its edge flashing a newly-filed silver, could sever his head as casually as if it opening a coconut. He turn away and walk down the hill, the frenzied yapping of the tethered dog accompanying him.

30. MUDDY MORE WATER

The letter comes in the post just after Carnival. Indira reflects that there was a time when you used to look forward to the postman coming, eagerly anticipating surprise and delight. Now is a postlady coming and is only trouble she bring. So y'girl already steupsing when she fishing out the contents of the letterbox. Landline bill, cellphone bill, electricity due for disconnection notice, water bill, flyers for a furniture store, a power-washing service, the newest pizza outlet and what's this? A brown envelope with the council logo on it.

This she opens first. Inside, a single sheet of paper. A bill. No, an invoice: *For the demolition of a structure and the removal of construction debris from a building in Belmont, Port of Spain.* Demolition – so and so much. Removal – 4 truckloads to the Solid Waste Management landfill site at such and such a truckload. 2 workmen at such and such per hour. 2 drivers at such and such per trip. 1 supervisor, so and so. 1 operations manager, so and so. VAT @15% – so and so. Total: $25, 219.95

What the expletive deleted is this about? An invoice for the clean-up? Who the expletive authorised this? She glances at the name printed below the signature – MT Khan, City Accounts Manager. Who is MT Khan? The name ringing a bell. Where did she see or hear that before? She walks back into the bar. Bostic, you know any MT Khan? I have an invoice here from one MT Khan about the clean-up of the backyard. Demanding over twenty-five thousand dollars. Bostic lets out a low whistle and comes over to see for himself. Hmmm… he scratches his head… That fellow with the bleached, spiky hair. What's his name? Indira looks at him blankly. Bostic snaps his fingers. Remember? The little self-important one with the clipboard. The one you call to come and clear out the yard.

Oh, yes, my gods. Where's the card? I didn't pay much

attention to the name on the card – too taken up with the colour. She marches to the phone and pulls a violet card from under it. Yes. It's him. Here it is. MT Khan, Event Planner and Coordinator. How many jobs this man has, eh? City Accounts Manager as well as refuse contractor. A person is allowed to do that? Have an official full-time employment with the council and moonlight as a private contractor for council jobs? What's that? Insider trading? No. That's something else. Nepotism? Double-dealing? No. No. Right now I can't think what. But it smelling fishy to me.

Indira go to the bar and pour a neat Grey Goose. Bostic lift an eyebrow. Not Cuba Libre, her usual comfort drink. She must be really upset. She down the tipple without looking at it. The Grey Goose vapour must scour bright some connection in the grey matter because she slam her palm on the table. Wait, wait, wait. Bostic. Lemme look at that invoice again. I want to check something. Here is the item. Operations Manager. Who the arse is that? Him. He. Nobody else was here, so it has to be him. The expletive not deleted crooked little scamp is a whole blasted Trinity all by himself. Getting three sets of pay for doing his one job with three different titles. And billing me twenty-five thousand plus for the privilege.

Wait a minute. That video we seeing on TV all the time, the *Solid Waste Leave a Clean Scene Campaign ad showing the clean-up here. Is not he who shoot it? MT Khan?*

Cameraman and video producer too? A four-head, five-head Deity? Well. We will see about that! Get me Councillor Junior Ramluck on the phone. He can't be allowing this nonsense to go on in his office.

Hold your horses, Indira. Think about it. Who send the event coordinator? Ramluck. Who office the bill come from? Ramluck. Who office the clean-up crew, trucks, drivers, supervisor, operations manager come from? Ramluck. Who you think pulling the strings here? Yes. None other. So calling him would just let him know that you know he's the puppet master. And what will happen next? If you think he's going to back down on this bill, forget it. This is his transparency trump card. If this went public, people out there will be glad to see that the council making people pay for private work. You will look like you want special favours for free.

So what to do?

Ignore it. But prepare your counter attack.

How?

Draw up your own invoice.

Eh?

Bostic itemises, shooting up fingers like bullets from a police high-powered on rental to a gangster who putting down a week-end wuk.

One: loss of business when we close down after the fire. Two: employees salaries. Three: increased insurance premium. Four: loss of property – the shed, tools, car parts. Five: repainting of walls. Six: replacement of furniture. Seven: electrical rewiring and inspection fee. And a next thing. Don't forget how he organise an event that bring flambeau, gas in bottles and so on here, into your place and he didn't organise for not even one fire extinguisher. Think about it. He's not some random event promoter. He's a councillor. Wouldn't look good for a councillor to be careless about public safety.

He wouldn't be the first and he wouldn't be the last.

Is true. But it still not going to be nice for him if that go public.

For the first time since she open the brown envelope, Indira smiling.

You're right. He's made so many missteps already, the government would be only too glad to drop him like a hot tawa. Would demonstrate integrity in public life and get rid of an embarrassment same time. Catch two birds with one set of laglee.

She mixes herself a comforting rum and coke.

So where that leaves us?

Sitting still. Making no waves.

Easier said than done when tide running strong and wind blowing high. Bostic don't bargain for the strong tide of remorse for sins – many actually committed and even more indulged in the imagination – that befall a population in Lent after a year of licentiousness and wrongdoing culminating in the Chrisnival season just finish.

★

He introduced himself to Indira early next morning by showing her a yellow card.

240

The Reverend Pastor UR Sukker
God Ordains Alternative Lifestyles.
www.ministryofGOAL.com

Indira looks at the card, then at the bald little man, kitted out in black and gold football gear, complete with whistle. She flicks the card with her fingers.

You're this person? The pastor?

He takes the whistle to his lips and emits three shrill blasts. Goal!

You sure you in the right place? This is a pub.

Three more blasts and again, Goal!

Indira grabs the whistle.

What can I do for you?

Perchance I could have the honour of conference with the lady identified on the façade of this property as the proprietress and licensee, one Indira Gabriel?

She release the whistle. That's me.

Charmed, I'm sure. If it behoves you to bestow the pleasure of your company on your humble servant?

I already have a religion and I don't want to change it.

He rubs plump palms together.

Haha. Nono. Your conclusions are not appropriate to the situation here present. Not at all. May I have the temerity to offer a little business proposition that will bestow mutual satisfaction and benefit to the two parties here present, that is to say – me, party of the first part and thee, party of the second part?

OK. On two conditions. First. Do not blow that whistle again. Second. English is not my first language. So, speak simply. Understand?

Crestfallen, he nods. She indicates a chair.

Would you like a drink? We stock non-alcoholic beverages.

And alcoholic ones too?

What's it to be?

Vodka and lime.

Indira gives him his drink and sits at his table.

What's up?

It is my urgent and overwhelming desire to locate my esteemed edifice of worship on your salubrious hereditament.

Indira raises her arm, yellow card style.

Ahem. I want to set up my church here.

Under her lashes, Indira checks her exit route. A lunatic. An asylum escapee. I could dash for the door. The table will block him. I'll throw a chair if he lunges. Meantime, I'll humour him.

Uhhuh. Here. How soon?

Next weekend. Saturday.

Definitely mad. Weekends this place crammed with sinners with no desire for repentance. And I have no interest in them repenting either. There's the lucrative wages of sin to consider.

Here very busy on weekends, you know.

Not inside. HaHaHa. Your backyard. It's certainly De Rightest Place for a tent. The Ministry of GOAL is planning a nine-night crusade. My branch preaches Sport as a Way to Salvation.

Your branch?

The Salvation Tree has many branches. Its roots can be traced to the original Tree of Knowledge.

Indira's eyes dart from the pastor to the door, door to pastor and back again.

Other branches preach different things. For example, there's Chutney Promotion as a Way to Salvation, Highway Construction as a way to Salvation. Gay and Trans Life too. We cater for the full spectrum of Trinbagonian activity. It's an all-inclusive church.

Not many of those around. So?

You've been selected. What say you?

We haven't talked transfer fee.

He shoots her an admiring glance. Her stare freezes his hand as it reaches for the whistle. They agree on rental time and fee. Five to nine pm; half the rent by Thursday, the remainder on the last night. She'll draw up a contract for them to sign.

Had she checked her horoscope that morning she might not have acted so hastily.

In the coming weeks, Geminis will have the potential to muddy more water, rock more boats, and even fool themselves better than anyone else.

31. FOOL YOURSELF

At De Rightest Place, everybody and they mudder have something to say about Jah-Son's predicament with the water tank and pump and the confrontation between him and the new owner-occupier of Gran-Gran's erstwhile home. I Cynthia say people too advantageous. Wrong and strong and using force to misappropriate. Anil ask if Jah-Son have deed to the property, if Gran-Gran did have deed, and if they didn't and the new feller have deed, then is nothing he can do. Law is law. And how he lucky he didn't get chop up. He wouldn't a have a leg to stand on. KarlLee say he didn't like the phrase Anil using about no leg to stand on. Most unfortunate choice of words in the circumstances. Boyee say, How come you picking holes in what people saying when you self does get vex when people talk down your so-called artist work? KarlLee say, When you doing something worth talking about, and not just playing cards and drinking, let me know, so I can pass an intelligent opinion on it. Boyee stand up and pick up his empty Carib bottle while sizing up KarlLee. Bostic come round from behind the bar with a glass of ice water, put it on the table in front of Boyee, rest his hands on Boyee's shoulders to ease him down on to his chair, take the empty bottle from his hand, and go back behind the bar. I Cynthia say, Seriously fellers, what allyuh think Jah-Son should do now?

KarlLee eyeing Boyee hard and he say, There's a thriving industry in this country whose main activity seems to be righting *supposed* wrongs. All man look up at this statement because they suspect where this is heading and they don't want it out in the open like it normal, normal. KarlLee continue: All a so-called wronged party has to do is pay a fee that depends on the nature of the task and level of risk involved and, bingo! business taken care of. If you go along that route, Jah-Son, this interloper would cease to be a problem. Hold on, say Cecil, I don't think the boy should

243

be encourage to take the law into his own hands. You never know where that will lead.

Just putting forward another option, that's all, KarlLee say.

In the end they agree that you can't take on every battle that life present. Life can get too wearisome if you constantly fighting. Things that bigger than you can downpress you, crush the life out of you. Sometimes you just have to swallow your pride and walk away if you want to survive. If we hadn't done so for four hundred years, Cecil say, we wouldn't still be here. Jah-Son think to himself, that yes, maybe it *is* time to stand up for yourself, but not *by* yourself. Like the story about the bundle of twigs, hard to break when tied together, but easy to break one by one, and that maybe, if there'd been more solidarity in those four hundred years, it wouldn't have lasted so long, and if there was more solidarity now, the downtrodden poor people, who is the biggest majority, wouldn't get trample on so easy.

Meantime, Jah-Son also wondering whether he get help out with Miss Holder, or getting trample on in that too. He had was to fix up the place himself. Invest in all kind a bathroom fixtures and fittings and paint and wood and Harricrete, transport rubbish away, and give the fellers and them a raise for the help-out. Between a rock and a hard place. He had to find somewhere for them to live. But what price he paying? No rent, is true, but he have to drive the old lady wherever she want, and if anybody hot foot, is she. He up and down whole time he not at work in the bar. If not grocery, is market; if not market, is doctor; if not doctor is drugstore; if not drugstore, is by a friend to drop something or pick up something or is hairdresser, or church, or funeral. Is like he her personal chauffeur. But then he look at Maisie, and she happy with the little bedroom she and Small Man occupy; she like having a yard for the little boy to run around in, she like that she could step out and get transport to town or walk to town, no long dirt road to climb. Jah-Son glad that the place fence round and somebody with some respect in the neighbourhood living there too. Almost like living with Gran-Gran again. So he push aside the nagging thought that it looking like people taking advantage of him.

And it's hard to hold on to any self-confidence when he in De

Rightest Place. He noticing that the most conversation Indira having is about moneymaking schemes for the bar. Is not that she unkind or dismissive or anything like that. No, is only that she making him feel that his problems not really her concern. He can't think when last she take interest in him as a person; he want to think *lover*, but he drawing the line at such a leap. Last time was when she had the fall behind the bar and cut her leg. Now he wondering if when he take her upstairs and tend to her injury and what follow, she was only using him to scratch an itch. But at least, when he come to work, Bostic asking how he settling in, whether everything OK with Maisie and Small Man and so on, and how he finding driving Miss Holder.

He washing up last night's glasses and reflecting how he glad to have somebody, apart from his birds, to talk to about his personal life, if only because finding words for his thoughts and feelings helping him to understand his situation, and managing his feelings better. He does not discuss with Bostic his relationship with Indira. Is this because he can't find the words yet, or because he know that Bostic is or was best friend with Indira's husband? He not sure where Bostic see him in the situation, and too besides, he don't think Bostic want to know.

That has to be the cleanest glass in town. Careful you don't empty the water tank.

He looks up to see Fritzie standing there. He didn't hear her come downstairs. He didn't realise he was washing the same glass under the running tap for so long.

We waiting for you.

He looks over and sees Indira and Bostic seated at a table. When did anyone tell him about a meeting? He follows Fritzie and sits with them. Indira begins.

Two matters have come up and we have to discuss what to do. Bostic?

Hmmm. First of all, we have a bill from the Corporation for the clean-up. Plenty money. Secondly, we have a good offer from a pastor to rent the yard for a nine-nights crusade starting next Saturday.

Stop there, says Fritzie. You say Saturday?

Starting Saturday every night for nine nights, five to nine pm.

So what about the regular trade?

Everything will go on as usual, Indira say.

Indira, you ever look outside and see how much a car does be park up here any day and night of the week? Is a constant coming and going. The neighbours tolerant now, but if it had say fifty, even only thirty more cars park up for four, five hours, there could be trouble.

It's only for nine nights. People will adjust. What you say, Jah-Son?

I think Miss Fritzie have a point. But as is only a short time, might be worth a try.

What about the Corporation bill? The crusade money can cover it? Fritzie goes back to the first issue.

Bostic smiles and catches Indira's eye. It can, but we looking to see how we can get round that.

Jah-Son sees the shared glance. He wonders why he is at this discussion since everything already decided. He stands and pushes back his chair.

Well, everything seems OK. I'll get back to work.

Jah-Son wait, says Bostic. One more thing. We will have to open earlier to cater for people arriving for the crusade. So we opening four instead.

Yes, Mr Bostic. Saturday. Four.

He goes back to the bar and starts to pack away empties into their crates. Fritzie, too, wonders why she is in the discussion. She turns to Indira.

How this going to affect the soup business?

We'll make a big pot of corn soup for when the churchgoers leaving hungry at nine o'clock.

In addition to the daily soupa?

Can't miss a chance to cash in.

I will have to see. There is Precious to think about.

What's going on with Indira, Fritzie puzzles on her way home. She can understand Indira wanting to do the best for herself with the business, but she was never this hungry for money before. Every little scheme that come her way, she looking to get into. One day to the next, she going from Devil Mas to God Mas. And she expect everybody to fall in just so, like we have no life outside

246

the business. Is OK for Bostic, he and Indira on the same page, but I have Precious; Jah-Son have his own issues, including Indira self. Is like Indira have some demon driving her. She know I have to put Precious first, yet she drop this late work on me just so. I can take it or leave it, but that's not the point.

Jah-Son, finishing up at the bar, is thinking about life. *His* life. He reach this age thanks to Gran-Gran, God rest her soul. Now without her, he has a sister and a nephew to take care of. Maisie pulling her weight, working, raising Small Man. He hope the new boyfriend who visiting responsible and not planning to give her a next child and walk off like the last one. He must talk to her about that. But how he could take on a superior father role with his sister when he self have plenty cocoa in the sun? His relationship with Indira for one. He and Miss Holder for another. Gran-Gran house, the water tank, the pump. All the times when he back down, taking the easy way out. The only time he stand up for himself, he lose his job. And now, new working hours. Why? So Indira and Bostic could save they skin. How everybody taking him for a Good Friday bobolee, advantaging him so?

He packs away the glasses, the empties, wipes down the counter, sweeps and mops, his mind running on another track. This thing about her wanting to make a child. She want a child because she feel she getting old, but I don't think I ready to take on a next set of responsibility. When I make a child, I want to be even more involve than I am with Small Man, but she don't want a father for the child, only the child. Is like she don't really want me to be with her like I is her man. This is a next advantage?

★

I Cynthia don't know what possess Indira to let that bogus pastor set up tent church in the backyard. Saturday night, Sunday night, Monday, Tuesday, Wednesday – nobody in the neighbourhood could hear theyself think, far less listen to TV. Is only a setta testifying and preaching and singing loud enough to wake the dead. Is like the preacherman feel God deaf? I see poor Fritzie and Jah-Son staggering home late, tired, tired, whole night they serving food and drink.

And what you think happen Thursday? Mih sister holding a lil christening party fuh her latest grandson, here, home by me. Car

247

with macomere come; nowhere to park; car with compere come; nowhere to park; car with baby, baby mother, baby father, baby mother mother and father come and nowhere to park. The street full up both sides with congregation cars. When they do find a space, people have to walk blocks to reach a lil ice cream and cake party, a lil drink a rum on the baby head party. And when I put on mih music, a lil *Raise yuh han', wine down low*, it getting drown out by *Washed in the blood of the lamb* coming from the tent church. Was a mess.

Friday, tent church so popular, residents coming home can't park nowhere nearby. Prized vehicle they take out loan to buy, abandon blocks away fuh bandits to thief and take down to The Bamboo and strip fuh parts. Come Saturday and residents plan a retaliation. They park all they car on the street. They call friends and family to come and park up too. By four in the afternoon you can't even park a bicycle; it eh have no space. When the faithful come, is them who have to park far and walk, not we.

One woman come and pull up, blocking a driveway. She leave the engine running and dash inside the tent to leave the baby with the granny while she drive around to find space. When she come back, car gone. With six-year-old daughter inside.

She phone the police to report missing car with child inside but nobody answer the phone. Somebody take she to a police station, but the sergeant say where it was park is not his jurisdiction. At the right station, it have plenty people waiting to report accident, break-in, shooting and the officer taking report in longhand. When she turn come, the officer say he can record the missing car, but she have to report the *missing child* in the station where the child living.

Meanwhile, the news of the disappearance reach inside the tent church. The whole flock leave to help find car and child. Somebody say a resident call Traffic Branch about obstruction and somebody say they see a tow truck removing the vehicle. The faithful fan out to the various police car-pounds and eventually locate car and child. The mother pay the five hundred dollars fine, drive back to the tent to pick up the baby and she gone home with she two chirren. The faithful who engage in the hunt gone home too, so the eighth night congregation at GOAL Ministries is only people who live in walking distance. Plus Anil and Feroze. Them two not missing a chance to check out likely moneymaking schemes.

When Sunday reach, who putting god outa they thoughts to try to go to tent church in Belmont after what happen Saturday? Who devout enough to trade the present near certainty of having their car tow, for the distant possibility of entry through the pearly gates? The tent almost empty on the final night of the crusade. There is no torrent of tithes, only a trickle of offerings into the GOAL net.

Y'girl Indira ent get no payment from the pastor. He say, The goal posts shift. I Cynthia say, Indira score a own goal.

32. A LONG RANGE VISION

Standing there, podgy hand smoothing over his scant sleek hair, glinting gold molars greet Bostic as he opens the doors next morning. Councillor Mr Ramluck. Unresolved history does not incline Bostic to be friendly, but habit permits a measure of courtesy. He offers him a seat, a drink, and asks what he could do for him.

A word with the madam?

I'll see.

Gemini: It is time for you to think bigger, which means with a long-range vision and focusing your sense of mission. This is setting a high standard in a world where 140-character messages from rank idiots make world news, but so be it. Be prepared.

She did not. She really did not expect the 'rank idiot' of this morning's horoscope to put in such an early appearance. What could he possibly be here for? Surely it wasn't about that invoice. Big Sawatee wouldn't be so crass as to come to collect in person. That was work for little peewats like MT Khan. But if it was, she and Bostic had a counter claim for damages, all printed out and ready to serve. *Be prepared* isn't only for Girl Guides and fellers cruising Murray Street at night. She'll keep him waiting long enough to be on his second drink by the time she makes her entrance. Shower, dress as if on her way out to a business meeting. Hair in a nape bun, crisp white shirt tucked into waist of pinstriped dark grey slacks held up by olive green rattlesnake belt, matching Cuban-heeled pumps and handbag. Lavish squirts of *Impulse* by Calvin Klein behind ears, on wrists, behind knees.

Councillor, good morning. To what do we owe this surprise?

He rises, almost upsetting the table. Ah Madam. You look very... harrumph, harrumph... *nice* today. I came at a bad time?

She looks pointedly at her cellphone. I've got a meeting in town in forty-five minutes.

I'll take only a couple of minutes.

They sit.

Harrumph. You are aware that Local Government Elections is later this year.

Hard not to hear the loudspeakers blasting foolishness all hours of the day and night.

Hahahaha. Yes. Can't be helped. Got to get the voters excited. And?

I see that your backyard is not being used now. Church over?

The faithful need only nine nights, it seems. Politicians need longer?

Hahahaha. Well, as a matter of fact, we do. I'll get down to brass tacks. I'm looking for a Campaign HQ. I'm hoping you'd allow us to erect a structure in the back, where the old shed was.

She raised an eyebrow.

Replacing a former structure, so no permission needed. We'll use it until a month or so after the election, then it's yours.

Until next election?

He looks up a little guardedly.

With your permission?

Hmmm. Look. I've got to rush. Call me tomorrow. Let's talk further. Bostic, please see that the Councillor has enough refreshment.

I have to go, too. He follows her out. I'll call tomorrow morning.

She jumps into the pick-up, speeds off, makes a couple blocks and is back.

Bostic, what you make of that?

I think you need some legal advice, not barman opinion.

So I *really* have business this morning?

A junior agrees to see her at short notice. When she returns she is no happier than when she left.

Bostic, I'm totally at sea. This is way out of my league.

Hmmmm?

Can we talk privately?

I can't leave. Jah-Son upstairs with Fritzie. Is lunchtime.

I'll send him down and you come up.

Campari soda for her, Earl Grey for him and he watches as she

251

pulls at her earrings, pushes her bracelets up and down, undoes her hair and ties it up again.

What's up?

I don't know where to begin.

The beginning?

How long we know each other?

Trick question? No? Lemme see. Maybe ten, eleven years?

There's nobody else in the world I've known as long. Not even Solo. And you and me still holding secrets from each other, not so?

Bostic gives a wry smile. And *for* each other.

I need to discuss something completely honestly. No games. No hidden agenda.

About the Councillor's proposition?

It is.

After lunch.

When they close for siesta, Bostic goes home, spruces up and returns with a briefcase. Upstairs, he won't sit in the armchair she offers, but plonks his briefcase on the dining table, pulls out two upright chairs, sits in one and motions to the other. She picks up a folder from the coffee table and comes over. Bostic taps little staccato drumbeats on the table.

Right. Begin.

The Councillor's offer. There are plusses. First is a new structure we can use however we want – rent as temporary offices, fit out for short-term stay, meeting rooms, performance space whatever. The minus is his claiming it whenever he wants.

Bostic nods agreement.

My, *our*, dealings with him so far didn't work out well. He's behaved underhand. There is talk of him misappropriating funds, cooking the books. I don't want to be mixed up in all that.

What did the lawyer say?

She was surprisingly open. She said that if the Councillor loses the election and there is an audit of his term in office, anybody who has benefited from his spending could be called to account or at least have suspicion of shady dealings cast on their character.

Not good.

Not good at all. In this business I deal face to face with customers every day. I can't afford to risk losing their trust.

She stretches across and places her hand over Bostic's.

Help me work out what to do.

He leans back into his chair, sliding his hand from under hers.

You like the idea of rebuilding the back. The problem is that you don't want Ramluck to be involved financially.

Yes.

Why not take out a loan? Do it yourself.

I tried that before. It didn't work. Here's why.

She slides the manila folder over. He opens it and reads for a minute or two.

Joint ownership.

And no Solomon Warner to co-sign.

He opens his briefcase, pulls out a foolscap envelope, extracts a sheaf of papers and puts them before her.

Her lips shape the words. 'Power of Attorney. I, Solomon Warner... hereby grant to my dearest friend, Terrence Bostic...'

Her hand flies to her mouth. Oh my gods. The date is... She rises to her full height and looks down at Bostic.

Three days before he left.

Twin blue lasers shoot from her narrowed eyes.

All this time.

Her voice hardly rises, but the words explode through clenched teeth at his bent head.

You knew he wasn't coming back.

She turns her back on him.

I can't bear to look at you.

He picks up his sheaf of papers, replaces them in the envelope, puts it in his briefcase, zips it up and leaves.

She tells the Councillor that deliberations with her associates are ongoing. She will inform him of their decision. Yes. ASAP.

Bostic doesn't return to De Rightest Place. Not that day. Not the next. We had a little disagreement, she tells Fritzie when she asks. He's taking a few days off, she volunteers to Jah-Son. You can manage on your own?

But one pair of hands can't be upstairs with soup and downstairs with bar same time. She decides to leave the bar to Jah-Son and work alongside Fritzie.

What's really going on, Indira? I know Bostic since Solo opened the pub. He never take one day off.

Indira stops peeling a sweet potato.

Tell me something. What were they like, together?

Tight. Real tight. Thicker than blood. They say best friends since four years old. Would trust one another with they life.

She turns to Indira.

And with they wife. Even a young sexy one.

Why does Bostic resent me?

Solo must be leave him in charge of you. To make sure you all right.

I can handle myself.

Really? You think he comfortable seeing you toying with a young boy? He must feel guilty that he not able to safeguard Solo's interest.

Indira plays in her mind what Fritzie has said. She has no answer, so the conversation dies. In the bar, Jah-Son is coping, just about. Pulled in many directions at once – serving, collecting money, giving change, dealing with deliveries, the phone. By siesta he is dropping.

On the third day of Bostic's absence, Indira sets off for his home. They sit face to face across a coffee table.

What?

Silence from her.

You wanted honesty and you didn't like it when you got it. What you want now?

A truce and a partnership.

Talk.

With your power of attorney and my deed, we could go to a mortgage finance company for a loan to put up a building at the back.

Go on.

An apartment above. Below, offices. One big one, one smaller one. Rent the big one to the Councillor. The rent will more than cover the mortgage.

When?

Now.

You prepared to put up this place as security? Solo's dream?

It's all I have, Bostic. Solo isn't here. I have to take care of myself. I am not going to be young, youngish, forever. And then what? What will become of me?

He leans forward, slumps his shoulders and drops his head in his hands. She comes over, sits on the coffee table and pulls his head onto her lap. She puts her hands on his shoulders, kneading at the knots there.

Please, let's do this.

She feels his shoulder muscles tighten further.

I can't let this golden chance to secure my future slip away. You know me.

The steam of her, rising through her skirt, invades his nostrils. His stomach squeezes searing acid up his throat. He lifts his head.

No one knows you, Indira. His voice is weary.

In less than a week the mortgage is approved. Indira has the Councillor over to a meeting with her and Bostic.

Nice-nice-nice, he announces, rubbing his hands and settling into a chair.

JW blue? Bostic asks.

A double, straight. Miss Indira, ready to do business?

She pushes a folder over to him.

You tell me.

As he reads, she can see his fingers holding the document clenching tighter and tighter, his face getting redder and redder, the vein in his temple throbbing faster and faster. She fears he will pop an artery.

P-p-p-preposterous. It says here that I'll be renting an office from you. What about our earlier agreement?

Your earlier proposal, you mean? Well, I've talked it over with my lawyer in Mr Knightley's chambers and I was reminded about the Central Bank's recent directive on commingling of funds. It would be a risky proposition for me, and for you, Councillor, for you to invest in construction on my property, because the lines of ownership and liability, private and public, would be blurred. This is what they came up with as a clear business arrangement and a neat paper trail, for both our sakes – yours in public life and mine as a citizen.

The Councillor slaps down the document, and rises to leave.
I will find somewhere else to invest.

I'm sure you can do so quite easily. But, before you go, there's a small outstanding matter. Bostic?

Bostic hands him a sheet of paper.

An invoice? For damage to the shed? I'm not paying a red cent.

Councillor Ramluck, I don't think you would want to have this little media distraction while conducting a campaign for re-election? Would you?

Is that a threat, Ms Gabriel?

This is a conversation about responsibility, Councillor Ramluck. All above board.

He sits down, pulls out the chequebook with two signatures, and writes a cheque for the full amount.

Oh, another thing. Mr MT Khan seems overburdened with responsibilities. Perhaps this is one he could be relieved of? She presents him with the invoice from his office. He writes CAN-CELLED across it and signs it.

Anything else?

The rental agreement is entirely up to you, Councillor. Maybe you'd like to come back when you've consulted with the council? My lawyers would want two signatures.

Good day, madam.

The kickstart for the construction comes from that cheque. With Bostic hands-on, the workmen do not indulge in their customary foot-dragging. A late start to the rainy season also helps. The steel frame is up, walls fitted and downstairs ready for occupation as offices ten days before the due completion date. Indira posts a sign on the forecourt: To let – Modern, well-equipped office space. Enquire within.

I must say this is amazing. How did you get it finished so quickly, Ms Gabriel?

Councillor Ramluck, I didn't hear you come in.

Well, well, well, so when can we move in? The Campaign HQ is ready?

I'll let the project manager show you round. Bostic!

When they return he is effusive in his praise of the fittings, the furnishings, the finish.

Quality. Class. Where's the lease? I'm ready to sign.

I'll call Mr Knightley's chambers and tell them to expect you and the authorised co-signer. Tomorrow OK?

Campaign HQ opens in a week. Indira knows that the figure for the year's lease would have made his eye water, but she also knows of the risk of unidentifiable stains on beige upholstery, condoms flushed down toilets, cigarettes crushed on rugs, electrical fittings pulled from walls, air conditioners burnt out and other matters of tenant indiscretion. Best *Be Prepared*.

The Councillor's party hadn't been installed a couple of months when he told Bostic he wanted an urgent word.

I'll see…

No. Not her. You.

A raised eyebrow.

You the project manager for the building at the back, not so?

A nod.

I want to show you something. When you free?

Around two.

When Bostic knocks at Campaign HQ, the Councillor comes out, jiggling car keys.

It will take only a couple minutes.

We going somewhere?

Building site.

They stop at a block of apartments under construction, but not a workman in sight.

I fire everybody. Workmen holding down two jobs, one here, one on somebody else site, drawing day's pay both places, running overtime, materials disappearing.

Bostic, resisting the urge to point out similarities with staff at the Councillor's office, only raises his eyebrows.

You can take it on?

Meaning?

Bring your team and finish the job?

Bostic walks through the site. The frame is up, roof in place, exterior walls for five units, three untouched. Electrical plumbing, masonry, carpentry, finishing, still to be done. He takes pictures from different angles and in several locations.

Drawings, quantity survey, purchase records, stock list?

The Councillor, concentrating on the toe of his left shoe, doesn't answer. Bostic looks at his phone.

Time to get back.

When they are back at De Rightest Place, Bostic leans into the driver's open window.

Four o'clock tomorrow afternoon. In the bar.

Something's come up. We need to talk, he says to Indira. Jah-Son, can you hold on? It'll be an hour at least.

Upstairs, he outlines the Councillor's proposal.

Bostic, you're seriously thinking about doing business with that crooked old weasel?

We've had two dealings with him. The first was sorted out eventually. The second is ongoing, on track.

It wouldn't surprise me to hear he's been using council workmen, diverting council materials and been fiddling books. That's his modus op. We know that.

We also know he does do some legit business. Something above board for official scrutiny.

Last time, I had to persuade you. Now it's you trying to convince me.

Indira, I have to do this. I need a break from the bar, people's problems, petty quarrels.

He walks to the window and looks out. She can barely catch his voice.

I have to get away from you. And Jah-Son.

He turns to her, his voice now brisk, upbeat.

It's the kind of work that does my mind and body good.

She comes over and touches her palm to his cheek.

This is the first time you ever asked for anything. I can't say no.

The next morning, Indira calls a meeting with her associates.

We want to run something by you. It may or may not happen, but we'd like to know how you feel about it. Bostic?

Councillor Ramluck is building some apartments up Carr Place. He asked me to project manage it.

You don't think we had enough trouble with that scamp already?

Fritzie, we made that work for us. And this can. Indira?

Fritzie, Jah-Son, this will involve all of us. There will be changes, for the better, and we need all of us to be on board. It's time to think bigger. OK?

Bostic continues. Jah-Son, can you manage the bar business? All of it?

Yes. The day-to-day trade. I'll be here some evenings.

It usually needs both of us, Mr Bostic. It's a strain for one.

Fritzie, the soup. You and who?

Can't think of anyone interested in kitchen work. Everybody want to buy cook food, not cook it theyself. I could rope in Precious on Saturdays, but she still has another term at school. Who else?

Miss Indira, when this starting?

Bostic?

We would want the Councillor signed on the dotted line, all payment for labour in the bank or at least in escrow with Knightley *before* the elections. The tide could turn. We wouldn't want to be stranded.

So, in three, four weeks?

Bostic exchanges a glance with Indira, who nods agreement.

Let's say four weeks. *If* it's happening.

Lying in her hammock, Indira feels her head spinning. Too much is happening. Too much, too fast, coming at her from all sides. Decisions, decisions, decisions, bam-bam-bam-bam and no time, *no time at all* to think things through before, snap, next! She's racking her brain to remember when last she was the one who orchestrated the scenario? The painting of the front? As far back as that? Hmmmm... Lunchtime soupa, bistro... But everything else – the Devil Mas' event, the Tent Church, the building at the back – came at her from outside, not of her choosing, and all, all, were fraught with issues. No time to think before acting, so it's damage control all the way. And what about rest, relaxation, recuperation? What about reflection? When last did she lie down with a book, any book? When last lie down and do nothing, for that matter. Or lie down and... Even Jah-Son is out of her control – busy with Maisie, Small Man, the apartment, driving Miss Holder, the bar... They've been working him too hard of late. Better watch he doesn't go sour... And now this! Bostic off site as project manager for that, that *scoundrel*! If Bostic takes on this new project, everything will be turvy-topsy, upside-downside, for a few weeks until people get the hang of their new roles. I'll have a helluva job running back and forth keeping tabs on everything. Time to make a list.

> De Rightest Place Consortium
> Indira: *Personnel, property, projects, paperwork*
> Bostic: *Construction*
> Fritzie: *Food*
> Jah-Son: *Bar*

Not much of a list, Indira says to herself, but at least it's got clear responsibilities and it's on paper and not running around in my head. Even if the project with the Councillor does not materialise, Bostic is restless. He will want to find other projects to manage. Wonder whether Fritzie and Jah-Son will welcome their independence, though? Having their own little area of control inside the bigger business?

When Indira walks into the bar next morning, they are waiting. Fritzie, sitting bolt upright, her hands folded in her lap. Jah-Son at the far side, hunched over, looking at his cupped hands resting on the table. He doesn't look up. She greets them and asks them whether they've given the proposal further thought.

Fritzie?

Is a good idea. But I'm not sure I want to have to deal up with workers. Having to take all kinda attitude from some own way young girl.

Jah-Son?

I have more responsibility lately since Mr Bostic doing the construction at the back. But the accounts? I glad he still helping with that.

Indira senses some willingness to go along – if they could be persuaded that it could work for them.

Jah-Son, why were you dissatisfied at Stephenson?

260

Because I was stuck. No chance to progress.

Why do you like here?

I learn plenty new things and I grow with the business. What I don't like is not knowing from one day to the next what are my hours and responsibilities. Makes it hard to organise my day here and with Maisie and Small Man.

Fritzie, why do you like working here?

I don't feel I working. I with friends, helping out. Is like home, but I have company and I get a small change to spend. That's how I see it.

What you think will change?

I will have to supervise staff, deal with accounts, make decisions, more planning. Now, *that* is work.

All four of us will be doing something new. Fritzie and Jah-Son, you'll be taking control of what you do now, but with a chance to grow it as you see fit. Make decisions. Get the benefit.

Bostic adds his encouragement.

Jah-Son, I'll still be here.

Mr Bostic, I want to. But I can't do it on my own.

What if we take on somebody like Curtis?

We could try.

Indira turns her attention away from the men.

Fritzie?

I can't show less willing than Jah-Son. Plus, when I look at doubles-lady, nails-lady, hairdresser, they is all they own boss. Who is me that I can't be like them? Maybe I can get Maisie to work with me? Jah-Son, you don't think it might suit her better than 3Fs? Look, Indira, come what may, Soupa still on the menu.

33. NO CHICK NOR CHILD
NOR PARROT-ON-A-STICK

An old lady like Miss Holder, with one thing and another wrong with her, have no business climbing ladder to put up picture of her departed mother, no matter how dearly beloved. When Maisie come out of her apartment to go to work, she step into water cascading down the old lady back steps. She run inside and turn off the tap that overfilling a bucket in the sink. Is then she hear Miss Holder feeble voice: Help, help, help. She find the old lady lying on the floor, a ladder resting on her chest. When A&E tell her on the phone they ent have no ambulance to send, she call Jah-Son. He come with Bostic in the pick-up and they load the old lady on to the pick-up tray and Jah-Son head with her to the hospital, dropping off Maisie and Bostic first. Hospital decide to keep Miss Holder. When he reach back at De Rightest Place and Bostic ask him how things went, Jah-Son say, Dread. Miss Holder not conscious. I am the one who bring her in, so I am now her 'next of kin'. Is like Gran-Gran all over again.

Except it didn't go so. After two days, Miss Holder begin to recognise him and on the third afternoon, the ward nurse approach him. You Jason Chance? Today Miss Holder's niece visited. Miss Holder say to change the next-of-kin to her.

Jah-Son hurry to Miss Holder bedside.

You looking better.

Yes, much better. And guess what? My niece visited me today. I know her?

No. I met her for the first time today. Her father, my brother, went years ago to live in the States. He died there long time. She grew up with her mother somewhere in Central. We have a lot of catching up to do. Her name is Shamita. She's coming again tomorrow.

How she find out you here?

God moves in mysterious ways. The nurse is her friend and she told her that there was someone with her last name in the ward and it was the tenant who had to sign as next-of-kin. So she came to see if we are family. Isn't that a strange coincidence?

So, no more 'no chick nor child nor parrot-on-a-stick', eh? Praise be.

Maisie send a couple clean nightdresses and tell me to bring back your soiled clothes. What you want me to bring tomorrow? Food?

Shamita said she is bringing something to eat. But look in the radiogram cabinet and you'll find two photo albums. Bring them. My niece wants to look at family pictures.

Next-of-kin scam, declare Bostic. Very common. Old lady on her last legs, never married, living by herself in big house, few surviving friends, but only tenant for company. You get a tip off from hospital staff. You go where she living, scope out her house, knock on neighbours' gates, say you're the niece and heard she's sick and you come to see her. Neighbours helpful, offer advice, give away information and you now have a better story. When you first visit the old lady, you can say how your mother always talk about the big verandah, or the plum tree or the shop down the road. And the old lady then say, But my brother only bring your mother by me once and she remember that? Now you know that her brother is your 'father', not her sister is your 'mother' and you build on that. If by chance she doesn't take bait, you say, Sorry, my mistake, get well soon, and move on. There's always another old lady longing for family.

And the albums?

Best part. Sentimental old lady looks at the photos, goes down memory lane with twists and turns and detours and soon she doesn't know what she told you from what you feed back as intimate family knowledge, and soon you talking about Uncle Edgar, Auntie Clarissa, Cousin Louisa, like blood.

What does she want? Miss Holder doesn't seem to have money.

Miss Holder has a house on freehold land. Now she has a next-of-kin for her will.

Shamita take over the hospital visits and when she bring Miss

Holder back home, she move in too. A couple of months later, Shamita tell Jah-Son that Miss Holder want to see him.

That day Bostic waiting for Jah-Son to come in from feeding his birds and start on the bar chores. He look out towards the backyard. He see the boy sitting on the bench, the bunch of sucrier, the bowl of seeds next to him. Bostic still around because the building project hasn't yet started. Quarter hour pass and he look out again. Jah-Son still sitting on the bench. Half hour pass; Bostic look out again. Jah-Son ent move. Staring into space. He go out and sit next to Jah-Son. What happen.

Miss Holder asking for rent. How much? A thousand a month. Bostic let out a low whistle. How come? Is you who make that rat hole fit to live in. She say with Shamita living there, she have more expense. Shamita say I getting a discount. Plenty people offering two thousand for it. They sit together, neither saying anything. The shrill of the bar phone cause Bostic to rise. He put a hand on Jah-Son shoulder. Feed your birds. Then come inside. We will talk then.

34. LIVE, LOVE, BE HAPPY... IRREGARDLESS

It was a blessing in disguise that the deal with the Councillor fell through, even after the weeks Indira and Bostic put into the proposal. The sticking point was the many millions to be held in escrow and released to a schedule that De Rightest Place Consortium insisted on. Without that power to withhold monies at whim, the Councillor wouldn't agree and the Consortium wouldn't back down.

As it turned out, the Councillor's political party did not reselect him as their candidate. Someone posted some damning data on social media. It showed the outrageous sums paid out of the public purse for labour, property, goods, services to companies whose sole directors and staff were revealed to be the wife, son, daughter, sister, brother, mother, father, tantie and nennen of the said Councillor. Tweets screeched back and forth like a disturbed coven of cocricos. It suggested one name as the insider source. Traditional media, as ever in the wake of social media, took up the story. The Councillor's party was nimble enough to brand itself as the party of integrity by choosing someone else whose misdeeds were still unexposed. Who rolled up one Monday morning at Campaign HQ? None other than a newly reblonded, freshly spiked MT Khan, the new candidate.

At De Rightest Place, it was as if, by formalising roles and consolidating as a Consortium, the team was charged with a burst of renewable energy. Can't beat long-range vision and focused mission, reflected Indira. They roared ahead into accomplishing much in little time.

Bostic's little team of Kobo, Desmond, Kwesi and himself, hands-on, took on small jobs, refurbishing kitchens and bathrooms, as well as bigger foundation-to-finish jobs right there in that gentrifying Belmont neighbourhood. First Cynthia, then other neighbours, called him in to renovate and rebuild. He had a waiting list of clients who would tolerate nobody else but Bostic's team working in their homes, while they were still in occupation. In the open air, in the hot sun, in the pouring rain, Bostic could feel his chest expanding, his lungs opening up, his heatbeat slowing. He felt back to where he was before Solo came back home, but now his own man, no longer drifting, no more monkeys on his back. It wasn't the carefree adolescence with Solo he'd taken for granted as *life*, but it gave a peace of sorts. The rhythm of laying blocks, mixing concrete, smoothing plaster, laying tiles, nailing tongue and groove, bead and reed, running pipes and cables satisfied his body. His mind, now free from what had become a stifling claustrophobia in the daily presence of Indira and Jah-Son, could try to find some meaning to his life.

To whom did he owe what? Loyalty? Friendship? Paternal devotion? Love? And how to repay those debts? Did he owe himself, Terrence Bostic, anything? He spent weekends helping Jah-Son, teaching him the finer points of being a publican. He admired how the boy grew in skill and confidence and how sensitively he managed to train Curtis. Between them, things were running smoothly, and, in just a couple months, Bostic's role in the pub segued into genial uncle and regular customer.

Indira let the second office to a newly-qualified dentist. Precious, an early patient, in only for cleaning and polishing, instantly fell in love with the stark clinical beauty of everything in the surgery – immaculate white walls, gleaming steel equipment, white translucent disposable gloves, *and! and! and!* the spotless digital data-capture and storage. No paper. *My world!*

Can I work here?

There isn't enough work for me to hire a receptionist.

I graduate from school in five weeks. I willing to work free for the first month. Try me. Train me.

May I work here. I *will* graduate. I *am* willing. *Please* try me. *Please* train me.

Like you start already.

You're living with your mother? Ask her to come and see me. *Please*.

Touché. *Please* ask her.

The soup continued as usual, but Fritzie was encouraged by

Maisie to broaden their offering and to go into catering as well. Making pastelles with Gran-Gran's recipe, but without grinding corn kernels from scratch – Promasa was Maisie's sole concession to modern methods. People were hungry for things authentic, she said. They'd had enough of the stingy, dry mincebeef in thick cornmeal casing, wrapped in aluminium foil that was passing for pastelles these days. Indira found she could hardly get into her kitchen to boil a kettle for a soothing camomile infusion, what with banana leaves, wooden press, trays of cornmeal balls, dishes of raisins, olives, capers, bowls of chopped beef, chicken and pork on every counter and table. She prevailed on Bostic and his team, for the sake of the future of the Consortium, to create a new food preparation space. Her spare bedroom was captured and outfitted as a sleek work-kitchen with independent stair access down to a new room built on a corner of the forecourt. Daily soup prepped, cooked and served downstairs; catering of pastelles, pies, dips, fishballs, crab-backs, upstairs.

Indira challenged Bostic. And what about me? I need office space! He set about rationalising her sprawling living room. In one corner he set up a mini office complete with desk, computer with double monitor, an executive chair, a corkboard and a filing cabinet, and separated it from the living area by a pair of Luise Kimme carved and painted screens, depicting a woman in poses of inspiring serenity.

And what about her and Jah-Son? He's busy, she's busy, what can you expect? He's sometimes called, during his shrinking siesta time, to bring up a Cuba Libre for her and something for himself. In the cool, muted light of her bedroom, they bring each other up to date on work, on life. They de-stress with tender, affectionate familiarity, as lovers, as friends. Talk about a child to bring meaning to her life has ceased. The world of De Rightest Place Consortium was spinning smoothly on its axis.

Bostic's latest job was a simple one-man affair. While his team finished a newly renovated house, he undertook a small job for Geoff, the photographer, who wanted to display some of his best work at home. *Home! Atelier! Studio! Gallery!* All in one place, showing Belmont artisanal creativity at its *Acme!*

Well, what he wanted was the sitting room converted with

panels, fabric and display lighting into exhibition space. Bostic drew a few sketches while Geoff sat at his computer, making, as he put it, 'photographs out of snapshots' for his buddy, KarlLee, who wanted a selection of four by fives made from Sunity's Canadian holiday pictures. He wanted to surprise her with an album, because she was forever talking about the good time she had there.

Bostic was treated to a slide show of Sunity's snaps: Sunity in hat, gloves, coat, boots; making a snowman, throwing snowballs. Sunity shopping in a glitzy mall. Sunity sitting on Santa's lap in front of a gigantic Christmas tree. Sunity and Jassodra entering a nightclub, the sign over the door announcing *Tropical Jazz Club*. Sunity sipping a cocktail, Jassodra dancing, and, in the background, a band.

Saxophonist, keyboardist, drummer and a double tenor pannist. His clean-shaven head was only in a quarter profile, but the visible line of the jaw, the posture bent over the pans, the wrists held just so, his legs straddling space, owning his territory made Bostic's sphincter clench.

At home that night, Bostic lies immobile, staring at the ceiling. Then he get up, goes to his computer and googles Ottawa nightclubs. No Tropical Jazz Club. He googles Tropical Jazz Club, Canada. Dozens. One in Toronto. He goes to the website. There are pictures of the club, the bar staff, the waiting staff, the décor, the drinks, the menus. There is one of a band, but no musician looks like the one whose very shadow he could have picked out in a crowd at midnight. Still, he copies the contact data. He works at Geoff's house for two days, his head muffled in a fog of confusion, elation, anxiety and hope. Then he moves on to one job and another, and another, and another, like an automaton, until torrential rains bring a slowdown in construction and Bostic releases his little team to do their own thing until September, the end of the school holiday season, and the expectation of a *petit carème* to get things rolling again.

He spends day after day in bed, at home. Not rising to eat, to bathe, to do anything. He works back through his life – what he did, what was done, until he comes to that day when he learned that Solo was leaving the island for the first time. How he felt then – the searing pain of separation, the numbness afterwards – is fresh in him again. The years of moving like a robot, one foot in front the other, of the solace in drugs, of long spells of oblivion. His mind crawls forward to the second leaving, his loyalty, his faithfulness to the promise asked and given, to the dullness of duty delivered day after day, year after year. He tries to talk himself into seeing himself now, an older man, in his late fifties, able to do what he wants, what he chooses, no longer a powerless adolescent at the mercy of the world of adults and of convention, no longer a needy recoverer. But even so, from talk to action is a giant leap. He goes back to spending evenings in De Rightest Place; he plays cards and draughts; he eats whatever Fritzie and Maisie provide. But his spunk is gone, and Indira notices.

We haven't caught up in a while, she tells him one evening. Come upstairs. Let's lime like old times.

Drinks and toasts out of the way, she comes to the point.

What's up? You're not sick?

Just need a little tonic I suppose. Worked too hard last few months. Had to take a little break.

There's more than that. You're worried about something. Is it Jah-Son?

Relieved she'd misread, he goes along with her.

I feel I should do something for the boy. He's worked out well. Beyond my expectations. What you think?

We both should do something for him. Him and Maisie and Small Man. I feel bad that his last salary increase went straight into Miss Holder's purse.

What you have in mind?

What about the apartment at the back?

The one I never got around to finishing.

You didn't need to. We are doing fine with the rent from the offices.

Well, I'm not busy these days. Talk to him. Hear what he says.

Jah-Son approaches him as soon as he comes in the following evening.

Mr Bostic, can we talk?

At the table where they sit, Jah-Son fiddles with his hands.

Mr Bostic, I hope you don't take this the wrong way. When my

Grandad Felix died, I was a little boy, two or three. Gran-Gran raise me. When I was looking to change my job, is a woman, Miss Indira, who help out. I never had a father figure. I just want you to know that I am grateful for all you did, all you doing for me. You let me in the bar first time, even though I could see you didn't want an intruder. You train me to where I am. You put your trust in me. And now Miss Indira tell me you going to build the apartment for us.

He looks up at Bostic.

Gran-Gran didn't believe in christening, so I don't even have a church godfather. I feel she leave that space open for somebody to take up by theyself.

Bostic cannot hold the young man's eyes. His own are suddenly full. He stares long and hard at the back wall, at the pictures of good times gone by hanging there. He swallows a couple of times, exhales deeply and looks at the young man. He places both his hands over Jah-Son's.

Jah-Son, I'll be proud and happy to claim you as godson. And, if ever you want to, as son.

Thank you, Mr Bostic. I feel Gran-Gran smiling down on us now. Maisie and Jonathan will be so excited to know that soon they moving to a nice new apartment.

Jonathan?

Small Man say he's a big boy now and is time people start calling him by his real name.

You fudged that, didn't you? Bostic's conscience prods him that night. No, I didn't. I told him he could be my son if he wanted. Not the same thing is it? What should I have done? Drop my pants? Shown him the birthmark? No, but you could have told him you suspect he is your son. What good would that do? He'd be bitter that I didn't say so earlier. He'd become judgemental about his mother. What's mother, what's father anyway? Egg and sperm? Right now, he's happy, I'm happy. Good, answered his conscience. One less thing on your mind, then.

One less thing made space for another thing to grow. He'd been somewhat cowardly with Jah-Son – OK, very cowardly, but it was for the best, he was certain, at least at this stage. Let him get accustomed to godfather first before anything else. Creep before you walk. Baby steps. The other thing involves him taking from his wallet the piece of paper on which he'd written the contact details of the Tropical Jazz Club, reading it, then putting it back, then taking it out and reading it, every half hour or so when he wasn't working on Jah-Son's apartment. Why he read it over and over, he couldn't fathom. He'd memorised every letter, every number on that scrap of paper. It was as if holding the paper, touching it, reading it, made the hope it represented, more real, more tangible, more *possible.*

At the end of July, the Consortium handed over the keys to the apartment to Jah-Son, Maisie and Sm... Jonathan. Bostic is alarmed to see Indira looking washed-out, tired. When they are alone, he asks if she is OK. She says she's had an upset stomach for a week or so and with some other things going on she wondering whether she's entering menopause early. You planning on seeing a doctor? Yes. She's made an appointment with her gynaecologist for the following week. She's sure she'll be fine. Don't worry, old friend.

Why don't you ask Jah-Son to stay with you till you're better? Maisie and Small Man will be right here in their own apartment.

You know that's a good idea. I'll put it to him.

That evening he writes on an envelope:
Solomon Warner
c/o The Tropical Jazz Club
and he added the Toronto address.

Inside he puts a single sheet of paper in the middle of which he writes only his phone number. He seals the envelope, sticks on stamps and drops the envelope in the mailbox. He tells Indira and Jah-Son that he's thinking of taking a little holiday. Still lots of time before work picks up again in September. He'll let them know when he decides.

A week later his phone rings. A 1 416 number is showing. He picks up the handset. His hand is shaking as he brings it to his ear. He can hardly whisper.

Solo?

Blood!

I CYNTHIA – BELMONT MACO

There is no interval in the confusion of existence

When Indira declare dat De Rightest Place throwing a lil thanks-giving Saturday coming, all a we wondering what she giving thanks for? Everybody and they brother reach. Who does turn down chance to fete, lime and enjoy a lil freeness, eh?

And people looking well special too. Curtis and Kwesi cutting swag, looking like African princes. I tell Jonathan he looking smart. He say, Auntie Cynthia, you looking real sexy too. That boy getting real fresh-up with he lil self, eh. Even Kobo clean up nice – hair in big tam, beard trim, new shirt and pants. Is a waste of my ethnic outfit to wear it just for Emancipation Day, Fritzie say when I tell her how splendid she looking. And as for Miss Indira, I cyah remember when last I see she looking so good. She wearing a purple, one-size-fits-all long dashiki. Last few months of stress had she looking magga and drag down and old. But not today. It looking like she put back on some size. Face a lil more full. Everywhere looking more full-out and more relaxed than for a long time.

If yuh see decoration! Tables with lil cocoyea centrepiece sportin palm-leaf bird and grasshopper and lizard. I woulda never believe is Amber and Precious who do it. Didn't expect dem smart-phone generation girls to go all-out native on we. But when I make that remark to Precious, she tell me, Indigenous is the new modern, Auntie. Geoff walking around taking pictures of everything and everybody, making the ladies turn their head to capture hairstyle, headtie, makeup and all, like if is a fashion shoot he doing.

Fritzie and Maisie give we a real rainy season spread – big pot of breadfruit oildown with saltfish buljol, callalloo, and a big-big dish of zaboca salad. As we sitting down to eat, I see Jah-Son pulling out chair for Indira. She tell him something and he go and fix up a plate of food and bring it for she. Then she say something else and he bring a drink. Wait nuh, that looking like tambran juice? She not drinking rum and coke?

After we finish the coconut ice cream and sweetbread, Bostic say he have a announcement to make. Anil turn down the music and Bostic say, I know Indira won't mind if I use this opportunity to tell you don't look for me here next week. I'm taking a little holiday. Well, you coulda knock me down with a sneeze. Everybody surprise too. All the years we here, and as far I Cynthia can make out, in all the years since he and Solo set up this pub, we never hear Bostic say he taking no holiday. Cecil and Boyee guessing is Tobago or Barbados he going, Karl-Lee say, not he. Bostic not going a inch further than Mayaro. Sunity say, I feel so too. Feroze say, Don't forget me when you want taxi to the airport. Bostic not responding to they fassness. He only lifting eyebrow, holding heself inside heself as usual, but with a lil' satisfied smile, a lil' holding-back secret smile I didn't see from him for a long, long time.

But I Cynthia not getting a nice vibes bout this. Last time the man in charge a De Rightest Place say he going away, he never come back. Yes, is Solo self I talking bout. But nobody else seem concern, so who is me to raise it? What we raise is a glass to wish him a great vacation. Bostic say, Thank you everybody. Let's stand and toast the lady who is responsible for all of this. Speech, speech, Nelson the Admiral, bawl out.

Jah-Son go behind Indira chair and pull it back when she stand up. Y'girl hold sheself up tall, tall. She look round the room at everybody. She say, If I say all that is in my heart, I will get too emotional and I will cry and spoil the mood. So I will just say, thank you, my friends, for making today such a memorable day. I know that you want to know what are we giving thanks for? Well, I've been giving that question a lot of thought myself and when I think about what we went through the last couple of years, you, me, De Rightest Place, I can't count the number of hard times we went through. I don't have to give you a list. You know them as well as I do. But look at us now. We came through it. Today we give thanks for that. I wish everybody many more happy days like this, together here, in De Rightest Place. *To all of us!*

Well we drink, we hug up, we toast one another. Anil turn back up the music, soca blasting, the fellers stack up chairs and tables and the dancing start. Precious dancing with the dentist feller she working with. Curtis and Maisie. Feroze and Fritzie having a wild time. KarlLee and Sunity wrap up like a Hotte Shoppe roti. Jah-Son dancing with Indira, though he holding her like if she is a crystal shandilay and he fraid she break. I Cynthia take a lil spin with Cecil and Boyee and when I turn round I see Jah-Son and Indira leaving to go upstairs. I ask Bostic, What's up. He say, She feeling tired. I say, Everything all right? He say, She good. Jah-Son move in with her. She in good hands.

I leave the party in full swing to walk back down the road. All the time I thinking about how slippery life is. As soon as you feel yuh have a hold on something, jus so, jus so, it not there again. It slip away out of sight – or change into something yuh don't recognise. And if yuh don't like how it is, what yuh could do? Fuh people like we, is either take it as it come, or put up a fight yuh know yuh bound to end up losing – or yuh might even decide to run away from it.

The thanksgiving in De Rightest Place put mih at a point in the story that I promise to tell you at the start. Right now, everything nice-nice, even tho' it eh fix up tidy-tidy. It have plenty loose thread. Everybody life does always have some loose thread hanging down. It could be unfinish business; it could be question that don't have answer. Anybody who did ever have to deal up with will, probate, beneficiary, deed, executor – watch that word good, eh – will tell you that even death is not the end of a life. Gran-Gran, Miss Holder, they gone now, God res they souls, but they not really gone that far. They deeds live on through the people they was close to and through those who was close to those people too, ripple upon ripple.

Them loose thread that lef hanging, you could snip-snip and cut them off – like the Middle Passage slash through family-kin-home-language-religion-culture – our whole sense of who we is – or jus like history book say, how Alexander run a sword to chop through the Gordian Knot. *Or*, yuh could leave the loose thread jus so, for generation upon generation to tie up.

And it have all kind a tie-up. Some is like Suzanne, that French Creole woman Indira know, and *she* family tree, cousins marrying cousins to keep Emancipation compensation in the family and to keep the line pure – a leaf and branch and root thing. No part can't survive without the nex' part. Other kind a tie-up is like everything confuse, hold-back, shackle, not able to move forward, because that thread make outa mental chain. Like the prophet Marley say, that is mental slavery. Maybe both kind a tie up does end up being the same? I cyah see it have profit in neither of them. But at least people own they loose thread. Is *they own*. They could tie up theyself with it, or they could let it hang down jus so, or they could use it to weave a tapestry of they own story.

I Cynthia, Belmont Maco, I leaving the loose thread hanging down jus so. Yuh see, sometimes yuh does have to give people business enough space, enough time, for people to shape it fuh theyself. Yuh have to treat it with respeck. Respeck for the individual and respeck for the space too. We in this space, who come here by luck and chance, still finding weself, still *making* weself. Is a process taking it own sweet time. But one thing we sure of, that this place is De Rightest Place to be. Fuh all a we.

Barbara Jenkins was born in Trinidad. She studied at the University College of Wales, Aberystwyth, and at the University College, Cardiff. She married a fellow student, and they continued to live in Wales through the whole decade of the sixties. In the early seventies they returned to Trinidad.

Since she started writing in 2008, her stories have won the Commonwealth Short Story Prize, Caribbean Region, in 2010 and 2011; the Wasafiri New Writing Prize; The Canute Brodhurst Prize for short fiction (*The Caribbean Writer*); the Small Axe short story competition, 2011; the Romance Category, My African Diaspora Short Story Contest; and the inaugural The Caribbean Communications Network (CCN) Prize for a film review of the Trinidad and Tobago Film Festival, 2012. In 2013 she was named winner of the inaugural Hollick Arvon Caribbean Writers Prize. Her debut short story collection, *Sic Transit Wagon* (Peepal Tree, 2013) was awarded the Guyana Prize for Literature Caribbean Award.

She completed her MFA at the University of the West Indies, St Augustine, Trinidad, in 2012. She spends her time reading, writing, singing in a choir, serving on the board of an NGO and visiting her globally-scattered three children and eight grandchildren.

ALSO BY BARBARA JENKINS

Sic Transit Wagon
ISBN: 9781845232146; pp. 180; pub. 2013; price £8.99

The stories in *Sic Transit Wagon* move from the all-seeing naivete of
a child narrator trying to make sense of the world of adults, through
the consciousness of the child-become mother, to the mature
perceptions of the older woman taking stock of her life. Set over a
time-span from colonial era Trinidad to the hazards and alarms of its
postcolonial present, at the core of these stories is the experience of
uncomfortable change, but seen with a developing sense of its
constancy as part of life, and the need for acceptance.

The stories deal with the vulnerabilities and shames of a childhood of poverty, the pain of being let down, glimpses of the secret
lives of adults, betrayals in love, the temptations of possessiveness,
conflicts between the desire for belonging and independence, and
the devastation of loss through illness, dementia and death. What
brings each of these not uncommon situations to fresh and vivid life
is the quality of the writing: the shape of the stories, the unerring
capturing of the rhythms of the voice and a way of seeing – that
includes a saving sense of humour and the absurd – that delights in
the characters that people these stories.

In the title story – a playful pun on the Latin phrase on the glory
of worldly things coming to an end – the need to part with a beloved
station wagon becomes a moving and humorous image for other
kinds of loss.

"Barbara Jenkins writes with wit, wisdom and a glorious sense of
place. In stories that chart a woman's life, and that of her island
home, this triumphant debut affirms a lifetime of perceptive observation of Caribbean life and society."
— Ellah Allfrey, then Deputy Editor of *Granta* Magazine

"Barbara Jenkins mixes a lyrical prose style with a close and humane
eye for the human condition […] She is a major new talent emerging
in Caribbean fiction."
— Monique Roffey, winner of the OCM Bocas Prize for
Caribbean Literature 2013